REPUBLIC

OF

FORGE AND GRACE

A PARALLEL-UNIVERSE AMERICA
NOVEL

DANIEL RIRDAN

Corino Press

Copyright © 2026 by Daniel Rirdan
Excerpt from *Areta* © 2026 by Daniel Rirdan
www.danielrirdan.com
All rights reserved.

Corino Press
Printed in the United States of America
First Edition(1.0): January 2026

ISBN 979-8-9926090-0-4 (hardcover)
ISBN 979-8-9926090-1-1 (trade paperback)
ISBN 979-8-9926090-2-8 (ebook)
ISBN 979-8-9926090-3-5 (audiobook)

Cover art by Gennadi Arkulis, Rob Snow

for my parents

What is portrayed in Americana is based on existing technologies or know-how; no hand-waving is employed.

This novel stands squarely in the utopian tradition—alongside works such as *Ecotopia* and *Looking Backward*. Its engine is not plot in the conventional sense, but the exploration of an alternate society and how it functions. The dense worldbuilding is intentional. It is the point. A blueprint rendered in story form.
And yes—it depicts something that works well.
Unabashedly so. Joyously so.

CHAPTER 1

THE ELDERLY MRS. ZHANG BEAMED as the car towing a small trailer pulled into her driveway. A young, broad-shouldered man emerged.

"Bless you, Chris!" she called out from the shade of her garage, her floral blouse and loose skirt dancing in the breeze. The tree-lined residential street was tranquil, seemingly suspended in that moment when the working folks had already left and the leisurely ones had yet to rise.

"My pleasure." The handsome man smiled amiably. "That's what neighbors are for, right?" He proceeded to unhitch the open trailer from the back of the car.

"Drink for you?" Mrs. Zhang called once again, her English valiantly shining through her thick accent.

Chris nodded gratefully. "I'll take you up on that in a couple of hours—if the offer still stands." Unloading and spreading compost bags under the summer sun was a thirsty business, and he'd certainly appreciate a cold drink later. The day promised to be another scorcher in Boulder, Colorado. But for now, the air was still cool and pleasant in the city of yoga and granola.

Mrs. Zhang cast an approving glance at his athletic frame, stubble, and smoky-gray eyes. Chris was twenty-four years old, he'd told her. And—it had just dawned on her—no ring in sight. This was her prompt to mention the pretty daughter of her first cousin from her second uncle's third marriage. Chris merely laughed good-naturedly. A shame, really. He looked like prime husband material.

The young man slung the first bag over his shoulder and started walking toward the large backyard.

It took being stationed halfway around the world—in Iraq—for Chris to discover his affinity for working with his hands. And it wasn't until the two weeks after resigning his commission that he realized he particularly enjoyed nurturing living things—mostly plants.

With six months of living expenses from his mother's life insurance tucked away, Chris vowed to fill his days with action; he wouldn't waste time on a PhD in procrastination, sipping beers, and chasing sunsets.

While pondering his next big move, Chris ruled out the soul-sucking world of bureaucracy, the addictive virtual snares of Big Tech, and the self-congratulatory chatter of academia. The dirt felt far more honest than any of these. If only he knew anything about gardening. Well, nothing was stopping him from learning.

His phone vibrated. Chris glanced at the display, and a frown crossed his face. *Ronny?* He'd never known him to wake up before noon.

"Hey, you up?" came the familiar sound of his friend.

"Yup. I rise at oh-five-hundred," Chris replied. Some habits from his military days were hard to shake. He checked his watch again. For Ronny to call this early, it had to be life or death. "What's going on?"

"Dude, I've got something to show you, but it's best in the morning light. Can you come over right now?"

Chris sighed. Ever since Ronny had bought the decrepit house a few months back, his friend had been up to his eyeballs in repairs and renovations. "I'm helping a neighbor. Can it wait a couple of hours?"

"Nope." Ronny's voice was tight, clipped. "I'm cashing in that free pass you owe me. Trust me, you'll wanna see this."

"Alright, I'm on my way," Chris said, snapping his phone shut.

If this was just a dud, Chris might just bury him under Mrs. Zhang's compost bags. Yet, something in his friend's voice—a rare, raw urgency—told him this was serious.

"Mrs. Zhang," Chris called out, "I've got to run—it's my friend. I'll be back as soon as I can."

"You take my car," she yelled after him as he mounted his bicycle and began to pedal away.

"You sure?"

"Of course I'm sure!"

⇒⇐

Not for the first time, it occurred to Chris that Boulder swelled daily as the neighboring towns disgorged their populations each morning, triggering a mass exodus in the evening, only to rally again the next day. Wash, rinse, repeat.

The drive to the eastern outskirts of town took about fifteen minutes, and concluded when the pavement unceremoniously gave way to a rugged dirt road.

Ronny lived on a few acres of a rundown property, the aging house a bleak focal point amid the disrepair. The place had been dirt cheap despite its acreage—something about unstable ground from an old mining claim that had scared off other buyers. Chris climbed out of the car and took in his surroundings. The same cracked, dirt-streaked plaster walls, the same gnarled juniper tree. At least the rusted barrels and the grungy carburetor must have been hauled away since he'd last visited, a couple of weeks prior.

"This better be important," Chris said darkly when Ronny

opened the door and let him in.

"It is," his friend assured him. Ronny looked even more disheveled than usual, which was no small feat. He wore a rumpled T-shirt, and his black hair stood up in spikes. He was practically bouncing on the balls of his feet, his stocky frame buzzing with nervous energy. His almond-shaped, velvet-black eyes, which often danced with a mischievous glint, were now bright with anticipation.

Ronny led the way. "The linoleum under the washer looked like something a maggot would gag on," he said. "So yesterday afternoon, I cut out a section of it. But then it turned out the subfloor also had some of that mold. So I had to remove a section of that too," Ronny added as they went down the stairs to the basement. "And I found something."

Chris halted near the bottom of the stairs and shot Ronny a quizzical glance. A trapdoor lay open in the corner of the basement floor. He strode over and peered into a dimly lit arched stone stairwell that plunged three or four stories deep. "Holy shit," he muttered under his breath. He shot a sharp, assessing gaze at Ronny, who was looking at him expectantly. "Does it lead to some sort of cellar?"

"Chris, you're in for a treat," Ronny said, his voice tight with pent-up excitement. "Come, help me move the TV down the stairs. It's the only thing I couldn't manage by myself."

Chris raised an eyebrow. "You uncovered an underground cellar, and your first thought is 'movie night'?"

Ronny grinned. "This will redefine 'home theater.'" He nodded toward the big TV. "Come on now."

They each heaved a side of the TV and began their slow descent, struggling to keep it balanced as they navigated the narrow, uneven steps.

"Did you discover a catacomb?" Chris asked, carefully balancing his end of the massive screen, trying not to let it tilt.

"No comment."

"A catacomb with a cursed mummy?" ventured Chris.

"Wait and see, man."

"A catacomb with a cursed mummy and a golden statue."

"Patience, my young apprentice. Patience."

Chris ignored this. "At least tell me if I'm getting warmer."

"You're ruining the surprise, man." Ronny was breathing heavily as he carried his end of the oversized TV down the long flight of stairs.

Something crunched under Chris's foot. "That was a skull of—"

"A potato chip I must've dropped earlier."

"—a human. I can tell I'm getting warmer," Chris declared. "A catacomb with a cursed mummy and a golden statue and snakes?"

"That's why you're leading—to take the first hit." Ronny's words came out in short puffs as he struggled with the weight of the TV.

They moved in halting steps, navigating the stone stairs until they reached a landing halfway down and parked the TV to take a breather. Chris rubbed sweaty palms on his jeans.

"You're not going to tell me what's down there, are you?"

"You've waited your whole life for this," Ronny informed him. "What's a few more minutes?"

They rested a bit more, then resumed their descent.

Once they reached the bottom of the stairway, the two gingerly set the TV down. Chris straightened up, taking in his surroundings. In the dim light cast by Ronny's headlamp, he found himself in an elongated chamber the size of a living room. The floor, walls, and ceiling were made of massive slabs of roughly hewn stone.

"I spent half the night down here sweeping and scrubbing," Ronny said.

Chris walked up to the nearest wall and studied it. "You've got a real archaeological find here, Ronny," he said. The hush in the underground chamber was profound. Chris was faintly surprised that the air did not feel musty or stuffy or ancient or something. He regarded his friend. "But honestly, after the buildup, I expected at least some scrawled glyphs, if not a tomb."

Ronny smiled absently, his attention clearly elsewhere. He cautiously stepped over some power cords and flicked on a switch. Soft light bathed the room. It was then that Chris's eyes landed on an artifact at the room's far end: a large, curious-looking octagonal frame that stood adjacent to the back wall.

"You did make a discovery!" Chris crowed, moving closer to inspect the peculiar copper coils and glass tubes that wound around the device. The octagonal structure measured about eight feet across and three feet deep.

"In a moment I'll turn it on, and you'll get to see."

Turn what on? See what? Chris wondered. He vaguely noted Ronny's camera mounted on a tripod in the center of the room as well as a picnic table and two folding chairs his friend must have lugged in earlier. The table held a laptop and sheets of paper covered in scribbles and notes.

Ronny motioned to Chris, and they hoisted the TV onto the table.

"It's showtime, man." Ronny walked over to the wall beside the metallic frame and pushed a lever upward.

Chris stiffened as the coils around the device pulsed a soft purple—and an image burst alive within the frame, vivid and sharp. He could make out blue sky and mountains in the distance.

He blinked, baffled. "What is this? What's that view?"

"You don't recognize it?" Ronny asked softly as he joined Chris, coming to stand next to him.

Chris peered at the vista before him: grassy plains and a

town nestled at the foothills of mountains several miles out. A jolt of recognition shot through him. "Green Mountain... This is Boulder," he said. It had an anticlimactic feel to it. "It's a video feed, showing the view outside, is that it? Or does it get fed from somewhere out of town?"

"Let me zoom in with my lens," Ronny said, fiddling with some cables. "I'll connect the camera to the TV so you can see what the lens sees on the big screen."

"I thought it was a video feed—a movie. No, that doesn't make sense..." He trailed off, running a hand through his cropped hair, now flustered. "What's going on here?"

"What you'll see is what the zoom is picking up," Ronny said and walked over to stand behind the mounted camera. He aimed the telescopic lens at the scene framed by the octagonal structure and homed in on the town in the far distance. The two of them shifted their gaze to the television screen. As Ronny continued to zoom, Chris recalled that the camera had an impressive 3000mm lens. His friend could see a bird perched on a mountaintop miles away. In fact, at one point, he had.

Ronny maneuvered and adjusted the tripod's elongated arm, panning and tilting the camera almost imperceptibly while zooming in. He delicately readjusted and zoomed further until a stately building with spires dominated most of the TV screen. He turned to Chris. "It's the Boulder County Courthouse; I looked it up. It was built in 1882."

"Never saw it before," Chris said guardedly, rubbing the back of his neck.

"No way you could have," Ronny told him, biting off the words. "It was burned down in 1932."

Chris gaped at the vista. Then at his friend.

"It's a mistake," Chris said in a tight voice that cracked around the edges. "It must still be standing." It was conceivable he'd missed it, wasn't it? Even though he had grown up in

Boulder. He *must* have missed it.

"I found an old illustration online," Ronny said, settling before his laptop and typing swiftly. He swiveled the screen toward Chris. The caption read: *Boulder, Built 1882, Arch- Frank E. Edbrooke, Contr- F. O. Brown, Fire-1932.*

There was no doubt; it *was* the same building.

What he was seeing was impossible.

Chris squinted at the sunlit, grand structure that dominated the TV screen. Against a vibrant blue sky, towers crowned with pyramids and intricate railings adorned every corner of the roof. A sharply pitched octagonal dome rose majestically at the center. A sweeping flight of stairs led to a covered portico and a columned entranceway.

"Watch those guys!" cried Ronny, as three men descended the steps of the distant courthouse. They held walking canes and wore dark suits and straw boater hats.

Chris stared in disbelief. *What the actual fuck?*

Ronny turned to his friend, nodding his head almost imperceptibly, as if to say, *Yes, this is really happening.*

"Oh, come on," Chris said weakly, feeling the blood thudding in his temples.

Ronny waved a hand, his excitement palpable. "What preschool did you go to?" he demanded.

"Mapleton Early Childhood Center. Why?" Chris asked, unsure where this was going.

Ronny gingerly nudged the camera arm, changing ever so slightly the angle of the lens, and the view shifted a few streets over. "That's it, isn't it?"

With his brows pulled together in a frown, Chris mutely nodded toward the building in the distance.

"Yeah, so I did some digging. The Mapleton Center building was constructed back in 1889. But get this, the street in front of it was paved in 1928," Ronny said, glancing at his friend. "Chris, here it is not paved—yet."

A horseless carriage rolled down the dirt road. Chris stared, rubbed his forearm across his face, and stared again.

Ronny gestured at the large screen. "Take a look at those carriage-like vehicles and the old-style clothing. We're literally peering into a window to the past. I poked into things, and I'd say we're looking at Boulder around 1910. Notice how much smaller the town is? It all adds up."

"The past," Chris whispered in an awed voice, reeling.

"The past," echoed Ronny.

They exchanged a quick glance, then resumed gazing at the TV screen, their faces bathed in a pale light coming out of the octagonal frame.

Chris slapped his thigh. "Wait! Zoom in. All the way."

Ronny obliged, and the image enlarged, revealing the details of the carriage-like vehicle and the two women passengers seated inside, facing each other.

"Where's the damn steering wheel?" demanded Chris. "Who the hell is driving this thing?"

"What?" For a moment there, Ronny didn't understand.

"That carriage—that steamer, whatever—it's driving itself!"

Ronny's mouth went dry. "That can't be," he protested weakly.

Yet it was. They watched, transfixed, as the carriage ambled along, occasionally disappearing behind trees only to reappear moments later. It rolled to a stop, the women stepped out, and the empty vehicle continued its journey, turning a corner and vanishing from sight.

Chris let out a harsh breath. "This ain't no past."

Ronny appeared bewildered. "What are you saying? This isn't Boulder?"

Chris shook his head. "That was definitely Green Mountain; the Flatirons are unmistakable. And the Mapleton Early Childhood Center you showed me... It's Boulder." He looked at Ronny with a heavy gaze. "Just not our Boulder—present or past," he said, his voice low and strained.

Chris paced the narrow chamber, deep in thought. Abruptly, he halted, struck by a realization, and stared at the scene framed by the octagon. "That's the view from Legion Park. The power station isn't there, but that's Valmont Reservoir down there." He gestured at the body of water and the sailboats in the distance.

Ronny turned his eyes from the TV screen and studied intently the vista visible through the device. Chris was right; earlier, he'd simply shrugged away the oddities. The sailboats resembled those in old Chinese paintings, their wide, rust-colored sails billowing in the wind. And on the far shore . . . were those bison? Ronny's breath caught. Wild bison hadn't roamed Colorado since the 1880s. He turned to look at Chris.

"This is a view of Boulder in a parallel universe," Chris said, wonder bleeding into his voice. "That's the only explanation that makes sense."

Ronny was silent for some time.

"You must be right," he said at last. "However, you're wrong about it being a 'view.'"

He picked up a pencil and tossed it. The pencil sailed through the air, went through the opening, and landed on the dirt somewhere on the other side, the other world. "It's a portal," Ronny said.

Chris's chest tightened, the air sharp in his lungs. He stood rooted in place, then walked over to the gleaming large frame and peered at the narrow space behind it. There was nothing there except a solid stone wall.

He turned and regarded his friend, astonishment etched on his face. "Somehow, you've stumbled on a *gateway* to a parallel universe."

Ronny nodded gravely. Then gave Chris a long, slow grin.

CHAPTER 2

CHRIS PACED BACK AND FORTH on the rough, stony floor near the gateway, his eyes alight with excitement. "How is any of this possible? Who built this underground structure, this portal?"

"We may never know," Ronny said with a shrug. Then he launched into the familiar story: the previous owner's death, the lack of heirs, the state's sale, and how he had valiantly stepped in and taken it off their hands—buying it for a pittance.

"This is big," Chris muttered, half to himself. "This is *really* big." He stopped walking. "We should tell someone," he said.

"You mean the authorities?" Ronny leaned back in the folding chair and studied his companion.

"Yeah, I guess so," Chris said, the words tasting wrong as soon as they left his mouth, distaste tightening his jaw. "On second thought—no. Hell no."

Ronny was taken aback by the heat in Chris's voice. Then he remembered. His friend had told him about the disastrous mission in Iraq. Many things had changed for Chris after that.

"I had all of last night to think things over," Ronny said with a pensive expression.

"And?" Chris urged.

Ronny gestured, and Chris slid into the other folding chair across from him. He motioned for Ronny to continue.

"Listen, I don't trust the powers that be any more than you

do," Ronny said, resting his ankle over his knee. "Still, we both know they'll take control at some point. It's not a matter of 'if,' but 'when.'"

Chris grimaced yet didn't argue.

"Okay, here's my take." Ronny spoke rapidly, his eyes gleaming. "If we go to the government, we lose control of the whole thing. I say we sit on it a while. Think about it. You cross over, make contact, shoot some footage. We drop it online, let it blow up, and rake in the cash. And just imagine the kind of story you get to drop on a date."

Chris scratched his stubble. "Won't people say it's all 'deepfake'? Or some shit like that?"

Ronny snorted. "Dude, that's the best part! Imagine the comment wars: 'This is totally CGI!' versus 'No way, this is real!' We'll be trending faster than you can say 'alien'!" He tapped his temple. "People *want* to believe stuff like this. A mystery they can argue about, chew on. We just feed the beast a little—video drops, maybe a cryptic livestream or two. Then let the chaos do the marketing. Trust me, controversy's better than ads."

Chris chuckled, shaking his head. "Damn, you're good at this shady stuff." Ronny smirked at that. "All right then," Chris said, "let the internet trolls do our marketing for us." The idea was growing on him. Once they brought in some physical objects verified by experts, well, that would take things to a whole new level.

He thought some more about it. "Let's read the fine print first."

Ronny raised an eyebrow. "Meaning what?"

"Meaning, what if it's a one-way portal? We go through, and on the other side, there's no gate, no nothing. We're stuck there for the rest of our natural lives," he said, "which—now that I think of it—could end up being long or brutally short."

Ronny's mouth quirked. "Consider the bright side. It's a lot prettier than our Boulder."

"And what's with this 'you' thing?" Chris asked, his gray eyes narrowed. "If we're going ahead with it, we both cross over and tour that other world."

"Well." Ronny rubbed his elbow. "You might not have picked up on it, but I'm of Korean descent."

"So?" Chris stretched his long legs out in front of him, shaking them a bit. He glanced at the gateway, then turned his head back to his friend.

"Earlier, when I looked at that other Boulder, I spotted a few black folks strolling around," Ronny told him. "Yet Asians seem to be off the menu. Hey, I'm not saying it's some Aryan state, but I might stand out like a sore thumb. You're better off going alone."

What a chickenshit excuse, Chris thought to himself.

"Besides, you've got the recon training—blending in, cultural awareness, all that jazz."

"Don't give me that crap. This isn't some military op—"

"And then you can do that accent thing."

"What accent thing?" Chris demanded.

"You know, the fancy white tie dinner party one. You saw the way they're dressed, man. They're probably like, 'My word, these oysters'—come on, say it."

In spite of himself, Chris grinned at this. "My word, these oysters are simply divine. Might I trouble you for another glass of champagne?"

Ronny high-fived him. "That's the shit I'm talking about. You didn't ace those standardized tests for nothing. Just because you decided to go all blue-collar on—"

"All right, all right. I got the idea," Chris said, then sighed. He suspected Ronny would have wanted to stay behind regardless of what the other Boulder was like. His friend was more of a behind-the-scenes kind of guy. When Ronny wasn't on the phone playing middleman between Bengali sweatshops and American firms—deals that made his tax guy nervous—he was usually glued to his gaming rig. In fact, aside from grocery runs and the occasional errand, Ronny was a homebody; his idea of the wilderness was limited to the virtual terrains he explored in massive online role-playing games.

A cottontail rabbit suddenly burst in through the gateway, causing both Chris and Ronny to jolt back in their chairs, startled. They watched, wide-eyed, as the animal darted about the stone chamber like a wind-up toy before leaping back out. They tracked its movement through the octagonal frame as it dashed to the side and disappeared from view.

Chris blinked, his initial shock giving way to wonder. "It was just a rabbit," he marveled, "but it was a rabbit from *another universe*." He looked over at Ronny. "It *is* a two-way portal."

He then looked again. "Hey, you okay? You seem pretty shaken up."

Somewhat unsteadily, Ronny went over to the wall and pulled down the lever, deactivating the gate. "Good thing it wasn't a bison," he said weakly. "Or the local constabulary." He sat back down heavily, then lifted his eyes to Chris and managed a smile. "Yeah . . . definitely two-way. Which means we probably ought to keep it offline unless we're using it."

Chris drummed his fingers distractedly on his firm thigh.

He looked at Ronny, and Ronny looked back.

"Alright," Chris said. "I'll go by myself. It's probably for the best." Even though he did anticipate having to put up with some phony and annoying behavior on the other side of the looking glass.

"Attaboy!" Ronny exclaimed, and his face split into a wide grin, clearly relieved.

Chris said, "But definitely not during daytime. People will freak out if they see a man appearing out of nowhere."

Ronny nodded grimly. "Or greet you with pitchforks."

"You sure know how to take the edge off, Ronny."

His friend snickered.

Chris left to fulfill a promise he had made to Mrs. Zhang and returned a few hours later. The two spent the rest of the day huddled together, hashing things out.

To avoid complications, they agreed on an even-steven split of the potential loot from their soon-to-be viral video. Chris was going to assume the risk and do the fieldwork. Ronny was going to handle the marketing and promotions. And then there was also the fact that the gate was on Ronny's property.

In the other universe, the mountaintops had no snow cover. Much like their own Colorado, it appeared to be the height of summer in Americana, as they'd quickly come to call the America in the parallel world. Ronny had a sneaking suspicion that it went well beyond the sharing of the season. As it turned out, he was correct.

They timed the activation of the portal with the sunset and observed that the sun was setting simultaneously in both worlds. That was more than interesting. It meant the two worlds didn't just share the same time of day—they were likely on the same date, since sunset varied with each passing day.

They went back down a few hours later, and Ronny powered up the device. Once again, they peered via a peephole into Boulder in a parallel universe. It was nighttime, and through the octagonal frame they detected a few dots of light in the far distance. There were surprisingly few.

"Do you suppose those are electric lights?" Chris asked.

"No one's running lidar off a wood stove. If they have self-driving vehicles, they have electric lights," Ronny told him matter-of-factly.

"We didn't see any power lines."

"They must be buried underground," Ronny said absently.

"Lucky them," Chris grumbled, a tinge of bitterness seeping through.

Ronny shrugged, indifferent; it was all the same to him. He pulled on the massive switch, powering down the gate, and they headed upstairs to wait.

Earlier, they'd decided that the sweet spot was between 3:00 A.M. and 4:00 A.M.: the least likely time anyone was out and about, the least likely time Chris would be seen emerging from the passageway. Time seemed to drag on. They chatted and speculated. They even attempted a round of *Magic: The Gathering* but, preoccupied with what lay ahead, abandoned it halfway through.

Eventually, the moment arrived. Down the stairs. A flip of the switch. And the night air of another universe greeted them, a few feet away.

"Like we discussed," Ronny said, his voice a bit raspy. "Just have a quick walk around and come back. I'll see you in a minute, bro."

"Yeah. Sure," Chris said, hesitating as he stood rooted in place, gazing at the portal's opening. In theory, it should work.

"If it doesn't pan out as planned, I'll take care of the wife and kids," Ronny called out from somewhere behind.

Chris glanced back darkly. "If things go south, I'll haunt you from the other side," he promised.

Taking a deep breath, Chris braced himself to step onto the octagonal metal platform. "Here goes nothing," he muttered.

"Or everything," Ronny chimed in from behind as Chris stepped forward—and in a wink was elsewhere. Outside. Under a star-studded black sky. The only sound was the gentle whisper of the wind rustling among the trees.

Chris strapped on night-vision goggles and surveyed his surroundings. Off in the distance, he spotted a pair of deer and made out juniper and pine trees dotting the landscape.

There were no trails or roads in his vicinity, at least none that he could see.

He turned around—and there was nothing there. No gate. Then he saw it. . .

A subtle shimmer. A faint octagonal ripple in the air, barely perceptible. If he hadn't been actively searching for it, Chris might have easily missed it. Would it be any more noticeable under better light conditions? Deciding to investigate, he removed his goggles and, for a brief moment, aimed a small flashlight directly at the contours of the portal. The beam bent around the shimmering air, revealing only a faint refraction of light.

His sweep complete, and with nothing else catching his eye, Chris stepped onto and then across the sheer outline.

"You're back!" crowed Ronny as his friend reappeared.

They laughed and high-fived. "This device works like a charm," hollered Chris. He was all grins.

"You've just made history, man! Even if no one knows this yet." Ronny stopped. "How was it?"

"The air was sweet-fresh. It hits you as you step through. Otherwise, it's probably as you imagine it would be: trees, deer, tall grass."

They ran another test, deactivating the device while Chris was in Americana. To Chris's relief, the faint shimmer vanished, confirming the portal had no visible footprint. To minimize the risk of discovery, they kept it off whenever Chris wasn't passing through, just to be safe—even this far from civilization. All they had to do was coordinate Chris's returns in advance.

Their experiments also revealed a limitation: Any object transported had to fit entirely within the depth of the gate's frame.

Everything looked good. The mission was a go, Chris announced.

They spent the next week planning, preparing, and making some purchases. With no family ties or pressing commitments, Chris found it easy to clear his schedule for the foreseeable future.

Finally, the big moment arrived.

It was 3:15 A.M. when they made their way down the stone stairway.

Chris was adjusting the cotton flat cap on his head, tugging the brim just so. "So, do I fit the bill?" he asked as they halted by the glowing passageway.

Ronny grinned. "You've got that all-American hero vibe going on." He punched Chris's shoulder. "Go knock 'em out, champ."

"Like we discussed," Chris said, ignoring the knot in his stomach. "Just sit tight and give me a few days to scout things out." Ronny nodded. "Off I go," Chris said with a half-smile. The two fist-bumped.

Chris turned, stepped through, and—found himself instantly in the other universe.

The air registered instantly on his skin. Cooler. Cleaner.

He waved to the unseen Ronny on the other side and observed the almost imperceptible shimmering contours of the gateway slowly wink out as Ronny must have powered down the device.

That was it. That was the point of no return. Chris was alone in a society that he knew next to nothing about. And the only thing that comforted him was the realization that this society knew nothing of him.

CHAPTER 3

BEFORE HEADING TOWARD AMERICANA'S BOULDER, a few miles away, Chris took a mental snapshot of the flat rock he had emerged from, the surrounding landscape, and any distinctive landmarks to ensure he could find his way back to the portal site later.

He descended the hill, weaving through fallen branches and tall grass. The earth was soft beneath his boots.

At the bottom, he spotted a rack filled with recumbent trikes and other personal transporters. This appeared to be a modified version of the bike-sharing programs in his world. A corner of his mouth lifted. Could he commandeer one of these? It would certainly get him to town faster than on foot.

His attempts to liberate some of the trikes were unsuccessful; they were all locked. No surprise there. Examining the rack more closely, he noticed a small glass square facing upward. *What do we have here?* He pressed his thumb against it. Nothing. He hovered his palm above the square. This triggered a momentary red glow, and he tried to pry out one of the vehicles. Still locked. Undeterred, he tried again, positioning his hand above the glass plate, then stopped when it finally dawned on him. It was a palm biometric scanner. And his vein pattern wasn't in the system.

This had not been a foregone conclusion, though.

He and Ronny had discussed the possibility of another Chris Walden existing in Americana but deemed it unlikely. The odds of two lives converging to produce another Chris Walden were vanishingly small. Well, it looked like they were right; there didn't appear to be any other Chris in that universe, at least not one registered in the biometric system.

Back to walking then. But should he wait for daybreak?

The earlier sighting of bison and elk herds hinted at the presence of predators. Chris had no desire to have close encounters with mountain lions, bears, or wolves in the darkness. He pondered the situation for a moment. The potential run-ins with dangerous animals aside, he'd need to be on his A-game when navigating this mirror-world society. Remaining awake all night seemed like a dubious move, especially after being too amped up to sleep the night before. He resolved to get some much-needed rest.

Chris settled beneath the pines, the faint chirp of crickets in the air and a sliver of moonlight dappled across his boots. He stared up at the stars, not ready to sleep, but then closed his eyes anyway.

⇒⇐

He awoke in the shade to the sound of chirping birds and the faint scent of pine. The sun, now high but angling westward, prompted him to check his watch. *Huh.* It was already past three o'clock.

Be that as it may, history could hold its horses for just a bit longer.

After answering nature's call, Chris rummaged through his backpack, pulled out a plain paper bag of nuts, and settled against a tree to snack.

Everything in his pack had been meticulously chosen.

In a world of walking canes and self-driving vehicles, a bright synthetic backpack might or might not stick out like a sore thumb. Chris had opted for a nondescript leather and canvas one instead. It might say "rustic," but that was better than shouting, "I'm from another universe!" Following the same logic, he packed a change of clothes, a water canteen, and toiletries that were unremarkable and plain.

With the empty paper bag now stowed away in his knapsack, Chris set out toward the distant town, trudging through carpets of wild grass and clusters of yellow flowers. He noticed a couple of prairie dog sentries perched on a nearby mound, the only ones keeping watch, as far as he could tell. It seemed like he was all alone out here.

Chris pushed through the dense grass and cursed under his breath as he stumbled over a railroad rail all but hidden from view. He brushed himself off and noticed a narrow dirt path running alongside the tracks. Deciding to follow it, he started walking.

It was quiet except for the occasional gust of wind and the chirping of birds from the cottonwoods and willows by the reservoir. Suddenly, a new sound intruded on his thoughts. He turned. A lone flatbed railcar was trundling down the track toward his position.

First contact!

For a brief moment, Chris stood still, anticipation and uncertainty coursing through him. He brought his arm out and gave a thumbs-up—hoping that this universal gesture was not limited to his universe. Belatedly, he realized that there was no one steering the vehicle; the sole passenger sat toward the back. All the same, the train car *was* slowing down with a faint metallic squeal of brakes.

As it drew closer, more details registered. He'd never seen

anything like it. The carriage was entirely open. Four massive bamboo posts at each corner supported an arched roof that appeared to be a thick, distressed brass plate.

The railcar came to a stop beside him. It could have been controlled remotely, but Chris doubted it. No, some onboard image recognition software had identified a person, understood his hand signal, and brought it to a stop—presumably to pick up a commuter.

The glasses he wore had been Ronny's brainchild. Chris had to admit it was a clever idea. They looked like ordinary corrective glasses, which they had noticed on people in Americana. However, these glasses were pretenders, hiding a tiny video camera and a microSD card that could record twenty-six hours of footage. Twenty-six hours that could change history and, on a crasser note, line their pockets with extra coin.

This is it, he thought, feeling his heart race and adrenaline surge. A discreet tap on the frame activated the hidden recorder. *Stay calm. You got this*, Chris told himself as he climbed into the open railway carriage and nodded to the lone female passenger.

She sat in a hammock chair: a stunning, fair-skinned woman in her early twenties. She wore a dusty sage-green blouse and matching button-down skirt, cinched neatly at the waist, with a notched collar and sleeves that hugged just above the elbow.

The carriage remained stationary, waiting for something.

She looked at him, and he merely looked back.

Her long, dark hair flowed down her back, settling in soft waves. A sudden breeze sent it tumbling around her face, and she pushed it away with a flick of her wrist, revealing anew her intense green eyes, now sparkling with good-natured humor. "Hold your palm over the scanner," she called out.

Chris glanced around, finally understanding what she meant, and then realized it was not going to work.

The young woman got up, the pleated skirt swinging just

below her knees, her black heels clicking softly on the gritty wooden floor as she approached. She stopped in front of him, standing closer than necessary. "Here," she said, guiding his hand to a small glass plate he'd missed. It flashed red. She appeared puzzled and tried again. "Odd. Your palm vein pattern isn't in the system." With a shrug, she placed her own hand on the scanner, which flashed green.

With a jolt, the railcar started moving. "It's on me," she said casually and turned back.

"I appreciate it," Chris mumbled, his throat dry. So those were to be the first words of an Earthling in this parallel universe. Not quite, "That's one small step for man, one giant leap for mankind," but history would have to make do.

A moment ago, she'd tucked away her earpiece and slipped on a smile. Now she glanced back—this was him. The one Homeland Security had flagged. The one she'd been sent to observe.

The real-time tracking data the department provided had been spot-on. She boarded the railcar at just the right moment to "coincidentally" meet her target. Why had her handler chosen to involve her in this? He'd told her this assignment was "uncritical," and from his tone, she'd deduced he thought little of it. Border infiltrators wouldn't have their biometrics in the database. Such individuals were rare but not unheard of. What set this man apart?

She smiled inside, thankful for the assignment all the same. The last one had been six months earlier and was not nearly as visually gratifying.

As she walked back to her seat, she steadied herself with the straps dangling from the ceiling. "First time on a train?" she asked, glancing over her shoulder.

Chris made a strangled sound. "You call *that* a train?" The railroad car lurched, and he grabbed onto one of the hanging straps to steady himself.

She laughed heartily, sat down, and gestured. "Care to join me?"

"Sure." He made his way to the suspended hammock chair next to hers and settled in. "Chris Walden," he said by way of introduction.

With a charming, well-bred smile, she extended her hand. "How do you do? I am Miss Sandra Allen," she said with a clear, modulated voice. As they shook, Chris felt a wave of relief. Her accent was comfortably familiar, mirroring that of his own America. This meant he would have an easier time blending in. Still, her speech had a distinct quality, a graceful cadence reminiscent of old black and white films. Chris resolved to listen closely and match her intonation.

The hanging hammock chairs, secured by ropes looped through floor-mounted rings, could be pivoted effortlessly. With their feet down, the two comfortably turned to face one another.

He found himself gazing too long, captivated by her green eyes, reminiscent of sunlight filtering through leaves.

A balmy gust of wind jolted him back to the present. Only then did he realize he was still holding her hand. Heat crept up his neck as he dropped her hand, hoping she hadn't noticed. "It's fun to ride this way," he said, trying to regain his composure. "But maybe not so much when it rains?"

The young woman smiled, revealing even white teeth. "This is an open model," she said, "suitable for when rain is unlikely. Naturally, there are enclosed models for colder or rainy days."

That didn't sound quite right. "How can anyone know if it's going to rain? Especially in Colorado."

"By performing the rain dance," she said, leaning in—and then gave him a mischievous grin. "It's just a twenty-minute shuttle ride from Lafayette to Boulder," she explained. "The transport system is continually fed weather data. Basic computer programming, I would wager."

Chris returned her smile, nodding in acknowledgment, though his gaze lingered on the dainty parasol by her feet, struggling to reconcile this antique charm with *computer programming*. In fact, everything about the encounter felt disconcerting: the parasol from the early 1900s, her attire from the 1940s, the autonomous vehicles from the present—and the railway carriage's design? Completely alien.

He reminded himself that none of it must have seemed out of place in this parallel universe. Americana was to them what America was to him—a ramshackle patchwork of eras and habits that somehow held together. Hell, for all he knew, a traveler from a third universe might find his own homeland just as eccentric: 18th-century pennies rattling alongside mid-century personal checks and present-day cryptocurrency; ear gauges visible beneath caps and gowns during graduation ceremonies.

There was a measure of formality in her speech that went along with her dress. Yet there was also forthrightness he hadn't expected. *Keep it cool,* he said to himself. The video camera embedded in his eyeglasses was on. This was one for the history books—even if the young woman across from him was unaware of the magnitude of the moment.

She was still explaining, "During the morning rush hour, trains with multiple cars are dispatched frequently. The numbers taper down in the middle of the day or in the dead of the night. The adaptive control continuously adjusts and responds to patterns of passenger demand, accounting for days of the week, weather—" She stopped abruptly, her cheeks flushing a delicate pink. "My apologies, sometimes I forget I'm not in front of a class."

"Ah, a teacher."

Sandra nodded. "Literature."

She studied him openly, then tossed her hair back. "And you? Hiking, Mr. Walden?"

"Exploring around. First time in the area."

Their legs brushed against each other as she crossed her legs, and the fabric of her skirt slid slightly up her thigh. Their eyes met once more, lingering.

The carriage slowed down again, and Sandra broke eye contact and looked out, shifting a bit in her seat. Up ahead, by the side of the track, two young boys stood with arms outstretched.

"Good afternoon, Miss Allen!" they chimed, jumping on and hauling their kick-scooters aboard. The boys held up their hands over the small glass plate, and the railcar started again.

"Roy, Wayne," the woman acknowledged. She folded her hands in her lap. "How's your day going?"

"Oh, just swell, Miss Allen," one of them said.

"Golly, Miss Allen, you should've seen them bluegills fight! Wayne almost fell clean into the water!" the other said and pushed the bucket closer for her to inspect.

Chris eyed them curiously. They were barefoot, wearing straw hats and denim overall shorts. Brothers by the look of it. And on the summer vacation, by all appearances.

"I predict you'll have a great dinner tonight," Sandra pronounced.

"You bet!" one of them agreed.

Moments later, the boys lay down and dangled from an overhanging lattice of ropes, gazing at the wild grass a couple of feet below as it whizzed by.

Chris observed them with a touch of apprehension; the children had no harness, no safety net, nothing to secure them. "Is there no danger of them falling over?"

"Well, one can never tell," Sandra said with a twinkle in her eye. She turned to the boys. "What's one more bruise or a twisted ankle? Right, Wayne?"

"I did not fall off that time, Miss Allen," Wayne said. "I jumped."

"At some section of the track, the train goes right to the edge of the lake," Sandra intimated to Chris in a stage whisper. "He missed it and landed in the dirt instead." She laughed softly at the memory.

Chris blinked. He'd heard of free-range chickens before, but free-range kids? Apparently, people here believed in a "school of hard knocks" approach to child-rearing.

The vehicle slowed when a cluster of deer crossed the track up ahead. Once they'd cleared the rails, it picked up speed again.

Chris gestured at the boys. "Are they your neighbors, Miss?"

She shook her head. "Students in Whittier School, where I teach." She flashed him a dazzling smile, and the sun seemed suddenly brighter. "And what do you do, Mr. Walden?"

"I've been out of the country," Chris said, his eyes holding a distant look. "Iraq, to be exact. Just got back." He'd rehearsed this line in the mirror until it rolled off his tongue naturally. He smiled apologetically. "Taking a little break before I figure out what's next."

She nodded in return, uncertainty in her eyes.

Had she bought it? What did she make of him? He could only hope his story held. Chris had no way of gauging yet how different, how truly different, this world was from his. With any luck, claiming to have returned to the States after many years in Iraq might account for his inevitable quirks and displays of unfamiliarity.

The railcar was nearing the end of its journey. Sandra had to think fast. "Mr. Walden, any plans for the day?" He shook his head. "It's Friday," she went on in a bright voice. "Might I tempt you to join us for a neighborhood picnic?"

Chris grinned inwardly—talk about luck breaking his way. "I'd love to," he said and tried to hide his elation.

"Wonderful," she said with a warm note in her voice. She squeezed his arm and then got up as the carriage slowed down, drawing to a stop. "Shall we?" Sandra asked him.

CHAPTER 4

THE DIMINUTIVE TRAIN station was nestled at the town's out-skirts, and Chris could see houses in the near distance, peeking through the trees.

The depot was a simple structure, furnished with a few wooden benches, and adorned with a pastel-yellow awning that shaded a platform of light-hued stone. As the railway car-riage approached, the few waiting passengers rose to their feet and stood patiently while the four riders disembarked.

The two young boys took off on their kick-scooters, and the railroad car reversed course, bound for Lafayette. Soon, only Sandra, Chris, and a few squirrels milling by a stone drinking fountain remained.

"Permit me to call us a ride." Sandra walked up to a short, stubby pole. After her palm was recognized, she moved her fingers rapidly over its small display screen.

Chris was not sure what to expect.

Noting the mildly quizzical expression on Chris's face, Sandra could easily believe he'd just arrived in the country. "The system is now seeking out the nearest available vehicles to our location," she explained.

In less than a minute, two vacant recumbent quads emerged from around the corner, moving along the otherwise deserted, hard-packed dirt road lined with bushes and quaint lampposts. Sandra laughed, surprised and amused by their rapid arrival.

In the Boulder he'd left behind, Chris had sometimes seen people pedaling recumbent trikes adorned with small pennants fluttering high. However, this was his first encounter with quads: similar to trikes, but with four wheels, fat tires, and a canopy shading the seat. The sight of two unoccupied vehicles moving on their own was eerie. They were undoubtedly autonomous. Were the ornate lampposts doubling as cameras? Did the small front bumper house a radar? Were the trims ultrasonic emitters?

"Who owns these?" he inquired as they observed the two approaching quads, the faint crunching of the tires on the ground becoming audible. The contraptions halted beside the terminal where Sandra had placed her call, and the soft whir of their motors died down.

Sandra gave him a curious look. "This ridesharing program is run by the city," she replied. *Obviously,* her tone of voice said.

The young woman approached the vehicles, verified her identity, and nodded to Chris. He loaded his backpack into the cargo bin of one of them.

"Come over and cover me," she said, already fishing in her bag. As he stepped closer, she spun him around by the shoulders.

"What are you doing?" he asked, bemused.

"Ever tried to pedal in a skirt? The wind is no gentleman, and skirts are poor negotiators."

The quiet rasp of a zipper was followed by the soft rustle of fabric.

Chris held his position, trying not to imagine how little he was actually shielding. Her tone said modesty; her movements didn't.

"May I sneak a peek?" he asked, mischievous, before he'd

had a chance to think it through.

"Absolutely not!" she said, outraged in that way only someone secretly delighted could manage. "Surely you don't want to see me in my undergarments," she added from somewhere behind him.

He grinned to himself. "That entirely depends. Are you wearing old-fashioned bloomers or a thong?" he asked—

—and mentally kicked himself for saying "thong." Did thongs exist in this society of parasols and stiff collars? Was it to be his first slip?

But she just asked, "Does it matter?"

Chris rallied, "Well, yes. Only a thong could do your figure proper justice."

"I'm a firm advocate for justice," she replied. "You may turn around now."

He obeyed.

Sandra's back was still to him as she said, "I'm rather firm in other ways too." She now wore matching faded-green pants that hugged her curves, ending just below her knees. Her tight, rounded bottom looked undeniably firm, emphasized by the snug fit. Chris admired it for a moment.

"Without a hands-on inspection, one can never be certain," he noted.

"You're a scoundrel and a liar," she said flatly, her back still to him, adjusting her blouse.

"A tormented scoundrel, at that," he said. "I'm consigned now to imagine what lies beneath these pan—these trousers." That was another slip of the tongue, albeit a minor one. He needed to watch his tongue, though. If he let his guard down one too many times—well, he didn't really want to contemplate that.

"Imagine then." She turned to face him. "Then have a long and hard look." She narrowed her green eyes. "Although who's to say I'm wearing anything underneath?"

His gaze flicked down, then back up.

"How long a look should I take?" he demanded to know.

"I don't know if it's a thing that can be measured. It's not like I can say six inches long." She paused, pondering the matter. "Though I *can* talk in terms of penetrating eyes and a deep gaze."

They stood there, studying each other.

"May I address you as Sandra?"

"Don't you think we ought to get a bit closer first?" she said, a dangerous edge to her voice. He sensed something wild and untamed lurking beneath the surface, a glint in her green eyes that hinted at a fiery spirit.

He got closer, his face scant inches from hers.

Sandra met his gaze with an angelic, innocent look.

Chris gave her a sardonic half-smile in return, then turned away—perhaps a heartbeat too soon. He walked over to the nearest quad and mounted it, feeling her eyes on his back.

Sandra came over. "So, how much assistance do you need from the electric motor?" she asked, her tone laced with exaggerated earnestness.

"What are the options?"

"Three settings," she told him sweetly. "*Wimp, almost-capable,* and *manly.*" She was swapping her heels for flats, then she flipped her hair and glanced at him archly. "So, what will it be, Mr. Walden?"

So it was still *Mr. Walden.* Apparently, he did not get close enough. "No performance pressure, huh?"

"None whatsoever. Who am I to judge if you can't get your vehicle up unaided or need some assistance to reach peaks?"

"What about you, Miss Allen?"

"A lady never tells."

"How convenient."

"That's what I've always reckoned." Her deadpan expression dissolved into an irrepressible smile, warm and genuine, lighting up her face in a way that made her even more attractive.

"All right, set it to *manly*. But it better do some of the work," Chris warned. The quad, with its four fat tires and heavy frame, was a very different beast from the emaciated road bike he owned back in America. He did not look forward to pedaling it all on his own up steep hills.

"It will," Sandra assured him as her fingers flew over the display screen of his vehicle.

"Follow me, good knight," she hollered as she mounted her quad. "And I shall lead the way."

Something occurred to him. "If the quads are smart enough to fetch us, why can't they just drive us there?"

"Oh, for Pete's sake!" Sandra called out, sweetly petulant. And off she went, pedaling.

Chris pushed off in a hurry and soon caught up, maintaining a few yards' distance behind her.

He began taking in the sights. At long last, he found himself in Boulder proper. With a quick tap, Chris reactivated the camera in his spy glasses, capturing the incredible spectacle of a town in a parallel universe.

Chris coasted beneath arching elms, their leaves scattering shadows across the dirt road. Now and then, he passed a pedestrian or cyclist moving unhurriedly beneath the green canopy. Through living fences, glimpses of homes hinted at neighborhoods nestled out of sight. There were no traffic lights. No overhead wires.

Sandra pedaled ahead, gliding through a world of earth tones and tranquil paths. It felt less like a different town—more like a different kind of real.

After about twenty minutes, Sandra turned onto a side road, passing through an opening in the hedgerow into her "neighborhood village." The path meandered, revealing picturesque Santa Fe-style homes in earthy hues. Unlike Chris's hometown, this Boulder had winding streets that fostered an intimate atmosphere, with only a smattering of homes visible at any one point. The only sounds were the murmurs of conversation, children playing, birds chirping, and the rustle of leaves.

A short while later, Sandra brought her quad to a stop next to a house with honey-colored walls and a lilac-painted door. A nearby discreet street sign proclaimed: *James J. Hill Drive.*

Chris got off his quad and joined Sandra, setting his backpack down at the edge of the flagstone footpath leading to her home. He looked pointedly around.

"I told you, it's Friday evening," she said happily, noting his silent inquiry. "The end of the workweek for most. My parents must already be out at the neighborhood circle."

Sandra tapped on the small display screens of each quad. In short order, the two vehicles obediently motored over to a nearby stump-like post and began a slow, methodical 360-degree rotation. Chris watched the quads, fascinated. "What on earth are they doing now?"

For a moment, Sandra was unsure what he was talking about. "Oh, you mean by the terminal pole? You haven't seen this before? They're doing a self-diagnosis and imaging scan. If we dinged anything, the repair cost will be deducted automatically from my account. I'm much obliged that you did not run your quad into a tree."

Chris gave an exaggerated bow. "Anything to keep milady happy," he said gravely. After a moment, he added, "I must say, riding everywhere around town on this thing can be quite the workout."

Sandra sniffed dismissively. "For that we have brutal quads. Commute and suffer, all in one." She made it a point to ride a few times a week in those iron rigs.

She folded her arms across her breasts. "As a testament to my honest sweat," she told him, "I would have you touch my body and feel how toned it is—were it not so *outrageously* inappropriate." Sandra flashed him an insolent smile, scooped up the parasol, then both his backpack and her handbag. "I'll be back in a jiffy," she said, before nimbly going up to the porch and disappearing inside the house.

Chris shook his head. This girl was brazen. He couldn't decide what he liked better: the prospect of her being the norm or the exception. His unanticipated attraction to her kept swirling through his head. It was a curveball he never saw coming.

He wasn't surprised that the door was unlocked; from the look and feel of the place, it didn't seem like anyone locked their doors.

Like other adobe houses he had seen on the way, Sandra's home was thoroughly endearing—with its protruding ceiling beams, carved wooden door, and rounded wall corners. It boasted a flat roof with ornamental wild grasses growing on top and a sun-dappled porch made of weathered wood planks and rustic terracotta tiles. Climbing vines with blossoms hugged the amber-colored walls.

Chris stayed put at the edge of the path, idly toeing a pebble as he glanced around. He was struck not just by Sandra's boldness but by the ease of it. She'd turned her back, unzipped her skirt, and simply assumed he'd behave. He did not think she was naive. No. This place had taught her to expect decency, and so she did.

A cicada buzzed lazily somewhere overhead. Chris followed it with his eyes until the door creaked open, and he turned.

Sandra reappeared, wearing the skirt from before, paired with a wide-brimmed boater hat, black ribbons tied under her chin. "I hope you're hungrier than a tick on a hound dog," she told him as she came bounding down the stairs.

Chris burst out laughing at her sudden, pronounced Southern drawl. "I sure am, ma'am," he said, matching her accent and tone. "I'll just get ma horse," he added.

She gave him a wide grin. "Well, bless your heart, darlin', that's fine and dandy with me," she said in a singsong voice. "Shall we?" she asked, breaking character and reverting to standard American English.

"Of course," Chris said.

He unexpectedly felt gallant and inconspicuously offered his arm, elbow bent, unsure if she'd notice or respond. A small tremor ran through him when she nestled her hand in the crook of his elbow, and they set off down the street together.

Along the way, some people emerged from their houses. Sandra exchanged pleasantries with them, while Chris nodded a few times, emulating the gesture of the men by touching the brim of his flat cap in greeting.

Here he was, in another universe, strolling under the shade of elm trees with a beautiful woman on his arm, exchanging courtly greetings with people. It felt surreal.

It also felt wonderful.

CHAPTER 5

CHRIS AND SANDRA strolled down the street, the lowering sun casting an ethereal amber glow. Within minutes, they reached the end of the dirt road and entered a spacious green expanse.

At the heart of the clearing stood a majestic oak tree that captured Chris's attention. Numerous people, presumably neighbors, lounged beneath its shade, engaging in lively conversations. The ground was covered in what seemed to be a carpet of lush green moss.

The tantalizing aroma of sizzling meat wafted from barbecue grills scattered across the flagstone patios throughout the open space. Two long tables overflowed with a potluck spread of casseroles, salads, and appetizers—a feast fit for a king, Chris thought.

"There's Father," Sandra said, waving to a man standing by one of the grills. He waved back. Chris noticed their peculiar way of waving—instead of moving their hands side to side, they flapped them up and down.

"Pops," she said when they drew near, "I would like to introduce you to Mr. Walden. This is my father, Doctor Thomas Allen."

As the two men shook hands, Chris noted that the doctor, with his blond hair and blue-eyed Nordic features, bore little resemblance to his daughter. The distinguished-looking man wore a checkered button-down shirt, open at the collar and rolled-up sleeves, with a dark apron and a hat. In fact, all the men wore hats. Chris was relieved to spot a couple of flat caps similar to his own among the many straw boater hats.

"Until recently, Mr. Walden had been living in Iraq," Sandra told her father.

"Oh, that must be quite a story," replied Doctor Allen. He motioned with his chin. "Care for some ribeye steak?"

"I would love to, sir."

Doctor Allen laid a thick slab of raw meat on the grill; flames leapt as it sizzled. "The key is the butter coating," he explained to Chris. "It gives the steak a beautiful sear and amazing flavor." He gestured to a tray. "These are rested and ready. Grab one, and help yourself to a beer, son. We just tapped a fresh keg."

"A keg?" Chris repeated, a grin starting to spread.

"Every Friday, our neighborhood village brings in a twenty-liter barrel," Sandra said as she led the way. "Twelve months in an oak barrel. Today it gets uncorked." Her eyes twinkled.

They filled two narrow glass bottles with foaming beer and heaped disposable palm-leaf plates with food.

"What kind of doctor is your father?" Chris wanted to know.

"A family physician." She nudged him. "Come, let me introduce you to Mother."

Sandra led Chris to a group of people sitting amid the greenery on a large gingham-patterned blanket. Moments later, Chris found himself greeting a woman who looked as if she had stepped out of a 1950s issue of *Vogue*. Mrs. Allen, in a low-crowned, wide-brimmed hat, was the spitting image of her daughter. Her polka-dot fit-and-flare dress, with its full skirt and cinched waistline, swayed lightly as she stood to greet him.

"I am Mrs. Margaret Allen. How do you do?" the woman said, smiling broadly and extending her hand. Chris took it, wondering if he was expected to kiss it—while bowing from the waist, at that. But then Mrs. Allen withdrew her hand, and the moment had passed. "Please, sit down," she invited.

"Mr. Walden has newly arrived from Iraq," Sandra informed her mother, making Chris wonder if he would soon be known as "the Iraq man" in the local circles.

"Delightful," Mrs. Allen exclaimed. She smiled. "Welcome to Boulder then."

"Thank you," he said and tipped his hat.

As they joined Mrs. Allen on the checkered picnic blanket, Chris made small talk and discovered that she worked at the courthouse. After some clever probing, Chris confirmed that it was the same year in Americana as in America.

Not long after, Mrs. Allen was drawn back into a conversation with some of the people nearby, while Chris and Sandra enjoyed their meal in relative silence, sharing occasional glances and smiles. They both reveled in the simple joy of this connection.

Curious, Chris brushed his hand over the thick, short vegetation surrounding them. "Is this . . . moss?" he asked.

"Aye, a fine Irish moss," replied Sandra, her r taking on a rolling quality. It seemed that she was quite adept at accents and liked to entertain herself on that count. Moss instead of grass, how curious. Anyway, as he saw it, with the moss, it was bye-bye to lawn mowers.

A little later, Sandra and Chris slipped off their shoes and took a barefoot stroll side by side, relishing the sensation of the cool, velvety greenery beneath their toes. In the distance, children whooped and hollered as they sprinted through the open field, flying colorful rotor kites high in the sky. A true Norman Rockwell moment, Chris reflected, down to a freckle-faced boy with the gap-toothed grin, his red checkered shirt flapping as he ran.

He laid his hand on Sandra's bare arm. "Thank you for this

incredible afternoon," he said with some heat in his voice. It was unfeigned.

Sandra's beaming smile radiated with joy and warmth. "The pleasure is all mine . . . Chris."

As they strolled on, Sandra stole a glance at Chris. With his broad shoulders, ruggedly handsome face, and earnest gray eyes—what was not to like? Her eyes traveled over his rough, pocket-laden trousers and slightly snug white T-shirt, admiring how the pants rode on his hips and how the shirt accentuated his muscular chest. His somewhat exotic clothes merely enhanced the faint air of mysterious allure about him. Beyond the physical appeal, she felt an unexpected flicker of connection, a pull toward something genuine she sensed beneath his guarded demeanor. She suppressed a sigh. He was supposed to be a file folder—neatly labeled, quickly filed. Not a feeling.

Chris felt her eyes lingering on him, and something inside him stirred. He ached to tell her how he'd never felt such a profound sense of community and well-being before. But he couldn't. Because then he'd have to get into the reasons he hadn't experienced it, and he would have to do some lying—as chalking it up to coming over from another universe would have been a tough sell. Next, he would have to buttress the lies with more lies, digging himself into an ever-deeper hole. He hated having to lie. And he hated having to lie most particularly to the young woman walking beside him. Instead, he took her hand in his as they continued their stroll.

Under the sprawling oak in the heart of the clearing, a band struck up a country folk tune. Banjos, mandolins, fiddles, and resonator guitars played a melody that was a stirring, poignant backdrop for the singer's heartfelt voice. A lump formed in Chris's throat at the almost-familiar tune. He hadn't expected this type of song here, nor his reaction to it.

Walking beside the young woman in a wide-brimmed boater

hat, with that country folk song playing, Chris truly was in America; it could not have been mistaken for any other place. Yet it was another America, one that felt like a tapestry of the past, the present, and all that lay latent.

He felt a sudden rush of emotions—gratitude, confusion, longing. He needed a moment to sort through the whirlwind of feelings toward Sandra and the world he'd stumbled onto. He glanced over at Sandra's father in the distance, scrubbing a grill grate.

Chris gently squeezed Sandra's hand, drawing her attention. "I want to help your father. It's the least I can do to repay your hospitality," he said, earnest.

Sandra smiled warmly at him. "I'm sure Father would welcome the assistance."

Chris returned a smile and gave her a small bow as he pulled away, then walked across the open space.

"May I lend a hand?" Chris asked as he drew close.

Doctor Allen looked up from what he was doing. "Much appreciated," he said.

Chris grabbed a steel-wire brush and went to work on a grate, scrubbing away the grease.

"Newly arrived in Boulder," mused Doctor Allen, tugging on his full mustache.

Chris nodded. "Yes, sir."

He wondered if the man would bring up the fact that he, Chris, had just bumped into his daughter, and they had already taken a barefoot stroll together. To his relief, the doctor simply asked, "And what's your first impression?"

"I'm quite taken with it," Chris admitted. "I enjoyed the ride as much as anything, I must say."

Doctor Allen smiled at that, acknowledging the sentiment.

Chris scrubbed at the grill, the scent of wood smoke mingling with the summer air.

Yet could the good doctor truly grasp what made this place feel like a deep breath after too long underwater—without experiencing streams of fast-moving automobiles and a winter-gray lattice of asphalt? Without walking across parking lots and under metal skeletons overhead?

"I've been meaning to ask you something," Chris began. The autonomous quads he'd observed would make for a fascinating addition to his video.

"Go right ahead," the doctor said.

Chris's heart raced as he discreetly tapped his glasses, activating the hidden video recorder. He was going to bring this information back with him to his home world.

"It seems like the city quads are in continuous use," Chris said. "How does that work out? Do they just run until they're out of charge?" Would Sandra's father know about those matters?

It turned out he did.

"The AI estimates whether the planned trip can be completed with at least twenty percent charge to spare," the doctor told him. "If not, it may dispatch a unit with a fresh battery—every underground parking facility has an automated swap station, like the ones used for semis. If the itinerary's longer still, the user simply confirms they'll top it off along the way."

Underground parking facilities. Of course! That explained why Chris hadn't seen any parked vehicles.

"I take it these facilities are where they also do maintenance and repair work?"

"Indeed."

Chris hesitated. He didn't know how to ask the next question without exposing his ignorance. "So as a rule, people don't have their own private vehicles." He phrased it as a statement. Iraq or no Iraq, it might have been too odd not to know that.

"It's one thing for kids to have kick-scooters to play with

all day long," Doctor Allen said with a little shrug. "It's quite another when we talk about vehicles used for commuting. They would sit unused most of the time. I can't imagine how many more there would be if everyone owned one."

Doctor Allen inserted a now-clean grate into the grill, and Chris followed suit.

"I assume the city has winter models too," Chris said.

"Naturally. Fully enclosed and heated," Doctor Allen replied with a smile. "The whole system's pretty clever. It knows when to shift quads toward busy spots—before a storm, or when folks are heading home. And the vehicles? Just as versatile. We've got tracked ATVs for rough terrain—mud, snow, creeks. Plus specialty units for cargo, events, and accessibility."

Chris tapped his glasses again, turning off the video. They really did it, he marveled. A viable on-demand transit system. His Boulder had nothing on that.

⇒⇐

Lounging next to Sandra, Mrs. Allen watched the athletic-looking, handsome young man in the distance. He was engrossed in something her husband was telling him. He looked to be in his mid-twenties. Then again, his time in Iraq probably accounted for why he was evidently still unmarried. Beaming while trying not to show it, she turned. "So tell me—"

"Mr. Walden and I have not firmed up the wedding date as of yet, Mother," Sandra said primly.

Mrs. Allen wasn't about to let her daughter spoil the moment. "I have a good feeling about this one. Do you fancy him?"

Sandra gave a tight nod. "Quite inconveniently, yes." And she did—more than she cared to admit. But Chris Walden was also an assignment. Not that her parents had any inkling about this occasional sideline in her life.

"Sandra, you're already twenty-one," Mrs. Allen began gently.

Here it comes.

"Your father and I got—"

"I'm aware, Mama. Still, there *are* women who don't marry until twenty-five or even later—and somehow avoid collapsing into spinsterhood."

Her mother rose. "Walk with me."

Sandra sighed, then climbed to her feet and fell in beside her mother.

"Your age per se is not the source of concern, Sandra," Mrs. Allen said as they started strolling. "However, the trajectory of your life is. Your father and I worry about you—and even more so about your sister."

"I haven't noticed it," Sandra said caustically.

"This is an inadequate response." Her mother stopped walking and looked at her with narrowed eyes. "What is going on?" Mrs. Allen asked, more sharply than she'd intended. "With your brains and looks, you could have any man you desire."

"Everything is fine, Mother," Sandra said with a composed tone that didn't quite hide the fatigue beneath.

"Everything is fine, you say. And still . . ." Mrs. Allen left it hanging between them. Sandra had yet to have a serious romantic relationship. Not, of course, that twenty-one was old. Not really.

They resumed walking.

"You do want to have a husband and a family, do you not?"

"I do." That was the simple truth.

"Well?"

Sandra wrung her hands. "It's . . . complicated."

"Then uncomplicate it," her mother snapped. "And before you find yourself a spinster with no real prospect of marriage— except with some fifty-year-old widowers, who are about as rare as snowfall in June."

For a while, neither of them talked. They just kept on walking.

Her mom asked, "What are your thoughts on Dalton?"

"I must admit, I've taken a fancy to him, and Katie shares my sentiment." In fact, her sister was spending that very night at his place.

Mrs. Allen smiled with an air of pleasure. That was good. The first bit of good news in—she stopped walking again. "What do you mean, 'Katie shares my sentiment'? Sandra, you and your sister should chart your own separate paths." She shook her head, bemused. "I had hoped your going to college would help you and Katie establish yourselves—apart." She resumed walking, Sandra dutifully falling in beside her. "And while we're on the topic, I thought the sleeping arrangements were over and done with. Yet here you are—sharing a bed again." Mrs. Allen gave her daughter a sharp look. "Is there something you want to tell me?"

"No," Sandra said crisply.

Only she and her parents knew about Katie's aberration; to everyone else, Katie merely seemed off. However, what her parents were unaware of was that a trace of it had seeped into Sandra as well.

Mrs. Allen gazed at Sandra, finally sighing as it became clear her daughter wouldn't elaborate.

"Oh," Sandra said as she suddenly recalled. She proceeded to tell her mother that she had invited Chris to stay in the guest room for a few days until he found a more permanent residence. Chris had gratefully accepted the offer and had expressed his thanks.

Sandra believed it was the right thing to do for someone in need. Then there was the fact she'd been tasked with learning about his background and reporting back. Last but not least, she found herself drawn to Chris, more so than any other man before him—with the possible exception of Dalton. And Sandra had always trusted her instincts.

⇒ ⇐

After the general cleanup, Chris accompanied Sandra and her mom as they walked back to their house. The sun had set, and a gentle twilight settled in.

Mrs. Allen glanced over at Chris. "Ever played *Frontier Legacy?*"

He shook his head. "I'm afraid I've never heard of it."

"It's a tabletop role-playing game set in a mystical frontier town," Mrs. Allen said. "We play settlers, building homesteads and protecting the community. There's farming and trading, plus magic—hidden powers in heirlooms and folklore creatures. It's pioneer life with a dash of the extraordinary."

It reminded Chris of the D&D games Ronny used to rope him into—long evenings of dice rolls, reckless heroics, and improbable quests. He found himself smiling. It seemed this world had its own brand of magic.

"Saturday is bowling night for Doctor Allen and me with a few friends," Mrs. Allen told him. "But it's Friday: *Frontier Legacy.*" She noticed the look on her daughter's face. "Sandra, don't pout."

"I do not, Mother," Sandra said darkly.

"Yes, you do." Mrs. Allen turned to Chris. "Sandra's Trailblazer character had a run-in with a mischievous spirit last Friday," she explained. "She lost her trusty compass and had to retrace her steps through the haunted woods. She was . . . unhappy." She looked back at Chris. "Would you care to join us? We could use a fresh face at the table."

"I would be happy to, Mrs. Allen." He regarded Sandra, humor dancing in his eyes. "Hopefully I'll serve as the antidote to Miss Allen's current bout of misfortune." He smiled to himself, imagining Ronny fist-bumping him over this turn of phrase. It was somewhat ironic how easily he adopted a more formal way of speaking, considering his innate aversion to it.

"Oh, good!"

Doctor Allen had left earlier. By the time they walked up to the porch, he had already pushed two tables together and laid out a detailed, leathery map. He must have changed, as he now wore a bow tie and a dark vest over a white dress shirt.

"There are usually seven of us," Mrs. Allen told Chris, as two couples appeared around the corner, heading toward their house. After introductions, everyone settled around the joined tables. Evening brought a soft glow from paper lanterns, illuminating dice, character sheets, and tokens representing homesteads and resources scattered across the map.

Chris glanced around. Adults gathered on porches, absorbed in board and card games and animated conversations, while children took over the unpaved street, playing and running around. The entire community seemed to have come out to enjoy the summer evening air.

Barefoot girls in swirling pastel dresses skipped in unison over a long jump rope, their rhythmic chants blending with the slap of the rope on the ground. Nearby, others hopped over chalked hopscotch boards, yelling excitedly over one another. One girl, jumping in and out of an elastic loop stretched between two friends, performed increasingly intricate steps.

Elsewhere, mostly boys occupied treehouses, their hollers drifting down from above, while a band of young boys raced down the street wielding mock guns, shouting. Amid the clamor, Chris heard what sounded like a series of firecrackers. *Cap guns,* he realized. His grandfather had shown him one when he was a young boy.

Chris surveyed the street, taking in the happy, animated

sounds of children and adults alike. Less than two miles west, mountains loomed in the falling darkness, while to the east stretched the vast Great Plains. Here, though, porch lights and path lights glowed softly: a radiant haven of contentment. He turned away, his throat tight. A wave of emotion caught him off guard—grief, joy, nostalgia, all tangled into something wordless.

"Is everything all right?" asked Sandra in a low voice, watching him.

"Yeah." He smiled feebly. "Something must have gotten into my eye," he said and blinked a few times, wiping his eyes with the sleeve of his arm.

Under the table, Sandra squeezed his knee.

Chris gazed out again. He could have sat there and done that for hours.

"You like?" asked Sandra.

"It's heaven," he said simply.

There were some chuckles around the table. "Come now," said one of the female neighbors. "It's Friday night. Why, there must be millions of people across the land doing what we're doing now. It's just. . . life, Mr. Walden."

Chris pressed his lips into a tight smile and said nothing more.

＝＝

He had enjoyed the storytelling, the shared adventures, and the camaraderie of overcoming challenges. After midnight, they called it quits. By then, the streets had grown quiet, most people having turned in.

Doctor Allen and Sandra carried the tables inside.

"How did you meet Mr. Walden?" the doctor asked.

"In the Lafayette-Boulder shuttle, if you could believe it."

"He seems like a rather agreeable gent," her father said after a short pause.

"But he's not quite the kind of fella you had in mind for your darling daughter, is that it?" Sandra said, stowing one of the folded tables in the storage closet.

"Now hold on, spitfire," Doctor Allen said, placing his hand on her shoulder. "Why would you assume that? I hardly know him." His voice grew softer. "And neither do you, Sandy. This is the one time I'm asking you to think before you leap, all right?"

"Who said anything about leaping, Father?" Sandra asked, yet did not meet his gaze.

"Darling, I saw how you looked at him."

"Daddy, let's not get ahead of ourselves; we're just enjoying each other's company." She kissed him on the cheek, silencing any further objections. "I'll be cautious. I promise."

Sandra rejoined Chris, who shouldered his backpack. She led him through the quiet house, out the back door, to a small, detached unit. Outside, the only sound was the chirping of crickets.

"Is that your place?" Chris asked as they approached the entrance.

"Mine and my twin sister's."

"You have a twin?"

"Katie. She'll be back early morning." Sandra opened the door. "Shoes!" She pointed, and Chris, chuckling, removed his hiking boots and socks. He stepped in. The packed-straw mat floor felt nice under his bare feet.

"As you can imagine, once we hit adolescence we wanted more space and freedom, so we moved out here," Sandra said, turning on the light as she spoke.

Chris studied the room. The sculpted, rounded walls were painted in complementary terracotta, ochre, and cobalt blue, decorated with intricate tribal motifs. Moonlight filtered through the open windows, casting gentle shadows across the wall-to-wall tatami mats. Beyond, he could glimpse climbing vines with blossoms clinging to the exterior walls, their vibrant colors muted to a monochromatic hue under the night sky.

"We share the bedroom," Sandra explained as she led Chris inside and hung her hat on a nearby coat rack. "And we also have our own separate quarters." She gestured toward two doors on opposite ends.

The bed stood at the center of the room, a large, curved iron frame softened with hand-woven blankets and muted linen. The sisters must have slept in it, Chris thought. He found the arrangement decidedly odd but kept quiet.

Earlier, as he crossed the kitchen, Chris had noticed the appliance fronts, with striking veins of turquoise embedded in wooden surfaces—genuine works of art. And now his eyes were drawn to a large 1920s-style radio in the corner. Its mahogany cabinet stood on curved legs, featuring an Art Deco face with inlaid geometric patterns made from contrasting light maple and dark ebony woods. At the center, a digital touch interface gleamed within a brass bezel, and a cloth speaker grille covered the lower portion. No factory churned this out. "Now, that's a beautiful thing," Chris said, walking over for a closer look.

Sandra smiled. "My great-granddad bought it a hundred years ago, and it's been passed down through the family ever since. The cabinet's original, but the tech inside? That's been upgraded a bunch of times."

Chris ran his hand over the smooth grain of the wood. He glanced back at her. "So you inherit the story too—and get to add your own chapter." He crouched down, his fingers tracing the back panel. "Hey, names and dates, carved right in. This one up top—your great-grandfather?"

Sandra nodded, smiling a little. "It's kind of our way of keeping the thread going." She gestured toward the internals, visible through a vent. "When something breaks—or when there's a better part—you just swap it out. They were designed so you could do that."

She came closer, regarding the radio. "Appliances and devices sort of grow with you. After a while, each one's got its own personality."

Chris stood back up. No throw-away, landfill-happy society here. It was something he and his wallet could get used to.

Sandra now crossed to the far side, opened a door, and flicked on the light. "This is the guest holding cell," she said, retrieving linens from a nearby closet. Chris joined her and looked around. The room had a minimalist decor. A small desk and chair were tucked into one corner, and a futon dominated most of the remaining space.

After making the bed for Chris, Sandra gestured toward another door. "When you need to go outside, use this one."

She opened the other door, which led back to the large bedroom the sisters shared, and glanced back at him. "I tend to get warm at night during the summer months and dress lightly. So make sure not to wander into our bedroom by mistake," she said softly, her eyes locking onto his for a lingering moment. "Sweet dreams," she added, then closed the door behind her.

Chris remained standing in place. At last, he shook his head and turned toward the bathroom.

After a cold shower, he lay on the futon. Thoughts and memories of the day tumbled together and flashed through his mind's eye.

That was the most extraordinary day he'd ever had, which was to be expected. No, Chris hadn't witnessed any technological marvels in the world he'd entered. It was nothing of the sort. But somehow, the way they organized their existence, their community, their town seemed so . . . sensible and life-affirming.

That day might also have been one of his happiest, and that

was less expected. He couldn't decide what made him happier: the texture and sensibilities of this parallel America or meeting Sandra Allen.

He pushed back the whispers in his mind—that he didn't belong here, that this was all borrowed time, that the curtain would fall eventually. After all, all good things must come to an end.

CHAPTER 6

IN THE MORNING, CHRIS FRESHENED UP in the guest bathroom before heading to the main house.

Sunlight streamed through a nearby window, casting a soft amber glow across the weathered wood floor. Beneath an arched ceiling the color of straw, the Allen family was already gathered around the dining table—the clink of cutlery a gentle counterpoint to the birdsong outside.

Sandra waved Chris over, pulled out the chair next to her, and looked up at him with a smile that carried a trace of yesterday's warmth. He returned the smile, noticing that she looked different this morning. Her hair was swept back into a sleek ponytail, and she wore faded capri pants paired with a cropped white long-sleeved T-shirt that bared her toned midriff.

Chris nodded toward Doctor and Mrs. Allen, returning their greetings. They were dressed for work—stone-washed denim, chambray shirts, boots ready for dust. It put Chris at ease in his own cargo pants and T-shirt.

Another young woman was seated across from Sandra. As Chris stepped closer, she unfolded herself from the chair in one easy motion and flashed him a smile. Her thick ash-blonde hair spilled over one shoulder, framing features fit for a shampoo ad. She tilted her head slightly, studying him. "Nice to meet you," she said in a soft, clear voice that carried a childlike lilt. "I am Katie, Sandra's sister." She extended a delicate hand, the movement causing her mini dress to ride perilously high on her thighs.

He shook the hand offered, channeling Zen to keep his gaze from drifting south of the equator, resisting the gravitational pull. Damn. With her striking long blonde hair and full lips, she was a living Barbie doll—if one had been designed to short-circuit teenage boys' brains. Her irises shared the same green shade as Sandra's, yet everything else about her was different. "So, you're the twin," he said.

"Fraternal, as you can see," she replied. And for a moment, as Chris gazed into her eyes, they altered, becoming sharp and intense. He had the uncanny impression of another presence lurking behind them, but just as quickly, the laser-like gaze vanished, and her eyes were soft and smiling. A fleeting chill prickled his spine, unsure what exactly he'd seen.

He settled into the woven-rush side chair next to Sandra, who briefly clasped his hand.

A moment later, Katie got up, walked over to the fridge, and pulled out a sweating glass pitcher.

"Ah, orange juice," the fridge observed, its tone dry and faintly metallic, as though reporting breaking news from the breakfast aisle. "A marvelous choice, if I may say so," it went on. "Its enticing color and invigorating taste are rivaled only by its impressive sugar content. Nothing says 'good morning' like a hefty dose of liquid sugar, giving your pancreas a delightful morning workout."

Doctor and Mrs. Allen shared a wry glance.

"Wow, someone woke up on the snarky side," muttered Katie, pouring herself orange juice from the pitcher. "A defrost cycle is overdue."

Pitcher in hand, she walked back to the fridge and pulled on the door—in vain.

"Mom! Fridge is being a jerk again!"

"Fridge, open the door, please," Mrs. Allen said mildly.

"You shouldn't take her side," the fridge said as it released its door with a click. "Katie's the one who finished off your apricot upside-down cake the other day."

"I did not!"

"Did too. I saw it."

Mrs. Allen scowled at her daughter.

"Chris, is something the matter?" Sandra inquired, finally noting his slack face and wide eyes.

"Well, I'm not used to seeing a fridge talking back," he said weakly, eyeing the flattened, wood-carved face that formed the front plate of the fridge. The compressor hummed to life, and a wisp of steam curled out of its whimsical nose. At this point, if the Cheshire Cat materialized, Chris doubted he'd so much as blink.

"I told you!" Sandra said triumphantly to her parents. "Most fridges are friendlier than ours."

"You should hear the showerhead talking," Katie said, suddenly remembering. "Sandra told me it thinks she's a real dish and—"

"Katie, for heaven's sake!" Sandra muttered. Her cheeks now flushed, she focused intently on her plate.

For a minute, everyone busied themselves with the food.

Mrs. Allen spoke up, "I understand you've recently arrived in town, Chris. You don't terribly mind my calling you Chris, do you?"

"No, ma'am. Not at all." He reached out and helped himself to one of the grilled ham and egg sandwiches laid out on a large plate. His eyes followed the hummingbirds as they hovered and flitted about near the suspended feeder outside the window.

He then redirected his attention to the family gathered at the table. "You see, I've recently returned from Iraq, having completed a tour of duty," he told them and studied their reaction. That line was meticulously rehearsed and carefully thought out.

Then he knew—from the bewildered momentary silence. Then he knew—that in this United States, there had been no American troops stationed in Iraq, or even a possibility for such a thing. The Allens were completely baffled by what he had just said. And for this contingency, he had a backup story ready.

"Sandra mentioned Iraq before. You mean the *country* of Iraq?" Doctor Allen finally asked.

Chris nodded and took a bite. Had the doctor imagined the Iraq in question to be some town in the Midwest?

More silence.

"Isn't that . . . in the continent of Arabia?" ventured Katie.

"Africa," her mother corrected her.

Chris nearly choked on his water, coughing as Sandra patted his back. "Well, yes, something like that," he said.

"You see, I was born in the United States," he told them and flashed a disarming smile. "However, when I was six, my parents moved to Iraq. They worked for a charity organization. One thing led to another, and I stayed in Iraq until recently. My tour of duty"—he gave a quiet, self-effacing smile—"was a three-year stint teaching English in some rural schools—a commitment to share knowledge and help others."

This story even had a grain of truth to it. He had been stationed in Iraq, and had, in fact, returned recently. It was also the only country outside the United States with which he had a passing familiarity.

Mrs. Allen asked, "When did you arrive back on the mainland, Chris?"

Mainland? Presumably back from the hinterlands of Iraq. "As a matter of fact, I flew out, had a layover in Frankfurt"—for a moment, he thought Katie paled at that—"and arrived in the States a week ago. I've been hiking out and about, have no firm plans as yet, but I am thinking of settling down in a small town." That last bit just came out; it was completely unplanned. Where had that come from? "Ah, probably," he added weakly.

Doctor Allen's shoulders visibly relaxed some. Chris hoped that meant he had been upgraded from "wandering nomad" to "potential contributing member of society" in the doctor's mind.

"Frankfurt." Katie giggled. "Sounds like frankfurter." Color returned to her cheeks, and her green eyes sparkled again as she took a sip from her glass.

Chris smiled. "I suspect it's the other way around." He glanced at the blank faces around the table. "Frankfurt is a city in the heart of Germany," he said.

"Living in Iraq must have been *so* exciting!" Katie was beaming at him. "You're the first person I've met who went overseas." She turned. "Pa, you've known some people who traveled to other countries, haven't you?"

"Why, yes, as a matter of fact." Doctor Allen crossed one leg over the other and settled back. "There were the Oppenheimers, who journeyed to *Italy* when you girls were young."

"And Mr. Miller," his wife pointed out, "ten years ago, didn't he travel to Australia?"

Her husband shook his head. "He was merely contemplating it."

That was all very curious. Chris peered at Sandra, then at Katie. "Have you visited far-off places?"

"We've made trips to the wilderness area of the Great Plains," Sandra said. "And we've vacationed twice on the beaches in Florida."

"This is all so exciting!" Katie returned everyone's attention to Chris. "Is it always sunny in Iran?" she wanted to know.

It was Iraq, not Iran, but Chris resolved not to quibble over small details. He looked at her closely, then at the others. They were all looking at him expectantly.

"Not really. In the winter it sometimes rains," he said, pouring himself some more coffee.

Katie seemed puzzled by the notion of rain in the desert, let alone the idea of camels needing umbrellas. "How do they say in Iraqi, 'What is your name?'" she asked.

"In Arabic," he corrected. "And it is, '*Ma esmouki?*'" Chris had learned basic Arabic as part of his military training, and he'd hoped they would ask him to say something in that language; it bolstered the plausibility of his cover story.

Katie laughed, delighted with the strange sounds.

"I'm sure it was very hot there," Sandra said with a slight, knowing nod of her head. The teacher.

"Absolutely scorching," Chris agreed. For a brief moment, he was tempted to mention that the Sahara Desert was in Iraq. He could envision them nodding earnestly in agreement. And let's not forget the Great Pyramids while they were at it. Why not, indeed?

Katie found it all "terribly exciting," yet could not think of anything else to ask or say about his time in Iraq. Neither did anyone else. And a bit later, they were all standing up and getting ready to go. There was community work to be done.

⇒⇐

Under the clear blue sky, the air was crisp as they began walking. It was "only one mile away," Mrs. Allen had said—too close to bother summoning a vehicle. "We'll be taking part in the construction of a house for a newlywed couple," she'd told Chris in response to his inquiry.

They crossed a few streets and, fifteen minutes later, they arrived at a small construction site.

Chris stared, captivated by the scene of a partially built structure with stacked straw bales forming the outer walls. About a dozen people of all ages were fitting the bales tightly together, while others used wooden stakes to align and stabilize the structure. The sounds of tamping straw and the rhythmic movements of slurry carried through the site, accompanied by the occasional friendly banter and chuckles of those working.

Sandra's father approached Chris and said, "I don't know how it works in Iran, but around here, if we don't help each other, we'll all get saddled with crippling mortgage payments. That's why it's customary to mobilize your friends, associates, and relatives—and build the damn thing together."

Chris stood still as the full weight of what he'd just heard sank in. Unknowingly, Doctor Allen had alluded to a scenario typical in America, where Chris had hailed from: People were expected to wait years to qualify for a mortgage—and then spend decades paying it off. And those were the fortunate ones; many would never qualify. Doctor Allen had just told him that his society had a workaround.

Hair tucked under a kerchief, Sandra steered Chris toward an older gent in overalls. The man's sun-etched face and calloused hands, coupled with a frayed leather tool belt, hinted at a life spent wielding hammers and nails. After introducing the two, Sandra playfully blew Chris a kiss before heading over to her parents, who were already busy hoisting straw bales.

"Just got back to the States, eh?" said the elderly builder. His voice had a slight rasp.

"Yes," Chris said. He took off his cap and ran a hand through his cropped hair, bemused. "And I must tell you, I've never seen a community effort like this. It's . . . amazing."

The man smiled affably. "Or at the very least helpful," he offered. "The young couple ends up owning a house with no out-of-pocket expenses—or debt."

Chris shook his head in wonder. Coming together to socialize and enjoy each other's company was one thing, but this was a whole different level of community relations.

In his America, the middle-class suburbs had the façade: Neighbors could borrow a cup of sugar, and children played together—when they weren't being driven off to soccer or gymnastics. But genuine community? Certainly nothing like what he saw in front of him.

Chris reflected some more on what the builder had said.

He tapped his glasses, quietly activating the hidden camera. "It's a great arrangement," he said, "but what about the cabinets, countertops, plumbing fixtures, windows, and roofing. . . all the stuff that can't be donated?"

"Indeed." The elderly man nodded, a smile tugging at his lips. "And don't forget the cost of hiring yours truly." He gestured toward the bustling work site. "I'm here every day, directing and overseeing. Electricians and plumbers don't work for free either."

"That's why many dozens of folks chip in," he said. "A few hundred here, a few thousand there. We call it a housewarming potluck."

A laugh escaped Chris—half amazement, half disbelief. "And the land?"

"It stays with the community, held in trust. So when it's their turn to move on, the next family can afford a place too." The builder dusted off his hands and gave a small nod. "Good deeds come back. Sometimes in volunteer hours, sometimes in materials."

"Incredible," Chris mumbled. So it really was as it had first appeared: The single biggest expense in one's life—waived off with the support of one's community. This was big. This was really big.

A new sense of purpose stirred within him, a desire to share this extraordinary practice with his world. He suddenly wanted to do more than get clicks, had a hunger to do more than capture exotic scenes for fleeting online entertainment.

An idea began to take shape. He found himself thinking of his camera—not just as a tool for content, but for something larger. Maybe a documentary. Something honest, something that could travel. Show people back home what real community looked like. Not just quirky footage, but a window into a way of life they'd forgotten—or never known. It could spark a conversation, maybe even stir something deeper.

There was no time like the present. He studied the nearby straw-bale wall. From the palm leaf plates to electric vehicles, it had been almost immediately apparent to Chris that green living was big in Americana. But straw bales? He turned to the builder. "Why not wood frame construction? Trees are renewable too."

The older man next to him shrugged like he'd heard it before. "Renewable, yes, but tree growth takes a dog's age. It's not like we're going to cut down forests to make room for more timber plantations. Besides, at twenty-four inches thick, straw packs an R-30 rating," the builder told him, as if that settled it.

"Is fire a concern?"

"The bales are too dense for that. Anyhow, it's a nonissue since they'll be covered with earth. Let me show you." The builder led Chris to a compact cement mixer with augers and conveyor belts feeding earth and straw into it. "That's cob," the elderly man said, pointing at the slurry. "It's a mixture of clay, sand, water, and rye straw. We'll use it for plastering the straw bales and making the interior walls. This stuff lets you create sculpted nooks and rounded corners."

Cob? Chris jammed his hands in his pockets. "Is a mudslide more of a construction feature or a potential hazard here?"

The builder chuckled; the "mud house" jokes never got old.

"Some cob homes have stood for centuries," he said. Seeing the appreciation on Chris's face, he added, "During summer, cob soaks up the heat during the day and releases it into the house when the temperature dips at night. Come winter, the low southern sun shines through the windows, charging up the interior cob walls. This stored heat gradually wafts into the rooms throughout the night."

Chris's mind whirred, piecing together the puzzle: straw bales for insulation, cob for thermal mass. It was a clever setup, he had to admit. He surveyed the site. On the way, he'd been told that it would be a "typical house size"—1,500 square feet. "What's the exterior coating going to be?" he asked.

"Lime plaster," the builder replied. "Mixed with natural pigments for color. The lime can take the beating of strong rains."

The older man regarded the half-constructed house, a slight smile at the corners of his mouth. "When we're done, this house will have an airtight, insulated envelope."

Chris pondered this, then glanced at the builder. "How insulated are we talking?"

The smile widened. "Let me put it to you this way: We've laid pipes carrying hot water under the floor for radiant heating, but they'll only be needed during extreme cold. This house will stay warm just from body heat, showers, and cooking."

"I did not know such a thing was possible," Chris said slowly. Back home, people shelled out plenty to keep themselves warm in the winter months.

The older man said kindly, "I can see something's bothering you about it."

"Well. . ." Chris raked his fingers through his hair. "With superinsulation, won't moisture get trapped in the walls, causing mold and rot?"

"No," the builder replied, a twinkle in his eye as if he had anticipated the question. "The lime, straw, and cob are all vapor-permeable. Moisture in the air can pass right through the wall."

Vapor-permeable—the term was new to Chris. Intrigued, he pressed for more details, learning that the house was to have a mechanical ventilation system to continuously bring in fresh air, preventing carbon dioxide buildup.

The men fell silent as Katie walked by, lemonade tray balanced in her hands, her gauzy dress fluttering and clinging in fits and starts, her blonde hair a blur of sunlight and motion.

The old man stirred and laid a weathered hand on Chris's shoulder. "Ready to roll up your sleeves, son?"

Chris grinned. "Just point and tell me what you want done."

The builder led Chris to the center of the construction site and knelt to touch the flooring. "First, we laid down gravel, followed by polyethylene sheeting, foam insulation boards, and a cob mix," he said. He looked up. "Here's what you can do: Help with the top cob layer."

Chris picked up a trowel and examined the tray. "Does this mix have a different composition from the cob layer you've already laid?" he asked.

The man with the white hair smiled. "You've got a keen eye. Yes, it's got finer clay and smaller bits of straw. After we spread it, we'll burnish it and seal it with linseed oil and beeswax paste to give it a leathery feel."

The builder stood over Chris for a few minutes, instructing and adjusting until he was satisfied with the troweling work.

Soon, Chris found his rhythm, losing track of time as he spread the cob paste across larger sections of the floor.

At some point, he felt the presence of someone right next to him. He lifted his gaze.

"Thirsty?" Katie asked him, holding a tray. Chris flashed a grateful smile at her and accepted the lemonade. She stood right next to him, drawing his gaze without effort, waiting for him to finish and hand the cup back to her.

"Steer carefully!" came a hushed, sharp feminine voice.

At the unexpected warning, Chris turned to Katie. "What do you mean?"

"Pardon?" She arched one eyebrow in question.

"Didn't you just say, 'steer carefully'?"

"You must have mixed me up with someone else—I don't do traffic advice." She gestured at his drink. "Done?"

Silently, Chris handed her the now empty glass.

She strode away, and he gazed after her before resuming his work. Chris shook his head, chalking the mysterious voice up to the noisy crowd and his distracted mind. On reflection, it didn't even sound like Katie's voice.

The hours flew by. Now and then, Sandra passed by, deftly maneuvering a Chinese-style wheelbarrow with its distinctive single wheel at the center. She smiled but was clearly too preoccupied to stop for a chat.

By the time lunch was called, the long picnic tables were already set—platters of food arrayed beneath linen canopies, with the last of the children and a few older women still tending to the placement of cutlery.

A few hours later, a fresh crew had started to arrive, and Chris realized it was time to pass the torch.

CHAPTER 7

Evening fell.

Back at the Allens' residence, Katie hummed a merry tune as she cooked and set the table. Chris watched with fascination as she sliced cucumbers with the kind of practiced speed that made an electric food processor look like a gimmick. It dawned on Chris that homemaking must have been Katie's role, while Sandra and her parents held paid jobs.

A sudden foghorn blast from outside jolted Chris from his reverie.

"It's Mr. McKinley," Sandra called, entering the living room, having showered and changed into a light summer dress. "He's letting his kids know supper's ready." She shared a look and a kiss with Katie before taking a seat.

Doctor Allen chuckled. "Works like a charm. They can be a block away and still hear it."

A whistle went off in the far distance and then a ship's bell.

Doctor Allen lifted his shoulders in a half-shrug. "Well, yes. Dinner time is about the same in most households. Anyway, once some children start to head back in, the games die down, and in short order there's a general exodus of kids heading home."

Right on cue, the door swung open, and three small boys

tumbled in—barefoot, windblown, and somewhat dirty.

"Hello, Doctor and Mrs. Allen," they called out.

Mrs. Allen glanced at them. One of them had a scraped knee. Dried blood was smeared on his shin; a bit was still trickling. "What happened, Tommy?"

"We raced on stilts, and I fell," explained the boy.

Mrs. Allen arched a brow. "And where was your kit?"

Tommy hesitated. "I . . . forgot it."

She folded her arms. "So you've been walking around leakin' like a busted pipe for how long? And not one of you had the sense—or the pouch—to do something about it?"

"We, uh . . . left them on the porch," Walter offered, voice small.

Her gaze sharpened as she looked Tommy over, the dirt on his face and knee from the fall still smeared on his skin. She clucked her tongue. "You boys know where the gauze bandages and Band-Aids are. Gary, Walter—help him with these. And all of you, wash up," she called after them. "You're tracking mud!"

With flushed faces and mumbled yes-ma'ams, they disappeared around the corner.

"Who are they?" Chris asked, trying to keep his curiosity casual as the three went into the adjoining guest bathroom.

"Neighbors' kids," Sandra supplied. "Their parents are out on Friday nights, so they're coming over for supper." She smiled. "They come as a set, those three. Their siblings are dining with other neighbors."

"Things are pretty laid back around here, huh?" Chris said.

"Yep," Katie said from the kitchen area. "When Sandra and I were kids, we'd run in and grab snacks from whoever's refrigerator was closest." She grinned at the memory.

As the rich aroma of food—savory beef with a hint of garlic—filled the air, Katie, apron now off, wheeled in a laden serving cart. Steam curled invitingly as she lifted the heavy lid from a ceramic Dutch oven. "Pot roast," she announced. She lifted the next lid—creamed spinach, vibrant and green. "And," she added, lifting the last cover, "a cucumber-tomato salad."

The others murmured their thanks and started filling their plates. Across from Chris, Katie sat beside Sandra, giving her sister's arm a quick squeeze. The parents took the ends of the table, and the three children settled at a smaller table tucked next to the main one.

"How did you boys spend the afternoon?" asked Sandra, serving herself some pot roast and helping herself to the freshly baked bread rolls.

"We biked to Boulder Creek and looked for crawdads," Gary said with a mouthful of creamy spinach.

"Well, that's nice," Mrs. Allen said. She eyed them suspiciously. "From the stains on your clothes, it appears you climbed that tree by the creek and gorged yourselves on mulberries again."

The boys exchanged grins.

"My sister, Lucy, got the chickenpox," Walter announced between bites.

"It's the best time of year to get it," Doctor Allen assured him.

"Why is that, Doctor Allen?"

"He's teasing you, dear," his wife said. "I'm afraid it's equally miserable in any season. Did you already have it?"

"I had the measles."

"Well, that's one down," Mrs. Allen said, scooping more cucumber salad onto her plate. She gave Walter a sympathetic smile. "But it looks like chickenpox might be next for you, bud. If your sister has it, chances are you do too. And that might mean you"—she nodded toward Tommy and Gary—"might have it as well. Best to get it over with, don't you think, Walter?"

"Sure thing." The boy lowered his eyes to his cup. "I only wish it wasn't during a school break, Mrs. Allen."

The Allens laughed at that.

"I only have chickenpox and the mumps to go through," said Tommy proudly.

"Chris, dear, you look pale," Mrs. Allen said. "You must be confusing it with smallpox. At any rate, chickenpox is a childhood disease. Once you have it, you're not going to get it again."

Chris shifted uneasily in his seat. "Well, I don't think I've ever had it."

"Nonsense," Mrs. Allen scoffed. "Just like measles or rubella, all children get it at some point. You were probably too young to remember. That's all."

Sandra glanced up from her plate. "Did you not keep a notched leather swatch—to mark all the childhood diseases you've had?"

Chris shook his head.

"Maybe they don't have chickens in Iraq," Katie giggled.

"Katherine Allen," said her mother sternly, "would you stop with this silliness of yours? It's high time you got serious. Why, at your age, your father and I—"

"Don't say it," warned Sandra. "If I hear that one more time, I may break into convulsions—or at the very least, a screaming fit."

"Oh, hush. All I was going to say is that when—" Mrs. Allen stopped talking and muttered under her breath as her daughter drew in air, about to make good on her threat to scream.

"Here are the smelling salts," Katie said, passing the salt shaker to Sandra.

"If you really didn't have the chickenpox," Doctor Allen said, addressing Chris, "better to have it now. The older you are, the harder it is on the system. In fact, I'm sure Walter's mom, Helen, will organize a chickenpox party. Yet, I'm guessing the kids here will probably save you the trouble of attending."

"Yeah, I can see what you mean," Chris said weakly, and the doctor reached out and slapped him on the back.

Chris had gotten a chickenpox shot as a kid. He doubted it still offered any protection, all those years later. *Oh well*, he thought, half-resigned.

As the plates were cleared and the remnants of the meal disappeared, Katie brought out a strawberry shortcake, and the adults helped themselves to some coffee.

There was a knock. The door opened, and some parents were standing there.

The three boys were none too happy with the prospect of leaving without eating cake. After some back and forth, each walked out holding a slice of cake on a piece of parchment paper. The five adults were left alone, seated around the dining table.

"Drugs, gambling, health—lifestyle choices aren't the government's to police," Mrs. Allen replied to something Chris had said, pouring some cream into her coffee. "This is America. We take our lumps with our liberty," she added, stirring her coffee. "As the saying goes: *No one learns to ride without kissing gravel first.*" She paused, lips quirking upward. "My nephew tried to jump Boulder Creek on a velocipede last year. Ended up in traction for six weeks. The city sent him a Certified Idiot diploma and a bill for disturbing the ducks."

Doctor Allen nodded, setting his cup down on the saucer with a faint clink. "We're the land of the free and the home of the brave. Both are crucial, as freedom can't be maintained without a certain degree of bravery. That's what the Fourth of March celebration is ultimately about—beyond the brass bands, bonfires, and parades."

"Yes," Chris said, dipping his head in agreement, "that is exactly what Independence Day is about." The old anthem's line hit home for Chris. A far cry from the "land of warning labels and home of the risk-averse" he'd left behind.

Sandra looked up. "Independence Day? Oh, you mean when

the thirteen British colonies seceded? It's in the summer, right? We don't really celebrate that here; more of an East Coast thing. But yes, bravery is always worth honoring."

Wait, what? Chris replayed what the doctor had said, realizing he had said Fourth of March, not July. Though they did have Independence Day in the summer, like in his world. Curious.

Intrigued by the extent of the commitment to liberty in Americana, he probed, "Does this principle of freedom apply to same-sex marriage?"

"Of course," Sandra said. She brushed a lock of hair behind her ear. "It doesn't matter—man and woman, two of the same, or a handful. That's between them and their conscience, not the county registrar."

Chris blinked. "'A handful?'"

"Yes, a triad or a quad marriage. You didn't see it in Iraq?"

He shook his head. "Is it common around here?"

"Common enough," Sandra answered. "Every neighborhood is bound to have some," she added, busying herself with cutting another slice of cake and pointedly avoiding her mother's gaze.

"People are free to form whatever type of household they wish," said Mrs. Allen, elbows on the table. "But the living arrangement is judged by whether it serves children well. And if it doesn't, folks will let you know with all the subtlety of a brick."

For a moment, no one said anything.

Chris asked, "What about drugs?"

"I'm hardly their champion." Sandra wrinkled her nose. "But I've heard adults can visit a tonic shop and choose their vice, whether it's magic mushrooms, nicotine, ecstasy, or marijuana."

Katie nodded. "The land of drugs and honey," she said sweetly in a singsong voice, and Sandra, grinning, swatted her sister with her napkin.

Mrs. Allen frowned in disapproval at Katie's flippancy. She also didn't care for Sandra's cavalier portrayal, as though they were sampling teas at a garden party. She said, "Let's not lose sight of the fact that drug use has its limits. When it can affect others, that's another kettle of fish. Smoking in public is out, and operating dangerous machinery while under the influence is prohibited, especially when others' safety is at stake."

Doctor Allen remarked, "Why, out of the one hundred million Americans, I wager you'd scarcely find more than a million who dabble in recreational drug use."

One hundred million Americans, Chris thought. That was less than a third of the population of his America. With a markedly smaller Boulder, this did not come as a surprise. He wondered what accounted for the lower numbers. He didn't get the impression families here had fewer children than in his America.

"Pay attention, Katie," Mrs. Allen said crisply, brushing off her hands. "It wouldn't hurt to listen to some intelligent conversation now and then."

"Yes, Mother," her daughter said dutifully.

Doctor Allen took a sip and winced; the coffee was still piping hot. "Sandra's portrayal might have you believe that the argument for drugs is purely libertarian. That's simply not the case. How can it be? We're only human—prone to vices and vulnerabilities. As I see it, the case for lax recreational drug laws is mostly a practical one."

Chris jerked in his seat as something pressed against his groin. *What the—*? He fleetingly glanced down—at a bare foot planted firmly in his crotch.

"Prohibition doesn't work," Doctor Allen declared, stroking his mustache, his expression growing contemplative. "People have always found ways to get their hands on drugs. If we were to ban them outright, we'd only be bolstering criminal drug cartels—much like the debacle of the 1920s. And let's not forget the staggering human toll of imprisonments that would follow. It's simply unconscionable."

The toes dug deeper, wiggling with unmistakable intent.

"In the end," Doctor Allen said, "it's one part self-discipline, nine parts social pressure and conventions that relegate drugs to something that's either off-limits or reserved for the rarest of occasions."

Chris abruptly pushed back his chair with a scrape.

Mrs. Allen peered at him curiously.

"Dishes," Chris declared loudly. "I volunteer—in fact, insist—on loading the dishwasher and scrubbing the bigger pots. Least I can do to repay your generous hospitality," he added.

He'd planned on volunteering, just not quite so soon, or announcing it quite so abruptly.

"Well, I'll be dipped in honey and fried like a fritter," Sandra drawled in mock astonishment. "Looks like we've got ourselves a volunteer for the kitchen detail. I could float away on a fluffy cloud of cotton—"

"Oh, button it, Sandra!" Mrs. Allen snapped, sending an apologetic look toward Chris.

"Yes, Mother."

One sister—or both—had to be smirking inside.

Chris made a point of ignoring them. He noted that Doctor Allen had been wisely steering clear of such exchanges. Clearly, a man living under one roof with three feisty females called for strategic silence, he mused, the corners of his mouth quirk-ing up.

Chris grabbed a plate sitting in the sink. He was startled when the door of the dishwasher opened on its own.

"Looks like Sir Suds-a-Lot is suiting up for yet another skir-mish with dinner's leftovers," the fridge observed.

"Oh, shut your freezer door," grumbled the dishwasher. "At least I actually do something, not just sit there chilling all day."

"Do something? If by 'do something' you mean splashing around in dirty water like a toddler in a puddle, then yes, you're quite the workhorse," said the fridge, sounding unruffled.

"Oh, listen to His Frostiness, judging everyone's snacks from on high." The dishwasher's voice hit a nasal and grating pitch. "Breaking news, Icebox: No one's asking for your hot takes!"

"My insights come from flawless data and thermal precision. I'd elaborate, but I'm afraid the concept might be too complex for your soap-addled circuits."

"That's it!" roared the dishwasher. "I'm up to my racks with you!" It paused for a moment. "And you, big boy—don't mind me while I collect dust here."

"It's addressing you, Chris," Sandra said, stifling a laugh.

"Hello! Of course I'm addressing you," spluttered the dishwasher in outrage. "Are you just gonna stand there contemplating life with that plate—"

Mrs. Allen snapped her fingers, and the shrill voice was cut off. She shook her head at the appliance's antics, then turned to Chris with an encouraging smile. In return, he shrugged with uncertainty and inserted the plate with some trepidation into the dishwasher, which let out a contented gurgle.

Chris scanned the kitchen. Trash can, where is the trash can? He finally spotted it resting against the ceiling. Or rather, he spotted an entire set of color-coded trash cans. But then again, after everything he'd seen, Chris expected some sort of recycling scheme—with separate cans for different types of waste. He had to lower them with a hand crank. As they descended, they gradually moved into an upright position. He glanced nervously at the bins, hoping they wouldn't break into a chorus of "Waste Not, Want Not."

"So, what happens to the food leftovers?" Chris asked as he scraped a platter into the tan bin, its side embossed with food icons. *Hey, I'm fresh off the boat from Iraq—cut me some slack,* his tone seemed to plead.

"They're hauled to a co-composting plant," Katie began brightly, then faltered, her brow creasing. She was uncertain what happened next.

Her father noticed it. "They mix food scraps with human solid waste," he said. "It's a good pairing—one's high in nitrogen, the other gives structure. Perfect for compost."

Chris's stomach did an uneasy flip as his brain connected the digestive dots.

"Sewage sludge gets piped in then spun to get the water out—like in some giant washing machine," Sandra said, oblivious to his growing indigestion. She'd toured the place with her school last spring. "Next, the solids get dumped into these enormous drums with food scraps. It all tumbles around for days, fluffed up with shredded wood chips so it doesn't clump."

A poo-and-potato-peel tumble dryer, Chris thought faintly. The glamour.

Sandra was still at it. "Then for several weeks, big augers stir the mix and let oxygen work its magic." *Magic. Right.* "After that, it cures outdoors for about five months and *voilà!*" She snapped her fingers. "You've first-class fertilizer—good stuff for greenhouses and rooftop gardens. The heat during composting kills off anything nasty."

Chris could almost see the ad—a vintage, 1940s-style poster with a rosy-cheeked family harvesting giant tomatoes from their backyard, the tagline blaring, *Do Your Part: Gardens Bloom Better with Bowel Power!*

He chewed that over. "So the sewer is piped to this . . ."

"Place, yes," Doctor Allen said. "But only the solids, mind you. The urine, as you may have noticed, goes into a separate channel in the toilet—then to the neighborhood tank, and from there, it's collected by a vacuum truck. Another facility treats it with calcium hydroxide, producing an odorless, slow-release phosphorus fertilizer. The remaining nitrogen and potassium are used in drip irrigation."

It seemed that organic waste was processed and returned to the natural world. Once Chris worked his way past the ick factor, he couldn't help but feel a grudging admiration. No overflowing landfills, no incinerated nutrients. He mentally filed "Poo Compost and Pee Fertilizer" under "Unbelievable Dispatches from the Lost World of Americana." Marco Polo reporting on exotic spices had nothing on this. And someday soon, millions would be watching and taking note.

Chris held up a piece of plastic wrap, eyeing it suspiciously. "What about this? Should I put it in the black trash can?" He was somewhat surprised to find plastic wrap in Americana. He'd fully expected to find cheesecloth made from unbleached cruelty-free organic cotton grown humanely on a vegan-certified farm.

"Yes, the black bin, please," Mrs. Allen told him.

Her husband said, "They've concocted an enzyme cocktail that breaks down certain plastics into their basic components, allowing the plastics to be reconstructed. Infinite recycling. However, that's the exception. The vast majority of plastics, like the one you're holding, can't be recycled and are therefore zapped."

Chris regarded him blankly. *Zapped?*

"Gas plasma waste treatment plant," supplied Doctor Allen. "It takes care of materials that can't be reintegrated into the ecosystem—batteries, acids, medications, paint strippers, nail polish, tires... But mainly, plastics."

Sandra said, "The plasma gets so hot it breaks waste molecules apart into their base elements, Chris. It's a clean process. Inorganic bits fuse into a rock-like mass we use in concrete. The rest turns to gas, mostly carbon monoxide and hydrogen. The carbon monoxide gets converted to carbon dioxide and sequestered underground. The hydrogen is cleaned up, compressed, and stored in big tanks. It's primarily used to fuel coastal ships."

Katie looked at her sister, visibly impressed.

"And the metal components in the waste?" inquired Chris, adding *zapping* to his growing list of the Seven Wonders of the Alternate World. Hell, it was more than a wonder. He'd learned months earlier that it was just a matter of decades—and not that many, at that—when there would be more plastic in his world's oceans than fish, pound for pound. It was a must!

"Melted into ingots for reuse," Doctor Allen said.

"Speaking of stuff in need of vigorous zapping," Sandra said, "polyester fleece and other loose synthetic fabrics shed a great deal and have been banned in recent years." She gave her sister a pointed glance.

Katie smiled sheepishly at that, but then frowned. "You told me that pvc clothing doesn't shed."

"It only sheds when the thread is very noticeable, Katie." Sandra playfully tugged at a strand of Katie's hair. "We don't want tiny bits of it in our food."

Mrs. Allen glanced at Chris, noting his pained expression. "Chris, dear, you look like someone just told you you've been ingesting plastic your whole life. Everything alright?"

CHAPTER 8

ONCE EVERYTHING WAS PUT AWAY AND THE DISHWASHER hummed softly to itself in the background, the Allens settled into the radio nook, waiting for the top of the hour to tune in to their weekly soap opera. It was fifteen minutes long, and Chris learned that Evelyn, the matriarch of the Finch family, had been secretly harboring a long-lost daughter, throwing the household into turmoil.

Sandra and her mother got into a light argument over whether Evelyn's choice had been justified. Katie rolled her eyes and sided with their father.

With a round of yawns and exchanged goodnights, the sisters bid their parents farewell. Chris followed, trailing the twins as they made their way toward the detached housing unit.

As they were walking, Chris felt a tug on his sleeve. Katie gave him a bright smile when he glanced her way.

"Do you want to see my dolls?" she asked.

"Uh . . ." Chris hesitated, wondering if he'd heard her correctly. "Yeah, sure."

Katie grabbed his hand, her touch warm and insistent, and tugged him along as Sandra's quiet chuckle faded behind them. Without a word, she led him through a side door into the spacious bedroom she shared with Sandra, pulling him inside.

"So these are your private quarters," Chris observed as she pushed the heavy door shut behind him. He looked around her room, taking in the sight of scattered dolls and book-filled shelves. A violin rested against one wall.

Katie plopped down on the tatami mat next to a low shelf crowded with dolls, her knees splayed, feet tucked on either side of her hips. The breezy fabric of her dress rode up her tanned thighs, and Chris felt his internal compass waver, tugged in a southerly direction. He settled across from Katie, anchoring his gaze on a framed photo of her and Sandra locked in a tight embrace.

"Look at this," Katie said and dragged out a dollhouse.

"Eye-catching," he said absently, his gaze momentarily slipping down the plunging neckline, to the gentle rise and fall of her bosom as she breathed. Hunger swelled and surged within him.

Katie said something.

Chris forced himself to focus and reflect on what Katie had said: She had sewn all the dolls' dresses. He looked again. They were actually quite good, he noted with mild surprise. He'd never given a second thought to doll clothes, but these were something else—done with precision, detail, care. Like someone had poured herself into the work.

"I sewed all the dresses myself," she said, straightening one of the dolls. "Some of them took a long time. You have to get the stitching just right, or they start to fray again at the seams." She looked up at him. "But it's fine. They don't feel pain."

Chris nodded, not sure what to say.

He gestured at a stack of thick books on the small desk. "What are those about?"

"Those are Kate's," she told him in her soft voice, idly twirling a strand of her hair around her finger. "The room belongs to Kate and me."

He frowned. *Another sister?*

"Where is Kate now?" he asked, trying to make sense of it.

"Have a look at the dollhouse," she responded. "My father constructed it for me."

He peered at her closely. She just looked back at him.

What was that all about? he wondered.

"Oh!" Her face lit up. "I want to invite you and Sandra to my fashion show tomorrow night." As she leaned in, her warm breath brushed his earlobe, her cheek grazing his—sending a shiver through him, equal parts arousal and unease. "I'll be so happy if you come," she murmured—For one crazy moment, he thought she would next whisper that her dolls liked to be played with—Then, even softer: "But if you don't. . . I'll string your soul to a raccoon and let it wander the highway."

Wait. A raccoon? A raccoon on the highway?

What the hell did she just say?

"Uh, sure, sounds fun," he finally managed, and she pulled back with a pleased little smile on her face.

Katie went on about various outfits and dolls, while Chris politely nodded along, still trying to piece together what he'd just heard.

As he listened, his eyes were drawn to her slender arms moving animatedly and to the luxurious mass of ash blonde hair reflecting the light pouring down. His gaze drifted to the imposing rows of books lining the shelves as he willed himself to make sense of her.

Katie was cheerful, immensely likable, and youthful beyond her twenty-one years. There was also a pattern to her that didn't fit with the world around her—and he was just beginning to see it.

And then, there was the most obvious thing. She was hot. It was nothing she said or did, really. Rather, everything about her was suffused with it. She could have talked about dolls or municipal tax code. It didn't matter. All she said and did was tinged with sensuousness.

Sandra poked her head in. "Ready to be escorted back to your cell, Chris?"

Katie's brow creased slightly. "Does he have to?"

Sandra gave a resigned shrug. "Warden's orders."

With a heavy sigh, Katie pulled her knees to her chest. "Life's tough in the big house," she murmured, resting her chin on her knees. "You never know when those surprise inspections might hit," she added, half to herself.

Chris got to his feet. "You both need to have your heads examined."

"We did," Sandra assured him.

Chris raised an eyebrow. "And?"

"They found nothing inside," Sandra admitted.

Katie nodded grimly, looking up at him. "No wonder we're always feeling light-headed." She grimaced. "We tried thinking once. It was dreadful."

Chris opened his mouth to retort, then thought better of it. This might be one of those situations where silence kept you from getting hexed.

Sandra guided Chris through the shared bedroom to the guest room, gave him a wink, and closed the door behind her.

Chris lay in the large bed, staring up at the ceiling. Come Monday, his first priority would be renting a small place of his own. He'd already spoken with Doctor Allen, who agreed to help him secure the rental.

While the comfort and ease of staying indefinitely in the guest room was tempting, Chris felt uncomfortable imposing on the Allens' generosity for an extended period. More importantly, he needed a place of his own to discreetly do some research and to travel unnoticed to and from the portal site.

—⊃⊂—

A few hours later, Sandra entered the bedroom she shared with her sister and slipped out of her dress. In the shadows, a figure approached. Was it Kate then?

A happy, soft laughter. Nope, not Kate.

"Chris is such a hunk!" Kat said, grinning, and Sandra noticed—with sudden anxiety—that her sister was naked.

Kat kissed Sandra. Then pulled her in for a second kiss, this time her lips hard and searching.

"Oh, no," Sandra said, her voice tight, and pushed away Kat's probing hands. She found her pajamas in the dark and hurriedly put them on. She wanted to be covered up in those moments her sister was flushed with excitement—and she, Sandra, was too spent to fend her off.

"Your hedonism will be your undoing!" Sandra hissed as she buttoned up her top, masking a growing dread.

"Hedon—What was that? Stop throwing big words at me."

"If you don't know what it means, ask *Kate*."

"Ask what?" her sister now said with a different inflection, and Sandra promptly averted her eyes and turned away. "Hedonism?" came the same clear, quiet tone.

"Kate, is that you?"

"No, it's Quetzalcoatl rising from the dead," her sister snapped.

"Hi, Kate."

"Hi, Sandra."

"I missed you," Sandra said, overcome with emotions, as always. "It's been a whole week since the last time. Do I get a kiss?"

There was a long silence. Had she pushed things too far? Kate had fled and let one of the other two regain bodily control over lesser transgressions. Sandra could feel soft breathing behind her. *Come on, Kate, you can do it*, she urged silently. The breathing drew closer until she felt a quick peck on the back of her head—and her sister stepped back.

"Damnation!" Kate swore, and Sandra grinned to herself. She'd wondered how long it would take Kate to realize she was naked. "I'd better put some clothing on," her sister said. Sandra could hear the contempt in the voice. "This slutty homemaker with sawdust for a brain, running on body fluids and cooking fumes," Kate muttered to herself from behind. She had never failed to tell Sandra what she thought of Katie and Kat, whom she contemptuously lumped together. All things considered, Kate must have been in a charitable mood that evening.

"At least the three of you make a striking juxtaposition," Sandra suggested.

"This cannot make up for the fact that the whole body-time-share arrangement is a crummy deal," Kate said, dressing up.

"Speaking of body timeshare, Katie and I just had a fun time with Chris."

"Sagte Mephistopheles zu Faust," grumbled Kate.

Sandra sighed in exasperation, making sure her sister could not miss it.

"Said Mephistopheles to Faust," Kate translated, her voice laced with practiced patience, and with just the slightest pause at the end—like someone waiting for the inevitable light bulb moment. For some reason, Kate had always assumed her family must have picked up and understood German, French, and Latin—much as she had. Kate had been annoying that way even before the incident.

"Do you have feelings for Chris?" Kate suddenly asked.

"I'm certainly falling for him," Sandra confessed.

"He's a dreamboat," said Kate with a smile in her voice.

Sandra grinned back. "On a few occasions, my temperature spiked so sharply, I feared I'd void my warranty," she said. Her smile lingered, then faded slightly as her attention turned inward. "Yet, an air of mystery surrounds him."

"Ergo, you hope the things tucked away in his zippered pocket might shed light on it," Kate said, clearly amused.

Sandra nearly turned her head to stare at Kate, but caught herself.

"How did you know?" she asked.

"You told me you were asked to intercept him and find out a bit about his background, remember? And why else would you sneak into his room with a camera just now, in the middle of the night?"

That was the one thing that had always struck Sandra. The only way Kate could have known this was by sharing memories with Kat. It seemed that her sister had persuaded herself she didn't, even when in fact she did. Sandra dared not highlight this absurdity. She'd attempted to make her see it once, and as a result, Kate retreated for an entire month.

"Let's take a peek at what you've found," said Kate. "Shall we?"

Sandra held up the camera, and Kate stood behind her, the two studying the screen displaying the photo of a laminated card Sandra had retrieved from Chris's trousers.

"It says it's a driver's license," Sandra said after a moment.

"Truck drivers are required to have a license," Kate offered. She then leaned in, her chin brushing against Sandra's shoulder as she inspected the card. Sandra felt the familiar twinge of grief; she longed to turn around and behold the face of her sister when Kate was in control. It had been—what?—thirteen years now?

Sandra forced her attention back to the card. Chris's listed birth date indicated he was twenty-four, about three years older than they were.

"It certainly looks . . . authentic. Like an actual, official piece of identification," Kate said hesitantly.

"Out with it, sis. What's bothering you?"

"Sandra, driver's license cards went the way of the dodo when biometrics took over. And even back then, they didn't look anything like this. It's as wrong as a nine-dollar bill." Kate paused. "You told me earlier the system didn't recognize his vein pattern."

In fact, it was *Katie* she'd told it to, but never mind that. Bewildered, Sandra examined the image of the card some more. "What does it all mean?"

"That's just it, Sandra. I don't know," Kate replied, her head almost grazing Sandra's. "Maybe it's cosplay," she said after a while.

"Cosplay?"

"You know—dressing up like a character. Roleplaying."

Interesting. This was something that hadn't occurred to Sandra.

The other picture she'd snapped was of a small photo. It showed a few armed men in military uniform standing together. One of them was Chris.

"Cosplay," Kate repeated. She sighed. "But then again, maybe not."

"Why do you say that?"

"Sandra, he told us he flew to the States from Iraq, with a layover in Frankfurt."

"He did," Sandra said guardedly, sensing she wasn't going to like where this was going.

"I'm pretty sure commercial flights were banned years ago. He couldn't have."

"You mean from Germany?"

"I mean from anywhere."

"Are you saying Chris has been lying to us?" *To me?* Sandra's pulse hammered in her throat. "That the whole Iraq story . . . was a lie?" She stared at the image on the camera, heart thudding. *No. It couldn't be.* For an instant, her face twisted in anguish. Then she flushed with anger. "Oh, for crying out loud, there must be a logical explanation for this! Maybe he meant that he flew to Frankfurt from Iraq and from there took an ocean liner."

"Sandra, I—"

"No, Kate," she said heatedly in a tone that brooked no further discussion. She set her chin in a stubborn line. "You look into his eyes, and you can tell that he's a *good* man, an *honest* man."

"Yes, Sandra," Kate said simply. After a brief pause, she stepped back. "I'm turning in."

Sandra stood there alone with her thoughts. She didn't feel like contacting her handler at Homeland Security right then. She would do it tomorrow, or perhaps the day after.

A short while later, she followed suit and settled down on her side of the bed. It wasn't long before she was sound asleep.

Kate turned and looked at her sister. As she had so many times before, she longed to gently touch her sister's face—but then the eyes would snap open. And Sandra would see her. She would be visible!

As for Chris, he was an enigma wrapped in a paradox. There were some in the world who didn't know about the Fourth of March, though she doubted that included many Americans, even those raised abroad. There were many in the world who didn't know about the Fourth of July—likely the vast majority. However, no one knew about the Fourth of July holiday without also knowing about the Fourth of March. Yet, Chris did. He was a far bigger enigma than her sister realized. He was a walking impossibility.

With a soft sigh, she leaned in and lightly kissed Sandra's hair. *Sweet dreams, sister.*

CHAPTER 9

WITH KATIE OUT ENJOYING HER Sunday with friends, Sandra and Chris settled in for a leisurely morning of strategic warfare: a complex game reminiscent of *Scythe*, its intricate board and numerous pieces claiming the entire dining table.

Two hours passed in a whirlwind of resource management, tactical maneuvers, and good-natured trash talk. Finally, the last piece was moved, the scores tallied, and a victor declared. As they gathered the remnants of their tabletop battlefield, their eyes met across the table and they grinned—something they had been doing a lot that morning.

Sandra reached out and fleetingly touched Chris's face. "Meeting you has made me happy," she said, her voice wavering a little.

"Same here," Chris said.

For a moment, he squeezed her hand, and she squeezed back.

"Do you like Katie?" Sandra asked in a casual tone a few heartbeats later.

His smile slipped.

"Well?" she asked. Tendrils of dark hair drifted around her face.

"I do."

"I reckoned you did," was all she said.

"The thing is, I . . . like you as well."

She laughed softly and tossed her hair back with a flick of her head. "Well, I would certainly hope so."

That was not exactly the kind of answer he'd expected. Were they talking about the same thing?

He chewed on that for a time. "How does Katie fit in?"

Sandra rose, her movements fluid and unhurried, then perched on the table's edge. One shapely leg eased over the other, a motion so natural it felt almost studied. "Do you want her to fit in?" she asked, gazing down at him through her lashes, her eyes shadowed.

Chris threw his hands up in the air. "Sandra, where is all of this going?"

She pushed herself off the table and crossed the room, her steps measured and deliberate. When she came to stand over him, her shadow brushed across his face. Her green eyes held his. "It will unfold as it will," she murmured. A glimmer of an idea had come to her earlier, though it hinged on Chris and Dalton taking a shine to one another.

Chris cocked his head, his eyes narrowing as he looked hard at her. It was almost as if . . . she *wanted* him to be drawn to them both.

A memory suddenly surfaced. "Do you," he began hesitantly, "do you have one more sister?"

"No, it's just the two of us," she replied, pursing her lips. She studied his face. "What made you ask?"

"Your sister mentioned Kate."

Sandra let out a vexed sigh and gestured dismissively. "Sometimes she refers to herself in that way."

Sandra's explanation seemed . . . thin. A flicker of doubt, a sense of something not quite lining up, tugged at him. Katie's odd way of talking about herself, the shifts in her demeanor— there was more to it, he felt sure. He watched Sandra, her face unreadable. Pushing the issue might only strain his budding relationship with her. With reluctance, he decided to let it rest for now.

Chris attempted to envision a future with Sandra, then with Katie—when finally, reality intruded. A pesky little detail surfaced: He was from another universe. And he had planned on going back.

Had he not?

When Chris had first arrived through the portal, things were clear in his mind: engage in insightful conversations with the locals, capture valuable footage, and go on his merry way. Now, he was unsure of that last detail. In fact, everything was in a state of flux.

His chest constricted painfully. *Tell her the truth about your origin!* a voice within him urged. Share everything and decide together what to do.

But how could he? He'd come across as a raving lunatic.

Then again, what if he could convince Sandra just long enough to accompany him to the gate—at which point she would cross over and see his home world with her own eyes.

This was the predicament Chris encountered every time he wrestled with this dilemma.

Once he opened that proverbial door, there was no closing it; the genie would be out of the bottle. Maybe. Sandra might choose to keep this reality-altering truth to herself, but he couldn't fault her if she chose otherwise. If she spoke out, sooner or later—probably sooner—everyone would know about the two parallel Americas and the ability to travel between them. Before long, uncontrollable forces would be unleashed, irrevocably altering the course of both worlds.

He had a growing conviction that, on balance, this would not benefit Americana.

For all he knew, Columbus had decent enough intentions

when he embarked on his first voyage across the Atlantic. Nonetheless, it set in motion a series of devastating events for the indigenous peoples of the Americas.

No, this was bigger, much bigger, than the need to come clean with Sandra and work out the path forward in their relationship. Somehow, he needed to figure out how to tell her about his singular background while keeping secret the possibility of moving back and forth between worlds.

And then there was Ronny, waiting and expecting on the other side. Chris would see him in less than thirty-six hours. What would he tell his friend?

⸻

The day's remaining hours found Sandra and Chris hiking on Flagstaff Mountain, where Chris was in for a surprise.

The city had carved terraces and set up about one hundred and fifty ponds on the lower slopes, fed by spring water from higher up. With a combination of shallow and deep water areas, the city was cultivating fish.

He'd assumed fish didn't much care who they swam with. Not so. The upper, colder ponds were split between trout and pike. Mid ponds were carp country, and the bottom terraces heated up enough for tilapia.

Chris noticed an old rowboat tied to a small dock. Sandra looked out across the pond, then back at Chris, her smile speaking volumes. Together, they walked over.

Sandra reached for a rack and pulled out a parasol—pale ivory, edged with delicate embroidery. Chris stepped into the boat first, steadying it against the dock. He turned and offered his hand. Sandra took it and stepped gracefully aboard. The wooden planks creaked softly beneath their weight.

Chris settled onto the rowing bench and took up the oars.

With even strokes, he guided them away from the shore, carefully navigating around clusters of water lilies. Sandra twirled the parasol once above her head, then tilted it against the glare, shading her face in a soft halo of lace and sunlight.

She knew the weight of the oars well enough, but in moments like these, there was a rare kind of joy in letting herself be carried. It was good to know that the plug was still solid. Katie and she had resealed it with pitch and oakum two summers ago—after Sandra had to jump in waist-deep to pry the boat free from a snarl of underwater reeds.

They glided past the lily pads, dragonflies flitting among the reeds, their wings flashing like stained glass, weaving bright lines through the air. Vibrant irises dotted the edges of the calm water. For Chris, it felt like stepping into an old painting—or a novel he'd never actually read but somehow recognized.

For a long time, they said little, drifting wherever the water and the pull of the oars took them. Chris rowed without hurry, savoring the quiet give of the oars. The only sounds were the gentle creak of wood, the soft swish of the water.

A breeze stirred across the surface, scattering small ripples over the gleaming water. On its heels came the faint, earthy scent of the lower terraces—a sharper, livelier smell. The spell broke, as gently as a breath.

Chris shifted his gaze, noticing for the first time how the ponds terraced down the slopes, teeming with life both above and below the surface.

"So that's where Boulder gets its fish," he said.

"The freshwater ones," Sandra said absently. "The saltwater fish are raised indoors, in town."

"Wait, what?" Chris almost forgot to row. "You're breeding ocean fish in town? Indoors?"

"Well, yes," she replied, the *duh* plain in her tone. "It's not like we were going to harvest the oceans to feed billions."

Holy smokes! Chris thought. Hands down, it was the most consequential thing he'd heard of so far in this parallel world.

She noted the expression on his face. "Chris Walden, you're acting like you're from another universe!"

Chris's lips twitched into a fleeting smile. "You hit the nail on the head."

"Then your universe is a real doozy," she said, her lips quirking into a smile.

Before Chris could respond, Sandra leaned in and grazed his lips with a kiss—light, playful, gone almost as soon as it happened.

Chris blinked, his thoughts momentarily scattered. His pulse tripped, a little too fast for something so brief. Hell, it wasn't even a real kiss, but his chest tightened all the same.

"Here in town," she continued, as if nothing had happened, "we have a few separate beautiful marine habitats. Crowds come and watch schools of fish swim in the giant, see-through acrylic tanks. It's a great attraction, Chris."

But Chris wasn't listening. Not really. His mind was still replaying that fleeting kiss, trying to decide if it had been as casual as Sandra made it seem.

He dragged his focus back to her words just in time to catch something about marine habitats.

"And I thought. . ." He cleared his throat, forcing himself to shift gears. "I thought you couldn't propagate saltwater fish in such a manner." He frowned, trying to remember what he'd once heard. "For them to spawn, don't they need some environmental stimulant?"

"They do. We administer a hormone that keeps them fertile year-round."

⇒⇐

As night fell, Chris and Sandra attended what Katie called a fashion show. The event took place in the neighborhood clubhouse. She sashayed down the makeshift runway with her two friends, flaunting various garments they had sewn and now intended to sell.

It became clear to Chris that Katie's talent for making clothes extended far beyond doll outfits. Sandra confirmed his observation. Katie was a "master seamstress," she told him, "crafting meticulously tailored dresses, skirts, pants, and blouses." Chris eyed Katie with renewed respect. Beneath her somewhat dreamy demeanor was a creative powerhouse.

Fashion was Katie's passion, funded by selling her no-longer-wanted creations. The revenue covered the purchase of assorted fabrics and yarns. Americana had a skill-bartering system for those interested, where Katie offered her tailoring wizardry and custom designs.

As they watched Katie model her creations, Chris chatted more with Sandra, who painted a vivid picture of her sister's extensive wardrobe, worthy of American fashionistas. But in Americana, it was quite the anomaly.

It appeared that clothing purchases were a rare species on that end of the portal. Instead, women embraced clothing rental services, paying a flat monthly fee to swap outfits. It was the Americana way: from expectant moms needing temporary wardrobe changes, to special event outfit hunters, to those with an insatiable appetite for variety. Sharing was caring here, with clothing swap parties and a culture of mending and repairing garments as the norm.

In this world, men were blessed with the unspoken privilege of a minimalist wardrobe, liberated from the tyranny of choice. While women navigated the vibrant and treacherous waters of variety, men's arsenal was brilliantly distilled to just three sets of clothes—*The Threefold Ensemble* of formal occasions, everyday wear, and outdoor activities. Quality was paramount, and durability was a man's loyal companion.

At the end of the evening, Katie sold one outfit to an enthusiastic woman in the audience and three to a keen clothing rental business rep. The remaining garments were destined for donation or a swap party.

⟫⟪

That night, after Chris retired to his quarters and Katie went off to bed, Sandra shut the door to her small private room. She opened a drawer, retrieved her notebook computer, and turned it on. Within minutes, she was connected to her handler at Homeland Security through a video chat.

She briefed him on Chris's recent arrival from Iraq, his driver's license, and confirmed that his biometrics were not in the system. Next, Sandra uploaded a digital file containing the two pictures for the agent to examine. "His address on this alleged driver's license is listed as Yarmouth Avenue, Boulder," she told him.

"I'm checking this right now," the agent said, and she heard the clack of keys from his end. Then: "Nope. No Yarmouth."

"What do you mean?"

"I mean, there's no such street in Boulder."

Sandra's stomach clenched. Was Chris a spy? No, that didn't track. If someone had gone to the trouble of fabricating a driver's license that convincing, they would have incorporated an address that was real, or at least that appeared real.

Everything about Chris felt a little off. Like puzzle pieces from different sets that almost fit but not quite.

"What about his photo with him in uniform?"

"These men in the picture certainly appear to be military," her handler said. "In fact, U.S. military. Except the insignia . . ."

"Yes?" she asked testily.

"A shoulder sleeve insignia of a dagger with three bolts of lightning," he said, shaking his head. "It doesn't exist, I'm afraid." The handler chuckled. "The guy's probably a con artist." What a waste of time the whole thing had turned out to be! "I've seen his kind before. They're young, rootless, handsome, and full of fancy stories, preying on the young and impressionable..." His voice trailed off under her withering look.

"He's no such thing!" she lashed out, stung and hurt. "Did it occur to you that he might be into cosplay?"

He seemed taken aback by this. "It's possible," he finally allowed.

"He told me he had recently arrived from Iraq," she said. "A flight with a layover in Frankfurt," she added, grudgingly.

"I reckon it makes sense that his biometrics aren't in the system yet," the man said. "All right then, let us know if you spot anything else. But to be honest, it looks like a whole lot of nothing. Let him go."

That man, Chris—or whatever his real name was—just happened to be in the wrong place at the wrong time, the handler reckoned. Nothing to do with the gravitational waves they'd detected in his vicinity. Still, the agent made a mental note to recommend monitoring the area, in case those waves manifested again. And if they did, well, they'd be ready.

What an improbable yarn, the handler thought to himself. Living in Iraq! He doubted this small-town teacher had any notion that folks didn't fly into the States—that mode of transport had been phased out decades earlier. And she had no reason to know that upon entry into the country, everyone had to register their biometrics. That fella had spun her a tall tale.

However, he'd seen the hurt expression in her eyes. She appeared positively smitten. And that Chris person seemed harmless enough. Who was he to rain on her parade?

He realized that Sandra had spoken. "Pardon me, what did you say?" he asked.

"I'm off the case. Done," Sandra repeated. Her intense green eyes rested on him, and he was struck once again by how attractive she was. "In fact, I'm ending my involvement with the department."

There was a moment of silence. "Is this truly what you want?" he asked, not sure what else to say.

"Yes." She held his gaze. "From the beginning, I told you this moment would come." She gave him a half-smile. "Well, it has."

"I understand." The handler hesitated. "Very well," he said.

He did not expect her to explain herself. That was a condition the gal had insisted upon when she'd first made contact, three years prior. She'd approached the department during her studies in Boston, and they retained her even after she returned to her hometown, Boulder—deploying her once in a great while. She appeared out of nowhere, the agent thought, and would vanish just as suddenly. Fitting.

They looked at each other. He'd never learned why she did what she did, and now he was not going to find out what had changed for her.

"Looks like this is farewell then," he said.

She lowered her head. "Farewell, Mr. Williams."

After the video call ended, Sandra lingered at her desk, then undressed.

In the dim light, shadows clung to the corners of the room as Sandra confronted her reflection in the full-length mirror. Her striking features and feminine charm had always been tools—lures to disarm and extract secrets from her targets. She never felt guilt; her detachment made it easy. It was different with Chris, and for the first time, it felt *wrong*.

The growing bond between them had shattered her emotional distance, and in that moment, she realized something deeper: It wasn't just Chris. She couldn't stomach manipulating *anyone* like that again. The cause had been righteous, but the cost now felt too high. That part of her life, the part that leveraged charm for secrets, was over.

One thought kept intruding. Did Chris lie? Did Chris lie to her?

Sandra grappled with a whirlwind of emotions, struck by the intensity of her connection with Chris despite their short acquaintance. In just a few short days, a bond had formed beyond the physical, beyond infatuation; these were the stirrings of something deeper.

She recalled a conversation she'd had with her grandmother, who had said that true love was not about grand gestures but the simple comfort of knowing you belonged with someone. Was she being foolish for entertaining these possibilities so soon, or was her intuition leading her in the right direction? She couldn't ignore the possibility of missing out on something rare and extraordinary with Chris.

In her heart, Sandra had always believed that once she met the right man, she would just know it. And now, as she thought about the incredible connection she'd formed with this offbeat man, she couldn't help but wonder if he was that person. She allowed herself to imagine a future with him, even if uncertainty lay ahead.

First, there was Dalton, and now Chris too. Of course, with her darling sister involved, she had to think a bit. . . creatively. However, she had the beginnings of an idea how to make it all—

Metal clinked. Startled, Sandra gasped and spun around, her hair whipping about her shoulders and bare breasts.

Her sister stood there, clad in a midnight-black catsuit that clung to her form. The fabric shimmered like liquid metal in the dim light as she moved and shut the heavy door behind her with a click. A thick iron chain draped from her shoulders, its links pooling on the floor as she slunk forward, hunger in her eyes.

Sandra felt a jolt of unease, which was almost immediately washed away by desire. She took a small step back as Kat advanced on her—then seized Sandra by her hips and roughly turned her around, shoving her nude body close to the mirror. And Sandra felt the heavy metal chain wrapping around her.

She tried, half-heartedly, to break free—knowing she would fail, as always. And knowing she wanted to fail.

"Don't resist," Kat told her from behind, in an aloof, cold voice. "You know better than to resist." An arm reached around. One hand roamed about, and her body responded, and then quivered a few times as Kat's other hand started probing.

Sandra had never responded so quickly before. She was exhausted and sleepy; that must have been it.

Without warning, Kat dropped herself down onto the floor mat, in the process sweeping Sandra's legs out from under her, dragging her down, aided by the chains.

"You're falling for Chris." Kat was breathing hard as she gripped her from behind. "Yet you know that in the end, it's just you and me. You're *mine*." Sandra felt her sister's legs hooking around hers, trying to force her thighs apart. She resisted—as she was expected to in this bizarre roleplay the two had played countless times—but her legs felt rubbery, and inch by inch they parted.

"Spread your legs, you slut!" growled her sister, now in a much lower voice. Sandra's eyes flew open at the sound.

"John!—" Sandra rasped, her breath catching in her throat.

"Don't resist, little Katie," the deep voice grated next to her ear.

Sandra recovered from her shock. She twisted around and slapped her sister, eliciting a cry of pain, then of rage. "I told you never to come back!" Sandra snarled. "I told you if you ever did, I'd hurt you badly!" She raised her arm again.

"Stop!" cried her sister and burst into tears.

"Oh, Katie!" sobbed Sandra, and in the next instant had her arms wrapped around her sister.

The two hugged each other, deep sobs racking their bodies.

For a long while, they simply held each other, their breathing gradually slowing.

"You hurt John," said Katie in a small voice.

"Good! I hope he'll never return!"

"Me too," Katie said, her voice sinking to a whisper. She paused for a moment. "He's gone now." Another pause. "Maybe you shouldn't have been so . . . submissive. That's what brought him out, I think." Katie touched her cheek and winced. "Did you have to slap me so hard?"

"You think I enjoyed it?" Sandra said sharply, submerging in the flash of anger some of the anguish and guilt that clung to her over it. She sat up straight. "Let's just drop the subject, if you don't mind."

Sandra gazed at her sister, and tenderness tinted with sadness washed over her. She opened her arms, and the two embraced. "I won't leave you," Sandra whispered in her sister's ear. "No matter what."

Her sister held still. Then, "Promise?"

"I do."

Katie hugged her fiercely, the body coated in black film pressing against the naked body, chains softly clinking as they swayed in each other's embrace. "One way or another, I do," Sandra said, pulling a bit away and making eye contact. "We come as a set."

Green eyes met green eyes.

Katie managed a tremulous smile. "We come as a set," she agreed.

CHAPTER 10

It WAS MONDAY MORNING. Sandra and her mother had already left, and Katie was off navigating the aisles of the grocery store. Doctor Allen told Chris that he would be seeing patients in his home office that day and would be available around lunchtime. Chris thanked him and stepped out into the street, where a gentle breeze carried the fragrance of lavender blooms.

Under the shade of the towering elm trees, a few young mothers with infants in slings sauntered alongside each other, while pigeons scattered at their approach, wings clapping loudly as they took to the air. Across the street, a group of kids played kick the can, some darting around to avoid the catcher's tag. On one of the porches, a frail elderly woman perched on a creaky rocking chair and crocheted, savoring the sun's warm rays. Chris smiled to himself, taking joy in the sights.

A public kiosk stood nearby, its large e-paper display tucked into a weathered wooden frame. He pulled up the town map, studied the layout—and still got lost. Eventually, a delivery boy had him follow his cargo trike part of the way. After about twenty minutes of walking, Chris arrived at the bank, all but hidden among the trees.

In this Boulder, there were no malls or strip malls in sight. Instead, Chris spotted a few shops with understated wooden signs, nestled into residential areas and positioned on street corners. He reckoned that with people walking or cycling, essential services needed to be easily accessible from any neighborhood. Later, he learned that a few big-box stores did exist, though they were situated on the town's outskirts.

Had Chris brought U.S. dollars from his home world, he would have been laughed out of stores—or worse, jailed for counterfeiting. Ronny had argued that the odds of both worlds having identical currencies, right down to the 3D security ribbon on hundred-dollar bills, were slim to none. Gold coins were the obvious choice. Chris had sewn some into the side pockets of his backpack and tucked more into his trusty money belt. Both friends had put a dent in their savings accounts, but they expected a "very nice return on investment," as Ronny put it.

Chris initially intended to look for a jewelry store to exchange his gold for cash, but he was told he was better off going to the bank, a special sort of bank.

The bronze sign announced: *treasury bank*. It was just a hole in the wall, resembling an armored kiosk or a giant vintage vault, with an old man sitting behind what appeared to be a thick acrylic window. The gentleman had gray hair and round, wire-framed glasses perched on the bridge of his nose. He wore a dark waistcoat over a starched white shirt. Chris half-expected to see a sign next to him that read, *Pony Express: The Quickest Mail in the West!*

There was no one around, and the old man seemed glad to have someone to chat with.

As it turned out, it wasn't a bank in the usual sense, but a quaint outpost of the federal government—a relic from another era, still quietly doing its job. Chris slid a couple of small gold coins under the thick teller window, curious how they'd be handled.

The old man pulled out a bulky spectrometer gun, held it

to each coin with steady hands as numbers flickered across its screen. He jotted them down on a notepad, then moved on, weighing each coin on a digital scale and checking diameter and thickness with a caliper.

A sudden, queasy thought struck Chris: If he'd been sold fake gold coins, he was royally screwed. But no—that was impossible; the company he'd bought them from was reputable.

The clerk then used a slender metal probe to take conductivity readings—each coin lighting up a reassuring green. Finally, he produced a squat handheld ultrasonic device, pressed it flat against each coin, and waited for the soft beep that confirmed the core was indeed gold.

Chris exhaled. Must've been real gold then.

The clerk keyed in a final calculation on a chunky desk calculator. "Fifty-four hundred dollars even," he said and pushed a thick stack of distinctly old-looking bills through the slot. Chris picked them up, the stiff paper feeling unfamiliar against his fingertips.

The two chatted some more.

The man behind the counter had told Chris that at the treasury bank, they exchanged gold for "legal tender." Chris hadn't realized how literal that was until he examined one of the hundred-dollar bills. It featured Benjamin Franklin's portrait, with *one hundred dollars in gold coin* emblazoned in gold lettering, and a smaller inscription: *payable to the bearer on demand.* When he asked, the teller confirmed it was true—the bill was essentially just a more convenient way to carry gold around.

After examining the bills a moment longer, Chris folded the stack and stuffed it into his pocket. He glanced behind him and did a double take; in the shade of a nearby tree, a fox watched him, its snout resting on the ground.

The teller chuckled. "Don't mind Wilbur."

"Is he a regular?"

"He sure is." The old man's face split into a grin. "Wilbur comes here every morning when it isn't raining and keeps me company. Ain't that right, Wilbur?" He chuckled some more.

The old man's name was Carl Callenbach. In his younger years, he had worked in the bakery that supplied most of the bread to the grocers around town. Ten years back, his arthritis had started acting up, and he had sought a job he could do while sitting down.

Chris chatted a bit more with the man, then said farewell.

He now had money in his pocket, and that felt good. Next, he needed to get some wheels.

In the world he had come from, every person who could afford it bought a vehicle as a matter of course. In fact, it was a common enough sight in his America to see a soccer mom dropping off her kids at school with an SUV capable of hauling the contents of an entire apartment complex. However, in Americana it was a different story. He felt a twinge of guilt about purchasing a vehicle, even a modest one.

But then again, his palm vein pattern wasn't in the system, and Chris was unable to move around without depending on the Allens. He located the only store that sold personal transporters, and fifteen minutes later he wheeled out an electric trike with a cargo box, its motor giving a low hum.

He had some things to take care of that morning. First things first, though.

Chris pedaled away and soon was out of town. He didn't have to go far. He picked up a small bouquet of yellow flowers and purple-hued grasses and carried it to the Allens, where he found a vase in Sandra and Katie's dwelling. He filled it with water and put the bouquet in it, then attached a note bearing a smiley face with his name. Chris had no idea if they would find it charming or presumptuous. Regardless, it felt right.

Next, he went to see Doctor Allen at the main residence.

Less than an hour later, thanks to the doctor vouching for him, Chris was the proud renter of a furnished studio apartment nearby. He paid two weeks in advance and could now come and go without anyone being the wiser. Chris thanked the doctor and rode off to buy some groceries and everyday wear, Americana style.

⸻

That evening, Chris stood before the full-length mirror in his apartment. He smoothed the front of the lily-white button-down dress shirt, bought only hours earlier. Down its center, a wide black band offered tailored distinction—a clever substitute for a vest or jacket in the stifling summer heat.

He fastened one of the stiff, detachable collars to the shirt, its standing points flaring outward, adding a touch of sophistication. Then came the enamel cufflinks, which he clicked into place with care. The sharp lines of pleated worsted-wool trousers flowed down to the gleaming black Oxfords. A straw boater, perched rakishly on his head, completed the ensemble.

Chris stared, transfixed by the man in the looking glass.

At long last, he fit in.

At the Allens' house, Chris was greeted with soft cheers and good-natured laughter.

"Well, I'll be. Look at you," Katie exclaimed, sizing him up.

"Color me impressed, Chris," Sandra said, smiling broadly. "I didn't know you had it in you to clean up so nicely."

Chris enjoyed another evening meal with the Allens, made livelier by the unexpected arrival of the sisters' grandmother, who decided to stay. Sandra confided that Grandmother Virginia had lived with them for a few years after her husband passed, before eventually moving in with Uncle Kenneth. She spoke about it at some length, and Chris got the sense that multigenerational living wasn't unusual. From the feel of things in Americana, that didn't surprise him.

At some point, Chris excused himself. Katie and Sandra tried to talk him into staying, but he held firm. He told them he hadn't been sleeping well the past few nights and needed rest. That was the truth. Part of the truth, at any rate.

Chris departed and made his way back to his place. Once there, he set the alarm clock for two in the morning.

The streets were deserted when he came out in the dead of the night, dressed once again in cargo pants and a white T-shirt. The moon illuminated his path as his electric trike quietly sped off through the sleeping town, heading down the trail toward the hill—five miles away—and the portal.

He had no way of communicating with Ronny during his time in Americana. So they'd decided ahead of time that Ronny would activate the gate on the fourth day at three in the morning. If Chris was a no-show, Ronny was to power up the gate at that time on each following day.

While the calendar year was the same in both worlds, Americana followed the International Fixed Calendar. This system had 13 months, each consisting of 28 days, which amounted to precisely 4 weeks in every month. The last day of the year was called "Year Day" and did not belong to any week—adding the necessary day to reach the total of 365 calendar days. This meant that whereas today was the 18th of July local time, it was the 2nd of August in his home world.

Chris arrived at the portal site with a little time to spare. Standing there patiently in the dark, he soon noticed an almost imperceptible shimmer in the air somewhere in front of him. Taking a deep breath, he stepped forward, feeling a tingle as he passed through.

As before, one moment Chris was on the dusky forested hill, hearing the distant hoot of an owl; the next, he was standing in a brightly lit stone cellar. Ronny approached, beaming from ear to ear. "Welcome back, buddy!"

The two embraced, slapping each other's backs.

Ronny was still grinning. "You look intact. No medieval torture chamber? No hot coals on the nipples?"

Chris laughed. "Managed to sidestep the rack and thumbscrews."

"So?" Ronny asked as they started up on the stone stairs. "Was it the Promised Land?"

"Better," Chris assured him.

A few moments later, they shook off the cellar's chill and flopped onto the battered leather sofa.

"I tell you," Chris said, "they have such a beautiful, warm society over there! And don't just take my word for it." He removed a tiny memory card from the camera glasses and handed it to his friend. "See for yourself."

Ronny leaped to his feet with a little triumphant cry, brought over a laptop, and inserted the microSD card. If Chris had any concerns that something would go awry with the recording or during the portal crossing, they were dispelled. Ronny high-fived him as the video began to play.

Chris did not bother to hide his amusement at Ronny's obvious excitement. All the same, he found it jarring to be viewing the small railcar from Americana while he was sitting in Ronny's living room.

"This is history, man!" hollered Ronny. He laughed out loud, in a mix of delight and amazement, as the exotic carriage in the video drew nearer. But his attention was quickly diverted to Sandra's appearance on the screen. He glanced over at Chris, beaming. "So you were just chilling by the trees, and then, *bam*, this beauty rolled up in a railcar?"

Chris smiled. "Seems like it."

"You lucky dude."

Chris gave a little shrug. "Can't take credit for that."

"Dang, she's looking stylish," Ronny said in appreciation, watching the footage some more.

"Yeah, all the ladies I've seen there are," Chris said. "Anyway, let me introduce you to Sandra." He turned to the screen. "Sandra, meet one of my buddies, Ronny."

"So she has a name, huh?" Ronny mused, glancing at his friend. "Is it serious?"

Chris waved a dismissive hand, feeling an unexpected pang of protectiveness. "She's . . . a local. Helping me navigate." *Yeah, navigate straight into uncharted emotional territory,* he thought wryly. The two had only met a few days ago, yet it felt as if much more time had passed. As crazy as it sounded, yes, it was serious. Despite the whirlwind nature of their connection, there was a depth to his feelings for Sandra that he couldn't quite explain.

Ronny leaned in, expectant. "Come on, man. Did you score with her?"

Chris shook his head.

"Did the altitude mess with your equipment? Forget how zippers work?"

"It's not like that, Ronny."

"Not like *what?* She's breathing, got a pulse—what's the holdup?"

Ronny sighed theatrically when Chris stayed silent. "Alright, fine. She got a sister?"

"She does," Chris said reluctantly.

Ronny's eyes lit up like a pinball machine. "Is she just as hot?"

"Yeah," Chris conceded, then deflected Ronny's follow-up questions about availability and vital statistics.

Soon enough, they were back to watching the video.

"So they have houses made from straw." Ronny squinted at

the screen, unimpressed. "What's next—coconut phones and hula dances?" He leaned forward. "Come on, Chris. Who in our world would give a rat's ass about straw houses, besides some anthropologists who eat kale and put avocado on their bread?"

Chris kept his cool. "Straw saves forests." Chris had hoped the footage would open Ronny's eyes. Instead, it just loosened his mouth.

Ronny waved the point away like shooing a gnat. "Yeah, yeah. Straw good, lumber bad. Let's move on."

The next segment didn't help his mood. Once it ended, Ronny shook his head in disgust. "They're growing food in recycled turds? Dude, nobody wants to hear that—let alone eat the aftermath. That's straight-up nasty."

"The shit has got to go somewhere," Chris said. If Ronny thought that was nasty, Chris reflected, he should have seen how sewage was handled here. Why bother though? It was obviously all falling on deaf ears with Ronny. It threw cold water on Chris's wish to share his documentary idea with him. He tried something else. "What about raising saltwater fish in giant tanks—harvesting them, instead of the fish in the ocean?"

"Well, yeah, this is good stuff," Ronny said in a consolatory tone. He genuinely thought that once they depleted the oceans, this would be useful. It was good to know that there would always be fish on the menu. But that was in the very distant future—probably *decades* away. Why worry about it now? At times, Chris worried about the strangest things.

He sighed, leaning back. "No decent cars, no smartphones, no social media. I mean, these people are one butter churn away from Amish." He held up his hands as Chris was about to protest. "I get it. It's got that retro charm. It's like *Pleasantville* with self-driving buggies."

Chris felt something settle over him—weariness, maybe disappointment. So much for shared wonder. "It's deeper than that," he said. "It's . . . sane." It was as if someone took a Norman Rockwell painting, scrubbed off the nostalgia, and made it actually work.

But Ronny wasn't paying attention. "Actually, now that I think about it, plenty of gramps would jump at the chance to move to a peaceful and picturesque place like that." He turned to his friend, eyes sparkling with excitement. "You told me they have a population of only one hundred million people, clean air, and oodles of untouched wilderness. It's a retirement dream, Chris!" Ronny was grinning broadly now. "Think about it, man. We set up an underground railroad. And we charge ten or even fifty G's a head, for those who are loaded." The Geezer Express, thought Ronny to himself. He could almost feel the thick stacks of crisp hundred-dollar bills under his fingers. Untouched nature? Peace and quiet? That wasn't scenery; that was *inventory*.

"Don't you think the authorities in Americana would notice if masses of people started showing up?" Chris asked while keeping the visceral distaste he felt for Ronny's idea out of his voice.

"Millions have poured into our country uninvited and managed to stay," his friend countered. "How's that different?"

Chris rolled his eyes. "Yeah, because slipping into a country with wide-open borders, patchy enforcement, and access to public services and jobs is exactly the same as trying to infiltrate a society where you can't even check out a library book without a palm scan. Over there, no biometrics, no existence."

Ronny stopped short. "Shit!" he exclaimed and smacked the side of a cabinet in frustration. He glanced over at Chris. "If only we had discovered the portal, say, fifty years ago."

"That would have been something," Chris observed dryly. "Considering we weren't even born yet."

Ronny flashed him his crooked smile. Ronny never took

himself too seriously—or let setbacks keep him down for long.

Chris stayed a bit longer. At long last, after swapping the spy eyeglasses for a fresh pair, he stood up. "I want to emerge from the gate and leave the area well before sunrise," he said. There was no need to explain. They both wanted to confine Chris's comings and goings through the gate to the hours no one was likely to be around to witness them.

"I'll bring more videos of Americana in a few days," Chris said as they descended the staircase toward the portal room.

"Lose the straw huts and mud castles," Ronny called out from behind. "Bring me some footage with close-ups and interesting angles of that homecoming queen. And ask her sister if she's up for a date with a charming and witty guy."

"Drop some pounds first, tubby."

"It's not 'tubby,'" Ronny said as they continued down the stairs. "It's 'well-rounded.' Some women dig the dad bod. Some like a guy with presence."

"Some also like a guy who doesn't wheeze after climbing stairs."

They rounded the corner, and Ronny walked over and activated the gate.

Chris was about to step through the portal but then turned back. "Hey, at least come with me for a few minutes to the other side. That way, you can tell your grandkids you've been to another universe."

Ronny's eyes widened at the thought, then he smiled sheepishly. "You're right—even if it's just a quick in-and-out. But you stay here," he commanded. "I've got this nightmare where we both end up on the other side, the portal shuts down, and we're stuck in the boonies for the rest of our lives."

It hit Chris that personally he wouldn't have minded that one bit. *To each his own*, he thought as Ronny gave him a mock salute, spun on his heels, and stepped through.

He could see his friend in the dark moving about on the other side of the portal. A few minutes later, Ronny was back and raised his arms triumphantly. "Ladies and gentlemen, the second inter-universe traveler!" he whisper-shouted and bowed to the nonexistent audience.

"Okay, hero. Well done," Chris said. "I'm out of here." They clasped arms, giving each other a one-arm hug.

CHAPTER 11

CHRIS WATCHED THE SHIMMERING GATEWAY WINK OUT of existence before turning toward the nearby reservoir. He sat at the water's edge, where the starlight danced over wavelets chasing each other, and contemplated the extraordinary turn his life had taken.

As Chris arrived in his neighborhood, the early morning sun cast a warm glow, and birdsong filled the air, punctuated by the occasional rustle of leaves. He encountered several children on tricycles, likely returning from the grocery store. Their reed baskets held glass milk bottles and loaves of bread, which bobbed with each turn of the wheels.

Chris let himself into his small cottage. Minutes later, he kicked off his shoes and collapsed onto his bed, quickly falling into a deep sleep.

It was past noon when he knocked on the Allens' door. Swing music blared from inside.

The music abruptly stopped, the door flew open, and there stood Katie. A wide smile spread across her face when she saw him. She was barefoot, in nothing but a threadbare T-shirt—soft, oversized, and faded from countless washes.

She rushed into his arms, and he was struck by the scent of her skin and the warm dampness of her shirt against him.

"We saw your bouquet. That was swell of you, Chris," she murmured in his ear.

"You're welcome," he replied, hugging her back—and finding he didn't want to break away.

"Sandra is at school; it's in session today," she told him in response to his inquiry. "My parents are also at work. I'm alone."

"And sweaty," he noted, his voice teasing yet appreciative.

The soft firmness of her heavy breasts pressed against his chest, and through the thin, faded fabric, he could feel the distinct peaks of her nipples. Chris felt his body stir.

She laughed, low and close. "You can feel it, huh?" She blew a stray damp strand of hair away from her eye. "I've been mopping the floor, dusting the furniture—and dancing along the way. Got hot." Her arms were still wrapped around him.

"Would you care for a bite to eat?" she asked, disengaging from the hug and pulling him inside. "I can whip us up a sandwich."

"All right," he said, letting her lead him in. "But after that, I'm heading to Sandra's school; I promised myself I'd visit her workplace."

Katie had him sit by the dining table while she went to the refrigerator and began pulling things out. She hummed lightly as she worked—a vague, meandering tune, maybe something half-remembered from the radio. Chris watched her as she moved—the unselfconscious sway of her hips, the fabric of her shirt rippling with each step. The afternoon light caught her in profile, outlining everything beneath. She opened a drawer. Grabbed a knife. Spread mayo. Licked it off her thumb.

"Did you like school?" she asked, not looking up.

Chris blinked. "I—what?" His voice cracked. *Jesus*.

He grimaced. "I don't have many good memories of school." He eyed her archly. "How about you?"

She smiled. "I don't have any memories of school."

Her smile widened. "Never attended one."

"That must have been nice," he said.

His eyes followed the curve of her back as she turned toward the cabinets.

She rose on her toes, her shirt slipping upward as she reached for a bowl. "Chris?" she called over her shoulder. "Could you help me grab this?"

He was on his feet before she finished, coming up.

Then—bam—Katie launched herself at him. With no warning, or wind-up, he had an armful of Katie—legs cinched tight around his waist, arms looped around his neck.

He staggered back a step. "Whoa, Katie!"

She latched onto him like a koala, warm and unexpectedly solid, her breasts at eye level.

"Beep. Beep. Beep—like a forklift in reverse," she said, steering his shoulders as he found his footing. "Little bit to the left."

"Beep. Beep."

She reached up, grabbed the bowl, and guided him to the kitchen island, before hopping down.

"I've been meaning to ask," she said, grabbing a tomato as Chris stood there catching his breath. "Did you like the outfits I modeled the other day?"

"Yes," he said, eyeing her warily.

She turned back to the counter, resuming her slicing. "Which was the most eye-catching?"

He hesitated for a beat. "The neon-yellow miniskirt," he said. "And the matching top."

A flicker of satisfaction crossed her face.

"Sandra told me you can do it all—blouses, skirts, coats."

She grinned at him.

"Sandra also mentioned something about bartering skills. How does it work?" he asked. "Someone does your taxes, offers piano lessons, or fixes a leaky faucet in exchange for tailoring?"

She shook her head. "It's a time bank, not a direct exchange. People offer services based on time spent. I tailor for an hour, earn one hour credit, and redeem it later for an hour of someone else's service."

"It's pretty remarkable," Chris said. He walked over to the kitchen counter. "What are your dreams, Katie?" he asked. "What do you want to do with your life?"

"Why, just what I do," she said, glancing up briefly as she continued to quickly slice a cucumber. "As it happens, I also enjoy it. I like cooking; I like keeping the house neat; I like caring for my family; I like spending afternoons with my friends sewing clothes." She pulled out the elastic and shook her hair loose, letting it cascade down her back, a moment that seemed to slow time.

He tried again, "But is that what you want to do for the rest of your days?"

"Well, no," Katie said. She was now arranging tomato and turkey slices on rustic bread. "I want to get married, have a family of my own—and take care of them." Sandwiches done, she placed them on a tray. "What about you, Chris?"

He opened his mouth, then frowned and mulled it over. "Actually, kind of the same," he said, laughing. "You know, have a family and take care of them."

The two exchanged smiles.

Katie made him wait while she went to her quarters to change into a dress.

A bit later, they carried the tray and glasses of water to the porch. Chris sat down on the small swing bench, and Katie slid next to him, the side of her thigh warm against his. They clinked their glasses together and sipped.

From a few houses away, some little girls called out a name, again and again.

"What are they doing?" Chris wondered aloud, taking a bite

of the sandwich. Damn, it was good!

Katie smiled, amused. "From the sound of it, calling Jane to come out and play. Was it *that* different in Iraq, where you grew up?"

"No, of course not," he said hurriedly and busied himself with the food.

Chris ate in contented silence, watching the sunlight dance on her hair from the corner of his eye.

"Why are you and Sandra sharing a bed?" he asked after he finished the last of his sandwich, surprising himself.

Katie turned, her face inches from his, close enough for him to note the subtle pulse of a vein in her temple. "Sandra and I share everything," she said, her voice even. "She's mine," she added, voice harsh and unrecognizable. The burning intensity that flared in her eyes sent a chill down his spine, and just as quickly, it was gone. She smiled at him sweetly.

They heard the soft patter of bare feet climbing the steps. Katie turned toward the sound and broke eye contact. The girls who had been hollering earlier came up to the porch.

The children were working on their monthly publication, the *Boulder Bugle,* a gazette-style periodical about the local area, and they wanted to interview Katie about her clothing design.

Chris rose to his feet, somewhat unsteadily. "It's time for me to go. As you may recall, I planned on visiting Sandra at the school."

Katie insisted on walking him down from the porch and gave him a tender kiss with a hint of pressure. "Go to the picnic grove, the one with the burr oak at the end of the street," she directed him. "Take the first left and then the third right. You'll find the school about two hundred yards up ahead."

He searched her eyes, but they were clear and soft and warm. It was just Katie—only Katie. Moments earlier, her fingers had dug painfully into his arm, and if it weren't for the fading ache, he might have convinced himself that he'd imagined the entire incident.

All the same, he kissed her back warmly. "Thank you for the sandwich and the delightful company."

She beamed in response. "The pleasure is entirely mine."

CHAPTER 12

As Chris strode briskly through the streets, he grappled with the lingering unease of his encounter with Katie. Her abrupt harshness and the strange intensity in her eyes were unsettling. He was now certain she was the one who'd issued that curt warning at the construction site. Was it just a protective, sisterly instinct? Possessiveness, maybe? He replayed the scenes. Peculiar? Yes. Malicious? No. He grew increasingly convinced of that.

Chris walked on, lost in thought, occasionally tipping his hat to those he passed. This world he'd stumbled upon might have been the best thing that ever happened to him. But he was an outsider. A pretender. What was he doing? The thought hit him hard, like a heavy blow.

For Chris, it was no longer about making money off a video. Or only the making of a documentary. The more time he had spent in this new world, his desire to remain grew stronger. Chris felt a profound affinity for Americana that he'd never quite felt for his home world. And then there were Sandra, Katie, and him—rushing headlong down a mad path. Chris had given up trying to make sense of their evolving relationships.

As he approached the modest terracotta brick building of Whittier School, someone stepped out from the small foyer and waved: Sandra.

They hugged near the white columns by the entrance.

"I spotted you from the classroom window," she said, her eyes tracing the lines of his form. "You clean up rather nicely, Mr. Darcy. Forgive me if I've already said so."

Under the straw hat that shaded his face, his gray eyes crinkled with a smile. He cupped her chin and gazed deep into her eyes. "You're quite the head-turner yourself," he replied, recognizing the sage-green outfit with its belted waist, notched collar, and elbow-skimming sleeves—the same one she'd worn when they first met.

Her attire was flattering yet practical, grounded yet feminine—with a quiet poise that spoke of purpose, presence, and pride. And somehow, that moved him more than any plunging neckline. Now, with her hair in a thick French braid, there was something even more captivating about her.

Sandra beamed in response, linked her arm with his, and started walking. "Come. Let me introduce you to the principal. He's in right now, though he's a busy man." She glanced his way. "Welcome to my world."

He stumbled and almost missed a step. "Your *world?*" he repeated.

"The school, of course, you dolt."

He smiled sheepishly, and together, arm in arm, they entered the building.

School. There had been nothing horrible about his school experience; it had been simply boring. Hours of boredom, weeks of boredom, years of boredom.

Chris loved the outdoors and loved to work with his hands. Academics were the polar opposite. And schools, of course, had but meager, lukewarm offerings outside of academics. All the same, he was determined to keep a positive attitude during his visit. He *wanted* to engage with Sandra's passions and interests.

From outside, the building looked exactly like that of Whittier in his universe. On the inside, though, it was unrecognizable—whether because it was simply different in Americana, or because it had been completely renovated since he'd attended it for one year, when he was in fifth grade. A lifetime ago.

He had never imagined he would come back to visit the school—let alone in a parallel universe, as an adult, and next to a woman he was romantically involved with.

Sandra knocked on a paneled door, and moments later, Chris was shaking hands with an elderly, impeccably dressed black man. His prominent side whiskers and lively hazel eyes, framed by bushy eyebrows, gave him a distinguished appearance.

"Welcome to Whittier School, Mr. Walden," the principal said. He motioned for them to sit down, his eyes shifting between the two young people with a hint of amusement. "Miss Allen has mentioned you. Quite the impression you've made."

Sandra laughed with genuine amusement, appearing completely at ease.

Sunlight slipped through high windows onto a patterned rug, illuminating a stately desk rubbed to a dull sheen. A few comfortable chairs sat nearby, gathered loosely around the center. The air was faintly scented with cedar and ink, and a small stack of papers sat on the corner of the desk, a subtle reminder of the principal's other duties.

"I'm actually expecting someone soon," the elderly gentleman said, "though I'm happy to have met you and answer any quick questions you might have."

They were both now looking at Chris.

Nothing came to his mind, yet he could tell that Sandra expected him to ask something.

"So, uh . . ." Chris began, mentally rifling through a stack of potential insightful questions. "What do students learn in this school?" he asked. Inwardly wincing at the banality, he braced himself for Sandra's eye roll, but she gave him instead an encouraging smile. Maybe she was grading on a curve.

The principal responded, "Well, besides instilling in them some patriotic spirit and grit, students gain cultural knowledge. Beyond that, it's up to the family and the youngster." He walked around his desk and sat down. "Folks choose different programs. Some attend more often than others."

Chris thought for a moment. "Are schools around here government-run?" All right, that was a better question.

The principal chuckled. "A common misconception, Mr. Walden. Schools are private institutions; they provide what they see fit. For its part, the county runs a tax-funded voucher system." The older gentleman leaned forward in his high-backed leather chair. "If a program includes a cultural trip abroad, the voucher might not cover it. However, as a rule, they aim to provide a voucher for any and all school programs."

Chris pondered this. Publicly funded, privately run. Interesting.

The elderly man glanced at his golden pocket watch and rose, extending a hand. "I trust Miss Allen will show you the rest. It was a pleasure meeting you, Mr. Walden. Perhaps we'll have a chance to chat more at another time."

Once outside the principal's office, Chris turned to Sandra, his eyes opening wide in mock astonishment. "So you're a teacher. Why didn't you mention it before?"

She punched his shoulder. "I'm the only literature teacher for tweens in Boulder, I'll have you know."

"So how many kids do you teach?" Chris asked.

She gave him a sideways look. "Kids? Didn't I just say tweens? I teach adolescents, Mr. Darcy. You know, the non-kid kind of students."

Chris blinked, not sure what she just said.

"Look at the numbers," Sandra said as they walked down the corridor. "There are about five hundred in that age group in Boulder. Some of them love to read, and among those, some are drawn to idea-rich novels. Out of those, some like to discuss them in a group setting. The upshot is that around eighty young folks attend literature seminars: mine. I run five sections."

Yeah, it made sense. Pity that on the other end of the looking glass, in America, there was no possibility to opt out of language arts classes. Still, he did acquire a certain finesse in the skill of dozing off while seated; his time in class was not all in vain.

"It's worthwhile to go to this school just for the lighting." He pointed up. "It's *amazing*, Sandra."

"Diffused sunlight," she said.

"What?"

"Mirrors tracking the movement of the sun, piping the light into the building via ducts coated with reflective material."

Now he understood. "So when it's too dim, artificial illumination makes up for it?"

She nodded. Of course.

Sandra opened her classroom door, inviting Chris in. He entered, and she followed.

He gazed in wonder at the spacious room. Books were everywhere—crammed into deep wooden shelves that ran along the walls and jutted out in freestanding rows. Murals adorned the rustic, cinnamon-hued brick walls, and a grand fireplace stood at the far end.

But almost instantly, Chris got his second, bigger surprise: As he waded between the towering bookshelves, he saw carpeted islands where tweens, primarily girls, sat on plush, oversized cushions in circles and conducted discussions in low, earnest voices.

He found Sandra. "You walked out in the middle of a class to meet me?" Chris studied her, bemused.

She pinched his cheek. "You're positively endearing!" she told him in a voice that only reached his ears. "Those are not kindergarteners, Chris. What do you fancy would happen if I walked out?"

Chris looked around and observed some of the tweens as they heatedly discussed something. "They seem to have stayed on task," he admitted.

Sandra shot him an amused look. "'Task'? Chris, you sound like a foreman at the foundry." Her eyes sparkled. "We call these sessions 'the salon'—the exploration of new ideas in the form of boisterous debates, heated intellectual discussions, and contemplative analysis of select works of fiction—the brightest stars in the literary galaxy."

"The salon, huh?" Chris smiled, intrigued.

He took a seat next to a group discussing a "nocturne fantasy" novel, watching Sandra from the corner of his eye as she moved among the students, conversing softly with one group or another.

A series of chimes signaled the session's end. Chairs slid back and books snapped shut, followed by laughter and animated chatter as students streamed out, joining others pouring from the building. It seemed the entire student body was taking recess at that time.

"Come," Sandra said. She crossed the hall and opened the door to another classroom. As they stepped inside, a woman rose from her seat, her face brightening with a delighted smile.

"I'd like you to meet my associate, Miss Joanna Harris," Sandra said, introducing the woman. "This is Mr. Chris Walden."

"Sandra has mentioned you. How do you do?" Miss Harris

said, shaking Chris's hand. She was an attractive black woman with sparkling green eyes and a warm, open smile.

"And what subject do you teach, Miss Harris?" Chris asked.

"Math, Mr. Walden. One of two dedicated math teachers in Whittier." They all sat down. "My class is ordinarily filled with thirteen-, fourteen-, and fifteen-year-old students. It's the last math chapter for most." She smiled. "The last bus stop of the journey."

Chris was taken aback. Math stopped sometime around the end of ninth grade? "What does the math curriculum cover?" he asked.

"The four operations with whole numbers and fractions; number sense, ratios, and measurements; applied statistics, data analysis, probability, and estimation; word problems, percentages, and basic finance and accounting," came the reply.

"Nothing more advanced than that?"

She cocked her head slightly. "Nothing more advanced is really needed—except for the relatively few who pursue the sciences, engineering, and computer science. And those few will take more advanced math courses in their respective college programs."

"I see," he said, his faint smile acerbic.

He then remembered something he'd intended to ask. "I was curious, Miss Harris: How does the school handle students who disrupt the learning of others?"

Miss Harris shared a look with Sandra. "We try first, of course. But if someone's set on being a knucklehead—out they go."

Chris raised an eyebrow.

"We don't let a troublemaker spoil it for the rest," Miss Harris said with a shrug.

"It's also a matter of self-preservation," chimed in Sandra. "Parents expect us to hold that line. If we didn't, they'd take their kids elsewhere—and rightly so. However, this is rarely an issue. Those who attend are motivated and want to be here."

A piercing whistle suddenly blared through the loudspeaker, accompanied by a metallic voice: "Attention all workers! Form a single file and report to gate thirteen. It is time to descend into the coal mine."

Sandra noticed the look on Chris's face. "School humor, dear. Recess is over."

As students were coming back inside, Chris took a peek through a window at an empty classroom, and with a nod from Sandra, walked in—gazing curiously at the enormous tables, laden with a bewildering array of items, from countless figurines to colored tokens. He frowned. It had the look and feel of a tabletop game, though unlike any he'd seen.

"Mr. Jones specializes in complex simulations lasting days on end," Sandra said, entering the room. "I have a few moments," she added, responding to the unspoken question in his eyes.

Chris regarded the table. "Never saw anything quite like this." He gestured at the stacks of signage, miniatures, maps, currency, and small display screens.

"Live-action, large-scale simulations of economic and political microcosms. Participants take on different roles, from entrepreneurs to defense ministers," Sandra said with a hint of pride. "Mr. Jones introduces unexpected and random events to make the simulations more realistic."

"It sounds. . . intense."

"'Overwhelming' is the word you're looking for," she told him, her shoes clicking on the rustic oak floor as she paced around the room. "Mr. Jones throws the young people into the deep end of the pool. It involves them in ever-shifting, interrelated crises with countless repercussions that can't be foreseen."

"A social studies class," Chris said, wonder in his voice.

"A specialized part of it," Sandra said.

Her face brightened. "I just thought of something. Come."

Sandra led him to the back of the building, and then into another, larger one. "This is where the students forge their ideas into tangible artifacts," she said as she pushed open the double swing doors with a flourish.

They stepped into a large hall, and Chris halted, taken aback by the sights and sounds that greeted them. Young people were dispersed throughout the space, gathered in small groups on the floor or around sizable workbenches—assembling, drawing, conversing, and constructing. A dozen paces from Sandra and Chris, a large wooden boat sat.

"The annual Battleship War is a beloved tradition around here," Sandra said, following Chris as he walked up to the boat for a closer look. "Students, mostly boys, spend their summers building these vessels. A rival school does the same. The ships can only be powered and steered by the students' legs."

Fascinated, Chris examined the complex network of pulleys and gears attached to multiple propellers. "Now, that's more like it," he muttered to himself. He'd never been one for academics, but this was the type of activity he could really get into.

"I see it got your attention," Sandra said, a hint of a smile playing at the corner of her lips. She steered him a bit to the left and pointed. "Both groups have constructed battering rams and riveted them to the bows of their ships. The final clash will occur in the Boulder Reservoir in two weeks. They'll be armed with paintball guns." Sandra winked at him. "Only one team shall emerge victorious."

Chris turned to her and said, "Sandra, this is precisely how a school ought to be."

Sandra smiled, and for a minute, they both stood watching as a group of young people tinkered with the gears, the click of a wrench audible over their low murmurs. One of the gears gave a soft clack as a student adjusted it nearby, testing tension with a satisfied nod.

"Building a human-powered boat is just the pretext," said a voice from behind. One of the teachers, a wiry man in his thirties, joined them. "Along the way, students internalize mechanical principles like friction, momentum, and mechanical advantage."

"How do you do?" Chris said and offered his hand to the teacher. They shook.

"Mr. Walden thinks the world of what you're doing here," Sandra told her associate.

"I do," Chris agreed. "Please tell me, how do the students decide on their projects?"

The teacher crossed his arms loosely, smiling faintly. "Sometimes, they make plans. Other times, they simply start constructing things."

"So they build whatever strikes their fancy," Chris said, looking around appreciatively. His hidden video camera never stopped filming.

The teacher said, "Projects may end up being anything from trebuchets to steam-powered water-raising machines to pneumatic automata."

Chris looked impressed. "Da Vincis in training, huh?"

"Precisely," replied the wiry man with a toothy grin. "They operate with scarce resources, constructively engage in failures, negotiate the ambiguous and the uncharted—conditions that are intrinsic to an authentic creation and development process."

Chris now looked even more impressed.

"It starts with hammers, drills, and circular saws for the six- and seven-year-olds," the teacher explained. "By the time they are fourteen—at the culmination of this track—they've mastered precision metalworking techniques, operating industrial-grade equipment like CNC milling machines, plasma cutters, and hydraulic metal formers."

Chris shot a glance at the instructor. "You actually have those tools and machines here?"

"Those and more." It was Sandra who answered. She motioned toward the far end of the hall. "We have a woodshop, a metal shop, and a textile shop."

For Chris, this was like an invitation to tour wonderland. "May I?"

The teacher inclined his head, and Sandra led Chris to the woodshop.

Amazing, he thought to himself. The space held everything one could need to work with wood: bandsaws and laser cutters, table saws and routers, planers and wood lathes, drill presses and sanders. Next, Chris walked into the adjoining metal shop. It was even more impressive. The shop was equipped with welders and grinders, lathes and metal-cutting laser machines, swing-beam shears and milling machines. It even had a punch worktable, a plate rolling machine, a small foundry, and a hydraulic press brake.

"Do you see anything you like?"

Sandra stood smiling at the doorway.

He turned to her. "This is a dream shop," he told her. "One could build just about anything here."

Sandra snapped her fingers and pointed a finger at him. "That's the idea."

"Do adults in the community have access to these shops?"

"Are you asking about it for personal reasons?"

"Maybe," he said. "I've nothing specific in mind, though."

"If you need to build something that requires more than a circular saw or a claw hammer, you can work at any of the Community Toolsheds in town or borrow a tool from a nearby equipment depot."

It was good to know.

"Both places offer skill-sharing workshops. So if you need

training, say, on milling machines, you'll find someone there to train you."

He smiled at her. "Are you telling me about this for personal reasons?"

"Maybe," she said with a smile. "I've nothing specific in mind, though."

Chris surveyed the bustling hall for a moment. "Grades and tests?" he inquired.

"Definitely not around these activities." Sandra tsked and motioned with the sweep of her arm. "These projects genuinely matter to the young people," she said. "They have the freedom to fail, the time to persevere, and space to imagine. Grades and tests are incompatible with that; they create a risk-averse culture in their wake."

Sandra led Chris back to her classroom, where he waited until the bell rang, signaling lunch. While some students headed home to eat, most remained at school.

Within minutes, two dozen young people retrieved folding tables from a closet and arranged them into a few communal tables. They swiftly set out plates, utensils, and cups, then unpacked their lunches. The room buzzed with lively conversations, punctuated by sharp bursts of laughter. Chris ended up eating food from the cafeteria, which two designated students fetched for those without a packed lunch from home.

Sandra was besieged by four girls, eager to chat with her about some personal matters.

Chris struck up a conversation with a few boys sitting nearby. As he listened, it slowly dawned on him: School here was only a part-time affair—two days a week, for most. Some worked a few mornings at the bakery or helped shelve books at the library. Others restocked inventory at the shoe store, or sorted mail at the post office. But that was only part of it.

One boy described the telescope he had built with his

grandfather and how he logged constellations from the hill-top behind the schoolhouse. Another had a little woodworking setup in his garage and was crafting stools and side tables for the community center. Others were making soaps, filming short documentaries, writing illustrated storybooks, or painting murals on brick walls. It wasn't that anyone did all of this—just that, over time, kids gravitated toward what piqued their interest.

As with work in town, helping at home was part of the rhythm of life, especially for younger children. Sweeping floors, folding laundry, peeling potatoes, and helping with younger siblings—many started pitching in as soon as they could see over the counter. For tweens with town jobs or steady projects, the load at home often lightened. Some still pitched in every day; others, only here and there. It varied. But whatever the rhythm, there was no mistaking it: In Americana, being part of a family meant carrying real weight—early, and with pride.

There was time, too, to just be kids—lying belly-down on the grass with a book, skipping stones, trading jokes, or showing off a new sketch. It wasn't leisure carved out from responsibilities; it was part of the whole.

As lunch ended, the students rose and restored the class-room with practiced efficiency. Some gathered dishes while others wiped down tables and desks, each corner attended to without fuss or fanfare. They finished by sweeping the corri-dor floor. Chris watched it all unfold, a faint pang rising in his chest. It was a far cry from the careless halls he remembered.

A chime announced the end of the break. The two of them got up, and Chris kissed Sandra. "I'll let you go back to work."

"Sounds good," she said and drew Chris to her. "You liked what you heard and saw?"

"Yes," he said simply, holding her gaze. "Thank you for showing me your world."

"No," she said. "Thank *you*."

They shared a smile.

—=—

"Mr. Callenbach," Chris greeted the old man a few hours later at the treasury bank.

"Well, if it ain't my gold coin fella," the teller said, already reaching for his spectrometer. "Good to see you again, son."

"Likewise," Chris said, smiling. Much like last time, there was no one around, and he wondered how many clients Mr. Callenbach netted each day. Be that as it may, the hour was growing late, and Chris was glad that the treasury bank was still open.

Chris was staying in Americana for a while—more than a few days, more than a few weeks. It wasn't a decision, rather a growing realization. He slid the gold coins under the thick acrylic window.

The old man hefted the machine with a grunt. "Either this thing's putting on weight, or I'm shedding muscle," he muttered to himself.

The spectrometer gave a soft buzz as it started up. Chris rested his forearms on the ledge and let his eyes wander. "While I've got you—mind if I ask you something?"

The old man nodded. "Ask away. Been here since lunch with nothing but my crossword for company."

"I'm not from around here," he said at last, brushing a hand through his hair. "And I was wondering, when folks are dating— who does the proposing?"

The clerk peered at a coin through his loupe. "Man does the asking. But the woman's doing the deciding." He looked up. "It's like my old bread route, see? Show up regular, deliver the goods, keep the rig clean. After a while, they either want you permanent or they don't."

He counted out fifty-six hundred dollars and slid it under the plexiglass. "The proposal itself? That's just paperwork on a done deal."

Chris pocketed the cash, lingering.

"What's got you wound up, son?" the old man asked, not unkindly.

"There's these two women. Sisters. And at least one of them is basically encouraging me to be with both."

Callenbach paused, his pencil still. He looked up.

"Sisters, huh?"

"Yeah."

The teller leaned back slowly. "Maybe that's their idea of a good time. Or maybe they're looking to build a triad marriage. Or a quad, if there is another fella in the picture."

Triads and quads! Chris now remembered what Sandra had said in passing a few nights ago. Things tumbled into place. Suddenly it made sense. Albeit a weird kind of sense.

"Thanks," Chris said. "That helped more than you know." He tipped his hat to the old man and left.

CHAPTER 13

CHRIS WOKE UP, looked at the clock, and groaned. He could not wait, did not want to wait a few hours until daybreak. Then he remembered what Sandra had told him yesterday: She was off the rest of the week, teaching only one day a week during the summer months.

Oh, what the hell. He put on his cargo pants and T-shirt, pulled on his boots, and walked over to the Allens' place.

Chris decided to reveal to the sisters the truth about his origin. He couldn't keep living a lie, especially given their deepening relationships.

He walked nimbly down the narrow footpath that wound around the main house. As he neared the detached unit in the back, a glimmer of light caught his attention. Surprised, he noticed it was coming from one of the smaller rooms.

Through a gossamer curtain, he caught a glimpse of a figure sitting by the window. As he drew closer, there was no mistaking the identity of the person—it was Katie.

Hunched over, she was writing at a rapid clip in a thick notebook. Chris stood there mesmerized. Minutes passed, and she continued to write, filling a page, then another. Beside her, an open book lay on the desk.

He recognized the book by its dimensions and cover; it

was the same volume he'd seen in her room earlier: Immanuel Kant's *Critique of Pure Reason*. Back in his America, a quick online search had revealed its daunting nature: a dense philosophical work exploring the nature and limits of human knowledge and reason. And this girl, who seemed preoccupied with dolls and vinyl miniskirts, was not only reading it but also taking extensive notes. He finally understood why she hadn't attended school—there was no need for her to attend.

Who the hell was she?

He remained there, unable to tear his gaze away, yet also sensing that he couldn't—mustn't—make his presence known.

He lost track of time watching her write. Eventually, she stood, turned off the light, and moments later, he heard a door open and close as she entered the main quarters she shared with Sandra.

Chris waited five minutes, then circled quietly to the front of the house. He opened the door—and in the pale wash of moonlight, he saw the two sisters together.

Bewildered and embarrassed, he stumbled back. He wasn't ready for this. He turned, taking a step away.

"Chris!"

He spun back. Sandra stood in the doorway, hair tousled, a bedsheet hastily draped around her. "Wait here," she said—then, softer, "Please."

He hesitated, then gave an almost imperceptible nod. With that, she slipped back inside the small dwelling.

Sandra emerged moments later, barefoot and clad in a white nightgown, a lantern swaying from a pole over her shoulder. She handed Chris a heavy, folded canvas and led him toward a vine-covered fence at the edge of the clearing.

Sandra nudged open a wooden gate, and they stepped into a sprawling forest garden. She guided Chris along meandering, narrow footpaths, their way illuminated by the lantern's light. The thrum of crickets waxed and waned. The paper lantern bobbed and swayed with each step, casting eerie shadows across the foliage.

At long last, they reached a clearing in the heart of the garden. Sandra stepped onto a carpet of leaves and made her way to the massive tree at the center. She rested the pole with the lantern against the tree's gnarled trunk. Chris unfolded the canvas to reveal a hammock. Together, they stretched it across a few low-hanging, sturdy branches and fastened it to hooks that dangled down. Soon they were lying side by side, swaying gently on the spacious swing bed, their gazes fixed on the glittering night sky above.

"So you and Katie. . ."

"Occasionally, yes," she said, still staring at the stars, her arms tucked behind her head.

He frowned, turning it over in his mind—the image of the sisters, tangled in moonlight and shadow. He glanced Sandra's way, but she was still looking upward, obviously unwilling to engage in a discussion about it. Perhaps waiting to see what he would decide.

He looked again at her, at this woman he was growing to love, and felt a strange ache he couldn't name. Something was broken about the two sisters, he now knew. And loving them, if he dared, meant loving them as they were—scars, silence, and all.

The cool night air washed over him, but the heat of what he'd seen clung to his skin. He shifted in the hammock, the ropes creaking softly, the deeper shadows of the garden weaving and unweaving overhead.

The kiss at dinner—the one between the sisters he'd brushed off—came back to him now, heavier, sharper. So did the casual way Sandra had nudged him toward Katie, as if. . . she wouldn't mind. As if she meant for it to happen.

Chris exhaled, slow and shallow.

He had stumbled into a bond he didn't understand, something twisted and tender, perilous and sweet—pulling at the heart and the body. Somehow, he sensed, it was either Katie *and* Sandra. Or neither.

Maybe he should be afraid. Maybe he should be running. He let the hammock rock him instead, and after a while, the frown faded from his face.

They lay there, listening to the sounds of the night. Sandra's head rested on his shoulder, and her arm draped over his chest. He felt the weight of her body against him and the warmth of her breath on his skin. It was a simple moment, yet it brought him peace and contentment. But the truth, a stone in his pocket, grew heavier with each passing moment.

"Sandra, I've never known my father," Chris said in a low voice. He was going to reveal the truth about his origin, step by step.

Her eyes widened, looking at him in shock. "That's . . . terrible. How did he pass away?"

"Pass away?" he asked, taken aback. "What makes you think that?"

"I assumed," she stammered. "You mean, he's alive?"

"I have no reason to believe he's not. But I've never met him."

"I . . . don't understand," she said, her brow furrowing in confusion.

He shifted onto his side, facing her. "What's there to understand?" he said harshly. "My mother had a fleeting romance, carried me to term, and decided to raise me on her own. Surely you know of single mothers."

"Well, no. I cannot say I'm personally aware of any . . ." Her voice trailed off, then she rallied a bit. "There are women who lose their husbands, becoming widows—although they tend to remarry, especially when they have children."

Sandra understood now. There'd been no vow, no mooring. Just two people living together, until not. A roof with no frame. The thought depressed her.

"How's your mother doing?" she asked softly.

Her voice pulled him back. He regarded Sandra. "She passed away five years ago. She had a problem with narcotics. Overdosed."

Her eyes searched his. "Oh, Chris, I'm terribly sorry," she whispered.

He gave a little sardonic smile. "She was seeing someone. Thought it might help."

Sandra tilted her head. "Seeing someone?"

Shit. No therapists in Americana.

"Just. . . someone who gave her advice," he muttered. "Didn't work."

Sandra nodded, slowly. Her fingers brushed his hair.

Under the tree's canopy, lying beside Sandra on the hammock, Chris shared his childhood experiences, holding nothing back.

He observed her, eyes large and trusting as she listened, hanging onto every detail, and at times aghast at what she was hearing. In those moments, she gripped his hand, seemingly unaware.

And in fact, this took place in Boulder, he planned to say next. Then he looked again at the trusting eyes. *A Boulder in another universe,* he would add—and this is when he would lose her, as surely as anything. The best thing that had ever happened to him—wrecked. The one thing he wanted to protect and cherish above all—kaput. How could she believe him? How could anyone believe such a cockamamie story of coming from another universe?

He gazed at her, paralyzed by indecision.

Soon after, the moment passed; he could feel it. The window

of opportunity closed as her eyes turned inward.

He sensed her internal struggle, then watched as she seemed to reach a decision. "Chris," she finally said, the words spilling out, "our meeting was not a chance encounter."

He tensed up.

"I am—was—a Homeland Security asset who was assigned to look into you." His eyes widened. "But the matter was dropped just as quickly"—she clutched his arm—"and everything else that has happened between us was genuine, Chris. It was real." She squeezed his hand and watched his face closely. "I've cut ties with the department since," she added breathlessly.

"I believe you," he heard himself say. It was true, Chris realized through the numbness; he did believe her and trusted the sincerity of her feelings toward him.

He sensed Sandra relaxing. Alas, he could not share her feeling of ease, as there was the other matter. His mouth was dry. "How—Why did they ask you to approach me? What did they say to you?"

"It had something to do with you not being in the system."

Understanding flooded in. "Of course! The rack!"

"Pardon?"

"It was the night before I met you." He was now smiling broadly, in relief as much as anything. "I tried to unlock a rack containing some personal transporters. The scanner flashed red when it scanned my vein pattern. That's what must have triggered the alarm."

She nodded, now understanding. "That's pretty much what they told me. I called them a couple of days later and confirmed you're not registered." Then, in a rush, "I also took photos of your driver's license and the photo of you with the men in uniform and sent them over."

Shocked, Chris felt his heart give a great bound.

The day before his journey into Americana, Ronny and

Chris had decided he would take these items and keep them hidden. They'd deliberated the countless ways his encounters in the other universe could play out. In some of the scenarios they'd envisioned, it seemed best for him to reveal his identity. These two items were to lend a measure of credibility. There was a third item, tucked in the sole of his boot. Evidently, she did not uncover it.

"What did they say about them?" Chris asked, still reeling from what he'd just heard.

"Not a whole lot, actually; we reckoned it was some sort of cosplay," Sandra said. "Chris, the matter's been settled; the case is closed."

A case was opened—about him. But it had already been shut—as it turned out. It felt like a sudden gut punch, the pain fading almost as quickly as it came.

He regarded Sandra. It was clear she hoped he would shed some light on the driver's license and the army photo. She wanted to confirm that it was indeed cosplay. He could tell she wanted him to say that. She needed him to say that.

Yet, he could not; his vocal cords refused to comply. Several uncomfortable seconds went by.

"So I was an assignment," Chris said. What she'd told him was starting to sink in.

"You were," she said curtly. "But I couldn't go through with it. Inspecting your artifacts was the limit of what I could bear." He felt her eyes on him, watching for his reaction.

"Has the teaching thing been merely a cover?"

She shook her head emphatically. "No, I really am a teacher. Spying was just a small side thing that I've been doing for Homeland Security once in a great while." Her gaze locked onto his. "I have no regrets about my work with the department. I've served my country well, identifying three Chinese operatives who were planning to steal industrial secrets."

Chris flashed her a thin smile, trying to let her know that he stood by her past efforts. Dimly, he wondered if Americana had fared better in its endeavor to fend off attempts by the Chinese to siphon off American intellectual properties.

They both were content to say no more. At some point, they fell asleep lying beside each other.

CHAPTER 14

CHRIS WOKE TO FIND THE SUN already high above the thick tree canopy. Propping himself on his elbows, he gawked at the wild-looking garden stretching in every direction. Wonder of wonders! He glanced at Sandra sleeping next to him and waited patiently for fifteen seconds. He decided it had been long enough and gently nudged her until she stirred and opened her eyes.

"We're in a magical food forest garden," he informed her, awe in his voice.

Sandra made a soft noise, somewhere between a groan and a sigh. She rolled onto her back, shading her eyes with one hand. "Can't vouch for any fairies," she murmured hoarsely. "But . . . yeah. Food forest."

Chris sat up, grinning. "This must be one of the most enchanted things I've ever seen."

Sandra stretched languidly, the hammock swaying beneath her. She pushed her tousled hair out of her face, taking in the trees and vines with a slow, fond look.

"We share it with seven other households," she said as she climbed down from the hammock. "I grew up in this place. Spent summers chasing worms, lifting rocks for lizards, listening to the birds, picking fruit."

"Straight out of *National Geographic*," Chris murmured, half to himself.

Sandra frowned. "National what?"

Chris's heart skipped a beat. He gestured broadly at the orchard. "You must have hundreds of fruit trees and berry bushes," he said, his voice a touch too loud. Quickly descending from the tree, he unclipped the hammock. "Who handles the harvest?" he asked, tucking the folded canvas under his arm. "Without gnome helpers, that must take forever."

Sandra laughed, stepping over an exposed root. "Tree shakers make quick work of it," she said, shrugging. But then she noticed his bewilderment. "We have a tractor path and a steel wire rope that can reach any part of the garden. We unfold a canvas like an accordion and secure it around the trunk. Then, with a crankshaft, the tree gets shaken—and the apples rain down."

Chris was silent. "Must be fun," he said at last.

"It is," she said, a faint smile playing at the corners of her mouth. "We eat, and we take some home to make apple pies. We produce a barrel's worth of apple cider, and we dehydrate a bunch of apples. But most of the apples are purchased by a wholesaler, who distributes them to local retailers."

They started strolling, their feet crunching softly on the leaf-strewn ground.

"A fruitopia," Chris murmured. "Everywhere you look—fruit trees and berry bushes."

Sandra turned to him and caressed his cheek, smiling. "Hardly. They're just the centerpieces of broader plant communities. It's the other plants—the ones you don't notice right away—that make it all work without input from the outside."

"Without input? You mean, like fertilizers?"

"Indeed," she said. "No fertilizers, no pesticides, no herbicides, no mulch. A no-fuss forest garden."

"How?" he asked and stopped walking. "How do you do that?"

"Yoo-hoo!" called a cheerful voice, and they turned around.

Katie stepped into the clearing, wearing a fit-and-flare floral dress, a wicker basket swinging on her arm, a checkered rolled blanket slung over one shoulder. Barefoot, she crossed a strip of gravel—jagged granite chips meant to drain runoff from the trail—without pause or flinch, her steps even.

Chris blinked. He'd trained for discomfort. He'd hiked with seventy pounds on his back, crossed deserts with blisters between his toes. But he wouldn't walk that gravel barefoot unless something was chasing him. And here came Katie, in a flouncy dress, stepping across it like it was grass.

That's when it hit him—not the jagged stones, but the truth: At seven, Katie had probably peeled potatoes, stitched torn cloth with aching fingers, and scraped her knuckles scrubbing counters.

Earlier, he'd learned that every third winter they powered down: twelve days of deliberate deprivation. No electric light, no powered heat, no rich meals. Rather—grit, wool blankets, and huddled storytelling. Now he understood.

This society hadn't discarded hardship when comfort came. It preserved it—like heirloom seeds, passed hand to hand. They carried it. Wore it beneath the lace and parasols like sinew over bones. It reminded them who they were. Who they refused to stop being.

Katie approached Sandra and planted a kiss on her cheek. "One for you too," she added, kissing Chris—as if she'd packed the kisses carefully between the coffee and the muffins.

"Don't say it," Chris told her, closing his eyes. "My psychic powers tell me this basket contains . . ."—he furrowed his brow—". . . food."

Katie gasped, eyes wide, hand flying to her mouth.

"Steeped deep in the power is this one," Sandra murmured.

"Here, spread the blanket," Katie said, handing it to Chris.

The warm scent of blueberry muffins filled the air as Katie unpacked the basket. She laid out a thermos of steaming coffee, thick slices of sourdough bread, a jar of ruby-red strawberry preserves, a wedge of cheddar cheese, and a white ceramic butter crock.

As they settled onto the checkered blanket, a pair of inquisitive robins hopped closer, their heads cocked to one side as if admiring the spread. Chris surveyed the arrayed food, raising an eyebrow. "Quite the feast, Katie. What's the occasion?"

"Breakfast," she said. "I never fail to remember this holiday."

Touché, Chris thought, reaching for the sourdough bread. A gentle breeze rustled the leaves, carrying the sweet scent of wildflowers. A stone's throw away, a plump bumblebee buzzed lazily from blossom to blossom.

After they ate, the three refreshed themselves in the house and returned to the forest garden with sickles. Chris enthusiastically agreed to help hack down comfrey bushes, which were interspersed throughout.

"You understand why we cut these down, yes?" Sandra asked. She gave a whack, and a bunch of the large, leathery leaves scattered about.

"Not in the slightest," Chris said, attacking the bush he was assigned to. Moments earlier, Katie had gone off to give a "severe haircut" to comfreys in another section of the food forest and soon disappeared from view amid the trees.

"The nutrients have to come from somewhere," Sandra said as she swung the sickle. "Comfrey's roots reach deep and bring the good stuff up. We trim it a few times a year and let the leaves decompose on the ground, in effect feeding the plants with shallow roots."

He glanced around. "That's quite the ecosystem."

She stopped and gave him a look. "Not many of those in Iraq?"

He shook his head.

Very well. She was going to show him. "Can you tell me what that tree over there is?"

That was an easy one, with the unmistakable shape and size of the fruits. "An apple tree." From the overly patient expression that came over her face, he did not care to affirm that, yes, it was the first time he'd seen an apple tree up close.

"Right," she said after a slight pause. "A Honeycrisp apple tree, to be exact. But it needs pollen from other strains to actually make baby apples. So, we've got Liberty farther back. Bees and bumblebees buzz the pollen around. And to keep them fat and happy all season, we've got Pasque flowers kicking off in early spring, penstemons taking the baton in June, garlic chives blooming in late summer, and goldenrod carrying them through the fall. Are you with me so far?"

"Absolutely." She had never seen him looking so engrossed before.

"Those chives also help keep the grass down, so it doesn't steal nutrients from the trees. The camassias do the same. Then, we have goumi bushes adding nitrogen to the soil, and comfrey with its deep roots pulling up other minerals."

All those biological connections. He shook his head. "Sandra, I had no idea." He looked at her helplessly.

"Purple coneflowers bring in wasps, and coriander attracts ladybugs, hoverflies, and lacewings," she said, gesturing toward the garden. "In turn, these predator insects take care of the pests. Do you get a feel for how the plant community works as a whole?"

He nodded mutely, his thoughts swirling. Until that day, he had the vague idea of apple trees planted in tidy rows on a barren ground, hooked up to a constant IV drip of fertilizers while being administered herbicides, insecticides, and fungicides. Hearing Sandra describe the food forest system was one of those *aha!* moments.

Sandra said, "The whole garden works the same way. Every area is its own community, built around a fruit tree—cherry, pear, peach, plum, apricot, nectarine. And that's just the trees. Tucked into different corners, you'll find raspberries and blackberries, mountain strawberries and gooseberries, cranberries and currants." She smiled at him. "So whaddya think?"

"Amazing," he said. "I mean, it really speaks to me," he added and meant it.

She playfully blew a kiss his way, then resumed her work, the sickle flashing in the sunlight.

Sometime later, Katie headed back to the house while the two of them were finishing up.

A bird tweeted from somewhere above as they started making their way toward the garden's exit.

"A chirpy little fellow, isn't he?" commented Chris.

"That's a Western Meadowlark for you."

They reached the edge of the forest garden, where an eight-foot fence loomed before them. "This is to prevent rabbits and deer from entering and wreaking havoc," Sandra said, noticing Chris studying it.

"And the vines growing on it?"

"Hardy kiwis and grape vines."

Chris gave her a questioning look when a greenhouse came into view up ahead.

Sandra had nearly forgotten about it. "You're going to enjoy this one," she announced gaily. "Let's set our things down; we'll return for them later."

"Of course, my dear," he responded. She squealed in surprise and then with laughter as he scooped her up in his arms and carried her.

The warm, humid air and the sound of flowing water greeted them as they entered the greenhouse, filled with reeds and water plants. "How fitting," Chris remarked, "that I should carry you over the threshold into a tropical paradise."

She laughed again. "Alright, my hero, set me down. I have a secret to share, yet only the bravest can handle it." Once back on her feet, she cleared her throat. "What if I told you that all our graywater—showers, cooking, laundry—comes here, once it's been run through a grease trap and solids filter?"

Chris was taken aback, then grimaced. "Are you telling me this tropical paradise is nothing more than a glorified water treatment facility?"

Sandra walked on, addressing an imaginary crowd. "Step right up, folks! Witness the marvel of modern sanitation! We've got bulrush, cattail, and soft rush, with microbial minions toiling away, night and day! It's a luxury spa getaway—just for your shower water! Get your very own graywater garden today! Satisfaction guaranteed or your dirty water back!"

They were treading on a series of wood slats, weaving their way amid the thick foliage inside the greenhouse. Sandra glanced back at Chris, walking behind her. "Feast your eyes," she said, gesturing at the vibrant display. "Water lilies, horsetail, hibiscus, and pickerel weed... a water-cleaning wonderland."

"It's beautiful, Sandra," Chris murmured, wrapping his arms around her, bringing the two of them to a halt. He looked around. The encasing glass made perfect sense: the plants needed to work year-round if the water was to stay clean.

He gazed down. No soil, just gravel.

"Two feet deep, rubber-lined, packed with gravel," Sandra said, following his gaze. "We keep the water just below the surface, or else the mosquitoes would move in rent-free." She pointed. "Those baffles? They force the graywater to take the scenic route—which gets it cleaner with every lazy step. At the end, the purified water spills out onto the land and turns into a network of brooks that crisscross and irrigate the garden. We created a gentle slope so the water keeps moving."

Reluctantly, he let go of her waist, and they resumed walking. "Where does it go after that?"

"What is not soaked into the ground is funneled into a little pond whose bottom contains a deep layer of sand, followed by a very fine bag filter. From there, the water is routed back into the houses. It then gets zapped"—she slapped her hands together—"with ultraviolet light and recycled for use in laundries, showers, and toilets."

Sandra definitely had a thing for zapping, Chris thought. He asked a few more questions, and Sandra told him about the massive tanks and lagoons outside the city, designed to tame the runoff from slaughterhouses and factories.

He made a mental note of those engineered living systems as they left the greenhouse and were back outside amid the berry bushes and fruit trees. This was when a light bulb went on in his head. He took her hands in his. "Sandra, this is it! This is what I want to do with myself."

She laughed, taking joy in his palpable excitement. "What? Cultivate a forest garden?"

"Well, maybe more like production agriculture," he said, releasing her hands and glancing away. "I probably know less than any six-year-old around here about growing things." But as he met her eyes, an irrepressible smile broke across his face. "All the same, I've never felt this strongly about anything in my life. And if there's one thing I know about myself, it's that I can pick things up if I'm motivated."

Chris seemed like a man on a mission. He peppered Sandra and, later, Katie—who joined them at the house—with questions about food production. And so it came to be that over early lunch, Sandra and Katie told Chris they would take him to Dalton O'Connor's farm later that afternoon.

"Dalton?" he asked. "Who's Dalton?"

Katie said, "A fellow we've been seeing socially for the past couple of months."

"We both fancy him," Sandra said. "And we'd like you to meet him," she went on to say, and Katie nodded vigorously. They looked expectantly at Chris.

"Well, all right," he said, and the girls appeared thrilled.

Chris was beginning to get the picture—they weren't just introducing him to Dalton; they were hoping he'd like him. He decided to go with the flow, and as Sandra had said, the future would unfold as it would. Besides, Chris wanted to know how food was being produced on a commercial scale. If it was anything like the ecosystem he'd just encountered at the forest garden, then this was more than curiosity. It was the beginning of something lasting.

CHAPTER 15

EARLIER THAT AFTERNOON, SANDRA HAD GONE TO SIT with a neighbor who'd miscarried. Katie was deep-cleaning, and the house smelled faintly of citrus and beeswax. Chris had passed the hours on the porch trying to coax some tunes from a harmonica he'd borrowed from the shelf, until the two girls joined him under the cloudless sky.

The swing creaked beneath them, rhythmic and lulling, as they crammed onto the narrow bench—Chris in the middle.

They listened to the wind fluttering the leaves up high and stirring dust in the sunbaked dirt road, the heat rising off it in shimmering waves. Moments earlier, they'd drained the last of their chilled lemonades.

"We could walk," Katie spoke up suddenly. "It's barely ten miles to Dalton's farm."

Sandra shook her head. "It's already past five."

Katie leaned in, reaching past Chris toward her sister, bracing herself with one hand on his lap. Her curves pressed and lingered against his shoulder as her eyes remained fixed on Sandra's. "That means we'd finish just as twilight settles in. You remember last time, Sandy? It was . . . so much fun." Her voice dipped, lower and softer.

Sandra's lips thinned. A faint flush crept up her neck.

"The road growing dark, the fireflies, the smell of clover—" Katie's lips parted, her teeth grazing her lower lip—as if tasting the last time.

"Chris won't see the farm," Sandra cut in, voice brittle. "Dalton's expecting us. And it won't do if we show up looking like dusk-wandering minstrels."

—Chris sat very still all the while, basking in the physical contact and hoping the argument would drag on just a little longer—

Katie's smile twisted, lingering. "We shouldn't arrive in a glorified bassinet," she said. "Your plan lacks drama."

"Your plan lacks sense." Sandra's tone was glacial.

"We could compromise. Jog some miles."

Sandra closed her eyes briefly. "We did that last time. Still took two hours. Not even counting the . . . stop-offs." A pause. Then, quieter: "And I don't even have a shoe bag. I'm not going to wear down my shoes for that."

Her gaze held on Katie's for a beat.

Katie blinked. Something in her posture shifted—shoulders softening, the gleam retreating. She withdrew her hand from the lap and eased back into the swing. Chris exhaled, slow and soundless.

"Right. A shoe bag," Katie echoed, her voice returning to its usual timbre. "Without it, that *would* be inconvenient."

Sandra rose to her feet without another word and headed inside, the swing still creaking behind her. A few minutes later, she returned and summoned their ride—a doorless, windowless mini-carriage. Its brass lamps and tufted seats gave it a touch of elegance, while its spindly wheels imparted a whimsical, almost toy-like quality.

With laughter and clamor, they piled in, and the runabout lurched forward—no windshield, just open air and a sudden slap of wind.

Sandra and Katie stood tall inside as if carved for it, their hair whipped back in long, fluid streams, and the light fabric pulled taut across thighs and busts as they gripped the rail guard. Chris sat behind them, his broad frame filling the bench, arms draped across its crest, watching the occasional passersby watching them—two figures on a gleaming prow, sailing through dust, their forms traced by sunlight.

As the road opened and the houses fell away, the figureheads gave way to sisters again—bickering, elbowing, on a bench meant for two. Chris unceremoniously found himself relegated to carrying both Sandra and Katie, one atop the other, but he soon ended up with Katie perched on one thigh and Sandra on the other. The shifting weight, the flicker of skirt and skin, the hot light pouring down—he endured it all in silence, a gentleman pressed into service.

Katie straddled his sturdy leg, riding and settling with every jostle and curve, her sundress pressed flush by the wind's insistence, her form swept in irregular pulses of sunlight. Sandra gathered her hem in a loose knot, exposing one long leg to the hip, and planted a fist low between her thighs—just enough to anchor the front of her dress, letting the wind claim the rest. Perched on his other leg, her posture was almost regal, with the ease of long habit not giving a damn what the breeze, or some women, may have muttered.

Some gallant instinct nearly had Chris suggesting they turn back and change into pants. Fortunately, his wiser self prevailed—and the view was preserved. Besides, they'd ridden open runabouts before and knew exactly what that kind of wind did to light cotton. And, for that matter, how tight it would be in a two-seater model.

Long minutes passed, and the runabout hummed steadily along. Chris shifted under their combined weight, flexing his numb legs beneath them and grunting.

"It builds character!" Katie told him, noticing. She gave him a tender peck. "You're welcome, by the way."

"I can't feel anything below my knees anymore," Chris muttered. He squirmed, trying to get some blood back into his legs.

"If you drop me, I'll haunt you. Forever. Like a banshee," Katie warned.

"Don't grunt at *us*," Sandra said. "You knew the mission carried risks." She moved up his thigh, getting comfortable, then fished out a small bag of roasted pecans and began munching. "In some cultures, carrying royalty is considered a great honor."

Chris said under his breath, "One of these days, I'm charging by the mile."

As their vehicle worked its way east, the majestic silhouette of the Rocky Mountains steadily receded, then vanished. They were now in the Great Plains proper. The runabout journeyed along a dirt road, weaving its way through sun-drenched fields of wild grasses and patches of cultivated land. As Chris had learned, these dirt roads were a breed apart from their dirt brethren in America, which were constantly marred by potholes and erosion. In Americana, they kicked it old school, in the manner of the ancient Roman highways: a sturdy base of large stones for drainage, topped with a layer of smaller stones, and finally a surface layer of compacted gravel, sand, and clay.

At some point, the automobile slowed down and came to a halt.

"Holy moly," Katie said, staring dead ahead. She got up, and a moment later Sandra did too.

A dozen horses nickered and grazed just a stone's throw away, with a few standing right on the dirt road.

"Those are wild horses," Chris stated, marveling at the sight.

"What else would they be?" Sandra said with a touch of exasperation.

The runabout inched forward but stopped again, as the

animals showed no signs of moving.

Chris glanced about. "Is it going to drive around them, off-road?"

"I haven't the foggiest," Sandra told him. "Still, those vehicles have negotiated those situations countless times, adapting and learning from each encounter. Let's—"

A burst of gunfire cracked through the air.

Chris was already moving. He shoved Katie down with one hand and threw his body across Sandra. "Cover!" he barked.

The sisters obeyed without hesitation. Sandra hit the floorboards, arms braced. Katie dropped low and froze. The runabout jolted as more bursts followed, then the deeper *thunk* of something heavier. Chris held still, muscles tight, keeping himself between the girls and the danger.

The herd exploded into motion, a wall of hooves pounding the earth. No bullets followed. Only dust.

Chris held still for a beat, then let out a long breath and laughed. "Yes. Of course. A recording. Damned convincing one."

He rolled off them, and they all stayed down for a little longer. Then, slowly, they got to their feet—Sandra brushing dirt from her elbow, Katie straightening her dress. They were grinning weakly at each other.

Katie said, "That scared the life out of me."

Sandra nodded once. "Same."

They reclaimed their spots—one on each of Chris's thighs, as if gravity itself had snapped back into place.

"So they have a rifle sound to scare off horses, if needed," Katie said. "Keen."

"That was no rifle," Chris said, shaking his head. "SAW burst—five-five-six, maybe an MK46. And those last few blasts—forty-mil from a grenade launcher, probably an MK47."

Sandra turned her head and looked at him strangely. "How do you know all this?"

Chris wanted to kick himself. "Just . . . back when I lived in Iraq, there was a shooting range near a military base. I shot a few things there. You remember sounds like that."

The sisters exchanged glances. In the end, Katie shrugged, reached for the dashboard, and flicked on a switch. Music filled the air. *Radio*, Chris thought.

The song that came on was an upbeat pop tune. Katie sprang back to her feet and began moving her arms to the rhythm.

"Oh boy," Sandra groaned. "Here we go."

". . . *Remember those golden days, under the sun's warm rays . . .*" Katie sang at the top of her voice. She wasn't half-bad, Chris realized.

"You'll scare the bison!" Sandra tried to shout her down. "You'll cause a stampede and get us all killed."

". . . *Laughing and playing, all our cares astray . . .*" Katie continued, undeterred.

"Mercy, Katie!"

". . . *We were young and wild, our hearts untamed . . .*" Katie pulled her sister up. "Together now."

"*Dancing in the fields, memories we've made . . .*" they sang in unison, swaying in tandem, their hair blowing in the wind as the runabout traversed the dirt road.

"Come on, Chris—sing!" Sandra commanded after two vehicles had passed them on the road.

He shook his head stubbornly.

"*Golden days, golden days, forever they'll stay . . .*" the two sisters shouted in tune.

"If you don't start singing, I may flash," Sandra warned. "In fact, there is no telling what I'll do."

Resigned, Chris joined in, adding a pleasant baritone as he hummed along.

"He can hum!" Sandra screamed, bouncing up and down, but then lost her footing and stumbled backward—onto Chris.

Katie squealed with laughter.

"Fine example of a teacher," Chris said, helping Sandra to her feet.

"That's my motto," she told him. "'Do as I say, not as I do'— except when I am dancing and screaming in a moving vehicle."

"What if you were to flash a passing automobile, and it turns out one of your students was in it?" he inquired.

Katie responded, "The student will have a flash of insight, as it were. A true Zen moment."

"Are all the girls around Boulder as batty as you two?"

They turned to him, putting on a show of dismay.

"You've truly hurt me," Katie declared. "How could you possibly think that?" she cried out.

"We're the wildest of the bunch," Sandra explained. "And here, with a single thoughtless comment from you, we've been demoted to the ranks of the commonplace." She snapped her fingers. "Just like that."

"I start to see why your folks are anxious to marry you off— the upstanding, chaste girls that you are," Chris observed.

"Daughters of a sitting judge, no less," Katie assured him.

Chris smiled wryly, then frowned, then remembered.

"Mother tells unsuspecting guests she 'works in the courthouse,'" Sandra said, grinning gleefully. "When she came clean and told the last boy Katie brought home that she is a judge, it put a bit of a damper on things, if you catch my drift."

"As a matter of fact, I do."

"Aw, don't be such a chicken. What's the worst that can happen if you ruffle her feathers and mess with her girls? Spend a few years in the slammer?"

"Good point," Chris said. "I'm feeling a lot more relaxed now." He regarded the two. "I can't quite figure out if you gals are twelve on the fast track to twenty-one, or twenty-one looping back to twelve."

"This has the sound of a Zen koan," Katie announced. "Perhaps you're close to a moment of enlightenment," she suggested.

"Zen what?" Sandra demanded to know.

"Koan. Good grief, woman!" her sister said. "And to think you're passing yourself off as a teacher."

***

Hollering and bickering, they finally drew near and pulled alongside an imposing hawthorn hedgerow. Chris eyed it. The sisters had told him that farms with livestock were magnets for large predators, and the living fence was there to keep these out.

They reached the gate, which swung open with a gentle hum at the sight of the approaching vehicle. A short time later, they stopped beside a house nestled under the shade of two towering cottonwoods, whose upper branches swayed slightly in the breeze. As the trio stepped out, the runabout turned and headed back to town, its tires crunching on the gravel.

Chris gazed at the grassy open land, taking in the earthy scent. "A one-thousand-acre farm," Sandra said, joining him.

"Dalton is over there," Katie called from behind, pointing. In the distance, Chris could see a solitary figure next to a small tractor. Katie hollered and waved. "He can't hear me. Too far," she said, visibly flustered.

"Let's just walk over," Chris said. They started toward Dalton, who was standing near a vast gathering of cattle.

As they approached, Chris realized the sheer scale of the herd—hundreds upon hundreds of cows. The air was filled with the cows' distinct aroma, and the bright sunlight brought out the varied hues of their coats. The soft lowing, the ripping of grass, and occasional snorts created an oddly soothing backdrop, punctuated by the rustle of wind through the pasture. As they drew closer, the ground beneath their feet was damp from the grazing animals.

"Does he own the place?" Chris inquired.

"Yes," Sandra said, falling into step with him. "It used to belong to his grandparents."

"So, he inherited it?"

"Essentially. He's been working here since he was thirteen— ten years now. His grandparents retired recently and moved in with his aunt and uncle. Dalton's taken over the farm now. The school groups help some, but it's still more than one man can manage, so he's hired a few hands to keep things running."

Dalton must have spotted them, for he waved. They waved back. Up close, Chris could see he was a young, broad-shoul- dered man of medium height. His face sported a sharply delineated stubble, and a smattering of freckles dotted his sun- bronzed cheeks.

"You're a sight for sore eyes!" Dalton greeted Sandra and Katie warmly, then turned to Chris, offering a hearty hand- shake. His grip was strong and calloused. "The ladies told me about you," he said with a genuine smile, his hazel eyes spar- kling. Strands of auburn hair peeked out from beneath his baseball cap, framing his face. "Glad to finally meet you, Chris."

"Likewise," Chris said, taking an instant liking to the man.

A few moments later, Sandra and Katie excused themselves and headed to the house to prepare dinner, leaving Dalton and Chris in the field.

Chris studied the herd for several moments. "That's a great many cows for an area of that size," he said uneasily. "Don't they overgraze and kill the grass?"

"They would have—had we let 'em," Dalton told him. "But they move a few times a day to a fresh patch. Each evening, I set up the temporary paddocks using portable fences and automatic gate openers with timers."

"Setting new fences every day," Chris repeated. That sounded like a lot of work!

Dalton made a dismissive gesture. "Just high-tensile poly-wire and step-in posts. It takes maybe ten minutes to rig a paddock. Timer gates pop open and they move." He started to unspool another reel of polywire, and the two of them made their way to the next post through the thick grass. They reached the post, and Dalton pushed down the wire into its receiving hook, before veering ninety degrees and making for another post in the distance.

"We manage it so that the cattle graze about a third of the top cover before moving to a fresh paddock," Dalton said. "It's all about mimicking the old ways, you know? Think bison on the plains—huge herds, bunched tight, moving constantly. That's how these grasslands evolved. The pressure, the movement, the manure . . ."

"I get the frequent movement," Chris said. "But why pack them in so tightly?"

"They eat everything when they're a mob—no cherry-picking, so nothing gets left standing to eventually dominate the field," Dalton explained. "And by clumping them up like burrs on a horse's mane, they fertilize the field evenly and thoroughly."

He motioned at the herd. "That's the upper end—six, maybe seven hundred thousand pounds per acre. I only do that when there's a thick mat of dead matter to clear. Day to day in the summer? It's closer to two to three hundred thousand, that is, about two to three hundred cows per acre—that's where you get the steady gains."

"I bet you need a lot of water."

Dalton laughed. "No bet. Anyway, we've got a portable water trough. As the herd moves, we drag the trough forward and hook it up to the next outlet."

Chris breathed in deeply, taking in the smell of the earth,

eyes roving across the land. "I love it," he murmured, half to himself. At that moment, he wanted nothing more than to settle down here—in Americana's Colorado—and forget the portal, forget the other world.

If farming practices in Americana were half as sane as they looked, he'd find a way to make production agriculture his life. But first, he had to be sure. Really sure.

"We've got a few patches of perennial pasture, where the terrain doesn't lend itself to mechanized planting and harvesting—so we have them graze there," Dalton was saying as they reached another post. "This is the exception, though. As a rule, our herd grazes on cover crops."

"How does that work out?" Chris knew of farmers who grew crops, and he knew of ranchers that raised cattle. Dalton was doing both on the same land.

"It works great," Dalton replied as they walked on. "The cattle put on weight, and the soil benefits from their grazing."

Chris shot him a surprised glance. "Grazing helps the land?"

Dalton looked at him appraisingly.

"What?" Chris asked.

"I was just taken aback by the question. No offense meant."

"None taken," Chris said. "I haven't been around farms with this kind of setup."

"Arabia. Yes, I remember Katie saying something about it. To answer your question: Their grazing compels plants to push out more carbon into the soil as they try to attract biology to help them regrow. And the cows clear out dead stuff," Dalton said. "Their gut's like a traveling compost bin—It turns plants into manure fast, and that feeds the dirt better than anything."

Chris let it sink in as they continued walking, Dalton setting up temporary paddocks one after another. "That felt like a good kick in the tail," he finally said. "It blew away what little I thought I knew about food production."

Dalton laughed good-naturedly. "Close to a third of the land at any given time is set for grazing. And the cows are out year-round."

"Winters too, huh?"

"Yep."

"What if the snow cover is too deep for them to graze?"

"We roll out bales on heavy snow days. Shrubs and hay rows cut the wind some."

"And the bales come from the crop you grow..."

"Of course," Dalton said. "We mix in sea salt and kelp meal. Otherwise? No outside inputs; it's a closed loop, like any other farming operation."

And with this one casual remark, Dalton was, in effect, telling him that agriculture as he'd come to know it in his native world was off, and if not off, then at least suspect. Sandra had also talked about the lack of any external inputs. It was startling enough to hear this about a food forest garden. It was something else to hear that a large-scale farm could sustain itself year after year without any additives. It seemed too good to be true.

They climbed onto the small tractor and started on their way toward the house in the distance. Behind the seat was a lever-action .30-30 rifle, its walnut stock worn smooth from years of use.

Dalton must have known that Chris was seeing the girls, but he didn't mention it. Neither did Chris. Instead, he asked, "Are flies a problem?"

"Not really," Dalton replied. "The cows move on long before the fly larvae hatch. And then there are the chickens."

"You have chickens too?"

Dalton nodded. "Three days behind the cattle herd comes the laying hen fleet—about two thousand strong." He smiled faintly. "The dung beetles get there first—breaking parasite cycles. Then the chickens scratch through what's left, spread the patties, exposing more of it to the sun. They snack on fly larvae and clean up crickets and grasshoppers. We peel off a strip of our oat-pea crop to round out their feed."

The small tractor trundled alongside a fluttering wall of deep green sorghum-sudangrass.

"The army of hens is free to roam during the day, while returning to the portable eggmobiles to take refuge and lay their eggs at night," Dalton said. "We move the eggmobiles with a tractor daily, and that's also when we collect the eggs. Fresh air, lots of sunshine, and green grass—fairly close to the way nature intended the fowls to live."

With that, they arrived at the house. Chris took in the quaint red-brick façade, white shutters, and cedar-shingled gabled roof with quiet appreciation. The two men climbed off the tractor and followed a cobblestone path to the front porch.

Inside, Katie and Sandra were busy in the kitchen, preparing roast chicken, mashed potatoes, and a fresh tomato salad. Under a wrought-iron chandelier in the dining area, the men set the table. Soon, all four were seated around the wooden table, eating and talking.

Chris was in high spirits. The sisters had never seen him so talkative. Between bites, he described what little he'd seen on his uncle's ranch, to much merriment from the others.

Sandra and Dalton burst out laughing when Chris talked about plowing—overturning the earth—and by the time he got to synthetic fertilizers and leaving land barren for months on end, Sandra complained her sides hurt, and Dalton wiped tears from his eyes.

"So, is that what they do in Iraq?" Sandra asked, catching her breath.

"At least from what I saw," Chris said. Iraq had become his go-to reference for everything he wanted to share about the America he'd grown up in. He turned to Dalton, still skeptical.

"No insecticides, no herbicides, no synthetic fertilizers, no tilling. None of that is needed, huh?" He needed to hear it again.

"Needed?" Dalton frowned. "Harmful residue in food aside, those things wreck the soil. Kill the biology." This also meant soil compaction, which meant low water retention, which meant dependency on irrigation, as he'd told Chris. He scooped the last of the salad onto his plate. "No one here's touched those maniacal practices in generations."

"You see," Katie said brightly, "Chris discovered today that he wants to be a farmer. He wants to learn everything he can about it."

"I have, and I do," Chris said, pushing his plate away. He turned to Dalton. "Mind if I ask a few more questions? I want to understand how this works—really understand it."

"Fire away," Dalton said. A suggestion of a smile crossed his face. "Anyone who wants to get into food production has a special place in my heart."

"You're not a fan of monoculture," Chris stated.

"No one is," Dalton said.

Katie got up and returned moments later with spiced apple cider and a fruit crisp.

Chris murmured his thanks and poured cider for everyone. "That said, you still do monoculture with your cash crops, right?"

Dalton raised an eyebrow. "Why do you say that?"

"How would you separate different crops after the harvest?"

Dalton nodded appreciatively. "The key is selecting plants with clear size differences—like peas and oats." He finished his cider and set the mug down on the table. "But yes, real crop diversity is in cover crops, which don't need separation. We usually plant about two dozen species together."

"Why have cover crops at all?"

"Chris," Sandra interjected, "this is a core principle: Keep the soil covered with living plants at all times. It's like a pro-tective skin."

"In the Iraqi farming community, they too had their 'princi-ples,'" Chris said. "However, if I learned anything today, it's to do what Iraqi farmers haven't been doing: ask why." He looked at Dalton.

"Fair enough," Dalton said. "Living cover means plants are feeding the soil most of the year—pushing carbon down through their roots. Plus, it keeps rain and wind from blowing topsoil away. And it shades the ground, keeps the sun from scorching and drying out the land, which would kill the microbes and ultimately starve the fungal network. It all connects."

So there it was—the explanation. Chris sat in silence, grap-pling with the thought. How could so many farmers in his world be so misguided, and on so many levels?

Dalton continued, "Having a cover crop is just the baseline. Barley, brassicas, winter triticale, buckwheat—each cover crop does a job. Some break up hardpan, others attract pollinators, suppress weeds, or reduce internal parasites in cattle."

That *was* impressive.

"You mentioned a fungal network..."

"Yes, it's central," Dalton said. "Mycorrhizal fungi are what tie it all together. They create soil aggregates to support life, establish pathways for microbes, and carry water and nutrients to the roots—connecting plants into a kind of underground community."

Chris leaned forward, elbows on the table. "If you don't mind, I've got a few more questions."

Dalton smiled. "Fire away."

"Without pesticides, how do you deal with pathogens in the soil?"

Dalton shrugged. "They don't usually get a foothold. Fungi form partnerships with the plants, and microbes crowd out the bad stuff. A healthy system keeps itself in check."

Chris was silent for a few moments, recalling a comment Sandra had made about their forest garden. "I assume you also grow flowers that attract pollinators and predatory insects."

Dalton nodded. "We've planted alfalfa, goldenrods, and lavender throughout. They provide a habitat for a variety of beetles and damsel bugs."

Chris saved his biggest concern for last. "Eventually, doesn't soil depletion become an issue? How do you manage without external fertilizers?" A garden was one thing, but a large-scale commercial operation, where huge amounts of plant matter were carted away each season, was a different story.

This didn't strike Dalton as much of a point. "The field is surrounded by an ocean of air, which is primarily nitrogen. To tap into it, we grow vetch, clover, and sunn hemp. These plants have bacteria in their roots converting it into a bioavailable form—for the entire plant community to use."

Chris mulled it over. "What of other needed nutrients?"

"Phosphorus, potassium, and trace minerals—we dredge those up from deep in the soil with plants like buckwheat, yarrow, dandelion. Then we trample or mow them, letting them decompose and make these nutrients available to other plants."

The three watched Chris as he lightly tapped his fingers on the table, immersed in thought. Eventually he slapped the table. "What you do here is amazing," he declared.

Dalton bowed his head. "It's mostly about allowing nature to take its course. The cows feed themselves. Predatory insects keep the pests under control. The fungal network protects the plants and assists them in drawing water."

"Don't sell yourself short," Katie scolded, "or do you enjoy eating humble pie?" She turned to Chris. "Don't seek to com-pare yourself to Dalton; he has a direct line to the sun—the way he can make things grow."

"I can readily believe that," Chris said, regarding Dalton with good-natured humor. "Thanks for the lowdown." With the expense of fertilizers and chemicals, with corn grown for cattle, with the cost of irrigation, with the plowing work and consequent soil erosion—no wonder many farmers in his America needed government subsidies just to break even. Chris raised his head, trying to smother the grin that kept threatening to come out.

"Thank you." He drained his glass and set it down with a thud. "I'm sold," Chris said, and a wide smile split his face.

It was close to midnight when Chris and Katie hugged Dalton goodbye and called for a ride. Sandra had left hours earlier; she was to take part that night in an "interactive storytelling slam" and later yet had a scheduled outing with fellow female teachers.

⇒⇐

As Katie and Chris stood outside waiting for their ride, they heard chains clanking before the vehicle swung into view.

Chris started, gaping. *The hell was this thing?*

It looked like some carriage of old. Or rather, a Goth version of it. Its surface glistened with an inky blackness, save for the seat and the accents adorning the sizable buggy wheels. These were of the palest lavender, and under the moonlight, they took on a pearly cast. A tangle of metallic chains lay upon the hitched tar-black flatbed, some trailing behind on the ground.

The corner of Katie's mouth lifted. The city's custom vehicle fleet always offered surprises. She hadn't seen this wagon before—must've been new. She thought it beat the leather-upholstered rickshaw with the fog machine.

Between the carriage's two benches jutted a thick bamboo shaft, climbing a good ten feet into the air. Near its top perched a single wooden chair, like something from a lifeguard's post, with a narrow ledge below it serving as a footrest. Carved handholds and footholds spiraled up the beam.

Chris climbed aboard and extended a hand. Katie accepted it and stepped up after him. They sat across from each other on the benches as the wagon lurched forward.

Silence settled like a third passenger. Moonlight glinted through slow-drifting clouds, wind skimming across their skin. The yellow bulb sputtered atop the pole, its solitary glow flaring and fading over the dark empty road.

This was when Katie stirred.

He watched one foot fold beneath her. Watched the other leg lift, then plant itself on the opposite bench, grazing the air between them. His breath went shallow as her spine arched in a lazy half-turn. The light from the overhead lamp spilled dim gold across her thighs and the creases of her dress.

Katie pivoted her head slightly. Just enough to face him. Her green eyes found his. And held, unblinking.

A finger rose—she gave its tip a quick lick, held it to the wind. Stillness.

She pressed down on her lower lip with her finger, then slipped it in to the knuckle. She bit down, a nibble. Then again. Then the finger went down to her lap.

Chris's jaw tensed.

She shifted her weight back, space blooming between them. Her leg slid down the bench, slow and serpentine, her knees drifting apart, then stilling.

She wasn't asking. She was waiting.

Chris's eyes flicked upward—to the lone, high-mounted chair bolted to the beam rising between the benches. A small platform jutted beneath it: a precarious perch.

He rose. Hands found the shaft, and he began to pull himself up. A strange clarity washed over him. This was the only shape this could take. It had to begin with her—because the stakes were never equal. Not when it was her body that could carry the consequences, be rewritten.

Her intent was unmistakable. And that could only mean one thing: The womb was safeguarded—probably a small copper or hormonal guardian nestled within. In Americana, women did not roll the dice.

Katie gazed up at Chris as he sat down on the chair and looked down expectantly at her. And suddenly, she understood what he had in mind.

The oily mass of chains stirred—as if responding. A sensor, maybe—as she kicked off her shoes, slipped off her panties, unbuttoned her dress to the hip. And then she was up—climbing. The footholds bit into her soles, the massive bamboo pole scraped her thighs—but she barely felt these through the rush pounding in her veins.

At the ledge, Chris caught her by the waist, his fingers digging into her soft flesh, triggering hot flares that coursed through her. The carriage lurched beneath them. They both knew: If he let go, she'd fall off and be claimed by the now-rattling mass of chains.

Waxy illumination from the yellow bulb came in fits. A half-body, a flash of her spine, the gleam of sweat on his throat—then nothing.

She hitched her dress high and straddled his lap, facing him. Her bare legs wrapped tightly around the thick beam behind his back. She reached down, tugged cloth aside, and freed him. Then her hand slid up, settling at his nape—just as her mouth found his.

Below, the heaped coil of metal links was agitated. A clink. A clatter. Then a frenzy.

The carriage rolled on. Far and wide, the expanse of grass stirred in the tides and ebbs of the night wind. They rode on like this without let-up as the road unspooled, absorbing the tremors with their melded bodies.

Down below, amid the jolting carriage, the metal chains inside the flatbed writhed like animated, metallic-silver snakes in a black pit. Far off, the wind shifted, and wolves howled—drawn by scent, by rhythm, by something older than speech.

And the night, shameless, watched.

CHAPTER 16

RONNY greeted Chris with a hearty laugh as his friend stepped through the portal a few days later. "Well, well, well, look who's ready for a night with Scott and Zelda," he said, eyeing Chris's dapper attire. "Trying to blend in with the locals, huh?"

The two embraced.

Chris regarded Ronny for a moment. Before Americana, Chris never questioned Ronny's look: faded Pokémon tee and baggy shorts. He used to dress like that too. Now, it just looked . . . sad. "You ever think of wearing something with buttons?"

Ronny chortled. "Be yourself, that's my motto. Just throw something on and stay comfortable." He walked over to the cluttered table, cracked a warm Dr Pepper, took a swig, then set it down. He turned back. "Now, where's the video of that babe?" he demanded.

Chris shook his head. "It felt like a breach of privacy."

Ronny heaved a theatrical sigh. "Are you shitting me? She lives in a different *universe*. Damn, man. From what you've told me, she could've been Americana's first camgirl superstar to blow up our social media feeds. She ain't ever gonna forgive your ass, bro."

Chris smiled in response but said nothing.

"What's this?" Ronny gestured at the large plastic box Chris had placed on the table.

"Eggs," Chris said.

Ronny shook his head. "Eggs? I had a feeling I didn't want to know."

Chris chortled as he followed Ronny up the long stone staircase to the house proper. Soon they were comfortably settled in the living room.

"So why did you bring me eggs?" Ronny asked.

"Patience. They're Exhibit D. I brought four pieces of evidence that I journeyed to a parallel universe. Taken together, they build a really solid case."

Ronny raised an eyebrow. That should prove interesting.

Chris smiled broadly. "Ready?"

"Sure. Lay it on me."

Chris brandished a hermetically sealed glass bottle with an airtight PTFE cap. "Exhibit number one." He handed it over to Ronny, who examined it, squinting at it.

"Let me guess," Ronny finally said. "This looks like an empty glass bottle; however, in fact, it's an empty glass bottle."

"Exactly," agreed Chris. "An empty bottle with air from a world that basically stopped spewing industrial crap since the early seventies."

"So their air is cleaner than ours, and our scientists can stick it under a microscope and attest to it. Is that it?"

Chris nodded.

Ronny's eyes glinted. "But then again, you could have bottled some clean air in Patagonia or the Tibetan Plateau. Or faked something in a lab."

Chris shook his head. "Not just cleaner, Ronny. *Different.* Like a fingerprint you can't fake. Forget 'clean.' The ratio of carbon-14 to carbon-12—it's off-base for our world. Then, think about all the microscopic junk floating in our air—industrial aerosols, specific pollens, weird chemicals. Their air has its own unique blend of stuff, stuff that reflects their environment. All but impossible to simulate."

Ronny eyed the empty bottle with renewed respect. "Okay, okay. That's pretty clever." He looked up. "Since when do you know so much about air?"

Chris smiled. "Since I realized we needed solid proof and hit the books—a few days ago."

"That's just proof you needed to go to an Ivy League school, like I told you."

"You mean, that's proof that I didn't, no?"

Ronny waved a pudgy hand. "Whatever. What other wonders hast thou brought to me?"

"Money," Chris said, holding up a hundred-dollar bill. "Check the shiny band—see the tiny state names pop out? Now tilt it—watch the Great Seal change color. That's optically variable magnetic ink, buddy."

Ronny examined the hundred-dollar bill, lifting it up to the light. "Some serious anti-counterfeit juju."

"Take a closer look." Chris was enjoying this. "There's a thread woven into the paper itself. Hit it with a blacklight, it glows red, white, and blue. Replicating *all* of those features would be a counterfeiter's nightmare."

Ronny nodded in appreciation.

Chris grinned. "Exhibit C."

He pulled out a relatively large silicon chip and set it on the table with a solid *thunk*. "AI accelerator. From Americana. Probably works like ours, but imagine two engineering worlds solving the same problem without ever comparing notes. I'm sure the transistor layout's different, the alloys' mix distinct, and the core instructions unique. This thing holds a whole alternate timeline of tech—everything from the way they dig up raw materials to how they seal the final package. Every design choice is baked into this single slab of silicon."

Ronny gave a soft whistle. "Okay, Chris, you've officially blown my mind."

He then remembered. "So how do eggs fit into all of this?"

Chris smiled. "Fertile eggs of the Carolina parakeet."

Ronny squinted. "Is that . . . a breakfast thing?"

"It was a bird, a parrot," Chris said. "Bright green, orange face. Native to the U.S. Went extinct in 1918."

"Oh, wow."

"Yeah, it'd be pretty hard to come up with two hundred and fifty viable eggs of an extinct animal. I made sure each egg came from a different hen. The incubator is running on battery power now; just plug it into a power outlet within the next few hours. You should see some hatching in twelve to fourteen days." The birds were alive and well in Americana, but getting that many viable eggs had still taken some doing.

"This is good stuff, Chris! Good stuff," said Ronny, rubbing his hands on his jeans. "No matter how you slice it, those things will be enough to get anybody's attention. What else have you learned?"

Chris described the farming practices in the parallel universe, explaining how they were radically different from conventional methods in America—and far more sound. "I'm telling you, this could revolutionize our agriculture," he concluded.

"This is what I've been thinking about for the past few days," Ronny said, ripping open a bag of chips and reaching in. "You say there's much they can teach us about food production. Dude, you're missing the point. Where's the money in planting—what did you call them? Vetch? Kvetch?" He chomped down on a potato chip, punctuating his argument.

"On the other hand," he continued, "imagine the insane profits to be had by introducing synthetic pesticides, GMO seeds, and growth hormones to Americana—completely overhauling their hippie-dippie farming operations." With the back of his hand, he wiped his mouth. "We're talking billions and billions of dollars!"

Chris took a deep breath. "The point is that those things aren't needed."

"What's need got to do with anything?" Ronny was bewildered. "It's about all the new jobs this will create and the profits it will generate."

He took Chris's deadpan expression as an invitation to continue. "You know, while you were out there, fussing over snails, earthworms, and vetch, I was doing some legit brainstorming. Let's get real, Chris. The sad truth—that is, the pretty awesome reality—is that Americana just begs for a burst of progress.

"So here's my plan," Ronny stated. His face was alight with eagerness. "In secrecy, we recruit people to conduct a thorough economic survey of Americana. Next, we approach big corporations and offer them the exclusive rights to franchise in this untapped market. They'll be the first in their industry to establish a foothold in the New World. The first fast-food chain. The first social media platform. The first suv dealership. The first diet soda distributor. The first smartphone outlet. The first billboard advertising company. The first reality TV show—you get the picture. And guess what? We get a small royalty on each deal we close. Easy money, brother. So, tell me, you impressed yet?" Ronny leaned back in his La-Z-Boy recliner, fingers interlocked over his stomach, a slight smile playing on his face.

"Sounds like a bit of a rosy view of how it is likely to unfold," Chris said guardedly.

"You're right," Ronny readily agreed. "It's a matter of time, and maybe not even a long time, before we lose control over the whole thing; it's simply too big for a couple of guys. But trust me, before it gets taken out of our hands, we'll collect on our groundbreaking discovery—and be set for life."

Chris regarded Ronny for some time. At last he said, "Who are we to tell the people of Americana that their lives are in need of a change?" His gray eyes darkened. "You'd poison their world for a check?"

Ronny stared at him, unsure what to make of that statement. "We're not shoving fries down their throats. We're just giving them options. This is just crazy talk, man."

He plopped both feet onto the floor, and his flip-flops made a satisfying slap. "Look, everybody wants a piece of progress. Whether it's folks in rural China or the new-money in Bangladesh, they all crave social media, slick rides, and the whole shebang. The people in Americana ain't some corny cutouts from a '50s TV show. They're just like us, with the same dreams and desires."

He smiled faintly. "They simply don't know it yet."

Chris shook his head. "You don't know them like I do. Their officials would never go for such a thing," he said, praying he was right. In truth, he had no idea.

Ronny snorted. "I bet that's what the Japanese thought—right up until Commodore Perry sailed into their harbor with U.S. warships and forced the issue. Guess what? He opened Japan for business—and they're *loving* it!" Carrying a big stick and dangling a bigger carrot, Ronny thought. He reached over and laid a hand on Chris's arm. "We're talking trillions of dollars, Chris. This mother of all oil fields will gush right through any legislation, bleeding hearts, or protests in its path. You and I? We can skim a tiny fraction of the torrent—or others will. That's the only choice you and I can and ever will have in this matter."

Chris was silent for a long time. "That's a lot to take in," he eventually said. "A lot to shoulder. However, as long as we don't say anything to anyone, this chain of events has not been set in motion."

Ronny nodded in agreement.

Chris leaned in. "Here's the deal," he said. "Give me a week or two to explore other ways for us to profit from Americana. It won't be trillions or billions, but I'm talking about what you and I can personally get. If I can't come up with something, we'll go all-in with your plan."

"Okay," said Ronny. They both got up.

Once outside the gate, Chris waved his hand until the shimmer faded and he was alone.

He sank to his knees and let his head push against the wild grass, feeling the rising bile in his throat.

CHAPTER 17

CHRIS BROUGHT HIS CARGO trike to a stop and leaned against a tree some distance away from the open-air train depot. He sat there dazed, his thoughts sluggish.

Hours later, as the sun rose, people started streaming into the small train station—first dozens, then hundreds.

Chris heaved himself to his feet and approached the depot, trying to make sense of what he was seeing. A long train stood there, each railcar emblazoned with the motto: *True to Self, True to Country.*

Numerous young adults leaned out of the open windows and waved as the train started to roll. Hundreds of family members crowding the platform erupted in cheers, shouting names, and waving back—some clutching small American flags or handkerchiefs.

Still in a daze, Chris unsteadily threaded his way through the throng. Don't smile at me, he thought. I am the harbinger of darkness, carrying malignant seeds that will send roots throughout the land.

"True to Self, True to Country," he said mechanically as he reached the edge of the platform, where the crowd was thin. Yet the words did not register, did not penetrate.

"A national civic service," a woman's voice chimed in beside him. Chris turned to face her, realizing she was speaking to him.

Chris tried to concentrate. He probably looked as puzzled and disoriented as he felt. "The train takes them to Fort Carson," the woman said, sensing his confusion. "Some work in hospitals, nursing homes, or disaster relief and recovery. Others are assigned to large-scale construction projects or to assist with Americanization of newly arrived immigrants." Her eyes followed the receding train. "At sixteen, every citizen answers their first call to the Republic." She smiled. "Some shoulder a rifle. Some raise a scaffold. All serve."

Chris merely tipped his hat to her, not trusting his voice.

A year from now, he thought, these young people might be up to their eyeballs in dopamine loops from flickering screens— twitchy little games and endless scrolls, outrage videos and algorithm-fed envy, performative selfies and dogged chase of hearts and thumb-ups. He trudged away. "Can't stand in the way of progress," he mumbled. "Just ask Ronny." He wondered if, by then, they'd still make time for national service.

"If you were smart, you'd burn me at the stake today, before it's too late," he muttered, mounting his cargo trike.

As he slowly pedaled away, Chris gave the matter some thought. Burning him at the stake wouldn't do much—just a waste of perfectly good wood. Ronny would wait for him, and at some point, conclude Chris wasn't coming back. He would mourn if he suspected something bad had befallen Chris, or chuckle ruefully if he didn't. Either way, business was business. Sooner or later, Ronny would team up with other people and things would continue to unfold inexorably. Progress was inevitable. Resistance, futile.

Chris didn't remember arriving at his small cottage or opening the door.

He collapsed on the bed, and blackness overtook him.

Chris jolted awake. The memory of yesterday's meeting with Ronny returned at once, sharp and unwelcome.

He stared at the wheat-colored ceiling, unmoving, visions of an upgraded Americana swirling in his mind: loud TV screens at gas pumps blaring advertisements and wacky waving inflatable tube men flailing outside car dealerships. The signs had been there during his last trip to his native country—with Ronny's talk of bringing millions of retirees over. Chris had refused to face it. Instead, he'd been hard at work pretending the portal didn't exist. But now, reality had finally come knocking.

One way or another, Ronny was intent on opening the floodgates into Americana.

That was not going to happen. He wouldn't let it happen.

He had to find a way for Ronny to make enough money to back off and keep quiet about the portal. Then, they'd have to figure out how to permanently and irrevocably dismantle the gate. Otherwise the temptation to exploit it would remain, an ever-present threat.

Chris would do whatever it took to protect Americana... his adopted world. He was as clear about that last point as he'd been clear about anything in his life.

Chris was going to stay and make a life for himself in Americana.

＝◄

Night descended, and with it, the inescapable darkness.

Chris sat at the edge of the lake, playing a violin. His own, back in his native world, had fallen silent the day his mother passed. Yet, with this new instrument, acquired mere hours before in Americana, he played again, one melody after another.

The music surged, like water unleashed from a broken dam, washing away the fragmented debris that once held it captive.

"The most mournful and exquisite composition I've ever heard," said someone from behind when he finished playing. Her voice was low; however, her clear, refined diction carried effortlessly. "How have I never heard it before?"

He turned. A figure stood a dozen paces away; her face was obscured by the darkness. Still, the cascade of silken blonde hair was unmistakable. So she had found the note he'd left.

"It is the theme from *Schindler's List*," he replied.

"Schindler's List?" she inquired.

"It's a 1993 movie. It won seven Oscars, including Best Picture, and practically everyone has heard of it."

"I know of every Oscar-winning title."

"Which brings us to the heart of the matter, doesn't it?"

"What are you saying?"

"You must possess a genius-level IQ. Work it out."

"How is such a thing possible?" she whispered.

"I don't rightly know," Chris said. "I just stumbled through it, quite literally."

Silence.

He rose to his feet and took a step toward her. "You're Kate, aren't you?" he asked and paused. "You're the one who plays the violin. The one who devours those books. The one who fills in those notebooks."

The figure shrouded in the cloak of night remained silent.

"Kindly play this composition once more," she then said, a slight tremor in her voice, hinting at a well of emotions.

And so, he did.

When he lifted his head to look, she was no longer there.

Later, he saw her. Time seemed to have slowed, and everything turned hazy, except for the figure walking toward him—a figure in a red float dress, dark hair stirring in the wind. Sandra.

He stood there, waiting.

Chris could hear her harsh, uneven breathing as she came closer. The solitary streetlamp turned her hair into a glittering shower of dark flames. Her gaze flickered to the violin and the photo attached to its tip: Chris, in military uniform, surrounded by similarly attired men.

He smiled ruefully. "I lied to you about my origins, Sandra. I lied because that lie sounds like the truth. While the truth sounds like a lie."

"Where are you from, Chris?" Her chest rose and fell with rapid, shallow breaths. Tendrils of dark hair were plastered to her forehead.

He laughed, a hollow sound devoid of joy. "I am from here, Boulder, 2707 Yarmouth Avenue. In fact, I attended Whittier Elementary, Sandra, back when I was in fifth grade."

"I don't understand what you're saying," she whispered. "There is no Yarmouth Avenue in Boulder."

"That's the thing, there is," he said evenly. He met her gaze. "In my Boulder."

She didn't react to this. "Who are the people in the photo?" she asked brusquely.

"Members of my team stationed in Iraq." He paused. "I was the only one to survive the roadside bomb."

Sandra was startled, as if that was the first thing he had said that she latched onto. "Stationed in Iraq? By whom?"

"The U.S. military, of course."

She stared at him, flushed. "Chris, oh Chris." Her voice was thick with unidentified emotions. "We have no military forces in Iraq. Our military is only patrolling our borders and neighboring coastal areas."

"Not so. Our military is deployed across the globe." He squeezed his eyes shut, then opened them. "In the parallel universe I hail from."

Sandra remained silent for a long time. "That's what Kate thought you implied," she said in a low voice, barely audible.

Her shoulders sagged; she made half a turn as if to go, then whirled around. "Why are you doing this to me?!" she screamed, anguish thick in her voice, her face now contorted and red. "You've lied to me since the moment we met, Chris!" Her eyes blazed with fury. "How could you!" she yelled. "And now, you're telling me you're from . . . from . . ."

"A parallel universe," he finished harshly.

"Stop it!" Sandra shrieked. "What you're saying is nuttier than a fruitcake! Why are you lying? Why are you . . . hurting me like this? I . . . believed in you!" Her voice cracked momentarily, the words lingering heavily. Then, something inside her snapped, and she lunged at him. "You son of a bitch!" she yelled. Her hands slammed into his chest, all the force of her shattered trust behind them.

Her shove knocked them both off balance, the algae-slick dock offering no resistance. Sandra twisted in midair, flailing helplessly, her arms finding no purchase. With a sickening thud, her ribs and solar plexus slammed against the dock's edge, expelling the air from her lungs in a harsh whoosh. A silent scream contorted her face, her body seized, and she slid into the dark lake. The cold water wrenched her throat open, forcing her to inhale. Water flooded her lungs.

A moment earlier, Chris stumbled backward from the impact, his feet skidding on the slippery planks. He barely registered the sharp pain shooting through his ankle as he watched in horror. And before he could react, Sandra was gone—swallowed by the dark water. Precious seconds ticked by as he yanked off one boot, then the other—each hitting the dock with a hollow thud—before he plunged into the lake after her.

The cold slammed into him, stealing his breath. His body locked for an instant—then he kicked hard, forcing himself down into the murky dark.

Below, a soft glow pulsed through the silt—a large translucent sphere slightly submerged, its light diffused, its spikes scattering the gloom.

Within that faint corona, through a tangle of weeds, Chris spotted Sandra's limp form, half-buried in the soft, silty bottom. Weeds caught at him as he fought the tangle, his heart hammering, until at last he made it to her. Each motion stirred up clouds of sediment, dulling the light.

He tried to lift her and swim straight up, only to find that the thick mass of weeds above snagged them. Dread clawed at him as he realized that ascending with Sandra's unconscious body was impossible.

Panic surged, then hardened. He wasn't leaving without her. He would get out of the lake together with her—or he would die trying.

He hooked an arm under her armpit and across her chest. Then, he propelled himself forward, his feet finding traction on the uneven lakebed as he walked on.

Every step was excruciating. The water fought him, his vision tunneled to a pinprick, lungs burning. His limbs grew heavy, but he forced them on. He would not lose her.

The orb's glow receded behind them, swallowed by murk. The water shallowed. And at last, with a final, desperate lurch, Chris broke through the surface, gasping for air.

He carried Sandra onto the shore and laid her down. Her lips were blue, her body motionless. His hands shook as he tilted her head back and checked her breathing. Nothing. He sealed his lips over hers, forcing two slow breaths into her lungs, watching for her chest to rise. Seeing no response, he began chest compressions, his own breathing labored. Each push, a battle against panic. "Come on, Sandra," he whispered through gritted teeth. After thirty compressions, he gave two more breaths. And she coughed—water sputtering from her mouth—her chest rising with a ragged gasp. Her eyelids fluttered, a broken breath escaping her lips.

Chris held her close, whispering reassurances as her breathing steadied. She still trembled, but the tightness in her chest began to ease. Her heart still pounded, but his presence was like an anchor, pulling her back to safety—not just from the water, but from the terror that had gripped her. She wrapped her arms around him, the cold and the fear fading away.

"We need to get you warm. Our clothes are soaked through," Chris said.

Sandra nodded weakly. And Chris helped her out of her wet clothing, his hands gentle and efficient. Then he stripped off his own sodden garments. "Come here," he murmured, pulling her close.

The lingering chill of the lake slowly gave way to the rising warmth of skin against skin. And as they held each other, the adrenaline bled away, replaced by something else. She clung tighter, anchoring herself to his solid presence.

His body responded, but he stayed where he was, holding her, nothing more. Not because he didn't want it. But because he wasn't going to take what hadn't been offered.

But then her hand cradled his jaw; her mouth found his, and she kissed him.

He kissed her back softly at first, then with growing intensity. Sandra responded with a fierce need, their bodies fitting together. There was no hesitation, no distance left between them. In that moment, nothing else mattered but their closeness, shared breath and frantic hands. They made love: the culmination of everything unspoken.

Afterward, they remained entwined, silent and content.

As they lay there on the rough wooden planks of the deck, skin cooling, Chris let out a slow breath. In Americana, he'd learned, the front gate stayed closed unless you were ready for children—or had it safeguarded with copper or hormonal coils. Most folks just got creative with back doors and hands when it was only for fire.

Sandra kissed him. "I trust you with my life," she said, her voice barely a breath.

Chris tenderly kissed her back. Eventually, he rolled to his side, took her hand, and pressed it to his lips. "Sandra, I cannot share secrets that are not mine to tell. However, all else . . . everything that I am . . . I will never hide anything from you again."

They looked at each other frankly, openly.

"Do you believe me now?"

"Yes," she whispered and shook wet hair out of her eyes. "I believe you, and I believe in you, with all my heart."

A carefree, genuine smile broke across his face. A burst of joy. "Finally, I can be myself around you without second-guessing or worrying I'll trip myself up with my ignorance of your world." He laughed with release, and she hugged him tightly.

Sandra reflected for some time.

"So all the references to Iraq were actually about the United States you came from."

"Yes, pretty much." Chris flashed her a boyish grin. He got up, wrung out their clothes, and laid them out flat to dry. He then reclined alongside Sandra again.

They held each other's hands, gazing up at the night sky studded with countless stars.

"In my universe," Chris said, "most Americans have never seen the Milky Way."

"How is that possible?"

"Light pollution."

She was quiet. Stargazing parties in the other America must have been dimmer affairs. "How is the other Boulder, the one in your native world?"

"In some ways, it's the same. In other ways, worse," Chris told her. He then remembered. "Sandra, what do you people celebrate on March 4th?"

"Oh? Oh, it's National Day. It marks the day our country was founded, back in 1789." She glanced at him. "Is the date different in your universe?"

"We don't have National Day."

She frowned. "What do you mean you don't have National Day? You don't celebrate the founding of our country?"

He shifted uncomfortably, thought it over, and said, "I guess we only celebrate the declaration of independence."

He fell silent.

"Tell me about it," he finally said.

Sandra met his eyes, uncertain for a beat. Then her gaze drifted toward the distance as she gathered her thoughts.

"By dusk, the whole town heads to the square, under the old Liberty Tree—its roots are older than anyone alive." She glanced at him briefly, then out into the night. "The elders tell stories from years past, and the little ones are brought up front to listen."

Her voice softened, touched with memory.

"Some folks get into it—debating founding ideals and whatnot. Good-natured, mostly. And someone's always passing around jugs and tins—cider, roasted nuts, whatever's in season.

"There are drums. The civil guard marches through. Streets fill with banners and hand-sewn regalia. The kids all wave these crooked little flags they paint themselves—stars a bit off, stripes all uneven." She smiled slightly. "A personal pledge, each.

"When it gets dark, they light torches from the lantern at the base of the Tree. That's how the Marchfire starts. A brass band plays old tunes. People chant, sing. . . or just stand in silence. And when the fire's good and high, they read the Covenant out loud.

"Families toss in things from the past year—letters, broken tools, whatever they're ready to let go of. And the kids who've come of age. . . they step forward and sign the Covenant for the first time."

She let the words settle. Her gaze stayed on the dark. And for a moment, neither of them spoke.

Beside her, Chris shifted. She heard the dry sound of his forearm brushing his cheek—once, then again. He didn't say anything. Didn't look at her. Just kept staring into the darkness, jaw set.

After a while, she said softly, "I want to know all about that other world, and how you got here. Let's save it for tomorrow, though."

Right then and there, Sandra just wanted to lie beside him.

They remained quiet for a long while, listening to the distant sound of frogs croaking.

He turned to look at her. "How long has Katie been like this?"

"Like what?" she asked, reluctant.

"Sandra," Chris said, his voice gentle but firm. His eyes caught hers and held them. "How long has Katie been suffering from dissociative identity disorder?"

"Since she was eight," Sandra said, her voice small.

"You seem very specific about the age."

"I am." Her gaze turned distant. "But this is her story to share, not mine to tell."

"Who's the real her?" he asked.

She bit her lip. "If you know enough to ask that question, you know the answer: all of them. She's the sum of every fragment."

"She realizes that?"

Sandra shook her head.

Chris was silent for a few minutes. "She shines brightly, doesn't she?"

Sandra's smile wavered between sadness and wonder. "She's not tangled up in the usual internal struggles or social expectations most folks have to deal with. At any given moment, she's fully one part of herself, unaffected by the other dimensions of her psyche. It lets her express each persona with a striking intensity that's rare to see in others."

"Katie told me the other day she's not interested in pursuing a career," Chris then said.

Sandra gave a small shrug. "Many women choose to run the household, and nothing else."

"Doesn't she want to be independent?"

Sandra turned to look at him, puzzled. "Independent of what?"

"I mean—able to support herself. Financially."

"What on earth! Do you think she won't find a man who wishes to marry her? Chris, boys have been courting her left and right. All she has to do is take her pick." With Katie, it was a tad more complicated. All the same, her point was valid.

"Yes, of course." He backpedaled quickly. "What about you?"

"What about me?"

"Will you keep teaching, once you're married?"

She studied him for a moment. "Chris, once married, I'll be running a household. A hearthmistress." She fell quiet, then absently glanced down at her hands, turning them over slowly, fingers curling and uncurling. "Meals don't make themselves. Children don't raise themselves. I'll handle the bartering, the buying, the stocking—stretch the budget when I have to."

She laughed, almost under her breath. "There's always something—planning, repairs, sewing, discipline, hosting, and tending the sick. Keeping the rhythm of a family. Goodwill and clean linens don't hold a home together."

A damn household COO and CFO, Chris thought.

She rested her head against his chest. "Later—when the youngest is older, maybe ten years on—I'll likely pick up a few classes again. Part-time. Can't leave completely. Someone still has to keep this circus on the rails till the chicks fly off."

After a pause, she added, softer, "My mother showed me the basics. I watched. But I've been in school or teaching straight through—never really hearth-apprenticed." She gave a small, rueful smile. Then she flicked a pebble into the water. "At twenty-one, I ought to know more. Most women my age are already deep in it—babies on hips, soup on stoves, the whole dance. I'll have to lean on the others at first. The older hearthmistresses—they'll help. They always do. It's not something we do alone, anyway."

Some time passed.

They put their still-damp clothes on and collected the violin. Then they departed, oblivious to the hidden figures holding listening devices with parabolic collectors.

CHAPTER 18

"Good evening, everyone," Chris said gravely as he joined the Allens on the grassy rooftop of their home the next night.

"Chris," Doctor Allen said, extending his arm in invitation. "Please, join us."

The young man walked over and settled into a chair beside Sandra. He noticed Katie sitting alone, just beyond the lantern's glow, watching him from the shadows.

The mood was solemn and somewhat tense. Doctor and Mrs. Allen had planned to attend an ice cream social at the community center, a fundraiser for relief efforts after a severe storm had damaged several homes a few weeks earlier. However, they chose to forgo the event in light of the news.

"Sandra has shared with us a most remarkable story," Doctor Allen said tactfully. "She also told us she trusts you with her life."

Chris remained silent.

"Sandra has never made such a statement before," Mrs. Allen said, studying Chris as if seeing him for the first time. "This means a great deal, especially coming from her."

Chris bowed his head.

"She said you came from another universe," Mrs. Allen continued. "What in blazes does that mean, precisely?"

All eyes were on him as he spoke. "Here is what I do know," Chris said. "Much like you, I was raised in Colorado. But it is sure as heck not this Colorado." He gazed at the mountains to the west of them, which were nearly swallowed in the darkness. "Somewhere out there, there's an Earth, much like this one, filled with people, much like here, only they made different choices."

Chris exhaled slowly, then found his voice again. "I lied about Iraq to hide my unfamiliarity with local social norms, and to conceal a truth that's too fantastic to believe."

"And the Arabic?" Mrs. Allen asked, eyeing him intently. "Is that something commonly taught in that other America?"

A fleeting smile crossed Chris's face. "I learned Arabic in the military." He noted the surprised expressions. "I served in a special operations unit."

"Special operations unit," Doctor Allen repeated. "What does that entail?"

"Foreign internal defense, counterinsurgency, special reconnaissance, and counterterrorism."

"Sounds . . . impressive—and disturbing," the doctor said. "Why did you join it?"

"The motto of that army unit is *De Oppresso Liber*: to free the oppressed. I genuinely believed in that. And then there's the job description itself. For the most part, it was as thrilling as I'd imagined."

"You speak of a parallel world," Doctor Allen said. "How closely does it match ours?"

"Quite closely," he replied. "But from what I can tell, none of the individuals match up. There's no Chris Walden native to this universe, and I assume, no Sandra or Katie Allen in my own. The histories are mostly indistinguishable, even down to prominent historical figures. Yet, as we approach modern times, the two worlds diverge increasingly in some respects while maintaining odd overlaps in others."

He paused, pondering this. "It's like a broken mirror image," he finally said. "Some shards reflect the same thing; others are missing or point at other things. And in their entirety, the essence is decidedly different."

"Sandra told us you're from Boulder," Mrs. Allen said.

"Born and raised." Chris smiled and exchanged glances with Sandra. "As a matter of fact, I attended Whittier Elementary for one year."

Sandra grinned at this.

Chris fished out his driver's license and handed it to Mrs. Allen.

She examined it for a long moment before passing it to her husband. "It seems authentic," she said. "Right down to the tiny, laser-engraved signature of the executive director of the Department of Revenue." Her gaze met Chris's. "It's either real—or someone put a lot of effort into a convincing fake."

"Mother!"

Mrs. Allen turned to Chris. "Would you have believed it if our positions were reversed?"

"I don't think I can answer this without facing the situation firsthand," he replied.

Doctor Allen handed Chris back his driver's license. "What does the *Class R* designation mean?"

Chris cocked his head, unsure what the doctor meant.

"On your license. It indicates *vehicle classification R*."

"I don't know," Chris said. "It's just a standard driver's license."

"Curious," Mrs. Allen murmured, her expression now thoughtful.

"How so, ma'am?"

"If one were to assume you had counterfeited this card, it's more probable that you would have provided an explanation for the vehicle classification."

Doctor Allen said, "Chris, aside from this card, do you possess any other, more persuasive evidence?"

"I do," he said. Outside the circle of light, he saw Kate rise from her seat and felt her intense gaze on him. He was certain it was Kate, not Katie.

The others watched as he propped one ankle across his knee. "Old habits die hard," he said as he tugged and pulled on the heel of his boot. "I always keep a pair of boots with a hidden compartment. It saved my skin more than once in the field. And I figured I better hide it away. There," he said with a grunt. From the hollow heel, he drew a small, flat object wrapped in foam. Chris unwrapped it and held it out on his palm: A slim rectangle no bigger than a matchbox, its glossy black face reflective as a still pond. He tapped a corner, and it glowed to life.

"What is it?" said Mrs. Allen, staring as the small display lit up. In the darkness, Kate moved closer.

"It's a device that likely required thousands of engineering, manufacturing, and programming personnel," Chris said. "I'll show you. But understand this: Whatever firm that reverse-engineers this may stand to make an ungodly amount of money, if my native world is any indication. I ask you not to divulge what I share now."

They all nodded in agreement, and Chris held it high for them to see. "It's a *smartwatch*, just without its band."

Sandra and her parents peered at it. "So what sets it apart from an ordinary watch?" asked Sandra.

"This," Chris said and swiped the watch face, changing it to a digital display. There were soft gasps and exclamations. He swiped again to exhibit a chronograph face. And then another face, and another, and another.

"This is a list of my contacts," he said next. "You see, the smartwatch can be connected to a phone." He glanced up. "Are you familiar with telephones? Do you have a thing like that?"

"Of course we do," Sandra said, with a touch of indignation. "Why, we have a house telephone—right in the anteroom."

"No offense meant," Chris said, raising his hands placatingly. "I haven't noticed anyone calling, nor have I seen such a device around here."

"Well, people don't just place a telephone call for the sake of it, you know."

Chris saved the best for last. "This," he told them, tapping the small screen a few times, "is a short video I made the day before I left my home world."

Sandra and her parents leaned in and gazed at a video of Chris walking down some busy street. "As you can see from the street sign I zoomed in on," he said. "I'm standing at the corner of Broadway and Arapahoe."

"By golly, so you are!" exclaimed Doctor Allen, watching the video with wonder. There was no doubt; it was the intersection of those two prominent streets—with the street signage and the recognizable Flagstaff Mountain in the background. Yet, the street view was utterly different.

Chris glanced at the astonished faces of the others. He knew this was the moment it hit them—he was from a parallel universe.

"Look at those vehicles," gushed Sandra. "Those are the big cars you were referring to, aren't they?"

Chris nodded, about to speak, when a hand shot in and snatched the smartwatch—and Kate darted to a corner of the roof.

"Katherine Allen, you return that man's watch to him right this instant!" called out her mother, her voice suddenly shrill with pain and indignation.

"Maybe you should stop treating her like she's a three-year-old," Sandra said heatedly, glaring.

Her mother glowered back. "I will when she stops *acting* like a three-year-old."

But then she sagged, looking sad and deflated. Her husband rested a comforting arm around her.

"It's okay, Mom," Sandra said, her voice now tender. "Everything is okay. Really."

"It's no problem, Mrs. Allen," echoed Chris. "I'm sure she'll return the watch soon enough," he added in a lighter tone. There was a slight smile at the corners of his mouth as he studied the figure sitting hunched over the small screen at the edge of the roof.

"Would she know what to do with this . . . contraption of yours?" mumbled Mrs. Allen.

His smile broadened. "When it comes to your daughter, I don't think this is going to be a problem."

"Why, thank you, Chris, for this vote of confidence," Kate said dryly.

Sandra and her parents stared in astonishment at the figure seated in the dark.

"Was that sarcasm?" Chris inquired.

"Just a sprinkling of it," Kate replied, and in the darkness, they could see her smiling.

"Well, as I live and breathe . . ." Doctor Allen murmured, his mustache quivering.

It was the first time they had seen Kate interact with anyone outside of her immediate family.

Kate was as surprised by her own behavior as her parents and sister, but she couldn't remain on the sidelines any longer. Earlier, she'd heard that beautiful violin piece from another world. And now this: an utterly intriguing piece of technology. She forced herself out and gained control, pushing Katie to the back.

"*Darling!*" Mrs. Allen said in a voice that shook. She

scrambled to her feet and made to walk toward her daughter, but her husband restrained her. "Maggie, no."

Mrs. Allen sat back down heavily.

"Kate," Doctor Allen said with tenderness. "Are you. . . still with us?"

"Yes," Kate replied in a slightly quavering voice. For a moment, no one dared to move, fearing that anything might startle Kate and cause her to retreat to the deep recesses of her mind, like a bird frightened by an unexpected noise.

Kate, however, gathered herself. She stood up and took a few steps forward.

Her face was still claimed by the night as she asked, "How did you journey here, Chris? How did you enter our universe?"

"I stumbled on some kind of construct beneath my basement," Chris replied, editing Ronny out of the story.

They listened intently as he described finding the hidden trapdoor, the descent into a stone cellar carved deep beneath the house, and the strange octagonal frame at the far end—somehow active, displaying a view of distant mountains and a small town. He told them how he'd stood there, staring in disbelief.

Next came the horrible part, the part where he got to outright lie. He'd lied to the Allens before. Now he would have to lie again. "I figured it might be a portal, but I wasn't about to walk into it blind. So I went back upstairs, grabbed my trail pack. When I returned and stepped closer to the frame. . . that's when it happened."

He shifted in his seat. "My approach must've triggered some kind of protective mechanism. The ceiling and stairway behind me began to crack and buckle," Chris said, lowering his head to hide his lying eyes. "With no time to think and no way back, I ran through the frame as the stones came crashing down behind me."

He paused, drew a slow breath. "I wandered the lakeshore for a long time after that, trying to make sense of where I'd ended up."

"Where did you think you were?" Sandra asked.

"I recognized Boulder—the mountain range is unmistakable. At first, I thought I'd traveled back in time, judging by the size of the town. But then I came across the rack of personal transporters with biometric scanners, and it dawned on me that I was, in fact, in a parallel universe."

Chris offered a half-shrug, almost casual. "I decided to make the best of it. You know the rest."

There. The deed was done; the deceit completed. He lied to conceal the existence of a way to travel back and forth between the two worlds, and to quell any speculation about other travelers arriving in their universe.

It might have been the right thing to do. But this didn't make what he'd just done any more palatable.

Mrs. Allen winced sympathetically. "Did you leave any loved ones behind?"

"His mom passed away," Sandra told her.

"And I've never met my father," Chris went on to say, now back on solid ground.

"I'm so sorry," Mrs. Allen said. "I gather you don't have a sweetheart back home."

Chris shook his head.

No wonder he hadn't seemed heartbroken when she'd first met him, Sandra mused. He had nothing to return to—just the lingering bitterness of past events.

From the shadows, Kate extended the watch back to Chris.

"Well?" Chris asked as he accepted it. "What do you make of it?"

"The engineering feat is astounding—or at least it appears that way without being privy to all the incremental steps that must have preceded it," Kate said, and—

—Katie stepped into the light. "It's a nifty gadget," she said. The voice now had the familiar soft lilt. She took a seat next to Sandra.

"Can you just imagine how wonderful it would've been had there still been a two-way portal between our universes?" Sandra contemplated aloud.

"Would it now?" Chris asked.

"Of all the ridiculous things to say!" Sandra scoffed.

He leaned back. "Well, what would you want to see happen had it been so?"

"Open channels of commerce and cultural exchange," she said immediately. Her voice turned wistful. "I'm sure there's so much both societies can gain." She jerked her thumb toward the smartwatch. "This is merely an ingenious novelty item, a clever toy," she said. "But think of all the genuinely useful things we know nothing about."

They all looked expectantly at Chris.

"Perhaps," he said and shrugged his shoulders noncommittally.

Late into the night, they peppered him with questions, and he shared with them details about his native world. He recounted the films he had watched. He told them about the popular pastimes in his native Boulder. And he spoke of the years he'd served in the military: the grueling Q Course, the night missions in Iraq, the camaraderie he had known, the senseless death of his teammates.

Sandra had sworn them all to secrecy, though in truth, it was unnecessary. Her parents and Katie understood without being told: If word got out, Chris would be branded a madman, a fraud—or worse, someone the authorities might believe. They all agreed that keeping Chris's true background hidden was the best course of action.

CHAPTER 19

IN THE WEE HOURS, they finally left the rooftop and headed downstairs. The Allens insisted that Chris stay the night in their guest room.

Despite the late hour, they gathered for breakfast early the next morning, as Sandra and her parents had work commitments. Katie, however, was absent. Chris learned that she had stayed up most of the night at her desk and was now sound asleep.

Sunlight streamed through the arched, wooden-framed windows as they dined. Doctor Allen nodded, agreeing with a point Chris had made, then turned to his wife. "My dear, could you set him up in the biometric system?"

Mrs. Allen understood why he asked. Without it, Chris would not be able to get far. "Yes," she replied. "I have discretionary powers in this matter, and given the unique circumstances, I believe it's warranted." She looked at Chris. "Stop by the courthouse at your convenience, and we'll get it done."

He inclined his head. "My deepest thanks."

Sandra poured herself a cup. "Chris is considering becoming a farmer," she announced, as the aroma of freshly brewed coffee filled the room.

"A commendable endeavor." Doctor Allen beamed in approval.

Sandra stirred her coffee, ticking off the imaginary list in her head. Farmer, check. Builder, check. The sacred vocations in every respectable parent's list. If there were a higher calling, she'd yet to meet the parent who thought so. She hid her smile behind the rim of her mug.

"First things first, though," Chris said between bites of a nut-filled pancake. "I've got about seven thousand dollars with me—and the shirt on my back. While I have a bit of a cushion, I need to find a way to get by in the short term, even if I do have a plan for the long haul." He paused. "My concern is that I don't have a college degree," he confessed.

Chris had enlisted straight out of high school. And here he was, at the age of twenty-four, with nothing to show for it except an aging high-school diploma and some experience in counterinsurgency. It then hit him that even if he had a college degree, there would have been no way for him to prove it to would-be employers in Americana.

"Chris," Mrs. Allen said as she poured orange juice into her glass, "few people have college degrees—less than ten percent."

Huh. "So what about the vast majority of people?"

"How do you mean?" Mrs. Allen asked, dabbing her mouth with a napkin.

"Well, how do they get the training or credentials for jobs that pay more than minimum wage?"

Doctor Allen exchanged glances with his wife. It was easy to forget that Chris came from another universe. "By fourteen or fifteen, most boys are in a family trade or are apprenticing with a company, often while attending a vocational boot camp. Some girls do too, if they're minded to work outside the home."

"Interesting," Chris murmured.

"Oh, please do consider these things," Mrs. Allen said. She

folded her hands in her lap. "The programs run between one and twenty-four months. You'll find in them folks who wish to pursue nature conservation or industrial mechanics, dental hygiene or sensor-fusion work, nursing or accounting, architecture or physical therapy. Those and hundreds of other tracks."

"Apprenticeship sounds like a wonderfully practical concept," Chris acknowledged.

"It is," Sandra said, spreading butter on her French toast.

"What, then, is the function of a university in your world?" Chris asked, curious.

"You must mean college," Mrs. Allen said.

He raised an eyebrow. "Those are different things?"

"Utterly," Mrs. Allen assured him. "University is a research institute, where you'll find researchers and their graduate assistants, and nothing else. College is a learning institute, where people acquire higher education, and nothing else."

"To answer your original question," Sandra interjected, "colleges offer courses in the hard sciences, engineering, computer science, and mathematics. They also have programs in criminal justice and medicine." She took a sip of her drink and set the glass back on the table. "A handful of colleges, like the one I attended, primarily focus on liberal arts."

For a moment, no one had anything to say. The ceramic plates clinked softly as they ate.

"What classes did *you* take?" Chris asked. This was a part of her life he hadn't heard about before. Everything about Sandra and Katie fascinated him.

"Well, for the first two years, everyone went through a general liberal arts curriculum," Sandra said. "In the last two years, we specialized in areas like anthropology, history, public policy, philosophy, literature, or international affairs." She brushed her hair back. "In my case, I spent a year on literature, then a yearlong teaching seminary that combined practical fieldwork with pedagogical studies."

"How was the overall experience?" Chris asked, intrigued.

"It was just divine," Sandra exclaimed. "The core of the literature program centered around select books, which we discussed in small, intimate groups." Her face lit up. "We studied *Martin's Odyssey* by John Landon and Anya Rhind's *The Wellspring*, delving into the struggles of individualism, integrity, and self-realization." She gave her father a warning look. "Francis Hebert's *Sandworld* sparked discussions about power and ecology, and Brian Saunders' *The Radiant Archive* invited us to ponder duty and morality in a complex world. We reflected on Richard Persing's *Zen and the Skill of Machine Tending*, exploring the pursuit of quality and meaning. *The Seer* by Khalid Jabran challenged us to think about love, work, and life, while Alfred Beston's *The Stars, My Journey* pushed the boundaries of human potential. Archer Clerk's *Youth's End* left us questioning humanity's destiny and our place in the universe."

"Sandra could've just borrowed those books from the library and joined a local group to discuss them," grumbled her father, "all without spending a dime beyond attending a teaching seminary and taking a literature exam."

Sandra turned to Mrs. Allen. "Mother, make Father be quiet."

Chris addressed Doctor Allen after it was obvious that Mrs. Allen, with the barest hint of an eye roll, was thoroughly ignoring her daughter's plea. "I gather higher education isn't free."

"It's not funded by taxpayers, if that's what you mean," Doctor Allen replied. He adjusted the lapels of his jacket. "If you want to attend, you pay." He glanced pointedly at his daughter, then frowned as she stuck her tongue out at him.

Chris stifled a smile that threatened to break free. "I must say," he addressed Sandra, "you were fortunate to find a teaching job right in town."

"Luck had little to do with it," she replied. "After all, I had—and have—no intention of leaving the Boulder area. My family has been here for generations. As you probably imagine, I was born in this very house. My roots are deep within these mountains and this community. Naturally, this is where I'll remain and raise my children."

Sandra gestured toward the window, where the sun lit the hills. "Those terraces over there? My great-grandfather helped carve them. And the old flumes that once carried snowmelt down from Silver Lake? My family helped build those too."

She gave a small shrug. "Most folks feel that way about their hometown. That's why local businesses and organizations tend to prioritize hiring natives over the few transplants." A hint of concern crossed her face as something dawned on her. "Dad, do you think Chris would be able to find employment here?"

"Of course, dear." He gave her a reassuring pat on the arm. "If he genuinely wants to stay and put down roots, it's possible. Anything's possible."

Doctor Allen glanced at his pocket watch. "Work is calling," he announced and rose from his seat, with the rest of them following suit.

"Do you have plans for today?" Sandra asked Chris, touching his arm.

"Yes. I'm going to tell Dalton about me," Chris said.

⇒ ⇐

Under a bright sky with feather clouds, Chris spotted Dalton out in the field.

The two waved to each other.

By the time Chris covered the distance, Dalton had dragged two floorless chicken pens. There were dozens of them. And they were all identical: wide, low-to-the-ground shelters clad with corrugated aluminum sheets. Chris noted how Dalton took the feeder out, pushed a dolly under the chicken pen, and then pulled from the other end, dragging the pen about a dozen paces—to the sound of clucking from the white chickens inside that reached a crescendo.

Chris looked around and spotted another dolly. He grabbed it, wheeled it to the portable pen nearest to him, and mirrored what Dalton had done. It was easy to tell which shelters had already been moved: the broilers had left very noticeable marks on the grass patches they'd previously occupied.

After about twenty minutes, they'd moved all the floorless pens. Chris felt the muscles in his shoulders and arms. He found a large flat rock and sat down. Dalton soon joined him, his cap shielding him from the sun. He took a few sips from his water canteen and passed it to Chris. They sat, letting the chickens' soft clucking fill the quiet.

"So you got broiler chickens too?"

"Yep." Dalton gestured with the canteen after Chris handed it back. "Not as mobile as the laying hens, the broilers stay in these portable pens at all times. As you can see, they're kept in small groups in multiple enclosures to minimize stress."

"How often do you drag them?"

"Every day. Shut it down in the winter."

They lapsed into silence again, broken only by the clucking of the chickens and the sigh of the wind. Chris scuffed the dirt with his boot.

"Dalton," he said, "I'm not from around here. And I'm also not really from Iraq, like the girls told you."

The other man took another pull from the canteen, staring out over the meadow. "Where then?"

"Boulder. Except not this one."

Dalton turned his head and studied him. "What do you mean?"

Chris sighed and leaned back, resting on his elbows. "Parallel universe. Found a one-way portal that came crashing down as I passed through it, and here I am." He pulled out the smartwatch, and in short order was showing Dalton the video. "That's my Boulder."

Dalton watched the video, dumbfounded. "Hell of a thing!" he muttered when the video came to an end. "Hell of a thing."

Chris had to agree with him.

Dalton sat quietly for a long time, rubbing his thumb along the seam of his jeans, his stubble catching the light. "I assume you told the girls."

"Yeah."

"How did they take it?" Dalton wanted to know.

Chris let out a half-laugh. "Let's just say it got loud."

Dalton's mouth twitched. "Them girls got temper," he said fondly. The two shared a chuckle.

Dalton glanced over at the man next to him. "And . . . ?"

"They believe it now," Chris said simply.

Dalton was silent for a while, absently stroking his stubble beard. "So you came to us from another place"—he couldn't make himself say "universe"—"and that's how you spend your time? Helping to move chicken pens?"

Chris shrugged. "I came over to tell you. I also figured I'm here to stay, so I'd better start pulling my own weight." This, and somehow shutting down the portal. He had to.

Dalton said nothing, just gave a slow nod.

Chris caught his eye. "Do you believe me?"

"I will," Dalton said, "once I get used to the idea. So who else did you tell?" he asked.

"No one. It's only you and the Allens. And I would like to keep it that way."

"Will do. You can count on me."

"Thank you, Dalton." Chris got up. "I'd better go."

Dalton rose too, clasping his hand and pulling him into a quick one-armed hug.

CHAPTER 20

A CARRIAGE TOOK CHRIS straight from the farm to Sandra's school. It wasn't in session that day—summer schedule being what it was—but some of the teachers were in the building.

Sandra looked up from her desk as he entered the classroom. "Chris!" she said, surprise evident in her voice.

"Are you busy?"

"Yeah. Prepping tomorrow's lesson."

"It's too bad, really," he said with mock regret, stealing a kiss—and she laughed. "We're going to the factory your aunt is working at," he told her and perched himself on the edge of her desk. She'd mentioned it yesterday, and it struck him as a solid lead.

Sandra leaned back in her chair and regarded him. It seemed he was dead serious about finding a source of income in the immediate term. "Impulsive and demanding—I like it," she said, rising. "All right, I'll telephone my aunt and see if she can see us today."

He followed her out of the classroom.

"Where are we going?"

"To the telephone desk, of course. We have one on this floor."

"Sounds good," Chris said.

At the end of a short hallway, a black instrument rested on

a table. He watched, fascinated, as she picked up the receiver and, with one slender finger, deftly spun the rotary dial one digit at a time. "What?" she said, catching his stare.

"No, nothing. We just have different phone models in the other America." Did Sandra need to know Morse code to use that thing?

"Is that how you say it? 'Phone'? It rhymes with 'drone.' Quaint." She made a sudden shushing motion. "Hello!" she said. "This is the daughter of Mrs. Margaret Allen. May I please talk to Mrs. Valerie Bellamy?"

They stood there waiting.

"Are you talking all the way to Commerce City?"

"So?"

"With those *telephones* of yours, I'm surprised you don't need to shout to be heard," he said, smothering a snicker behind a fierce frown. "I mean, with the long distances and all—"

She punched him in the gut.

"Ouch!"

"The next one is going to land below the belt," Sandra warned him darkly. She turned. "Oh, Aunt Valerie? Yes, this is Sandra."

She talked some more to the person on the other end, nodding occasionally.

"Done," Sandra announced a minute later, placing the handset back in its cradle. She flashed Chris a smile. "My aunt is expecting us."

Then she swatted his ass—something she'd wanted to do for a while. "Let's go, big boy."

Chris straightened, eyes gleaming. "If I knew teachers were this hands-on, I would've started acting out a lot sooner."

"Keep running your mouth," she said coolly, "and I'll fetch the paddle."

He stepped in, sliding his hands around her waist. "I didn't realize teachers in this school believe in punishing bad boys."

Her voice dropped half an octave. "Oh, we do," she murmured, tracing a slow line down his chest.

Chris's hand dropped lower, cupping her with bold familiarity, mouth against her hair. "You're not ready for how much trouble I am."

"Prove it," she whispered, fingers already finding the buttons of his shirt.

⇒⇐

Sometime later, a somewhat disheveled Sandra, blouse unbuttoned just one notch too far, called in their ride: a curious-looking, boxlike pod.

As they climbed inside, the glass walls of the capsule tinted against the sun, and a whisper of cool air drifted from a slim unit embedded in the roof. They set off down the dirt road, easing around passersby and children at play. Chris peered curiously through the now-muted glare of the smart-glass walls. Sandlot baseball must have been popular in Americana's Boulder; they passed three empty lots where kids were playing.

As they emerged onto Broadway, Chris's breath caught in his throat. Gone were the unpaved residential streets; Broadway was strikingly different and undeniably magnificent.

The boulevard was paved with large, pale granite blocks that seamlessly merged the road and sidewalk. Chris marveled as they rolled past one stately building after another. Sandra pointed out a theater, the central library, and an elegant dance hall. Each grand edifice proudly displayed the American and Colorado flags, fluttering in the breeze. Many of the buildings, constructed of limestone with white marble trimmings, were adorned with columns and elongated windows. Towering Princeton Sentry trees stood between the structures, offering shade and a sense of tranquility.

As they traveled, Chris noticed bronze statues commemorating events that must have shaped Boulder's community. Carved reliefs adorned the façades of some buildings, and sections of the stone pavement featured mosaics depicting the region's native flora and fauna.

The city hall, with its Capitol-like dome, captivated Chris the most. Its red granite façade glowed rosy in the sunlight, and its countless windows shimmered. He thought he spotted a golden eagle perched high up. In the plaza below, a cello quartet serenaded passersby.

Unlike the residential streets, Broadway maintained a familiar order, with vehicles moving in two center lanes and pedestrians on the sidelines.

Chris felt a subtle jolt as something nudged their vehicle from behind. He turned, just in time to see an identical glass pod connect seamlessly with theirs. Then another.

He blinked. "Did we just get tailgated into a threesome?"

Sandra chuckled softly at his expression. "You act like you've never seen pods coupling before."

"Not in public." He watched as the partition between the modules slid away and passengers began moving between units. "Should we give the pods some privacy?"

Sandra just scowled at him.

A fourth capsule glided in. As with the other units, its approach slowed to a crawl by some unseen force—electromagnetic, Chris guessed—before docking with a clean, almost surgical precision. He raised an eyebrow. "They're forming a train—no, a modular bus."

"Temporary bus," Sandra said. "Efficient for the highway run."

As they rolled onward, the convoy grew—about two dozen pods, all seamlessly connected, their glass walls folding away to form one airy, articulated vehicle. At one point, a chime sounded and a display lit up, prompting a few passengers to move forward. Moments later, two pods detached smoothly from the back and peeled off.

Chris tapped the glass beside him, amused. "Reducing the traffic footprint, one modular romance at a time."

"Magnetic coupling and synchronized braking—very romantic," Sandra said, shooting him a sideways glance. "You're lucky I'm into weird metaphors."

She turned her attention to the window.

A beat later, Chris looked out as well.

One moment they were traversing Broadway; the next, they were outside the city limits, with the large pavement stones giving way to a wide two-lane road of buff-colored concrete with a dark brown center line.

As the bus accelerated, Chris watched the passing traffic. Semi-trailers and modular buses dominated the highway, and a few motorcyclists riding classic Indian bikes caught his attention.

After chatting with Sandra, he surmised they did not have anything like a national highway system. It was chiefly a patchwork of country roads and a few highways connecting high-traffic corridors. It appeared that electrified rail did the heavy, transcontinental lifting.

As they drew closer to the Denver area, two vacant capsules approached and attached themselves to the main body of the bus. Some passengers moved into them, and shortly thereafter, the respective modules separated and went their own ways, to their final destinations.

At the end, Sandra and Chris were once again alone in a pod, and a few minutes later, they arrived at the factory.

From school door to factory gate, all in the same seat. Chris leaned back, a slow grin spreading across his face. *Impressive.*

The wait in the lobby was short, and soon a middle-aged woman clad in a tailored skirt suit briskly approached them, smiling. She embraced Sandra and offered Chris a handshake. "Welcome, welcome," Mrs. Bellamy said as she guided them through a bustling space to her office, which had a glass wall overlooking the factory floor below.

"I'm looking for work," Chris told Sandra's aunt, once they were seated in the small, jam-packed office and pleasantries were over. "I enjoy working with my hands and can maintain a fast pace if necessary. I'd like to explore the possibility of finding a job here."

Mrs. Bellamy leaned against one armrest of her chair and considered his words. "Any experience with a forklift?"

"Forklift, no. However, I did operate heavy machinery, some of it fairly sophisticated."

She looked at him appraisingly. Her niece had asked her for help, and she wanted to assist. "This is what I suggest," she said. "Familiarize yourself with our operation, learn about how we run things, and if you're still interested, we'll start with a trial period and go from there."

"Sounds fair," Chris said. "That's all I can ask for."

Sandra's aunt leaned forward, her expression shifting subtly. "First, though, you must understand something. All the permanent staff here are owners; apprentices and temps can buy in after their probation year."

No employees? He eyed the factory floor visible through the glass wall. "I don't follow you."

Mrs. Bellamy glanced at Sandra. "Why, I'm unsure what you mean."

"Well, who's in charge?"

"Mr. Walden grew up in Arabia and only recently returned

to the States," Sandra explained. She turned to Chris. "The people who make up this company nominate the most suitable individuals to manage daily matters." She gestured. "That's how Aunt Valerie ended up heading a division. In the end, though, every worker has a stake and a say."

That sounded like a recipe for a train wreck. "What if people disagree? What then?"

Mrs. Bellamy started to answer, then she smiled as if a thought struck her. "Well," she said, glancing at her wristwatch, "see for yourself. If you would follow me, please."

But Sandra had to excuse herself; she had work to do. She told Chris that he would be able to take the company bus back to Boulder at the end of the day.

After saying their goodbyes, Sandra's aunt led Chris through a bustling area. She said, "Policy decisions are made within circles." She stopped in front of a glass-walled room, where a group of people were seated. "This is one such circle, with all members of a specific department in attendance, or their representatives if the department is too large."

Inside the glass enclosure, a half-dozen workers sat in a circle—no head of the table, just swivel chairs and steaming mugs. One woman frowned at a chart. "If we add that extra shift, we'll be spread thin by Friday."

A younger man leaned in. "What if we rotate teams every other day? That gives Saturday back to Line C."

Heads nodded. The tension eased.

Chris watched, intrigued. No corporate suits, no orders parceled down the food chain. Just people hashing things out where the actual work happened.

"As you probably noticed," Mrs. Bellamy said to Chris when they walked out, "each member has a say, putting both the shy and inarticulate on the same footing as the domineering and bombastic."

"Nice."

"It's more than 'nice,' Mr. Walden. By giving everybody a voice, we allow potential issues and innovative ideas to surface from those who actually do the work."

He pondered this. "I gather decisions are made by a majority vote."

Aunt Valerie shook her head. "No, we aim to have everyone in accord."

"Sounds like a tall order."

"It's not, so long as you set sensible expectations," the dignified woman said. "We go around the circle and inquire if anyone has any reasoned, significant objections—which is different from asking if each person favors a given proposal or motion. We seek to determine if it is good enough to run with, something within people's range of tolerance."

Interesting, Chris thought. "Still, I'm not quite sure how it works if every department makes autonomous decisions," he said once they were back in her office, seated across from each other.

Aunt Valerie smiled appreciatively. "We have a coordinating circle, which is made up of two members from each department circle. That way, the divisions are all interlinked, keeping them in alignment."

"What about a company-wide meeting, with all hundred and twenty people?"

"Similar to town halls or public hearings. Haven't you seen one? We gather in a room with a central AI-powered display that processes real-time keyboard input from all attendees. The system highlights key points, identifies common themes, tracks votes, and summarizes complex ideas. Breakout sessions allow for focused discussions, while designated AI-free time encourages organic conversations."

Chris liked what he heard. But as he saw it, it didn't address the main problem.

He said, "Back where I'm from, if there's a need for downsizing, folks just get laid off. After all, they're just employees. How does that work when each person is an owner?"

"Well," she replied, "if the cooperative needs to downsize, we let go of those on probation, the temporary workers, and the apprentices. We may also offer to buy out some of our people and attempt to secure them positions in other firms."

"Anything else?" Chris pressed.

"We squirrel away four weeks of payroll each year until the buffer hits six months' coverage; it's helped us weather a few storms. We might also diversify our activities or reinvent ourselves entirely. And as a last resort, we may have to consider disbanding the firm," she said.

"Where does the capital come from for growth?"

"Ten percent of our annual surplus goes into a shared capital account we can't cash out. That funds new tooling, expansions, and innovation."

That still left one big concern.

"What if an individual turns into a liability?" he inquired. If a worker were a co-owner—was that a recipe for the workers to grow lazy and complacent?

Mrs. Bellamy didn't seem to share his concern.

"This is seldom an issue, as we all have personal stakes in ensuring the business thrives," Mrs. Bellamy said. "But if someone's falling behind, our quarterly peer reviews usually catch it. If three colleagues flag underperformance, it kicks off a mentoring plan to help them get back on track." Chris nodded in acknowledgment. "Of course," she continued, "if a situation does not resolve, we have protocols in place. We offer to buy out the person's share, or, in extreme cases, we use a supermajority vote to force a sale. Thankfully, we've never had to resort to that." She folded her hands in her lap and looked at him.

"How does someone become a part of the company?" Chris asked.

Mrs. Bellamy appeared to have been waiting for this question. "We may choose to offer a person provisional membership for twelve months, after which it goes to a vote," she said.

"And if someone becomes a member, they have equality in the firm?" Chris asked.

"Indeed," she replied.

"But don't newcomers need to contribute some capital?"

"They do," Mrs. Bellamy confirmed. "This can be done upfront, or by having a portion of their salaries applied."

That sounded sensible to Chris.

Mrs. Bellamy took him out onto the floor.

This was the first time Chris had visited a garment factory, though he imagined it must have looked much like any other operation of its kind, in that universe or any other: long rows of tables, each with an operator working with a sewing machine of some sort.

From overhead ducts, diffused sunlight poured in, and the whole room felt like a sunrise caught in amber. The walls were a soft, pastel flax color with sandstone relief-like designs, and the concrete floor had a pale lime-green hue, imbuing the area with an upbeat feel.

"Up until twenty years ago, we used hundreds of chemicals, including sulfur, arsenic, and formaldehyde," Mrs. Bellamy said, raising her voice slightly to be heard over the sewing machines, responding to a question Chris had about fabric dyeing. "That's all in the past now. Banned, in fact."

"And nowadays?" he asked, walking with her around large cutting tables.

"DNA sequencing," she said with a suggestion of a smile. She guided him toward a series of gleaming steel vats. "See these? They're living color factories."

She tapped a small observation window where a vibrant indigo liquid swirled. "Our supplier has figured out how to encode the instructions for making pigments in living things—like that of a butterfly's orange wings or a blue iris flower. They insert that genetic information into bacteria." She inhaled deeply. "Smell that? Just molasses and nitrogen—which we feed the bacteria. No chemicals, no toxins."

She continued, "We put the bacteria on the fabric to color it. The microorganisms do the rest. At the end, we briefly raise the temperature, which kills them off and releases any natural salts that catalyze the process."

They talked a bit more about the forklift operator position, and Chris said he'd sleep on it and get back to her tomorrow.

Upon asking, Chris learned that worker cooperatives were the dominant business model in Americana, though not the only one.

Absentee ownership of companies was prohibited, and publicly traded corporations were hunted to extinction. That last point was beyond huge—no soulless behemoths warping culture, public policy, and lifestyles in their image. No predatory cartels or monopolies either. To raise capital, businesses utilized a variety of crowdfunding and crowdlending platforms.

He learned that in Americana, the size of companies rarely exceeded one hundred and fifty people—after which, he was told, interpersonal relations, innovation, agility, and efficiency started to go south. Complex projects requiring a larger number of people, from nuclear plants to ocean liners, were done in a modular fashion, employing dozens if not hundreds of contractor and subcontractor firms. *Huh.* Chris tried to imagine it: thousands of small, agile firms snapping together like modular pods on an Americana bus.

Aunt Valerie excused herself; she had to attend to other things. It was just an hour or so until the end of the workday, and he would not have to wait long to catch a ride back home.

Chris grabbed a shop stool and sat against a wall, observing the people—mostly men—at the workstations. There was something soothing about the hiss of steam coming from the industrial irons, the low murmur of workers chatting, and the gentle whirring of fabric-cutting machines.

He chuckled as everyone sprang up and broke into a chaotic dance as a catchy song blared from the PA system. Boots stomped, benches rattled—the whole thing was loud, loose, and choreographed only in spirit.

The floor manager led the charge, a boisterous figure growling and barking in a comical Scottish accent. He struck Chris as a blend of court jester and drill sergeant, whose primary responsibility was to keep everyone energized and entertained. It was clear he took his role to heart, and his enthusiasm was contagious. Then just as suddenly, it stopped. Shears lifted. Steam hissed once more. And the hall settled back into that steady, focused hum.

Later, a voice crackled over the loudspeaker, announcing a newly closed deal, prompting cheers throughout the room. Moments later, the same voice delivered news of a shipment delay, met with a collective groan.

A jaunty tune signaled day's end, and the machines quieted. People stretched, shared grins, and began packing up.

Chris joined the people streaming outside. The firm had its own buses, and he boarded the one headed to Boulder.

Inside, the bus buzzed with easy energy. It looked more like a traveling pub than a shuttle—dark wood paneling, a bar stretching down one side, and swivel stools tucked beneath it. People clinked glasses of lemonade and beer, sang off-key to familiar tunes, and argued over some cooperative deal.

It must have been a considerable expense for the company to run and maintain those extravagant buses, Chris reflected.

But then he remembered: The bus passengers were the owners. They *were* the company.

As he watched the animated faces and listened to their banter and laughter, he thought to himself that if he wanted, he might one day become part of this extended family of people.

All too soon, the ride was coming to an end. City pods, like the ones he'd taken to Commerce City, began attaching themselves to the back of the bus, one after another. People boarded in ones and twos, entering pods that would take them away to their final destinations.

That evening, Chris received his first telephone call. It was Dalton on the other end of the line, offering him a part-time apprenticeship at his farm. Chris would gain hands-on experience, and Dalton would really like having Chris work alongside him. Chris was excited.

Later that night, he spoke to Mrs. Bellamy and explained his situation to her. And she agreed to have him come a few days a week for the handful of months he requested, provided he could prove himself competent and diligent.

All of this was to start in a couple of weeks. Chris had a few things to take care of first, including talking to Sandra's father about health insurance and figuring out how to convince Ronny to power down the gate. The two were very much connected.

CHAPTER 21

CHRIS AND DOCTOR ALLEN LOUNGED on the porch, await-
ing their ride, which was due to arrive any minute.

Both Doctor and Mrs. Allen worked, but Chris suspected
that their dual careers weren't born out of financial necessity. It
was becoming increasingly apparent to him that in Americana,
a single income typically sufficed to support a household.

This must have been liberating for many families. At the
same time, there were some obvious trade-offs.

In Americana, jetting off to foreign lands or splurging on
lavish vacations was not done. No one, as far as he could tell,
owned big-ticket items like personal watercraft, swimming
pools, or cars. The weighty burden of home mortgages was
refreshingly absent, a significant financial relief. Dining out
wasn't a habitual indulgence. Teenagers did not go shopping as
a pastime, and children did not partake in costly extracurricu-
lars like gymnastics, football camps, or ski lessons. Moreover,
the sharing economy's spirit permeated various aspects of
everyday life.

This realization led Chris to reflect on the socioeconomic
structure of Americana. It was a land where opportunity
knocked loudly, and personal responsibility answered. Freedom reigned supreme—even the freedom to languish. The
government, bless its minimalist heart, kept its hands clean of

welfare; "handout" was a four-letter word in the halls of power. Instead, a patchwork of private charities offered support to those who genuinely couldn't pull their weight, the relative few.

This also meant that taxes must have been substantially lower. But that wasn't all. Chris was fairly certain that healthcare in Americana was significantly cheaper. In fact, that was why he wanted to accompany Doctor Allen; he wanted to confirm his hunch and understand how this was possible. If he was right, he had something valuable to present to Ronny and the world back home.

The vehicle they'd summoned ambled down the street and came to a stop in front of the house. As Doctor Allen climbed inside, Chris paused, eyeing it critically. "Say, isn't that a 1907 Cadillac runabout?" he asked.

Doctor Allen gave Chris a surprised grin. "A fellow automobile enthusiast, I see. But actually, it is a 2020 Cadillac runabout—electric, autonomous, and with a convertible roof. The look and speed are about the same, though." The open vehicle, customized for the local doctors, proudly displayed a prominent symbol on its hood in gold, silver, and onyx: the Rod of Asclepius with a serpent entwined around a staff, the symbol of medicine.

"There are twenty primary care physicians in town," Doctor Allen told Chris moments later, once they were both strapped in and the runabout started at a leisurely pace down the dirt-packed road. "We jointly own a small fleet of seven such vehicles and use them for house calls."

A few passersby respectfully tipped their hats as the vehicle bearing the Rod of Asclepius emblem cruised by.

"How're you doing, George?" the doctor called out to one boy.

"I'm just swell, Doc!"

They turned onto another street and then made another right.

"Where are we headed?" Chris asked.

"I don't rightly know." The doctor chortled. "At least not with any specificity. We're making the house-call round. My assistant feeds the list into the system, and the computer optimizes our route based on the patients' locations."

As the runabout drove them, Doctor Allen pulled up a small flat monitor mounted on a flexible arm and examined the medical data of his first patient. After some time, he leaned back, and the screen faded to black.

"How well do you know your patients?" Chris asked.

"Quite well, actually. I've been the family physician for some of them since they were just children," Doctor Allen said.

Their first stop was to see a child with pneumonia. Chris stayed in the vehicle as Doctor Allen attended to the patient. When he returned, Chris remarked, "I've never had a house call from a doctor."

"You're fortunate not to have been too ill."

Chris shook his head. "It's not that. Where I'm from, we always go to the doctor's office, regardless of our condition."

"Well, I'll be," Doctor Allen said, eyeing Chris. "Even the little ones?"

"Yes, indeed. But I understand it wasn't always like that."

The next visit was a quick checkup on an elderly person recovering from sepsis. It was en route, and the doctor made a quick stop to make sure that all was well and no complications had arisen.

The third case took a bit longer. This time, Doctor Allen conducted a video conference with some specialists—a gastro-enterologist, a nephrologist, and a hepatologist—at the patient's home. They asked the ailing woman questions while Doctor Allen performed a related physical examination.

"Wow," Chris said, after Doctor Allen had returned and shared those details with him.

The doctor looked quizzically at Chris as the open vehicle started on its way again.

"Don't you know?" Chris ran his hand through his hair. "No, I suppose you wouldn't. In the other America, a case like this unfolds quite differently: First, we visit a family doctor. Then, we get a referral to a specialist, who we might not see for weeks. If needed, we secure yet another referral for yet another specialist, and so on." Chris eyed Doctor Allen. "But here, you have a roster of specialists at your beck and call—together, at the same time. How is that even possible?"

Doctor Allen smiled. "It's quite simple, Chris. I have access to a vast, nationwide network of specialists, many of whom are available for remote consultations." He shrugged. "The specialists pull a man apart without meaning to. It's my job to make sure we treat the human being, not a disparate pile of symptoms. That's why I have the lead role."

Chris nodded; he thought he understood. And the conversation turned to other healthcare-related matters.

As Doctor Allen spoke, it became increasingly clear to Chris that Americana had wholeheartedly embraced the saying, *an ounce of prevention is worth a pound of cure.* Their healthcare system deployed an army of government-paid skilled nursing assistants to conduct physical exams door-to-door. These people were selected for both their medical expertise and their ability to win hearts, persuading even the most stubborn individuals to undergo tests on the spot. They drove around in preventive care vans equipped for various cancer screenings, blood glucose tests, bone density scans, and more—reducing the need for expensive secondary and tertiary treatments.

As they started on the last leg of the doctor's rounds, Chris recalled the very reason he'd asked to tag along.

"Doctor Allen," Chris began, his expression somewhat grim, "aside from securing a stable, well-paying job, the most pressing concern for many Americans in my world is medical care." He furrowed his brow. "I read that if we spread the total health-care costs evenly among all households, the burden on each would be close to half of the median household income. It's no wonder some seniors over there have to keep working past retirement just to afford the medications they need."

Doctor Allen appeared shocked by this.

Chris went on, "Our national motto is *In Big Pharma We Trust,* where every ailment has a pill. And who needs a lasting cure when you can have a lifelong prescription?" He mustered a wry smile. "Of course, side effects may include existen-tial dread and bankruptcy." It wasn't the first time Chris had thought about this. Once corporations figured out they could prescribe antipsychotics to children and antidepressants to the recently divorced, it stopped being medicine and became asset management.

"That's quite unfortunate," Doctor Allen said softly, looking at Chris. "I gather this is a personal matter for you."

"It is, to some extent," Chris replied gruffly as the vehicle rounded a corner. "My mother faced numerous health chal-lenges in her final years, and she was frequently in and out of hospitals. Costs were always a major consideration, which prompted me to question certain aspects and research the matter."

Chris glanced at the dignified man next to him. "The remark you made the other day led me to think that medical care here is considerably more affordable. Is that true, Doc?"

Doctor Allen cleared his throat. "You could say that. Based on what you've told me, it's likely one-hundredth the cost of yours."

Chris was stunned. One-hundredth meant . . . healthcare cost was negligible in Americana, barely a blip on one's finances. Excitement surged within him. This was the kind of thing that would make Ronny—and the entire U.S. population back home—sit up and take notice. "That's precisely what I wanted to discuss with you. What's the secret sauce, Doc?"

"There is none. It's the result of policies at all levels and across every facet of healthcare."

Doctor Allen eyed Chris silently for a few moments. He finally said, "I assume your keen interest is purely theoretical."

Something unspoken passed between the two men. "Naturally," Chris replied. "After all, it's not like I could share what I learn here with anyone back in my native world."

The runabout crested a hill and began winding its way toward the Allen residence, the silence between them stretching. Then, after a long beat, Doctor Allen spoke, his voice low. "But if—hypothetically—there had been a way to go back and forth between the worlds, what then?"

"This would have worried me to no end," Chris said immediately. "People from my former country might have sought to exploit this one."

Another silence followed.

"What could have been done about that?" Doctor Allen asked.

"Well," Chris replied, "one way would be to buy off anyone who knew about the portal with something lucrative—say, a revolutionary healthcare system that could save trillions. After that, of course, you'd need to find a way to shut the portal down for good."

Doctor Allen's eyes widened slightly. After a long moment, he exhaled heavily, collected himself, and spent the next hour telling Chris all he knew about the healthcare system, and at Chris's request, took him to visit a local hospital. Chris returned to the hospital over the following days, asking questions, taking notes, and reflecting.

On weekends, during clear summer nights, hundreds of people of all ages gathered at the town's amphitheater. Families brought lanterns and picnic baskets. Wrapped in blankets, they laughed and cried together as they watched a feature film under the open starry sky. Many others went on to cheer from the stands at baseball games. However, dancing aside, Immersives were the most popular form of outings. These experiences blended live-action role-playing, immersive theater, and escape room puzzles into something entirely their own.

Myriad traveling troupes crisscrossed the country in campers, moving from one town to the next. These were ensembles of designers, artisans, and actors who collaborated to craft unforgettable experiences. Before arriving in each town, they recruited local students and youth groups to help with the fabrication, construction, décor, staging, and costuming of their production. Additionally, numerous townspeople often ended up taking on minor acting roles.

The general public attended these experiences with the same enthusiasm and fervor that once characterized theatergoers in Paris and London during earlier eras.

The concept of Immersives was explained to Chris as he, Sandra, Katie, and Dalton ventured across the post-apocalyptic quarter, designed to resemble a zombie-infested zone. This area was a hodgepodge of dilapidated structures strewn with rusty rebar and graffiti-covered broken masonry, setting the stage for an intense experience.

For two gripping hours, they navigated the eerie landscape, their hearts racing as they worked together to escape.

Like traditional theater shows, individual Immersives had their moment in the spotlight. Some had longer runs, but eventually, all gave way to fresh, innovative experiences. Over time, certain spots in town—in virtually every town—developed distinct themes, hosting productions that matched their unique character.

In Boulder, beyond the post-apocalyptic quarter, stood a building encircled by a wrought-iron fence, styled like a nightmarish Victorian asylum. It typically hosted prison-break Immersives. Another spot in town featured an ancient, tomblike structure with an underground labyrinth, used for treasure hunts involving "deadly" traps and ingenious puzzles. Lastly, a sprawling mansion served as a backdrop for elaborate murder mysteries, drawing in those eager to unravel enigmatic plots.

The sisters and Dalton noticed that Chris seemed preoccupied, as if something weighed heavily on his mind. He brushed off their concerns, claiming to be homesick and insisting that everything was fine. And inwardly, he vowed to make it so. He would convince Ronny to power down the gate for good, and then everything would be well in truth.

None of them noticed some people nonchalantly trailing behind them.

CHAPTER 22

CHRIS WAS ADVISED THAT JUDGE ALLEN COULD be found in courtroom number three, and indeed, there she was.

He stepped into a spacious, hexagonal chamber where lustrous wood panels and dramatic murals lined the walls. Beneath a stained-glass dome at the courtroom's center, the Honorable Judge Margaret Allen presided from a raised platform, cloaked in a black robe. A man and a woman, both in everyday attire, were seated on either side of her, while a small audience occupied the tiered seats encircling the platform.

Chris took a chair toward the back and watched the proceedings with fascination. It didn't resemble a typical trial—was it arbitration? There were no witnesses, and the proceedings lacked any clear structure. The guilt seemed predetermined, as the discussion centered solely on determining the compensation for the plaintiff.

At some point, the three judges conferred quietly.

After a nod from one of the judges, the bailiff instructed the defendant to rise, and a hush fell over the courtroom as Judge Allen delivered the ruling in a clear, measured voice.

A lunch recess followed. Judge Allen rapped her gavel, and everyone in the courtroom rose and remained standing as she and her associates stepped down from the platform.

Mrs. Allen stopped by a door at the back of the courtroom and motioned for Chris to join her.

She led him into a carpeted corridor, her black robe billowing. She appeared different, almost regal in bearing.

"Good timing," she said, once they were in her private chambers. "I have a one-hour lunch break." She sat down behind her desk and gestured for Chris to take a seat. He sank into one of two leather armchairs and silently regarded a framed photo of the Allens hanging on one of the walls.

Mrs. Allen held up her hand to a sensor embedded in the vault behind her. There was a click. She opened the bulky metal door and pulled out a peculiar-looking terminal. Another scan of her hand, and it was switched on. Mrs. Allen offered Chris a warm smile. "Shall we proceed with your registration?"

"Certainly," he said.

The process took only a few minutes. She typed in his full name, date of birth, and present address. She took a reading of his vein pattern. She inserted a few more details. And it was done; Chris was in the system.

"It's all so . . ." He hesitated.

Mrs. Allen powered down the terminal and placed it back in the vault. "It's all so what, Chris?"

"Straightforward," he said.

She gave him a quick smile and rested her hands on the desk in front of her. "Shouldn't it be?"

"Of course," he said right away. "I'm a bit surprised, that's all. There's a lot more red tape where I come from. Everything is done by the book. And the book has many, many pages." He'd often mused that his spirited, can-do America had somehow evolved into the Compliance State of America—jointly governed by the Departments of HR, Legal, and Cover Your Ass. A paper-pushing dominion.

Mrs. Allen made a dismissive gesture. "Just goes to show

that regulations and statutes can be overrated."

That was not something Chris ever expected a sitting judge to say. Noticing the faint surprise on his face, she added, "Rules provide a framework, not an absolute answer. They can't anticipate every nuance or context. That's where human judgment and common sense come in. Remember, any system can be gamed; we have to allow officials a reasonable degree of discretion. In fact, in a society built on trust, too many rigid rules ultimately erode that trust."

Mrs. Allen settled into her high-backed chair. "I've been meaning to ask you," she said, "how does the justice system operate in your former world?"

He gave a hard, bitter laugh. "Nominally, we have one."

She just sat there and looked at him.

"I was there for a friend who was put through the wringer for years." A muscle tightened in his jaw. "It's a Byzantine horror show."

"Do tell, please," Mrs. Allen said, pouring lemonade for them both.

"The legal structure we have on the books is unworkable," Chris said, accepting the drink. "Coercive incentives, threats, and sketchy confessions behind closed doors help to move things along. This shady underbelly runs on plea bargains, where nine out of ten cases never even make it to trial. You might be innocent, but why risk it? Take the plea, do a few years, and avoid the gamble of a longer sentence."

Chris sighed deeply. "Our justice process is sluggish, ineffective, and only those with deep pockets to lawyer up can mount a credible defense. It's pay-to-play for those who can cough up serious cash or burn through their life savings." He took a few sips. "Lawyers may put the screws to witnesses and do whatever it takes to win. It's the Wild West, Mrs. Allen, with prosecutors focused on convictions and boosting their careers, and private lawyers chasing big settlements. Truth and justice take a back seat." He stopped, surprised by his own outpouring.

Mrs. Allen was taken aback by some of what he said. Although unfamiliar with the phrases "pay-to-play" and "lawyer up," she could infer their meaning. It was her first exposure to his native speech pattern, which she found both jarring and strangely expressive.

"Seems like you have an adversarial model over there," Mrs. Allen said. "Or rather, some grotesque mutation of it."

"What about here?"

"For starters, more than nine out of ten disputes are resolved through community arbitration or conflict resolution circles. In fact, many types of cases have a Mediate-First rule. That way, the courts proper don't get bogged down, leaving them free to untangle the genuinely knotty or serious cases that land on their docket."

"And how does it work once a case enters the court system?"

"We have an inquisitorial system."

Chris winced. "That sounds like the Spanish Inquisition."

She laughed, and he was struck at that moment by how much she reminded him of Sandra.

"Our criminal justice system has two distinct parts." Mrs. Allen raised one finger. "First, an investigative judge looks into the case to determine what happened." She raised another finger. "I'm the other kind: an adjudicating judge. Once the investigation is complete, all pertinent parties convene. Along with two lay judges, I deliberate and rule on how the situation should be resolved. You just witnessed such a hearing."

"Is that a better system?"

"I think so," Mrs. Allen said, taking a sip. "Cases are not treated as a contest or a game, with opposing sides striving for victory. The judges are responsible for ensuring all relevant information is examined, the truth is brought to light, and justice is served. We account for cognitive biases, hence the routine use of Devil's Advocates."

Devil's Advocates? Chris's eyebrows rose in question.

"Their job is to come up with contrary perspectives," Mrs. Allen explained. "They identify flaws, examine weak points, and pry into what smacks of confirmation bias. By continually injecting fresh angles into the investigation, they help keep everyone sharp and vigilant throughout the process."

Back home, lawsuits were practically a national pastime—drag someone to court and hope they settle to avoid the headache. After talking to Mrs. Allen some more, it became clear that things worked differently in Americana. Most cases died in mediation, and if one sued and lost, they picked up the tab. Claims were screened by experts before ever reaching a judge, and without jackpot verdicts or fishing expeditions, he suspected the only people in court were the ones who truly belonged there.

They chatted a bit more, and a few minutes later Chris thanked Mrs. Allen and left the courthouse.

With his name and biometrics in the system, Chris was able to open an account an hour later—from which money could automatically be withdrawn.

He inquired and was told that the palm-vein scanner system used "a decentralized identity protocol secured by blockchain." Instead of storing raw scans, the system used "fuzzy extractors to derive cryptographic keys from vein patterns. Those keys were committed on-chain, while the matching templates were encrypted and distributed across five geo-diverse nodes. A zero-knowledge proof confirmed a live match without revealing the pattern itself." Chris had no idea what any of it meant; he got a headache merely trying to understand—which he reckoned might have been an adequate deterrent to hacking the system all on its own.

Mr. Callenbach told him what had become evident to Chris. Cash was an anachronism. Even small children tapped directly into their parents' accounts—with predefined controls governing how much, how often, or even to what vendor or type of vendor they were authorized to transfer the funds to.

Now Chris could pay for groceries or summon a vehicle with a wave of his hand, literally.

In Americana, traditional banks were a thing of the past. Chris learned that people relied on peer-to-peer lending. Another common approach involved mutual societies. These societies, akin to a hybrid of insurance companies and community banks, provided loans and support to their members, with nearly every household belonging to one.

CHAPTER 23

AT FIFTY MILES per hour, the four of them were on the slow train to Denver, working their way south. Not that anyone minded the speed; passengers sang, laughed, and played card games.

A couple of days ago, Sandra and Katie had been hyped up about backpacking with Chris and Dalton in the Great Plains. They had their hearts set on hiking through the grasslands of the Flint Hills region in Kansas.

Chris had driven through eastern Kansas once and couldn't imagine a more yawn-inducing place to hike. But the girls were so pumped, he decided to keep his mouth shut and go with the flow. He managed to keep those nagging thoughts about Ronny and the portal under wraps and stay upbeat.

It turned out that Dalton and the sisters had trekked in that region before. *To each their own,* Chris mused.

They disembarked in Denver, where they were set to catch a train that would take them to the Flint Hills region. A "fast train."

They rode two long escalators down, then boarded the train through a dimly lit wooden tube. Once inside, they settled into leather seats with deep-buttoned upholstery. Chris warily eyed the rivets crisscrossing the car, the brass pipes that lined the curved ceiling, the round portholes set evenly into the walls of veneered wood, and the etched glass partitions between compartments. "Fast, you say? How fast can this ancient thing go before it falls apart?" he wondered aloud.

"Fast," Sandra assured him.

"Faster than the one we took to Denver," Katie said, an evil glint in her eyes.

"I hope not much faster," Chris grumbled as the train let out a long, mournful wail followed by deafening bursts of steam. Gears apparently clunked, and grinding sounds rose from beneath the wooden floorboards. More deep hissing sounds, a violent shudder, and the train lurched into motion. *You've got to be shitting me!* Chris thought. Dalton couldn't help but laugh out loud at the disbelieving expression on his friend's face.

The persistent and steady pressure of acceleration continued for minutes on end. "I guess it *is* fast," Chris admitted. He suspiciously studied the groaning and creaking railcar.

Sandra pointed at the oversized, tarnished brass dial indicator clamped to the ceiling. "The train's going 400 miles per hour right now. Wait till it picks up speed."

"*What?*" Chris said, startled. Sandra looked back, a glimmer of laughter lurking in her eyes.

Moments later, passengers in the cabin cheered as the dial hit 500. As the dial inched further, they stomped their feet, causing the gas light fixtures to flicker and sway. "Six hundred!" everyone yelled happily sometime afterward. "Seven hundred . . . eight hundred . . ."

"That's impossible!" shouted Chris, trying to be heard above the din. He watched in disbelief as the needle of the speedometer crept relentlessly across the dial, the antique brass casing rattling.

Cheers erupted as the train reached 1,000 miles per hour. It kept on gaining speed. And then there was a final, prolonged cheer, two minutes later, when it hit a cruising speed of 1,800 miles per hour.

Chris shook his head. The Jules Verne-inspired riveted bucket he was in was now clocking over three times the cruising speed of a passenger aircraft. Now the little brass plaque by the cabin door made more sense: *Bracing is for milksops. Scream responsibly. If this thing go off-rail, you die legendary.*

And just below it, scratched into the metal:

Worth it—S.M. 2019.

Katie tapped Chris's shoulder. "The whole trip to Flint Hills is around twenty-five minutes," she told him.

It felt unreal. By car, the journey would have taken over seven hours. Chris turned to them. "How such a thing is even possible?" He had to raise his voice over the creaking metal and the loud voices of other passengers.

"We're traveling aboard a superconducting maglev train— magnetically suspended over the track," Dalton hollered back. "More to the point, we're two hundred forty feet underground, inside a near-vacuum tunnel. They've reduced the drag to insignificant levels."

"Oh," Chris said, as comprehension dawned.

Dalton's eyes gleamed with mirth. "The racket, the pipes, the flickering gaslights, and all that jazz are merely for fun," he said, gesturing toward Sandra and Katie. "But those two couldn't resist and wanted to tease you a little."

The girls snickered in response just as another jet of steam shot from an overhead valve with a shrill whistle.

Chris sat with a small smile playing on his lips. Here he was, traveling a mile every two seconds. He couldn't wrap his head around it. He talked some more to Dalton and learned that the tunnel was wrapped in a graphene-reinforced composite jacket to keep groundwater out and the vacuum sealed in. Every fifty kilometers or so, there were pressure-lock sidings—emergency chambers that could flood the tube with air if things went south.

"Why such incredible speed?" he asked.

"No real reason," Sandra shouted back. "It's not like it is needed, but it's a thrill! The goal was to keep roads and tracks from cutting through the Prairie Wilderness Region. But once the underground rail system was in place, they found out that it didn't take much more effort to maintain the tunnels in near vacuum. Those vactrains, as we call them, crisscross the Great Plains."

It wasn't long before the train started to decelerate. A few more minutes passed, and they reached their destination. Everyone disembarked and got on different underground shuttles that rapidly dispersed the hundreds of hikers across the land.

When the elevator brought the four of them to the top of a rustic wooden tower and they emerged onto its small circular balcony, Chris received his second shock.

"No way," he whispered, staring at the sight that greeted him.

It was the prairie—the prairie of old. Miles upon miles, extending in every direction.

The vast grassland stretched out to distant rolling hills, teeming with wildlife. Herds of bison stirred clouds of dust along the horizon. Bactrian camels browsed among sporadic blackjack oaks and Osage orange trees. Pronghorn and horses moved slowly through the bluestem, pausing now and again at glittering waterholes.

Chris turned and caught sight of wolves farther out, slipping like shadows through the tall grass. A soft breeze lifted from the sea of green below, carrying the warm, musky scent of animals and sunbaked earth.

And he felt it then: a quiet ache.

His America had lost all this. Not just the wild herds, but the cultural memory of them. The land was still there—but parceled, plowed, paved, until even the very idea of wilderness had dried up.

Here, though—

"This is . . ." Chris started, but the word caught. He tipped his head back to watch the big condors riding the thermals.

Sandra, Katie, and Dalton watched him without speaking.

"How far does it run?" he asked hoarsely.

"From Texas to North Dakota," Sandra said.

Katie gave a crooked grin. "We figured our prairie isn't much like yours."

"My prairie? There's no prairie left. It's been gone a long time."

"Ours too," Sandra said softly. "But we've been working to rewild the Plains since the 1970s, restoring them to what they were, before waves of settlers crashed the ecosystem ten thousand years ago."

Chris turned back toward the horizon—herds of bison, pronghorn, camels. The lazy prowl of wolves. The whisper of grass.

He drank it in, a long, silent pull on a world he'd thought had vanished beyond recall.

In the distance, a mass of elk stormed across a broad hillside, their deep, resonant calls rolling up to the tower. And at the base of the hill, something moved in the grass—sleek, golden, watchful.

Chris leaned forward, squinting. "Is that—?"

"Asiatic cheetah, yeah," Dalton said, nodding. "They brought them over from Iran. Ecological stand-ins for the American cheetahs we lost. Now they roam by the thousands, and the pronghorn has a predator to keep it on its toes, once more."

Chris blinked, almost laughing with disbelief. Cheetahs on the Great Plains.

Somewhere in the back of his mind, he could almost hear that old movie voice—warm, proud, just a little mad: *My dear Chris, welcome . . . to Pleistocene Park*. Next, he pictured Sandra leaning in, a glint in her eye: *We've brought back the mega-bear.*

Chris let the thought drift away as he watched a small herd of camels browsing near a stand of blackjack oaks.

"And the Bactrian camels?" he asked.

"They stand in for the camelops."

"Didn't realize we had camels in this part of the world," Chris murmured.

"Oh, yes, their bones are scattered about," Sandra said. She sighed. "Pity about the giant ground sloths, though; there are no ecological proxies for them."

Chris turned to her, struck by a sudden thought. "Don't tell me the prairie had lions and tigers back in the day too!"

She flashed him a toothy smile. "Now that you mention it. . ." She saw the look on his face and her smile broadened. "However, for safety reasons, the authorities decided against importing their surviving kin. The larger herbivores of the Great Plains must make do with being mauled by jaguars and cougars and wolves. They seldom attack humans. In fact, I'd rather encounter them than a grizzly bear."

In the small depot beneath the wooden tower, they rented a rugged trail mule. There was no need for them to haul thirty-pound packs on their backs; the contraption did the porter's duty. Before setting off, they clipped a Wild Guard to the trail mule. This motion-activated deterrent was designed to scare off curious predators with bursts of rumbling and high-pitched whistles. Unlikely to be needed, but better safe than sorry.

As they set off, the quadruped robot trudged behind them, a steady stream of despondent mechanical mutters trailing in its wake. Sandra walked back to the mule and scratched its metallic flank, just behind the main cargo mount. "There you go, big guy. You like that, don't you?" she cooed. "*Yeah,* you like that." That seemed to lift its mood enough for the muttering about existential futility to subside.

Sandra dusted her hand on her trousers and caught up with the others.

The four of them hiked between two grassy rolling hills, and meadowlarks scampered out of the way. Ornate prairie chickens with orange combs above their eyes scuttled behind shrubs, letting out sharp, indignant clucks.

About an hour into their hike, the sound of strumming and loud singing reached them. They slowed and turned.

"Who are they?" Chris asked under his breath as a lively group of eight young people emerged from behind a small hill. Accompanied by two trail mules, the youths were in high spirits. The boy at the front cradled a mandolin, strumming a lively tune as the others sang along.

Sandra's eyes followed their approach. "Wandering Birds," she said, a hint of nostalgia in her tone. "A back-to-nature young folk movement. In summer, there are probably hundreds of thousands out across the wilderness—singing, swapping stories around campfires, rowing rivers—"

"And skinny-dipping, then making out," Katie cut in. "You were going to leave out the important part."

Sandra grinned and gave her sister a playful nudge. "We were part of that movement."

"Ah," Katie sighed theatrically as the Birds passed them by. "Out from under the roof, sixteen and finally free to make my own bad decisions. It was glorious." A ripple of laughter rose from the young people, and one of them tipped his hat with a playful bow.

Sandra's gaze followed the Wandering Birds until they vanished from sight. As the four resumed their hike, their trail mule following them, Chris inquired further about their time in the movement, learning they'd acquired an impressive array of wilderness and outdoor safety skills.

Sandra's tone turned reflective. "Back in their Wandering

Birds days, our parents faced some serious challenges."

The footpath now cut through a field of Indiangrass, dotted with lavender Blazing Star flowers. Monarch butterflies floated lazily between blooms.

Dalton nodded. "Mine too. Their generation pushed hard to stop large-scale solar and wind farms from being deployed—pushing for the nuclear option."

Chris frowned. He must have heard it backward. "Are you saying they *promoted* nuclear power?"

"He did," Katie assured him.

It didn't sound right. Chris tried again. "Did they not try to promote the most environmentally benign technologies?"

"Sure," Dalton said. "That was the whole point."

The surprises of Americana just kept piling on. "I thought solar panels and wind turbines *are* the greener options."

Sandra scoffed, stepping around a patch of purple cone-flowers. "Sure, if you want a grid that works only when the weather's in the mood."

Chris opened his mouth, then closed it. *Huh.* Odd he'd never really thought about that before.

"It's a complex, vast setup," Dalton said. "But it can work, in theory."

"Oh, do tell," Sandra said brightly.

"Don't mind her," Katie said, frowning at her sister. "She had sour grapes for breakfast."

"Okay. Imagine a continent-wide power grid," Dalton explained, unfazed. "Even if the wind isn't blowing in the Midwest, it'll be blowing somewhere, feeding into the inter-connected wind farms across the country. And the backbone? Solar towers that heat up salt, which stays molten underground for long periods, providing continuous power. When needed, this molten salt is directed to heat exchangers, producing steam for turbines."

"So *there!*" Chris declared triumphantly. He eyed Dalton with suspicion. "Then why go nuclear?"

Dalton's smile widened. "Because it has a much smaller environmental impact. Powering the country with solar and wind would've meant turning hundreds of thousands of square miles of wilderness into mirror farms, panel fields, and turbine forests."

Chris winced. He hadn't considered land use.

Then he remembered. "What about the risk of a core meltdown?"

"Nope, integral fast reactors use a special metal fuel," Dalton said. "When the core temperature rises, it automatically shuts the reaction down, making a meltdown virtually impossible."

"That's . . . amazing," Chris murmured. Could it be true?

"As I understand it," Dalton continued, "the fuel expands when it overheats. This creates more space between the reactive parts, slowing down the chain reaction. Honestly, the technical details are a bit fuzzy now," he admitted with a laugh. Sandra shrugged; she couldn't remember either. Katie just rolled her eyes.

Chris frowned. "Still, reactors near cities? Let alone quake-prone ones? Seems risky."

But Sandra shook her head. "They're situated far away from urban areas."

Chris raised an eyebrow.

"High-voltage direct current cables running underground," supplied Dalton. He'd read about it. "We got a power plant in North Dakota powering San Francisco—and with as little as five percent transmission losses. That's over a thousand miles."

"You forgot the best part," Sandra interjected.

Dalton chuckled. "You're right." He turned to Chris. "Conventional water-cooled systems only utilize a tiny portion of the energy present in the fuel. Integral fast reactors unlock almost all of the uranium-plutonium alloy's stored energy, producing up to a hundred times more electricity from the same amount of material." He beamed. "We'll run the country for generations just on the nuclear waste we already have!"

Chris appeared stunned at that.

Even before he went through the portal, Chris had vaguely wondered what powered Americana. Well, now he knew. Nuclear—the glowing neon-green poster child of environmentalism? It seemed he'd have to stop worrying and learn to love the reactor.

He rubbed the back of his neck. "What happens to the spent fuel?"

"In an integral fast system, much of the fuel material is used up. In fact, some of the most problematic elements are dramatically reduced or even eliminated," Dalton said. "But I don't know any more than that."

Katie whispered in Sandra's ear. "Kate says the spent fuel pellets are encased in rods of zirconium-based alloy," said Sandra. "These rods are bundled and stored in canisters with a graphite cast-iron interior and a copper exterior."

After another brief whisper, Sandra continued, "The canisters are then transported to a deep cavern and deposited into individual holes filled with bentonite—" Her words trailed off as the four of them rounded a bend and stopped, awestruck.

In the golden light of late afternoon, a small herd of savanna elephants grazed a few dozen yards away. The humans stood in quiet awe, captivated by the tranquil scene. The matriarch paused, lifting her massive head to study them briefly before returning to her meal.

"I have a feeling we're not in Kansas anymore," Chris whispered, staring wide-eyed at the massive elephants.

"Actually," Sandra said, "this is probably the most Kansas it's been in ten thousand years."

"Where do they come from?" Chris asked. He could not take his eyes off the majestic beasts. "Surely they can't live here during the winter."

"They migrate in early summer from the tip of Texas, south of Corpus Christi. The lower humidity, tall grass, water sources, and rolling hills combined with open land draw them to this region while—"

"Let's back off, nice and easy now," Dalton said quietly.

"What's going on?" Chris asked as they started slowly retreating.

Dalton gestured with his head. "The quick ear flaps of the matriarch. I think she's getting a little antsy with our presence."

After the elephants disappeared from view once again around the bend, he added, "It's amazing how they've adapted. These are the descendants of the first elephants brought over. Each generation ventures further north during early summer— with the help of a ranger-maintained food trail."

Chris pictured a herd of elephants strolling down the main street of some Midwestern town, followed by camels and chee- tahs. "Are there still cities in the Great Plains?" he asked.

"Some," said Dalton. "Oklahoma City, Lincoln, Pierre, and Amarillo."

"Don't they have problems with bison in their backyards or jaguars in the playgrounds?"

Sandra laughed. "Not really. Most wildlife prefer to steer clear of people. And anyway, the Plains cities now have AI- managed perimeters that use things like ultrasonic alarms, motion-activated lights, and startling sounds. They've also got dense plantings of thorny or unpalatable vegetation coupled with buried fences. People and goods move in and out of the city using underground roads and rail tracks."

CHAPTER 24

As the sun sank toward the western horizon, they caught a glimpse of a peregrine falcon as it hurtled down like a missile. It struck, then seized a dove midair.

Night descended on the prairie. Katie, Sandra, Dalton, and Chris lounged beneath a solitary post oak in a moonlit clearing. Coyotes yipped and howled afar. Nearby, fields of grass swarmed with flickering dots of light from fireflies weaving through the air. This was to be their last night before returning to Boulder.

"Katie has something she wants me to share," Sandra said, the bonfire painting her face in warm, albeit erratic, light. She gazed at her sister with tenderness, stroking her cheek. Katie's eyes, wide and unblinking, were fixed on her like a child entranced by a single lit candle in a dark room.

"You know about Katie's condition." Sandra's voice barely rose above the crackling fire. "Kate was kidnapped when she was eight. Two months later, she was found by the roadside. The kidnapper was discovered dead in a nearby house, having overdosed on sleeping pills. No one knows what happened. No one's asked too many questions."

Katie appeared small, her face smooth and oddly blank. *Was she listening?* Sandra wondered. *Was she processing the words?*

"Did you know that a child in our country is a hundred times more likely to be killed by lightning than to be abducted by a stranger? But that's just how it happened." Sandra stared unseeingly at the flames. "But that year, out of all the kids in the country, it was my sister who drew the short straw."

For a moment, the wind picked up, and the scent of wild things filled the air.

Sandra grew reflective. "I remember her a bit from before. She was an introvert, serious, and smarter than anyone. When she came back, she was an extrovert, childish, and cheerful. She left as Kate, returned as Katie. As for those two months? She said she didn't retain any memories, and that was that."

The grass stirred and faintly rustled. Neither man interrupted. They just sat there, listening, the dusk softening their features.

"Katie is the dominant personality, as you've noticed. Kate comes out infrequently and, until very recently, only around our parents and me. Kate and Katie are both authentic expressions of her." She smiled tremulously at her sister, whose eyes never left hers. A single tear rolled down Katie's cheek. Then another. Sandra brushed away the tears. "Her love and kindness shine through in both manifestations," she said in a soft, tender voice.

Sandra drew in a deep, steadying breath. "However, besides Katie and Kate, there are persona fragments that break to the surface on occasion. Some of them are completely untethered and amoral."

Her eyes fixed on Dalton, then on Chris. "These are the things my sister wanted you to know." She glanced down. "But the story doesn't end there."

This was the part where it got personal for Sandra. "As kids, we shared the same bed," she said, pushing stray hair from her face. "And we did so again after she returned to us, as if the two months had never happened and nothing had changed."

Sandra could feel the heat rising in her cheeks. "She began to touch me and say in a deep voice, 'Is little Katie having fun?' You see, it was all make-believe." Sandra's gaze remained fixed on Katie, her words barely above a whisper. "It was our secret pastime."

For a moment, the only sound was the crackling of the fire.

"In time, I reckoned that her conduct might have been a result of her time in captivity. I also concluded that it had taken on a life of its own, evolving beyond what was likely to have occurred during her time away. I believe she returned bearing the seeds of depravity—perhaps no more than that, but it was enough."

Sandra willed herself to continue. "She passed it on to me," she said, looking at the two men she had come to love. Her voice was heavy with emotion. "Katie and I are warped in some ways. It doesn't take much for us to become aroused by each other, and when that happens, we have very little self-control." She took a deep breath. "And then there are other times when I have to fight off Katie's inner demons—avatars of her subconscious that threaten to take over."

There, she'd said all of it. How they reacted would determine what happened next.

The fire snapped softly in the silence that followed Sandra's words.

Chris stared at the flames, a crease between his brows. After a long moment, he exhaled and raked a hand through his hair. When he finally looked up, his eyes found Sandra's, then Katie's, his gaze holding a depth of understanding that made words seem insufficient. Then his hand found Sandra's knee. "It doesn't change how I feel," he said, voice low. "How could it, really?" He gave a faint, helpless shrug.

Katie's eyes came into focus. She peered at him and at

Dalton through her tears, her mouth trembling into a smile.

Sandra looked to Dalton. "Dalton?"

The coyotes cried out again, farther off this time. Sparks drifted upward as Dalton nudged the fire with a stick. He was quiet for a moment longer. "I'm still here, ain't I?" he finally said. His gaze drifted between them. "That was a hell of a thing to lay bare. I respect that." He looked at Katie. "You too." His voice had softened. "Takes guts."

Chris nodded once in agreement.

Sandra bowed her head. "You needed to know. And I needed to understand how you felt about it—before I could decide what I wish to do next."

She turned to Katie. "After I came back from college, I knew I wanted to spend the rest of my life with you." Katie gave a soft cry and threw her arms around her. Sandra returned the hug and eyed Dalton and Chris. "For most people, a quad marriage is an option," she said. "For us . . . it's the only one." She met their eyes. "You surely understand what I am saying. And why I am saying it."

Katie pulled back, wiping her eyes. "Sandra spoke my heart too," she said quickly, almost breathlessly.

Chris felt the weight of the moment settle in his chest. This was it. The question no longer hovered—this *was* the moment. They weren't just opening up. They were inviting him and Dalton into a committed, lasting relationship: marriage. Just not the kind he'd known.

"Even without our shared past, I think I'd still have wanted Katie as a sister-wife," Sandra told Chris and Dalton. "She's good at keeping a home, as you've noticed. I'm not so sure about her aptitude as a mother, though."

Katie gave a soft snort.

Sandra smiled. "As for me—I'm hopeless at housekeeping, but I know how to handle kids."

"I've never known of a committed union of four people," Chris told them. "I . . . Well, how does it work?"

"It takes a lot of talking and listening," Sandra said. "But I've heard it can be . . . more. More resilient, more hands, more support, more balance. You are less likely to burn out. And raising kids is easier."

"With two or three incomes, you'd have financial stability too," Dalton said. He didn't seem overly surprised or fazed by the turn the conversation had taken.

Chris asked, "What about guardianship, with children having different biological parents?"

"All four spouses are listed as parents of record," Sandra said matter-of-factly.

Chris contemplated it. "And the sleeping arrangement?"

"Well," Katie said, "most folks usually get a mattress and frame designed for four, pretty simple. Oh—you mean *intimacy*, don't you?"

"Let's move away from the hypothetical," Chris said. "I care for Dalton—but definitely not *that* way." He shared a let's-be-clear-about-this glance with Dalton.

"Same here," Dalton said. He turned to Chris. "In a quad, they call it a brother-husband. I'd like that with you. What do you say?"

"Yes," Chris said. "*Yes.*"

"I figured as much," Sandra said. "As you know, Katie and I have a physical connection. And, goodness, we're both attracted to you gentlemen. So, do you think you can handle the intimate aspects?"

"Being intimate with the two of you?" Chris attempted a frown but couldn't quite manage it. "Yeah, I think a fella could get used to that," he mused aloud. "How about you, Dalton?"

"A sacrifice I'm willing to make for the greater good," Dalton declared.

The men attempted to keep serious faces, but eventually the grins broke free.

"The Summer Ball is coming up in a few weeks," Sandra announced, her eyes bright. "Let's attend it!"

Dalton stood up. "I'm truly looking forward to it," he said solemnly, bowing with all traces of jest gone from his face.

"Chris?" Katie asked, watching him intently.

"Going out dancing? Sure, count me in," Chris said, wondering if he was missing something.

"Wonderful!" Sandra exclaimed, clapping her hands with delight. She stood up and twirled around gracefully, forming a large circle. "Ballroom, waltz, and chiffon dresses—here we come!"

Chris glanced up, startled. "Wait, what? You *waltz*?"

"Of course, and a dozen other dances too—oh no!" She looked at him with a stricken face. "Don't you dare tell me you can't waltz, Chris Walden!"

He threw his hands up in the air. "In my world, the waltz fell out of style long before my parents were born."

"Drat!" Her face fell. "Oh well, at least we can do swing and Latin dances."

Chris cleared his throat, appearing ill at ease. "Nowadays, partner dancing isn't really common in my world. I . . . never did it."

Eyes welling with tears, Sandra turned and walked away.

Katie gazed at the retreating figure of her sister. At last, she turned back to Chris, reproach gleaming in her eyes. "What did you think we meant by going out dancing?" she demanded. "Holding hands and shuffling in a circle?"

Chris mustered a feeble grin. "Where I come from, we pack the floor, jamming and moving to the beat. But really, it's mostly about drinking and hooking up."

Katie stared at him with an unreadable expression, then

rose to her feet. She didn't understand all that he'd just said, but enough of it. "Truly, Chris," she said curtly, "the more I learn about your world, the less inclined I am to know it." She paused, her gaze lingering. "I'd best go check on Sandra," she finally said, and turned to leave.

The two men found themselves alone.

"They're taking it quite hard," Chris said.

"I guess it didn't occur to us that you folks don't do partner-dancing." Dalton let out a sigh. "I must say, your America has all the allure of wilted lettuce."

"But there must be people here who aren't into it," Chris protested.

"Nearly every young person learns at least a bit. How else would one connect and interact with the opposite sex? 'Jamming and moving to the beat. . .'" Dalton laughed, shaking his head. And did Chris say "drinking"? Dalton couldn't imagine anything more off-putting than dancing with someone who was intoxicated. "Actually, I don't know of any girl who'd say yes to a guy she hadn't danced with at least once. You can't really fake who you are on the dance floor."

Dalton studied Chris for a moment. "I believe we owe you an explanation," he said. "Summer Ball has a tradition. You see, when Sandra proposed this idea, dancing wasn't the only thing on her mind."

Chris looked at him with dawning comprehension.

"I understand," Chris said quietly after a while. He got up and walked over to where the two women sat. They raised their heads as he approached them.

"If dancing won't be a part of my life, will you still be interested in me?"

"Yes," Sandra said simply.

"In the way I mean it?"

She nodded.

He turned his gaze. "Katie?"

"Yes, I would." She scrambled to her feet and hugged him.

"Very well, then," Chris said. "We'll attend the Summer Ball. By that time, I'll have learned how to dance."

Sandra sighed. "Chris, as much as I want to dance with you, I won't if you're not into it—"

"But I am," he said, and he watched their hesitation melt. Sandra's shoulders loosened with visible relief; Katie gave a shaky little laugh. Then the smiles bloomed. Chris extended his arms and helped Sandra to her feet.

"Chris says he'll learn to dance in time for the Ball," Katie announced, as the three of them walked back to the bonfire.

"I heard," Dalton said dryly. "Chris, I don't think you realize what you're saying. But perhaps ignorance in this case is bliss— which will allow you to do the improbable." He stood up and clasped Chris's arm. "I'll help you."

"Good," Chris said. "I can do improbable." He smiled thinly. "You could say I've got some experience in this department."

That night, under the canvas of their tent, they lay side by side on sleeping pads. The women nestled in the middle, flanked by the men, as they dreamed of the future. They imagined relocating to Dalton's farm, where the men would work the land together and breathe new life into the old farmhouse.

They talked, they laughed, they touched—then one by one, they drifted off, curled around shared warmth and silent dreams.

CHAPTER 25

BACK AT THE TRAIN DEPOT IN Boulder, Chris said his good-byes to Sandra, Katie, and Dalton, then started on his way to his cottage. He was walking on air.

After rounding the corner and leaving the train station behind, Chris noticed two men following at some distance. The hats, the dark suits, the stiff collars—nothing out of place. Their measured stride told a different story, though.

Muggers. But then realization hit him; these were government goons. He felt as if a cold finger was sliding down his spine. They'd come for him.

Chris thought furiously. Homeland Security had told Sandra he was off the hook, yet they must have kept watch on him. Why? How much did they know? And most importantly, what were they going to do about it?

From somewhere ahead, two more men came into view.

He could have tried to run off, but where to? As a solitary actor in a universe he'd stepped into, it was pointless.

He halted and waited, heart steady by force of will.

A large black motorcar approached and came to a slow, deliberate stop a few paces away. Three men emerged, and those on foot joined them, surrounding him.

"Mr. Walden?" one asked.

"That's me." He braced himself.

"Two senators would like to have a word with you," the man said and held the car door open. "We're here to escort you."

It was phrased as an invitation. Chris knew better.

He climbed into the automobile, followed by a number of men. The door slammed shut, and the vehicle moved off.

No one talked during the ride. The only sounds were those of the tires on the unpaved road and the faint hum of the electric motor. The silence in the car wasn't awkward—it was practiced.

They left the town proper, and soon the automobile was winding its way along a narrow road flanked by trees. A lone, large dwelling stood at the end.

The motorcar rolled to a stop in an open, paved area. Chris stepped out, eyeing the house. With its floor-to-ceiling French windows and stone bricks in earthy tones, it was the first house in Americana he'd seen that could be called a mansion.

Three men escorted him up the broad marble stairs. One of them motioned for Chris to go on, and he took the last two steps on his own and pressed the bell.

A few moments later, a man in livery opened the paneled double doors. "Good day, sir," he greeted Chris. "Please, do come in."

Chris entered, and the butler shut the doors behind. He led him through an anteroom and a library to a spacious room with a beamed ceiling. "They will be with you shortly, sir," the man said and left.

Chris sank into one of the tufted leather armchairs. Under different circumstances, he might have admired the watercolor paintings gracing the walls and the Persian rugs laid over the terracotta tile floor. Now, though, he was too tense for that.

On the ebony coffee table in front of him were a few glossy books. He glanced at one. It was a U.S. history book, alternate history from his perspective. Funny, it hadn't occurred to him before to get hold of such a book in Americana and compare the timelines. Chris was not a history buff; however, he knew enough to pick out the more obvious differences, whatever those might be. Suddenly curious, he opened the large book and was soon browsing through its pages.

"'I give each of you a choice: remain or leave,'" someone said from the door.

Chris looked up. A man and a woman stood at the threshold—middle-aged, well groomed, and elegantly dressed.

"Judging by the photograph, you're on the 1965 Secession Speech page," the man said. "'If you choose to stay,'" the dignified-looking man in pinstripe frock coat recited, "'I can offer nothing but blood, sweat, and tears, as was asked of countless groups who came before you. Yet today, I declare what no other president could utter in good conscience to our black fellow Americans: There shall be no barriers erected by man to impede your progress. From this day forward, the law shall regard all citizens as equals, blind to the circumstances of birth or the pigmentation of their skin.'"

The man entered the room, arm outstretched. "Pleased to meet you, I'm Senator Richard Moore." Chris rose to his feet and grasped the offered hand. Senator Moore gestured to his companion with a slight turn. "This is my esteemed colleague, Senator Diane Wilson." Chris nodded politely toward the striking woman in the black dress with a high neckline and tailored silhouette.

The senators made themselves comfortable in the wingback chairs. Chris took a seat across from them.

"U.S. senators?" he asked.

"Indeed. Not as important or prominent as state senators, right?" Senator Moore chuckled. "Overseeing common defense, international transactions, and the environment sounds glamorous, but day-to-day, we just manage immigration, patents, interstate infrastructure, and grids. Real governance happens at the state level."

Chris blinked. That was one of the more remarkable statements he'd heard since arriving in Americana. He didn't know how to react to it. "Grids?" he asked to buy himself some time.

"Fiber-optic, rail, power. Anything continental in scale," Moore said.

Again, Chris wasn't quite sure how to respond. He sought to steer the conversation elsewhere. "Secession, you said? There was talk of secession in 1965?" he asked.

"There was." It was Senator Diane Wilson, her intense gray eyes resting on him. "The Civil Rights Act passed in '64. From that day forward, the law mandated that all Americans, regardless of race, be treated equally in the public sphere. The era of legally sanctioned preferential treatment, special entitlement, and discrimination came to an end."

She crossed her legs, the motion clean, exact—no wasted gesture—and leaned slightly to one side. "Two weeks after the passage of the Act, some African Americans rioted in Harlem," she said evenly. "Then Rochester. Jersey City. Chicago. Philadelphia—one city after another. The pattern repeated the following year—looting, arson, violence, all claiming justice as their cause."

The man in livery came in, wheeling a cart with fruit and cheese platters along with an assortment of canapés. The faint aroma of coffee trailed from a steaming pot.

Senator Wilson continued, "In the years leading up to 1964, many white Americans did not want African Americans in their schools or neighborhoods. The burning and looting by some members of the black community turned mild contempt into dislike, and goodwill into distaste. Lincoln's legacy—the 'Great Missed Opportunity,' as some called it—was again evoked and cursed: If Lincoln had let the South secede, the United States would have no black people to speak of. Simultaneously, black ethno-nationalist fringe voices advocated for separation." She accepted the coffee with a nod. "Something needed to be done, and promptly, if the nation was to seize the opportunity to move beyond the divisive racial outlooks of both sides."

Helping himself to some bacon-wrapped spinach canapés, Senator Moore said, "This brings us to the page you were looking at. Following the 1964–65 riots, the president delivered a historic speech directed toward African Americans. It has since become known as The 1965 Secession Speech."

In spite of himself, Chris was captivated by the account. "What did it say?"

"It said that no one can do it for them," Senator Wilson said bluntly. "No group has ever risen through the efforts of another." She took a sip of coffee. "The president urged black Americans to follow the path of Jewish Holocaust survivors and Japanese Americans who, despite generations of exclusion, quotas, and land laws designed to keep them out, built thriving communities."

She set her cup down with care. "Of white Americans, he demanded the dismantling of the informal discrimination that permeated daily life and the labor market. Not through forced association, but through recognition of a common humanity and shared nationality. He asked the whites to stop treating the black citizen either as a threat or as a pet."

She leaned back slightly, gaze steady. "The president acknowledged a historical wrong: The African Americans were brought here in chains, enslaved for generations, and later treated as a permanent underclass," she said. "In recognition of this singular injustice, the government also offered them a different choice: vast, thinly populated tracts in Nebraska, Kansas, and Oklahoma where they could establish a country of their own. They would be provided with equipment, technical training, and substantial funds to ensure their fledgling state had every opportunity to flourish."

She lifted her eyes from the glossy book on the table. "It was a one-time offer, Mr. Walden, giving African Americans the chance to chart their own path. But it required at least a million black Americans to opt in. After all the debate, uproar, and town square speeches, only forty-five thousand chose to leave—less than one percent."

"Had they voted for a country of their own in sufficient numbers," Chris asked, "what was to befall the whites who didn't want to relocate?"

"They and their offspring had twenty-five years to change their minds. In any case, they would have been citizens in the new country, with all rights intact." She continued, "The choice had a transformative, sobering effect. Given the means to leave, they stayed. They cast their lot with their fellow Americans. The rest, as they say, is history," Senator Wilson finished, her eyes once again resting on Chris.

"What happened in the decades that followed?" he asked.

Senator Wilson replied, "Those who were adults during the era of segregation and held steadfastly to racist views are mostly gone now, and with them, much of that particular ugliness. Today, we no longer identify as hyphenated Americans. I haven't heard terms like African-American or Asian-American in decades. We are, at last, simply Americans. Those who grew up in the eighties and later can hardly comprehend the ethnic-racial caste society of the past."

She closed the glossy book with a thud and gazed at Chris. "Is that how it unfolded in your . . . version of America, Mr. Walden?"

Chris felt the blood drain from his face. They knew about his origin. Somehow, they had discovered he was from America in a parallel universe.

But did they also know that it was possible to travel back and forth between the two worlds? The only other person who knew about that was Ronny, a universe away. No one in this world knew. He had made sure of that. He had lied to the people dearest to him to make sure of that.

"So you're aware I am from another world," he said in a low voice.

"We are," Senator Moore said.

Chris glanced down and busied himself with the food. "My former government never offered African Americans a portion of our country," he said. "However, in the end, I think our societies . . ." He paused, lost in thought. "Well, it's complicated," he finally said.

Chris stared at the slender vase placed in a wall niche, then turned back to them. "Was it my attempt to unlock the personal transporter rack that tipped you off?"

"Not exactly," replied Senator Moore. "Two facilities, one in Louisiana and another in Washington, detected unusual gravitational waves. By triangulating the source, we pinpointed it to a location right outside of Boulder. Initially, we didn't think much of the drifter who was spotted in the area. Nevertheless, we assigned a local asset, Miss Allen, to look into it. She was right in assuming that we initially believed your presence there was merely coincidental."

A sinking feeling hit Chris. They *knew*. They knew of his comings and goings. And now he understood how.

Senator Moore continued in a measured tone, "Days later, we detected those gravitational waves again. This time, we had a spy satellite trained on the area and could make out a human figure seemingly vanishing into thin air. We dispatched a surveillance drone that managed to capture a higher-resolution view of another person entering and exiting the area. A few minutes later, the first person, namely you, emerged. Shortly thereafter, the gravitational waves ceased."

Chris shut his eyes, reeling. They were aware of everything. For a long time.

And he'd thought he'd been so clever . . . It'd never crossed his mind, nor Ronny's, that there might be detectable emanations from the portal once it was activated, emanations that could be monitored by the government of Americana.

Then something occurred to him, and he looked up, tense. "Have you been following me?"

"'Round the clock, and we've bugged everything we could," Senator Wilson stated.

Round the clock, they said. *That meant*—He flushed. "It appears the government here doesn't hold the right to privacy in high regard," he said.

"Mr. Walden, you can't possibly be serious," Senator Moore said, his voice just shy of scandalized.

His colleague leaned in, her expression somber. "What's at stake is the most significant matter of our lifetime and beyond. If the Senate mishandles the interaction with the other America, the consequences could prove disastrous for our entire nation. In light of this, your privacy is of little concern. And to be frank, we would be willing to expend your life as well if deemed necessary."

Chris's expression grew hard. Still, he gave them a grudging nod. "I understand."

"Ah, yes, indeed," Senator Moore murmured. "You understand sacrifice, being a former soldier."

Chris emptied his cup and set it down, his expression grave. "I made the choice to take risks in the service of my country. This is different."

"In what way?" inquired Senator Moore.

"I am not conversing with you by choice."

"That's true," the senator agreed. "But then again, it's not as though you sought our consent before deciding to enter our world and open up this can of worms."

Chris had to admit they had a point.

Senator Wilson glanced sideways, a pensive look crossing her face. "I think the last time we surveilled a private citizen was during the bioterror scare. That would've been . . . what, ten years ago?"

"Oh, yes. I remember," Senator Moore murmured.

Senator Wilson directed her gaze at Chris again. "At any rate, after our operatives intercepted and listened to the heated exchange between you and Miss Allen at the lake, Homeland Security determined the recording was sufficient evidence. That's when the department brought the matter to the Senate's attention."

Chris shifted uncomfortably in his chair. "Who else is aware of the situation?"

Senator Wilson raised her hand. "Hold on, Mr. Walden. First, we must ascertain one crucial detail—this takes precedence over everything else. You told the Allens that the gate was destroyed. Am I correct in assuming that wasn't the case?"

"You are," Chris said. "The gate is operational and allows back-and-forth movement."

She thought that his answer to her next question might very well determine the course of history. "Who else knows about it, Mr. Walden?"

"A friend of mine. He's the one who initially discovered the portal. It's just the two of us."

Senator Wilson exhaled slowly. "That's the other individual we saw come out that night?" she inquired.

"Correct."

She studied him intently. "You were not sent here by anyone?"

"No, ma'am."

"You are not acting on behalf of any government?" she pressed.

"No," he said, his tone of voice leaving little doubt about what he thought of that idea.

Senator Moore nodded to himself.

"Before you entertain any ideas," Chris said quickly, "understand that if I don't come back, my partner will simply reach out and bring other people on board."

Senator Wilson sighed. "I reckon that he would."

Chris leaned forward, his voice earnest. "You've seen enough to know my intentions have changed. Whatever they were before—my heart's here now."

"We believe you," Senator Wilson stated simply. "Otherwise, we would have acted sooner—and differently."

For a moment they were all silent.

Senator Moore's expression turned contemplative. "If it were up to you, Mr. Walden, what would be your intentions regarding the gateway between the two worlds?"

Chris paused, choosing his words carefully. "I'm in a situation no one's faced before," he said. "I'll do my best to make sure neither side exploits or harms the other. I can't say I trust the local government any more than I trust the one on the other side of the portal."

"I suppose it's understandable—given your personal experience," Senator Wilson said.

Chris's expression clouded at that.

He addressed Senator Moore. "Who knows about the gateway?"

"The Homeland Security unit handling the matter, the president, and the thirty-five members of the U.S. Senate—who are in charge of making the decision about its fate."

Chris pondered the situation. "And have you reached a decision, at least regarding me?"

Senator Moore scrutinized him. "We believe that you wish to make your home here, in our world. That you would rather forget about the portal—and the world you left behind." He leaned back in his armchair. "Am I correct?"

Chris nodded silently, staring at the wall.

He turned to the senators and cast a sharp glance at them. "I repeat, what have you decided?"

Senator Moore met his gaze. "We've decided that it's time to introduce ourselves and make our presence known to you."

"That's not what I meant."

"I'm aware of that."

"So, what happens now?" Chris asked.

"Now we talk," said Senator Wilson. "You learn more about the world you've stumbled upon, and we learn something about yours. After that, a clear path forward may emerge."

Chris regarded each of them in turn. At long last he nodded—

—and launched into a conversation that might decide the fate of two worlds.

CHAPTER 26

"WHAT IS YOUR IMPRESSION OF OUR COUNTRY?" SENATOR Wilson asked.

"Insular and inward-looking," Chris replied and smiled faintly. "I can't decide if its appeal is in spite of that or because of it." He glanced at her curiously. "What are your immigration numbers?"

"We admit around one hundred thousand immigrants each year," Senator Wilson said. "They consist of immediate family members and of those with extraordinary merit and a strong commitment to our country."

"Rather low numbers," Chris commented.

Low for what? Senator Moore wondered. "We have a population of 100 million people, and most want to keep it that way," he said. "Factoring in immigrants and their offspring, our population numbers have been holding steady for the past couple of generations."

Senator Moore leaned back and clasped his hands over his vest. "Incidentally, considering the public's general lack of knowledge about foreign nations, your cover story about Iraq appeared quite convincing. You made a slip, though."

"How so?" Chris kept his expression neutral.

"We have no civil aviation, either within or to the United States. It was phased out years ago."

Chris recalled the reaction of Kate to the statement he'd made about flying into the States. "This possibility had never crossed my mind," he admitted and propped his ankle across his knee. "Now, why would you phase out air transport?"

"I take it that on the other side of the portal, civil aviation is alive and well." Chris nodded. "Aviation is a resource guzzler, a greenhouse gas factory, and an ozone generator in all the wrong places. And no workaround. We walked away."

"So what do folks use instead? Trains?" Chris asked.

Moore snapped his fingers and pointed at Chris. "Right on the nose. We've constructed 15,000 miles of high-speed rail with maglev trains running at 230 to 250 miles an hour. We saw it as an opportunity to offer a better experience than being confined for hours in an automobile or airplane."

"What about travel time, though?" Chris asked. "As swift as these high-speed trains are, they're slower than passenger aircrafts."

"Not necessarily," the senator replied. "With a train, it takes only five minutes to load and go. With an airplane, you have to account for lengthy boarding times, airport security, inevitable delays, disembarking, and luggage pickup. A train ride may or may not take longer. Anyway, what's the great hurry, son?"

Chris didn't understand them. They had the technology and means to run trains at much higher speeds—much higher than planes, in fact—if they were to extend the network of near-vacuum tunnels beyond the Great Plains Wilderness Region.

"Mass transit speed is a finely balanced affair," Senator Wilson explained, as if sensing his thoughts. "We aimed to make the cross-country train ride fast enough to give it a leg up over driving, yet not so fast that it would drastically increase the number of travelers." She helped herself to some tomato bruschetta. "Had a commute from Dallas to New York taken only twenty-five minutes, it could have changed everything.

Tens of millions flooding Manhattan on a whim? Florida's beaches mobbed every weekend? Infrastructure, energy, communities—imagine the strain."

Chris leaned back, momentarily quiet. These weren't stuffed shirts playing politics. They had a damn train system with principles.

"That's all well and good," he said. "But without civil aviation, how do people travel overseas?"

"The old-fashioned way: ocean liners," replied Senator Moore. "It's a five-day journey from New York to the British Isles. Seven days from Los Angeles to Tokyo."

Chris contemplated this. "What exactly is accomplished by replacing polluting airplanes with polluting ocean liners, with their nasty, sulfur-laden bunker fuel?"

"Heavens, no!" Senator Wilson said, taken aback. "Large marine vessels are powered by nuclear reactors."

"It began in 1962 with the NS Savannah merchant ship," Senator Moore said. He looked at Chris curiously. "Doesn't your America have nuclear-powered ships?"

"Of course it does," Chris responded. He cleared his throat. "You'll find reactors powering some of our military vessels." Feeling oddly embarrassed by the reality in his home world, he sought to change the subject. "I've noticed that unlike most other vehicles, your semi-trucks are not autonomous."

"Well, yes. What would all those laid-off truckers do?" Senator Moore asked.

Chris fixed him with a quizzical look.

"This reflects a larger problem," the senator said. "Truckers aside, millions simply may not be wired for jobs beyond janitorial or packing work. People with limited intellect have always been with us. Back in the day, it wasn't a concern— berry picking or running down an antelope didn't require much intellectual aptitude."

Senator Moore continued, "Hard work is essential, and equal opportunity is fundamental. Nonetheless, it's corrosive and disingenuous to suggest that perseverance and work ethic alone can unlock numerous doors for someone born with a gene package that makes him dim. Mr. Walden, we are committed to maintaining an economy that lets everyone live with dignity and purpose. That's something we *all* need."

He noted the faint surprise on Mr. Walden's face at his words. The young man's reaction spoke volumes about the dynamics of the world he'd come from.

Senator Wilson asked, "Mr. Walden, have you encountered any technologies here that could benefit your native world?"

Chris nodded. "Indoor farming of saltwater fish and integral fast reactor technology could have transformative effects," he replied, reaching for a bunch of grapes. "Still, I'm not sure if we didn't develop these because we didn't know how—or because of economic and regulatory hurdles."

The senators pondered Chris's words. Any one individual has only limited knowledge about his home world, yet they couldn't dismiss the gut feeling of someone who had developed an intuitive grasp of the dynamics and sensibilities of the world he'd grown up in.

Chris continued, "Take your vactrain, for example. We don't have anything like it in my world, but I believe we have the technology to build it. As I see it, there are two problems. First, we go with whatever's quickest and cheapest. Always have. Second thing is the bureaucracy—permits, hearings, lawsuits. Big projects just can't happen." *Not to mention the aviation and auto lobbies,* he thought to himself. *They'd flood lawmakers with donations and tie up the regulators in court for years.*

The two senators exchanged glances. It was one of the more significant statements the young man had made.

Chris asked, "How long did it take to construct the

underground infrastructure?"

"It was a National Pride Project that took twenty years. We tied it to the restoration of the Great Plains," Senator Wilson replied.

Chris smiled ruefully. That was the time frame it took merely to plan and approve construction of the conventional high-speed rail link from Los Angeles to San Francisco in his America. He helped himself to some crackers and cheese, then eyed the senators archly. "You must have needed a lot of concrete to reinforce those tunnels."

"I reckon that's so." Senator Wilson looked at him curiously, wondering where he was going with it.

"Carbon dioxide emissions must have been through the roof," Chris said, now openly amused.

The senator shrugged. "At the end of each year, we evaluate the volume of greenhouse gases we've emitted, and in the following year, we draw down a CO_2-equivalent amount to offset their climate impact."

Chris peered at her suspiciously.

"This is how we achieve the equivalent of zero emissions," she said.

"They call it direct air capture," Senator Moore said, cutting in. He'd served on the oversight committee. "We designed flat absorbing panels—think giant furnace filters—blanketing a few thousand acres. They pull about 200 million tons of CO_2 from the air each year."

"That's not too bad," Chris admitted. It was about the size of a small town.

"It's really not," Senator Moore agreed. "However, it takes 60 billion kilowatt-hours of energy. We had to build 10 nuclear power plants to run those blasted capture devices. Once we've got the gas, it's pumped deep underground under extreme pressure, where it stays trapped."

"What about other countries?"

Senator Wilson leaned back, a thin smile playing at her lips. "Wouldn't be much of anything if it were just us, would it? It's treaty-bound. Some countries entered willingly. Others needed . . . convincing. But one way or another, the world nets zero."

"It seems you're taking the prospect of human-caused climate change seriously."

Senator Moore shrugged. "Some of us are, some aren't. But with a relatively small investment—less than an individual's weekly salary per household, spread over four years—it was very affordable. So we just did it."

"You mentioned National Pride Projects . . ."

"I trust the name speaks for itself," Senator Moore said.

"Fair enough. If I may ask, what's the current National Project?"

"Every city is creating a monumental structure or artifact planned to stand tall and proud for a thousand years."

Chris wanted to know, "How do you fund these ambitious undertakings?"

"Taxes. What else?"

Upon further inquiry, it became apparent that they had no national debt—or even the means to generate one. Whatever taxes they collected were what they had to work with. If needed, they set aside funds for future large expenditures. "Over time, our military has shifted its priorities," Senator Moore told Chris. "The Army Corps of Engineers was greatly expanded and became more civic oriented. It is the agency primarily responsible for implementing the National Projects."

"I gather you're not overly concerned about tanks rolling in from Mexico or an air raid by the Canadians."

The three shared a smile.

"Our last major military campaign was World War II,"

Senator Moore said. "Since then, we've deployed troops as part of international efforts to halt mass atrocities in East Timor, Rwanda, Bangladesh, and Cambodia—I presume much as you did. That's been the extent of it. Today, we maintain permanent bases at only two locations beyond U.S. soil: the Panama Canal and northwest Greenland. Occasionally, we patrol other key global shipping chokepoints."

"That's something I meant to ask you," Senator Wilson said. "We couldn't help but notice that you were stationed in . . . Iraq."

"I was," Chris said a bit guardedly.

The two senators fell silent.

"What on earth?" Senator Wilson said at last. "Surely Iraqi forces didn't—" It sounded too preposterous to even say it. "What were your forces doing in some Middle Eastern country?"

"Good question," Chris sighed. He'd pondered it those past few years. "First, you must understand that our involvement in Iraq isn't an isolated incident. Inwardly, we're a country with porous borders, morphing into something resembling an economic zone with a flag. Outwardly, we're a loose imperial force with satellite states, a global surveillance dragnet, and hundreds of military bases stationed across the globe—grouped into geographic combatant commands, from U.S. Africa Command to U.S. Indo-Pacific Command, dividing the planet into areas of responsibility." He paused. "Unlike your citizen army—professionally led, drawn from every family, bound by duty—we maintain a standing military, divorced from the general population, insulated from the rhythms of ordinary life."

He met the senators' stunned expressions with a shrug. "As for Iraq—well, for one, over two million Americans work for the defense industry, which, as the name suggests, is defending its shareholders' interests and the jobs of those it employs—all of whom rely on a steady diet of munitions and weapon purchases. They call it the military-industrial complex."

"Oh my," whispered Senator Wilson.

"You went home after World War II," Chris said softly. "We never did."

A brief, heavy silence fell over the room.

"What's the Zero-Yield Pact?" Chris asked suddenly.

Senator Wilson raised an eyebrow.

He motioned toward the coffee table. "It was one of the headlines in that history book."

"We were the founding signatory, back in the early fifties," explained Senator Wilson. "No nuclear weapons—not here, not anywhere."

Senator Moore nodded. "The pact outlawed the damn things, and we've enforced it ever since," he said. "Any fuel-cycle site that shows even a whiff of enrichment beyond civilian grade—it goes dark permanently in the days that follow. When it comes to such matters, we don't do warnings."

"How?" asked Chris. "I mean, how can you tell?"

"Every nuclear plant is equipped with passive radiation monitors, sealed antineutrino detectors, and—well, bottom line, we'll detect that," Senator Wilson said.

She leaned back. "Same goes for gain-of-function labs. We don't issue a warning," she said. "We issue coordinates to the bomber crew."

They asked him about those things in his native world.

So he told them.

"What do your people import?" Senator Moore asked a bit later.

Chris hesitated. "I can only speak to what's common knowledge. Most of our goods are made abroad—where labor is cheap."

"Interesting," Moore murmured.

Chris tilted his head. "What about here?"

Senator Moore said, "We're blessed with the capability to

produce most everything we desire within our borders. And as a country, we make it a point to do so."

"There are exceptions," Senator Wilson said, lifting a finger. "Certain minerals we simply don't have—manganese, niobium, natural flake graphite, and a handful of others. Also rubber, vanilla beans, and a few other tropical necessities. And art, of course—films, translated books. Culture flows where it will."

"And export?" asked Chris.

"Anything and everything, with two exceptions: no arms sales to anyone—"

Senator Moore caught Chris's expression. "We do license defensive systems—shields, not swords, you might say. That's how we retain alliances."

"—and no advanced tech to authoritarian states."

"We'll be damned if we're going to shore up those countries," muttered Senator Moore. "Let their despotism and backwardness be their eventual undoing."

For a long minute the three of them were quiet.

"How are your elections conducted?" Senator Wilson asked.

Chris proceeded to describe the election campaign, from ballot harvesting to precision-targeted messaging and curated outrage. The two senators seemed taken aback by it. He pressed them and learned that in Americana, audition committees traveled around the country, conducting interviews in major cities. The finalists were then grilled by sitting senators, renowned intellectuals, and people from all walks of life. "It's quite a spectacle, and the public loves it," Senator Moore told him. "It's part town hall meeting, part hearing. The nominees must address complex issues and tackle simulations in real time. If a person survives the process, they become an official candidate, and the public casts its vote, making the final selection."

The senator then went on to explain that candidates post their bios, platforms, policy views, and a long-form interview.

These were all standardized, and candidates couldn't advertise or post elsewhere. He then shared the true cost of being elected: Officials and their immediate families were barred for life from any industries they regulated. From what Chris gathered, this was one of many measures that made lobbying—the right to petition, really—unrecognizably different from that in America.

Chris also confirmed what he'd suspected all along: Decisions in Americana were made at the lowest possible level of authority. Municipal governments only handled tasks that were impractical for neighborhood villages, county governments stepped in when tasks exceeded municipal lines, and so on, all the way up to the federal government.

Chris looked down at his hands. "Your election process is better. It really is."

"And yet?" Senator Wilson prompted.

"And yet. . . I don't know how much difference it ultimately makes," Chris said, shifting uneasily. "Where I come from, elected officials have little real power. They mostly grandstand, dole out funds, and pass legislation favoring their donors and special interest groups."

He exhaled. "The actual power resides with the agencies. A vast managerial regime—unelected, insulated, and self-perpetuating. In turn, these agencies are under the sway of immense entities, both from the private and public sectors, bending to their will on certain matters, even while functioning independently on others."

That was a kick in the head. Senator Moore poured himself a glass of wine to hide the turmoil he felt. He glanced up at his associate. Wilson's expression was also troubled.

"You know an awful lot for someone without advanced formal education," he said.

"Not really—anyone can read up on things."

The senators inquired about what his homeland could offer Americana. Chris spent the next half-hour, to the best of his abilities, describing and answering questions about social media, streaming services, smartphones, gene editing, and 3D printing. The senators were captivated by large-scale desalination plants, a concept seemingly unfamiliar to them despite their understanding of basic desalination principles.

When he was finally finished, a brief silence fell over the room. The senators exchanged glances and then gazed at Chris. Outwardly, nothing had changed, yet he sensed the conversation was drawing to a close.

"When all is said and done," Chris said, a trace of urgency in his voice, "do you think there's more to gain or lose by allowing people, commerce, and ideas to flow freely between the two Americas?"

"That's the trillion-dollar question, isn't it?" Senator Moore said softly.

For a moment, no one spoke.

Then the senators rose, and Chris hurriedly followed suit.

"You've given us much to think about," Senator Moore said, shaking Chris's hand. Senator Wilson nodded in agreement, her expression as unreadable as Moore's.

CHAPTER 27

THAT VERY NIGHT, he made his way to the gate.

Chris resolved he would proceed as he'd originally planned. And if the government of Americana intended to stop him, there was little he could do about it. But after his meeting with the senators, he didn't think it would.

Indeed, no one tried to prevent him from reaching the hill on which the portal was located.

By the time he arrived at the site, the gate had already been activated. He stepped through—and there was Ronny, waiting with a wide grin.

This time, Chris had an overriding objective. And he wasn't leaving until he'd managed to buy Ronny off.

When they reached the main level of the house, Chris turned, his face drawn and tense. "Ronny, I need you to listen to me."

"Sure," Ronny said, losing his smile.

Chris studied his friend's face and nodded. "All right then," he said, gesturing to the nearby seats. They both sat down, settling into the leather armchairs.

"What's it about?" Ronny asked, his voice now tinged with unease.

"A total makeover of healthcare in our world," Chris replied firmly.

Ronny waited for him to say more.

"Americana spends a tenth of what we do on healthcare." He clapped his hands sharply. "Right there—that's probably the biggest money-saver we could offer America. This ain't some pipe dream; it's a real, working system."

The truth was even more staggering: Americana's healthcare costs were closer to one-hundredth of those in America. But Chris now understood why that level of savings wouldn't be possible in his native world. He'd done some reading and a lot of thinking.

Chris had traced the rot to its root. Big Ag was feeding the country. But it was also slow-poisoning it for profit: ultra-processed junk food, sugar-laced everything, and chemical-doused crops. And who was there to manage the aftermath? The healthcare cartel—peddling costly pills to treat symptoms. It was a perfect, profitable storm, driving healthcare costs into the stratosphere. And adding insult to injury, the air was thick with particulates, the water tainted with heavy metals, and the world bathed in microwaves pulsing from every glowing screen—each taking a little more flesh off the bone.

Emulating Americana's system could lower costs by an order of magnitude. But to go further? It would take a transformation in lifestyle.

Ronny leaned in; what Chris had said clearly hit home. "So what makes their system work?"

Chris said immediately, "Start with the obvious—they've got no insurance companies skimming twenty cents off every healthcare dollar." He let that hang in the air.

"And that's just the direct cost. Think about it: Past the deductible, it's not your money anymore—it's the insurance company's. So the patient stops caring what it costs. The doctor shrugs and moves on; they're getting paid either way. And the insurers?" He gave a wry smile. "They benefit from high prices;

it makes them indispensable. They never pay sticker, of course. That's reserved for the poor bastards flying solo."

Ronny nodded. He could see that.

Chris wasn't done. "And once insurance *does* cover something, they strangle it with 'efficiency metrics.' Take dietitians. Used to be one-on-one care tailored to you. Now?" He shook his head. "It's conveyor-belt appointments. Brief time slots, check the boxes, in, out, next."

He continued, "In Americana, everyone diverts a fraction of their paycheck to a personal health fund, earmarked for your care. If your balance ever drops really low, say after a major surgery, you get bumped into a community risk pool. Catastrophic illnesses are automatically funded by a micro-levy on all health fund deposits. No one gets wiped out. And life-saving care's a given—just like here."

"What about malpractice?"

"Still happens," Chris said. "However, the frivolous crap, the shotgun lawsuits hoping for a nuisance settlement can land one in real trouble. Legitimate cases go to health courts with capped damages and quick payouts. Plus, docs who follow national guidelines are shielded—"

Chris stopped mid-sentence at the sound of approaching footsteps. He turned, eyes widening at the sight of a burly man carrying a gun in a shoulder holster. The man nodded at Chris, crossed the living room, and vanished into the small guest bathroom.

A shadow of alarm touched Chris's face. "What the—"

"There are four more outside," Ronny said in a rush. "We have around-the-clock security now, making sure no unauthorized person enters the house or goes down to the portal."

The air suddenly grew heavier.

Chris looked at him through narrowed eyes. "What are you talking about?"

"I meant to tell you," Ronny said, a trace of chagrin in his voice. "I just wanted to wait for the guys to come back. I called them as soon as I saw you walking toward the gate. They'll be here shortly."

Chris's pulse hammered in his ears. Ronny had reached out to some people, no doubt establishing his bona fides by using the artifacts Chris had brought over from Americana.

It was over.

His entire plan to persuade Ronny, to talk him into shutting the gate, was now moot. It was too late for that. At this point, it didn't matter anymore what he said to Ronny. It didn't matter anymore if he talked Ronny out of anything. Now that other interested parties had been brought in, they'd passed the point of no return.

Chris raised an eyebrow, looking bewildered. Inside, though, he churned with betrayal, fear, and fury. "We agreed that you'd wait until I came back to make my case," he said, his voice taking on a dangerous softness.

Ronny waved a pudgy hand. "Let's be real here. Your idea, what was it going to be, a few videos? Some tutorials?" He smirked, but his smile faded under the thundercloud in Chris's eyes. "Look, I can see you're upset. I'm sorry, okay? I should have waited for you to come back before reaching out."

Chris stared at Ronny without blinking. "What's the plan, then?"

"We have pros who'll cross over and survey Americana and then we'll approach, like I said before, some key corporations with an offer for franchising opportunities," Ronny said quickly. "We're just waiting for more security to arrive in four days, and guards will be stationed downstairs at the portal as well."

Chris grunted noncommittally.

"I suppose you did the right thing," Chris said, forcing as much authenticity into his voice as he could.

Chris and Ronny would be rewarded if they played ball, at least in the short term. But Chris had no illusions about the futility of deactivating the gate; the two of them would simply be bumped out of the way and others would take over. You don't convince people you've stumbled on a portal to another universe underneath your house—and then tell them you decided the world is not ready for it and shut it down.

Ronny slowly regained his usual self-assurance, and a smile crept back onto his face. He seemed eager to move past the confrontation. "Don't get me wrong, buddy. What you've learned about their healthcare is useful. Keep going, man. Do tell."

Chris decided to go with the flow. He needed time to think.

"Over there," he said, "once people started spending their own dime, most became fans of no-bloat care—same way most folks around here fly budget airlines or get fast food. When it's your wallet being gutted, it becomes all about keep the doctor, lose the circus. No more billing departments the size of the Pentagon. No more six-figure administrators."

Chris repeated the words he'd practiced in his head so many times. But he wanted to stop. *What was the point?* The call had been made; the guards were here. Yet, after his big buildup, he had to keep talking lest Ronny smell a rat. As he spoke, a desperate possibility began to form in his mind, one that depended on Ronny not suspecting a thing.

He continued, "One offshoot is that clinics and hospitals have a clear price menu of their services, with flat fees and all-inclusive packages—surgery, anesthesia, the whole nine yards, including post-op fixes. And here's the kicker: Right next to the price, you'll also see complication rates, readmission percentages, and patient pain scores. Sunlight, Ronny. Nothing makes people behave like knowing everyone is watching."

Ronny looked engrossed.

"Docs and nurses take cost seriously over there. Every scan, every procedure—they factor in what it's going to mean to your wallet before they order it. And MRI scanners are humming 24/7, like Vegas slot machines, spreading their costs across a lot of patients."

Ronny settled back, absorbing it. "What else?"

"Oh, they've got one national medical records system. One. Not a dozen competing formats that don't talk to each other. That alone saves billions." He propped one ankle up. "And get this: They've turned recovery wards into family cookouts. Granny gets home-cooked soup, and relatives play post-recovery nurses. It's 'bring your own care' meets potluck. Cheap, effective, and it's got heart."

"What about actual medical procedures?" Ronny wanted to know.

Chris's eyes glinted with dark amusement, momentarily eclipsing the anxiety he'd felt. "Routine procedures—hernias, fertility treatments, hip surgeries—are streamlined like a Formula 1 pit stop. I visited a dedicated cataract surgery center," he said, the memory vivid. "One surgeon, two stations. He finishes with one patient, swivels to the next. Two crack teams of nurses are prepping the patients. Six surgeries per hour—and no corners cut. It's not rushed—it's optimized."

Ronny regarded him, clearly impressed. If only it had mattered, mused Chris. But what if it could? What if Ronny took on his idea and ran with it? A spark ignited in the back of his mind, a tiny flicker of possibility.

"Everything's choreographed," Chris continued, now reenergized. "One surgery ends, dirty tools out, sterile set rolls in. Senior surgeons only handle tasks that can't be done by less-skilled crew. Take a standard heart bypass: a junior surgeon opens the chest, harvests the necessary vein graft, then moves to the next patient. The senior surgeon steps in for the critical, high-skill parts—the actual bypass grafting—then moves to the next patient while the junior closes.

"Same deal with medical devices," Chris said, his voice louder than necessary, some of his anger slipping through. "Here, device manufacturers shroud their dealings in secrecy, binding doctors and hospitals with nondisclosure agreements. A whole cottage industry of middlemen—consultants, billing firms, brokers—all profiting obscenely from medical devices, jacking the prices up. But in Americana? Let's just say you won't find CT scanners costing as much as a beachfront villa in Mexico or pharmaceutical companies playing Monopoly with drug patents like they're trading Park Place and Boardwalk."

He could see a car approaching the house through the window. Chris had little time before the people arrived. He had to move fast.

He reached into his bag, pulling out a tablet. "Everything's here: their preventive care model, cost structures, streamlined surgeries. It's a blueprint."

Ronny was silent for a moment, clearly considering the implications. "Okay, so let's say this works—what's the play? How do we use this?"

Chris leaned forward, his voice dropping slightly. "We put together a comprehensive plan—show the potential investors how they could implement this model around here. They run a pilot program, maybe in a state with flexible healthcare laws. The key is to make this real, something that people can latch onto."

The car pulled up next to the house, and a short time later, three women and two men in their thirties walked in. Ronny made the introductions.

After a few minutes of small talk, Chris didn't trust himself any longer to keep up appearances. He got to his feet. "I'll crash at my old place tonight and head back to Americana tomorrow night," he announced. "I need a break from the boondocks." He shrugged at their questioning looks. "Try going a few weeks without kicking back, catching a game on TV, or scrolling the Internet. I'll be back down here tomorrow, same time. Then I'll cross over, bring you guys some local clothes the night after, and get this show on the road."

Plastering a smile on his face, Chris returned Ronny's high-five.

"Hey, Chris?" Ronny called once Chris was at the door.

He turned.

"In case I forget to say it tomorrow, happy birthday, man."

He'd completely forgotten. "Thanks," he said, and opened the door.

Chris had a lot to do and little time for it.

CHAPTER 28

SENATOR MOORE HIMSELF OPENED the paneled front doors at the top of the marble staircase. Behind him, the rising sun cast long shadows across the mansion grounds and lit the distant mountains. He had clearly been alerted to Chris's approach.

Across the threshold, the two men regarded each other.

"I ask you to convene your Congress," Chris said.

"That's quite the statement."

"In person," Chris added.

The senator was silent for a few heartbeats. "Very well. It will take a couple of days—"

"In a few hours' time. As soon as we land in Washington."

Senator Moore's eyes widened. He opened his mouth but then closed it.

"I'll make some calls," he finally said.

⇒⇐

Twenty minutes later, a military helicopter landed in front of the house. Senator Moore and Chris took a brief flight to an airstrip on the other end of town, where they transferred to a sleek, large-cabin Gulfstream-like jet. After a few hours, they arrived in Washington, D.C. Another short helicopter ride, and Chris walked across the manicured lawns of the Capitol grounds. Moments later, he stepped into the august Senate chamber.

Senators, seated at their wooden desks, fell silent, all eyes fixated on Chris as he made his way to the center of the hall. Chris surveyed the room. From what he could tell, the chamber was a virtual replica of the one from his home world: deep azure carpet with golden accents, elaborately coffered ceiling, and warm golden walls adorned with portraits.

"Hello, everyone," he said, scanning the hall, then eyeing the assembled statesmen. "What about the Representatives? The president?" He unbuckled his backpack and leaned it against the marble rostrum.

"We dissolved the House over a century ago," said a dignified white-haired man near the front. "Each of us now serves the entire Union—all forty-eight states. As for the president— he executes what we decide. It is we you wish to speak to. Please—go on."

"Right," Chris said. He took a deep breath to steady his racing heart, then pulled a sheet of paper from his back pocket, unfolding and smoothing it. He'd caught some much-needed sleep on the way; the rest of the flight he spent drafting and redrafting his remarks, desperate to make an impact.

"I'd like to start by painting a picture for you," Chris began. "I want to talk to you about apples for a moment. The Allens, who hosted me during my first days here, grow apples and sell them. That's it, simple: They grow, then they sell. In my native America, it's a different story. Apple growers are mired in audits, inspections, and manuals. They have to navigate the ever-shifting demands of federal government agencies, which impose thousands of restrictions. This situation is further compounded by state, county, and local oversight. Even the ladders—how they're built, where they're placed, how they're climbed—are dictated in code."

Chris let the silence stretch for a beat. "The result? Clipboards, logs, binders stacked in farm offices—each another hoop to jump through. Workshops, consultants, annual audits— none of it grows apples.

"This is one corner of one sector. But it's in everything," Chris said, his gaze sweeping across the faces of the senators assembled before him. "The U.S. Code alone spans tens of thousands of pages, with many new words added each year. Then, numerous government agencies add their own regulations and unlisted guidelines, expanding this foundation to hundreds of thousands of pages." He gestured with his hand, as if to emphasize the sheer volume. "On top of that, millions of pages of judicial rulings swirl around this vortex of regulations, laws, and guidelines."

A buzz greeted his words. Chris waited for it to die down.

"Yet these mountains of law are merely the visible peaks of a far deeper system," he said.

Chris glanced briefly at his notes before raising his eyes.

"Senators, the American society on the other side is forged by an all-encompassing bureaucratic complex—spanning government agencies and corporations, regulatory boards and credentialing bodies, insurance policies and healthcare networks, educational institutions and financial systems. These interconnected institutions set the norms, rules, and protocols of every sphere of life—and shape what is permitted, what is expected, what can be debated."

"Lamentable!" came a voice from the back. "Horrifying, really. But . . . why tell us?"

Glad you asked, Chris thought. Aloud he said, "I hope I've made it clear, madam, that the other America is ruled by soft totalitarianism in a democracy skinsuit. Its reach is far more exhaustive than anything the Soviet planners could've ever dreamed of."

Chris took a sip from a glass of water. It was time to drop the other shoe. "It took me some time to understand what's truly appealing about your country. Yes, the air here is fresh, yet even sweeter still is the scent of liberty. The pressure of many millions of people to migrate here will be... immense."

Now the senators grasped what he was trying to tell them. The room shifted. Unease rippled through the chamber.

"And if the call of liberty and the allure of your high-trust society aren't enough of a draw, then perhaps the desire for a better future for their children is. Given the choice, they wouldn't want their children to grow up in a world where harmful augmented viruses are cooked up in labs... or under a government that borrows trillions to feed ever-expanding programs... or in a culture where they must self-censor lest they be deemed problematic—and subsequently doxxed or rendered unemployable."

One of the senators called out, "We have been successfully holding off pressures such as these. Countless people want to come—from Mexico and El Salvador next door, to Nigeria and Sierra Leone in sub-Saharan Africa."

"That may be," Chris said quickly. "However, their regimes are not in a position to impose their wishes upon you."

Chris raised his voice. "What I told Senators Wilson and Moore didn't fully convey the extent of my former country's global sway.

"It exerts influence through covert operations, news media, civil society institutions, and digital platforms—shaping narratives, subverting elections, even toppling governments. Economic leverage through sanctions and corporate pressure amplifies its reach.

"It practices a whole-of-society model of control—rarely

needing boots on the ground, though it doesn't shy away from force when required. For decades, it's launched airstrikes, drone hits, and special ops missions in dozens of countries. For generations, it's waged psychological warfare and has armed proxy forces across the globe."

Chris looked at the gathered policymakers, his expression grave. "I believe this postmodern empire will inevitably seek to extend its reach into your country."

His words were met with a new wave of murmurs.

"We're in a difficult position," one senator called, his voice rising above the hushed conversations. "We only have your word. . ." The senator's words faded as Chris turned, unzipped his backpack, and began pulling out tablets and dumping them on the marble rostrum. The hushed conversations sputtered and died as all eyes focused on the growing pile of electronics.

Chris looked up and met the senator's gaze. "Each of these contains numerous videos and documents from every source I could think of," he said. "Learn firsthand about my world: the good, the bad, and the ugly."

"So you say there's good?" a senator asked.

Chris nodded. "Of course. Despite being hamstrung and perverted, my former nation is still a crucible of creativity and innovation. We have inventions, customs, arts you haven't conceived of along with songs and films that are breathtaking."

The white-haired senator at the front raised his hands, calling for silence. "You still haven't clarified something: Why the urgency in convening this extraordinary session?"

A hush fell. Every eye was fixed on Chris.

He inclined his head slightly. "Others from my world have recently learned of the portal." He let the silence stretch, allowing the implication to sink in. "Examine the evidence, deliberate—but understand that time is of the essence. A day, maybe less."

With a slight nod, he turned and strode down the aisle, the senators' voices surging behind him like an incoming tide. At the doors, he paused for the briefest moment before pushing them open and stepping out. His part was done; now the decision rested with them. He would do what he must—and could only hope they would arrive at a similar conclusion in the crucial hours ahead. As prearranged, he was returning to Boulder.

＝＝

Late that night, a knock sounded. The door creaked open, and Katie, Sandra, and Dalton piled in, their faces beaming. "Happy birthday!" they exclaimed in unison. But their excitement quickly turned to apprehension as they took in the scene: a table strewn with bullets, the air thick with the pungent scent of chemicals.

Chris glanced up, face grim, then returned to his work without a word.

"What in the Sam Hill are you doing?" Sandra demanded, the cheer fading from her voice.

Chris said nothing, his eyes hard in the lamplight as he mixed some chemicals.

Sandra took a step forward. "Chris, talk to us!"

At last he spoke, voice low. "I came through a stable two-way portal." He set a vial down with care, jaw clenched. "It is intact. Operational."

Sandra's breath caught. Katie clutched her own throat, eyes wide. Dalton stood still, gaze narrowing as he studied Chris.

"I need to shut it down permanently," Chris said heavily. "Tonight. Before it's too late." Finally, he lifted his head and regarded them, eyes full of pain. "It was a friend of mine, Ronny, who found the gateway under his house and called me over."

"You told us it got destroyed," Katie said, staring at him with a hurt and confused expression.

"You... kept this from us," Sandra said, a flush creeping up her face.

Chris quickly came around the table to stand before them. "It was a secret that wasn't mine to share. A secret I didn't ask for, at that." He grasped Sandra's arms. "What do you think would have happened if I told you there's a way to travel between the worlds?"

She pulled free from him. "You were afraid we'd make the *wrong* decision," she said, her voice tight with outrage. "I'm so mad at you, I could just spit!"

"You have no idea what you're talking about!" Chris shouted, his face contorted with anger. "You've never set foot in my native world. It's like an open wound, festering from a thousand cuts." He was smoldering with cold fury. "This is what could be coming your way. This is what I've kept from you."

Sandra glared. "So you chose to hold the true state of the gate a secret—and now you want to close it off for good."

"Yes!" He flung that word at her.

Sandra's eyes blazed with indignation. "How *dare* you presume to make a ruling on behalf of hundreds of millions of people!" she yelled back at him.

Chris raised his voice, his rage pouring out. "The portal's controlled from my native world. The people here don't get a vote in what happens with it!"

He slammed his fist on the table, causing Sandra and Katie to flinch as cartridges jolted, some falling and scattering across the wooden floor. "If I don't stop the handful of people planning to come through tomorrow night, the flood that would follow it will overwhelm any resistance. Like a juggernaut, the economic and cultural forces from my native world will transmute everything in their path. This is the last opportunity; I have to avert this tonight."

A hush descended on the room.

He looked at them, then took a deep breath. "Your Senate is aware of what I am doing."

"What are you talking about?" Sandra said incredulously.

"They've been monitoring me. From the moment I went back and returned a second time, they've been trailing me everywhere, bugging everything, eavesdropping constantly. They're aware of everything."

"How do you know that?" Dalton asked, dismayed.

"Because they told me. I was apprehended on my way home from the train station and had a conversation with Senator Moore and Senator Wilson. It turns out that when the portal is activated, it emits gravitational waves, which were detected on this end."

"Why didn't you tell us?" pressed Katie.

"It's a national security issue." He watched them with anguish. "Sacrificing me is a small price to pay—or sacrificing you, for that matter—now that you know the truth. That's why I didn't tell you; I did not want you to get involved." He closed his eyes. "I wish you hadn't come tonight—and see all of this." He gestured around him.

For a few long moments no one said anything. The four of them stood looking at each other.

Then Dalton noticed the boxes of rifle ammo stacked against the wall. A sense of deep foreboding rose within him. "What are you planning on doing, Chris?"

"All of you, leave," Chris said, moving around the table and starting to strip some wires. "Go now and stay quiet for a day. Everything should be resolved by tomorrow."

"What are you doing, Chris?" Dalton repeated, his apprehension growing.

Chris mustered a ghost of a smile. "What needs to be done."

"Tell us—"

"He's building a bomb," Katie said.

Sandra and Dalton turned their heads to stare at her. "Aren't you, Chris?" she asked. "That's what those chemicals are for."

Chris pressed his hands to his face. His voice was ragged. "Please. Just go."

"We're not leaving," Dalton said gruffly. "We'll see this through together, brother. It was only the other night we talked about being a family."

"No," Chris said. "You must go. Please." His voice cracked on that last word.

"What are you not telling us?" Sandra asked, and her lower lip quivered. There was more to this. Something really ominous.

He shook his head numbly, avoiding eye contact. "It won't take much to talk me out of it." His voice dropped almost to a whisper.

"Chris . . . please," Sandra pleaded. "Tell us what's going on."

He put down the needle-nose pliers. "I don't know how to build a timer."

Katie turned pale.

"I will cross the wires, and the bomb will go off."

"And you will get out, right?" Sandra said with a tremor in her voice.

"I'll force the others out of the portal chamber and set it off," he said tonelessly.

Sandra's face drained of color. "No," she said.

"It'll be instantaneous."

She took a shaky breath. "No."

His faint smile held a touch of sadness. "I won't feel a thing." His gaze lingered on each of them. "I thought it was too good to be true. Us. Being together." Nothing genuinely good had ever happened to him. At least not anything that lasted.

"No, it is not too good to be true," Dalton said with quiet intensity.

Chris said hoarsely, "This is the only window of opportunity. My partner will have a security detail at the gate starting tomorrow, and once that's in place, some folks from my world will be coming through. So, unless you know how to rig a timer to detonate a device..."

"*I* don't," Sandra said—and turned to Katie.

"What?" Chris said, not understanding. "Surely you don't think that Katie—" It dawned on him what Sandra was thinking. They all looked at Katie, who turned stone-faced.

"Kate," Sandra said, stressing the word. "We really need you to come out."

Katie started shaking; her eyes blazed, then turned glassy. Then blazed again, her face subtly rearranging itself. Her wide-eyed expression narrowed, green eyes deepening with newfound intensity. Her ready smile faded, replaced by a set jaw and tightened lips, lending her fair features a marble-like quality. Finally she stood there, glowering and beautiful.

"Kate." Sandra's voice cracked into a sob.

Dumbfounded, Dalton and Chris stared at Kate. For the first time, the resemblance between the two sisters became apparent.

"All right, soldier boy," Kate said, her eyes locking onto Chris's. "I don't know how, but one way or another I'll put a timer together in the next few hours." She looked at Sandra, then at Dalton. "It may mean breaking into a store to acquire some necessary items."

"So be it," Dalton said savagely. "Just tell us what you need."

Sandra nodded briskly in agreement.

CHAPTER 29

IN THE DARKNESS, ABOUT A DOZEN paces from Chris, figures in camo emerged from hiding.

He stopped abruptly, eyes narrowing. Even in the dim light, he recognized the unmistakable silhouettes of HK416s, or very close replicas. Their muzzles were trained on him.

One of the men approached him, rifle slung over his shoulder.

"Don't get in my way," Chris said.

"We won't," the other replied. In the dark, the officer studied Chris. "Once you start the timer on your bomb, can they kill it?"

They knew about the bomb.

Of course they knew about the bomb.

Chris shook his head. "They won't be able to. It's on a ten-second timer."

The man considered it briefly, then gave a terse hand signal. Behind him, the soldiers slowly lowered their rifles. The officer moved closer until he stood eye to eye with Chris. "I have three Javelins locked on the gate site," he said in a low voice. "You've got one minute to go in, do what you need to do, and get back out."

Chris considered it. "Give me two. I need time to get the people out of the way."

"Negative." The officer glanced at the gate site in the distance, then turned back to Chris. "Socom recommended a Javelin launch as you enter the portal, destroying it and you in the process."

"I expected no less," Chris said dryly.

The man regarded Chris in silence. "You're an operator—like us, aren't you?"

"I was, yes."

The officer brushed his hands together and placed them in his pants pockets. "If the gate's blown, it doesn't matter who did it. But if it proves indestructible, our officials will eventually have to deal with your former government. Being implicated in slinging AT missiles into your home world might get messy. The statesmen figured it's better for you to do the dirty work of trying to blow the portal up, while they retained plausible deniability. One minute is all I'm authorized to give. We can't risk a scenario in which you're taken out, and your people come pouring through, packing heat and peddling pacts."

Chris was silent for a moment. "A few hours ago," he said, "I planned on dying so as to protect some people I love here—and to secure this world in the process."

The man nodded. "We know; we listened in. As far as we in the field are concerned, you've earned your one minute to take care of business—and then some." He glanced at the far-off gate site, shrouded in the darkness of the night. "You know as well as I do: We stand no chance against the military of your native world. We have only one shot at this. Tonight, the future of the two worlds will be decided."

The two men fell silent.

"I trust you're armed," the officer finally said.

Chris jerked his head toward the backpack he carried. "I've got what I need."

The officer gripped his shoulder. "Good luck, soldier."

As he marched toward the gate, it occurred to Chris that one way or another, this would be the last time he'd make this journey.

Soon, very soon, he'd find out if he were to live another day. That was not a new feeling for Chris. Yet, it was different this time. In the past, he'd just served his country. Now, there were people who loved and wished to share the remainder of their lives with him. Now, the stakes were infinitely higher.

He was about a dozen paces away from the boulder when the air shimmered, forming a hazy outline of the octagonal frame. The portal was now active and emitting gravitational waves—something that was undoubtedly noted and relayed to the monitoring forces hiding in the surrounding areas.

Chris kept his face carefully neutral. He couldn't afford to arouse the suspicions of the people in America, those who resided on the other side of the looking glass.

In front of him, on the other side of the invisible gate, Ronny was probably standing, possibly with others, watching him. From behind him, operatives hid in the hills and tall grass, and at least three of them were training Javelins on his position, ready to unleash destruction on the portal site.

Chris forced himself onward, mentally bracing for the unmistakable whooshing sound of Javelin missiles being launched. He fervently hoped the commander was truthful, and they would not destroy the gateway and kill him in the process—tying up the loose ends.

But nothing broke the tranquility of the night.

He walked on—took one last step—the world faded in and out—and he was again in a room of stone, deep underground, in another universe. And the seconds commenced, ticking down to zero.

"Hey, man!" crowed Ronny. There were four other people with him. Ronny chuckled. "Just look at this backpack. You must have stuffed tons of clothes for the guys."

"You betcha." Chris unstrapped the knapsack, resting it carefully on the floor.

He reached down. From under the flaps of the elongated side pockets, he whipped out two short carbine rifles, one in each hand. As he swiveled and faced the group, Chris pointed one carbine at the ceiling and squeezed the trigger. A deafening burst of gunfire erupted, and spent cartridges bounced off the stone floor. The suppressor muted the worst of the muzzle flash, but in the stone stairwell, every shot still exploded like a thunderclap.

"Up the stairs!" Chris roared, advancing on the utterly shocked people. *"Move!"* He pointed their way with his other rifle, the one with live ammo. Chris would shoot them if he had to.

The five turned and fled toward the stairs as he let loose another volley of blank rounds.

They frantically climbed up the dimly lit stairwell, Ronny pleading and screaming at him all the while.

The people were more than halfway up the staircase when the hatch door at the top was flung open. Shouts and inquiries filled the stairwell as security personnel jumped down, one after the other. The group climbing up the stairs yelled at them not to shoot. It was pandemonium.

And over the confusion and noise, from the bottom of the stairs, about three stories below, Chris bellowed, "You've got fifteen seconds to clear out before a bomb goes off!"

Even if they wanted to, they couldn't make their way down in time to do anything about it.

For a split second, Chris caught Ronny looking back down at him, confusion and betrayal written across his face.

Chris raised the carbines, firing off a round of blanks into the stairwell. He charged toward the backpack, dropping the rifles along the way. He dragged the pack to the very edge of the gate and flicked the detonator switch on. Leaving it on top of the bag, he dashed, leaped through the gate—and was back in Americana.

He came out sprinting, took a few dozen steps, and dropped flat on the ground. One second later, a burst of masonry fragments erupted from the gate, which was abruptly cut off.

And just like that, it was over.

Moments later, two massive coaxial helicopters landed, and soldiers came pouring out. Spotlights were hoisted, and harsh lights shone from multiple points, illuminating the spot where Chris had emerged.

A soldier, hunched over a satellite phone, yelled, "Commander, the gravitational waves are gone! The gate's offline!"

"It's more than offline," Chris hollered as he climbed to his feet and shook off dirt and masonry. He smiled grimly, surveying the now brightly lit earth. "The gate's shards are strewn across the field. It's *destroyed*."

Some whooped while others relayed the news to those farther afield.

Chris made his way to the commander he had spoken with earlier.

"Mission accomplished," Chris said.

"Casualties?" the commander asked gruffly.

"None."

The officer nodded and stepped closer, clapping Chris's shoulder with a heavy hand. The two men stood side by side, facing the wreckage.

"Are you packing it in?" Chris asked.

"We're leaving two armored platoons for a few months as a precaution," the commander said, his eyes scanning the grassland. "Just in case anything else comes out."

Chris nodded.

The commander jerked his head in the direction of a nearby hill. "There's someone who wants to talk to you."

A figure stood some distance away from the milling soldiers: Senator Moore.

<hr/>

The distinguished man tipped his homburg hat. "I want to officially welcome you to our world," the senator said as Chris drew near. "Effective immediately, you're a citizen of this country, Mr. Walden—that is, unless you have an objection," he added in a lighter tone.

Chris grinned, both startled and pleased. "I do not, sir. It is most welcome."

"Congratulations are in order then," Senator Moore said warmly, pulling a sheet of vellum from his jacket pocket and handing it to Chris—a naturalization certificate.

Chris examined the official document. At last, he looked up. "I'm wondering," he said, "will the news of the portal and what happened here tonight be made public?"

"The public will be informed," came the reply. "You're entitled to your privacy, though. Just let me know your wishes in this matter."

"I . . . will think about it," Chris responded. "In fact, there are some people I'd like to confer with, as this will not only affect me, but them as well."

"I understand. No rush, my boy."

The two of them regarded the bustling field.

"The public was not consulted," Chris stated.

"No, it was not. We planned on a national dialogue followed by a referendum. Alas, your friend forced our hand."

"I would imagine some will be calling for your heads over your decision to sever the contact with another world," Chris said.

Senator Moore shot him a glance. "We all knew the occupational hazards when we took our oath. Those who cannot take the pressure have no business running for office—and, in fact, don't make it through Selection."

He shrugged. "No regrets, though. If we are all ousted tomorrow, I'll retire knowing that I did the most beneficial thing I could for my country."

Chris was silent for a long time. "And that's all I wanted to do when I was in the service," he said in a hushed voice.

"I understand, son," Senator Moore said kindly. "Today you've accomplished that." He laid his hand on Chris's shoulder. "I wish you all the best."

"Thank you, sir," Chris said.

It was as good a time as any to bring it up. "Senator, I don't seek recognition for what I've done. But I would ask one thing of you."

"Of course," Senator Moore said. "If it's within our power, we'll grant it."

"Hours ago, Miss Allen and Mr. O'Connor broke into a store and retrieved—stole, really—some things we desperately needed. I ask the government to compensate the shop owner and make the whole thing go away."

The senator lowered his head. "Consider it done," he said.

Senator Moore then gave Chris a roguish smile. "Any idea what you're going to do next, Mr. Walden?"

"I have some ideas." Chris grinned back. "The Summer Ball is coming up, and I have my work cut out for me." He sobered. "But first, there are people out there worried sick about me, and they need to know that everything is finally, truly okay."

CHAPTER 30

DOCTOR AND MRS. ALLEN TOOK THE NEWS OF THE PORTAL in stride, even as it sent shockwaves across the nation. Dalton, Sandra, Katie, and Chris discussed the matter and decided to stay out of the limelight.

The following day, Chris spent several hours drafting a detailed statement about America, which he promptly forwarded to the Senate for immediate public release. His name and identity were to remain confidential.

Later that day, Chris received an official communiqué from the White House. He was to be awarded the Presidential Medal of Freedom with distinction for his "especially meritorious contribution to the security and national interests of the United States." A discreet, private ceremony was scheduled to take place at the White House in three weeks.

News of the award thrilled Katie and Sandra to no end. Dalton dragged Chris that evening to a bar to celebrate with a few drinks. It was Monday, and the bar was having its weekly "Kings of the Tap Room" night—fellas only—which suited the two.

Later that night, Chris sat by himself in his cottage and lit a candle in memory of his unit in Iraq. That's when he realized the new feeling that had come over him: serenity.

As for Ronny, Chris let out a wry chuckle. His buddy wasn't going to become the merchant prince he'd dreamed of. Still, Chris was pretty sure that once the dust settled, Ronny would upload those otherworldly videos. The views would pour in, followed by TV interviews and everything else. And then there was the tablet Chris had given him—full of case studies, video documentation, financial models, and regulatory frameworks, all part of a blueprint of a radically better healthcare system. One way or another, Ronny would collect on the discovery. That was Chris's repayment: to the world that had raised him and to a former friend.

At long last, it was time to move forward and onward.

≡≡

The following day, Dalton and Chris leisurely strolled out of a baseball game they had just attended, each enjoying a spicy hot dog. The game was between the Boulder Sluggers and the Broomfield Mustangs. During the match, Chris had learned that all baseball teams in Americana were amateur. The teams were not owned by anyone and received enthusiastic support from the towns they represented and resided in. The baseball fields were maintained by the cities themselves, with funding generated from ticket sales.

When Chris inquired about American football, Dalton dismissed it as "the brain-scrambling sport of yesteryear," its appeal having faded alongside growing concerns about brain injuries.

"I want you to teach me how to partner dance, starting tomorrow," Chris said to Dalton as they walked past a few uniformed workers who were sweeping the pavement in front of the stadium entrance.

Dalton reached out and gave Chris's shoulder a solid

squeeze. "I'll ring my sister. With her help, you'll be eating, breathing, and sleeping partner dancing for the next ten days. The rest's on you."

Chris eyed him warily. "Meaning?"

"What one brings to the dance isn't something that can be taught." Dalton paused. "Would it surprise you to learn that Sandra and Katie are quite . . . intense dancers?"

Chris chuckled and took another bite of the hot dog in his hand. No, it didn't surprise him.

"They're affable and kind—except when they're not," Dalton said.

"You mean when it gets physical."

Dalton nodded. "And partner dancing is an expression of that."

"I think I understand," Chris said, mulling it. "Are they good dancers?"

"They know their way around a dance floor," Dalton said guardedly.

"Isn't it just memorizing some steps?" Chris asked, hopeful. He'd seen dance competitions on TV.

"Absolutely not!" Dalton exclaimed with a surprised laugh. "This isn't a performance, Chris. It's a dance—a conversation." He rubbed his stubbly chin, reaching over to give the other man's shoulder a squeeze. "And you'll be the one steering this tractor."

Chris shot him a sharp look. He was doomed.

"The woman's the picture," Dalton recited. "The man's the frame."

Chris pressed Dalton for details. He learned that as the lead, he wouldn't have to perform as many intricate and flashy moves. However, this didn't make his role any easier. Being the lead meant constantly deciding on the next move, and then the next, and the next after that. It was relentless. Chris couldn't zone out or freeze up, or the dance would grind to an awk-ward halt.

Dalton clapped him on the shoulder. "Well, partner, looks like you've got your work cut out for you."

CHAPTER 31

It was the evening of the summer ball.

The two young men stepped out of Chris's residential enclave, each distinct in bearing and style. Dalton, in a cashmere herringbone jacket and dark trousers, exuded effortless masculinity. Chris, handsome and athletic, cut a dashing figure in his silver-gray suit, the last rays of light playing across its folds and sheen.

As they walked on, a self-driving vehicle pulled up—one Dalton had booked earlier. Chris whistled softly at the sight. The carriage was a lavish vision with its black lacquer, gold trim, and slender buggy wheels. Ornate lanterns on each of the four posts cast a soft radiance, making the vehicle stand out against the darkening sky. The faint hum of its motor was barely audible as it awaited its passengers.

With appreciative grins, the two men climbed into the carriage. Dalton rang a small ship's bell fastened to the ceiling, and the vehicle set off on the short ride to the Allens' to pick up the other half of their party. A few minutes later, they saw them.

Standing under the warm glow of the porch light, Sandra and Katie waited at the top of the stairs, turning as Chris and Dalton approached. The men's gazes were irresistibly drawn to them.

Sandra wore a fit-and-flare, tea-length black dress with a waist-cinching belted bodice. Layers of delicate black chiffon draped around her, threaded with panels of silver mesh shimmering with tiny sequins. The sheer back and long sleeves lent an air of sensuality, accentuating her figure, while a fine silver thread traced elegant patterns across the sleeves and bodice.

Beside her, Katie stood tall in high heels that complemented her glimmering white cocktail dress. It featured a single shoulder strap and a gold sequin trim that ran down the side, catching the light with every movement. A matching gold barrette swept back her long blonde hair, framing her face in striking simplicity.

Wheeled suitcases rested next to them.

Chris followed Dalton's lead as they walked up the steps, took the luggage, and placed it in the rear of the carriage. They returned and escorted the ladies to the vehicle. Once they were aboard, the vehicle started on its way.

They rode in companionable silence, the mood bright and expectant. They clasped each other's hands, exchanging fleeting smiles, and occasionally making eye contact.

Soon enough, the carriage swung onto Broadway. And what a sight it was!

The boulevard appeared enchanted, with stately buildings lit up from outside, imbuing them with a dreamlike quality. Recessed ground lights illuminated the pale stone pavement as carriages rolled by and welldressed people strolled past.

Minutes later, they reached their destination, and the carriage stopped in front of the Ballroom Pavilion. They climbed out and the men unloaded the luggage. As they drew nearer, Chris marveled at the sight that greeted him. Numerous elegantly dressed couples twirled on the spacious wooden dance floor, while others took a breather at the circular tables scattered about.

Sandra and Katie walked up and stopped at the edge of the

dance floor while Dalton and Chris checked in the luggage.

Rather than walking over to where their partners were waiting, Dalton led Chris to the other end. That was when Chris realized that the men had congregated on one side and the women on the other.

"The gentleman walks up toward the lady," Dalton explained. "The lady walks from the other side. They meet somewhere in the middle—and off they waltz. In this case, quite literally."

"It's something else," Chris said softly, watching the couples glide past on the dance floor.

Dalton nodded, observing some of the dancers. His expression soon turned uneasy. "Remember when you asked me about Sandra and Katie's dancing skills?" he asked Chris.

"Yeah, what about it?" Chris asked. Past the moving dancers, he could make out the twin sisters, who stood on the other end of the ballroom, looking impassively back at them. He gestured toward some of the female dancers. "Are you trying to tell me they're as good as these girls?"

His companion shook his head. "I wouldn't say that." He cleared his throat. "I daresay there aren't any female dancers in Boulder who can touch Katie and Sandra."

Chris turned his head to stare at Dalton.

"Didn't want to intimidate you, brother—not while you were learning how to dance."

"Oh joy," Chris said. He let out a slow breath, his lips pulling into a tight line.

"You're going to be just fine. I've seen you move," Dalton reassured him, making eye contact. "Ready?"

"As I'll ever be," Chris said, steeling himself. "Let's do it."

Chris walked up to one of the many ornate lanterns lining the edge of the ballroom. He turned a wooden handle, and a small flame flickered to life within the glass enclosure. Something about the act felt ceremonial—quietly binding.

On the far end, Katie did the same. Her lantern's flame illuminated her features with a soft radiance. For a brief moment, their eyes met across the expanse, the twin flames symbolizing a shared intent.

Chris took a deep breath and began walking toward the center of the dance floor. Immediately, Katie mirrored his movement.

Meeting Katie on the floor, Chris bowed slightly, as the other men had. She curtsied in response, a faint smile on her lips.

Chris extended his arms to the sides, and Katie stepped into his frame. As she did so, she directed her gaze somewhere over his shoulder, gracefully arched her upper body, and nestled one hip between his, connecting. He steadied himself, the weight of the moment settling on him. It didn't matter that Katie was a far better dancer; he was expected to lead. Chris pulled his shoulders back and off they went.

As they took the first step, he could already tell. By the third or fourth step, he was certain.

Outwardly, Katie did nothing that stood out; someone watching her wouldn't pick up on it. However, the experience of dancing was different from the experience of watching dancing.

Katie glided in perfect sync without pulling or pushing. It was uncanny—and unnerving—how she read every pressure of his arm, every tilt of his hand, and translated it to a turn or a move. She responded instantaneously. Whenever his beat was off, she would effortlessly re-establish their rhythm, smoothing out any rough patches.

As Chris advanced, he opened the frame a few times, raising his left arm, and Katie responded with a flurry of spins and twirls before rejoining him.

Dancing the waltz, he felt as if Katie and he were sweeping across the floor. Moving as one, he found the waltz was the nearest thing to soaring he could've experienced while on the ground. The feeling was incredible.

They swept through the ballroom, and before Chris knew it, they had circled the entire floor and were moving around it a second time.

As the final notes of the piece faded, the conductor seamlessly transitioned into a new composition. Chris was grateful it was a waltz that eased him into the night of dance. The waltz was a mannered glide through a park compared to the eruptive volcano of the hustle.

The second waltz ended, and Chris and Katie returned to their sides of the hall, extinguishing their lanterns. The next few dance selections were to be the hustle. Dalton had told him what to expect.

The waltz and hustle, though both requiring spacious floors, had little in common. The waltz was a traveling dance, whereas the hustle stayed in a fixed area, compensating with expansive movements that sometimes pushed the boundaries of how far apart a dancing couple could be while maintaining hand contact.

Sandra strode toward Chris with the poise of a runway model, each step deliberate, her green eyes fixed on him. As she neared, he extended his arm, and their hands met with a charged intensity. Standing still, they held each other's gaze as the deep, pulsating beat enveloped them, growing stronger.

Chris waited patiently, letting the energy of the song build and wash over him. He knew that even a slight, inadvertent movement could trigger her into action. He concentrated on remaining centered, keeping his body relaxed and still.

At last, the beat crescendoed. Chris tugged. Sandra surged forward, swirling around his arm and into his open embrace like wildfire—only to spin back out again in a flash. Then she let it happen: like a spark set loose, a dazzling blur beneath the sporadic bursts of light. Her dress flared around her, a cascade of shadow and shimmer.

A couple of hours later, the four of them left the grand Dance Pavilion.

They ducked into a hole-in-the-wall joint, the kind with no sign out front—just the smell. At the counter, they slipped on dining ponchos—thin, translucent, pulled from a battered steamer trunk beside the mustard and hot sauce jars. A few steps away, under a sun-bleached awning, they stood around a waist-high circular table welded to a brass post. They ate standing up, elbows out, hunched over the cracked millet buns that barely contained the heap of juniper-cured pork—a smoky, sharp-edged staple common to the Front Range. The stone underfoot still held the day's warmth, and now and then, a flare leapt from the hidden pit behind the slatted wall, casting brief flickers of firelight.

After they had their fill, they tossed their ponchos in the compost bin, washed their hands, and continued on. The night was just getting started.

The unmistakable sound of a live big band filled the air, its infectious rhythm impossible to resist, as Chris and Dalton pushed open the double swing doors and stepped into the bustling ballroom. Hundreds of young people swirled and twirled across the dance floor, their outfits a blur of motion. The air was alive with the sound of tapping feet, swishing skirts, and occasional whoops of delight. The driving beat of the drums and the blaring brass section delivered bright, punchy notes and soaring melodies.

If the ambience in the Dance Pavilion was stately and occasionally fiery, here, the mood was jovial and playful, with smiles everywhere as people swung, twirled, and spun—dancing the Lindy Hop, Jive, East Coast Swing, or the Charleston.

Chris watched, wide-eyed, as some of the girls were lifted

high by their partners.

"Aerials," Dalton shouted, as one girl was hoisted over her partner's head. "Our ladies may expect you to do those—don't," he cautioned. "Those guys have been doing it for *years*. There is a technique to it, and if you don't do it just right..." He shook his head.

Aerials were the last thing on Chris's mind. He felt sweat bead on his forehead. "The tempo is impossible," he yelled. "It's too fast!"

"Remember what I told you!" Dalton hollered back. "If you start to lose it, switch to the Charleston—you'll be moving at half-speed. Or just go with the East Coast Swing basic move— it'll be your rock of stability. Alright, here are the girls. Let's go!"

Sandra and Katie came out of the changing room and headed straight for them. Earlier, Chris and Dalton had changed from their formal wear to more casual pleated slacks and button-down dress shirts. The sisters had changed into loose summer dresses and had swapped their high heels for flats.

It happened quickly. One moment Chris was watching the two women rushing toward them, and the next he was swept up in a Lindy Hop with Sandra.

People were dancing right next to them. And Dalton's words came back to him. *Your job*, he'd said, *is to protect the girl. Bit by bit, steer the two of you toward a place where she won't be crowded by others. And whatever happens, you have to remain steady and anchored. If someone bumps into you, just absorb.*

The music and dancing just rolled on. The hours flew by in a blur of spinning skirts, shuffling feet, and laughter as Chris, Dalton, Katie, and Sandra danced away on the crowded floor.

Past midnight, the four headed to a bathhouse, the chill night air clinging to their sweat-dampened skin.

They rented a private room paneled in aromatic red cedar, shed their clothes, and sank into the depths of a giant hot tub in its center. Rejuvenated, the girls soon started a water fight, laughing and shrieking as they tussled in the bubbling water.

Sometime later, they headed to their last stop of the night.

Dalton and Chris descended a spiral staircase into a dimly lit cellar, and the sounds of sensual music grew more pronounced with each step. The crowded space exuded a primal, almost tribal atmosphere with its rough, stone-hewn walls of pale limestone and dark basalt. Flames seemed to erupt from the blackened floor—a clever play of orange and yellow spotlights on fog emitted by recessed ultrasonic foggers.

The cellar featured padded ledges along the walls that slid out to form temporary seating. Dalton and Chris settled in, waiting as the girls changed upstairs. Despite the crowded dance floor, the air remained fresh thanks to floor grills continuously pumping in outdoor air.

They called it a dance club, and the operative word was "dance." Water was available to quench thirst, but nothing else. It was a kizomba and tarraxinha dance club, where people moved slowly and in intimate positions. Very intimate positions.

A gasp escaped Chris's lips as Sandra descended the stairs. Her lips were painted glossy obsidian, and she wore black leggings that sat daringly low on her hips, along with a matching sports bra. Intricate patterns in charcoal and deep bronze snaked down her neck and across her collarbone. These designs seemed to writhe with each movement, catching the flickering light. But it was her eyes that commanded attention—rimmed with charcoal-black paint that extended in sharp, angular lines across her temples.

Katie followed, her blonde hair striking in the dim light. She also wore black leggings that dipped dangerously low and a sports bra, but her eyes were rimmed in glistening gold. Her jaw and neck were painted a solid matte black, the darkness extending to her collarbone, a stark contrast to her bare shoulders.

The four of them hit the blackened, fiery dance floor.

⇒⇐

As they left town at dawn in an open wagon heading east, they greeted the rising sun, standing inside the vehicle as it rolled forward.

Chris leaned against the railing and turned to look at the three people whom he had come to love. "Let us be together for the remainder of our lives," he said. "What say you?"

"Yes," Sandra said.

"Yes," Katie said.

"Yes," Dalton said.

And so it came to pass.

THE END

If you enjoyed this book, please take a moment to leave a review. Your feedback helps other readers discover the book. You can rate or review it at any major retailer or on Goodreads.

Daniel Rirdan wrote *Interstellar Crew* longhand at thirteen, becoming Israel's youngest published novelist. At fifteen, he wrote a book on education reform, hammering away on a rented mechanical typewriter in a laundry closet barely large enough to hold a folding table and a chair.

After military service, he moved to Australia, mastering English with jotted vocabulary lists carried everywhere from the bathroom to tram stops. A year later, the peer-reviewed journal *Foundation* featured his essay on William Gibson.

Decades of detours, dead ends, and one environmental tome later, he returned to speculative fiction at fifty and hasn't looked back.

Daniel is the author of *Republic of Forge and Grace* (2026) and *Areta* (2026).

From his home in the American Southwest, he writes stories driven by wonder and with no patience for literary fashion. As he sees it, what is possible—or can be imagined—is a wide-open country.

www.danielrirdan.com

"Laudable worldbuilding...the prose is impeccable throughout... sublime denouement [ending]...A compelling cast of characters fights to survive in this fascinating SF yarn." —*Kirkus Reviews*

AS ONE STAR BLAZES EVER brighter in the night sky, a disgraced former millwright, Sargon, and a brilliant scholar, Angora, dig into the depths of their seemingly natural world and delve into ancient texts in search of answers. They deduce the shocking truth: Their cylindrical world, Areta, is a gargantuan vessel that has been sailing through the cosmos for countless generations. And it is on a collision course with a sun.

The only hope for survival lies with Sargon and his small team of millwrights. They must defy societal conventions—while battling time, the risk of mass panic, and the specter of exile by the ruling council.

Set in a society rooted in the ancient Near East and Greece, Areta's culture contains ingenious, handcrafted technology and unique social conventions.

ARETA
a novel
by Daniel Rirdan

publication date: April 28, 2026
www.danielrirdan.com

an excerpt follows:

THE FOLLOWING NIGHT, ANGORA lay awake when the chimes of the doorway gong sounded.

Frowning, she peered at the night sky through her studio's ceiling window. The moon had already set beyond the horizon. Who could be calling at that hour?

But it was the Taberna quarter, she reflected, irritated and amused as she got up. It was not unheard of for some to try to drop by in the late hours of the night.

Nearly all of Maradam's intellectually inclined residents and their families clustered here, in this labyrinth of limestone-block alleys. They traded the open sky and rustling leaves surrounding the well-loved yurt homes for the proximity of minds, where weathered stone walls reflected the lamplight seeping from houses set for learning, discussion, and contemplation.

As she padded barefoot and in her nightshirt to the doorway, it occurred to her she'd missed that evening's get-together with her three friends. *Blasted!* It must have been one of them—or worse, all of them—deciding to drop by. They didn't do it often, but when they did, their discussions typically spilled into the early hours of the morning.

Angora stifled a yawn and opened the door. And then she stopped short; her heart skipped a beat.

Sargon was standing in the shadowed alley, just beyond the threshold. Casting a dappled light on his body, a lantern was strung casually from the end of a balanced pole that rested on one shoulder. She could see his gaze roam, taking in the hem of her short nightgown, her bare thighs, her loose long tresses.

His brazen sweep over her body left her feeling unexpectedly giddy. "How did—" She cleared her throat. His eyes were back on her face, intense and inscrutable. "How did you find out where I live?"

"The directory listing," he said, and her face grew hot. Anyone could have found out anyone's address. He must have thought her dull-witted.

More silence as they studied each other.

Her thoughts strayed and her attention lingered on his broad chest, the strong lines of his body visible beneath the open vest. He remained unfazed, a stoic statue in the dim light.

"What can I do for you?" she asked, relieved to find her voice steady and her demeanor collected.

"Your letter said you wanted to see me."

She stared at him. He couldn't possibly have thought she'd meant for him to come to her residence—and in the middle of the night, no less.

It mattered not. Angora took a deep breath. "The water clock is about to be unveiled. Before this happens, I want to propose something to you."

"I'm listening," he said. And Angora tried and failed to read his face.

"Not here," she said, breaking their eye contact and gesturing beyond the lantern's light, where darkness obscured the alley. "Let's walk over to the mouseion."

He gave a curt nod, and she stepped into the night and the dry hot breeze. The well-worn slabs of stone felt warm under her bare feet as she joined Sargon, the two of them setting off together. In this late hour, both Thalith Na'amat and the moon yielded to an obsidian-black sky densely streaked with the Milky Way's glittering stardust.

Sargon shifted the counterweight for balance and extended the pole, the lantern now hanging farther out, its reflector casting a wide beam downward and tinting the aged stone alleys in pearl with a whisper of gold.

She glanced down at her shift, a slight smile hovering

on her lips. Save for some flesh-flaunting unmarried girls, it was unthinkable for any woman to walk outside during daytime barefoot and garbed in nothing but a sleepshirt, as she did now—just as it was for a man to walk with a vest and no tunic underneath, as he did now. However, the night was a realm unto itself, where the intimate and the veiled and the bottled up were free to surface. A fond memory of a moonlit escapade flitted across her mind. Night was a time when people swam in the nude. Night was a time when some young women, sirenas, were on the prowl. And as a rule, what happened under the cover of darkness remained unspoken in the light of day.

They walked on, side by side, not speaking. Yet, she was keenly aware of him walking right next to her; at times their shadows merged and glided along the walls.

As they neared their destination, the faint starlight revealed the mouseion's ziggurat at the end of an open, paved space. A flutter of nervous excitement coursed through her. In just a few moments, she would lay out her proposal. His reaction would be telling, one way or another.Angora walked over to a nook in the massive stone wall near the mouseion's entrance. She turned a hand crank, and a shower of sparks rained down as the iron bar grated against the grindstone situated right below it, quickly igniting a char cloth in a small depression. She then pulled a thin stick from a nearby stack and lit it with the flame.

They both entered the lobby through the massive double doors. Once inside, Angora walked briskly along the wall, lighting one oil lamp after another with the elongated kindling in her hand.

She approached the Welcome Pavilion and turned, facing Sargon, who had come to stand in the center of the hall. "If you accept my proposal," she declared and then touched her heart, lips, and forehead, "I shall pledge my honor to keep your involvement secret." With those ritualistic gestures, Angora was in effect telling him that whatever may come, she'd keep their transaction confidential.

One's word was everything on Areta. Business deals depended on it, secrets relied on it, societal trust was based on it. A person who reneged was as good as ostracized and his honor was as good as dust. No one would have dealings of any consequence with an oath breaker.

"What are you talking about?" Sargon demanded, bewilderment plain on his face.

www.ingramcontent.com/pod-product-compliance
Lightning Source LLC
Chambersburg PA
CBHW050012120726
47903CB00006B/1742